The Water Master

❧❧

Betsy Dickinson

❧❧

THE WATER MASTER

For information about Nightengale Press,

please visit our website at www.nightengalemedia.com.

Email: publisher@nightengalepress.com

Dickinson, Betsy,
THE WATER MASTER/ Betsy Dickinson
ISBN 13: 978-1-935993-79-7
A Novel

First Published by Nightengale Press in the USA

January 2016

10 9 8 7 6 5 4 3 2 1

Printed in the USA, Canada, European Union, United Kingdom, Germany, Australia, Russia, Brazil, South Korea

ACKNOWLEDGEMENTS

Writing a novel, particularly a first one, requires the support of some pretty cool people. First, they have to believe in you and second, they have to be good enough friends to be honest.

Tom Perkins, my half-second-cousin-once-removed (that's another book), was my first reader and gave me some excellent advice. My actual first cousin, Kirsti Hoffman was vital in the development of my main character and spent a good deal of time teaching me about plot and character development. Ron King read the first few pages and made a suggestion that changed the whole tenor of my book. Jonathan Kelley proofreads and edits for a living and provided that service to me at no charge. Special thanks for the support and long discussions, my friend! Every time I eat frozen yogurt, I think of you!

My sister, Harriet Dickinson Dorsey read The Water Master, cover to cover and into the night. When she said she couldn't put it down, I knew I had something. I can't thank you enough for your support and excitement.

Other readers and friends who provided guidance and moral support along the way were Jenny Sontag, Kathleen King, Barb Strote and Marilyn Heasley. Barbara Seiders made a valiant attempt at technology advice and I hope she still likes me after all that.

And to my husband, Rich Sowieralski, I'm so glad you love football! Thanks for leaving me alone to write.

Finally, to my editor and publisher, Valerie Connelly, who teaches as she edits. I had a ball during our Sunday editing appointments! I look forward to many more hours with you Val!

INTRODUCTION

My first foray into the Columbia Basin occurred after a year of traveling throughout the United States. I had a job interview scheduled in Pasco, Washington for my dream job. We had spent the last few weeks in the lush, green and wet Olympic Peninsula. As I studied the maps of the Southeastern part of the state, I saw that Pasco sat at the convergence of three rivers, the Snake, the Yakima and the mighty Columbia. I imagined a watery playground with lots of trees and green.

It was August. It was hot. As we drove down from the Cascade Mountains into the Yakima Valley the landscape changed from pine forests to sage desert. By the time we got to Pasco, the temperature was 112 degrees, the landscape was dried up and brown and there wasn't a person to be seen on the streets. I cried.

But the job was perfect. I stayed.

Over twenty years later, I'm still here. I have learned that the Columbia Basin and surrounding area is one of the most unusual geographic areas in the United States. Beauty is found in the long evenings of summer, and the most colorful sunsets in the biggest sky you will ever experience. On a good day, the Columbia River flows calm and blue, the water sparkling like a million tiny diamonds During a wind storm the water is angry and brown with white caps spotting the surface. After the storm, thousands of tumbleweeds, partially submerged, look like dead bodies on the turbid waters.

Ten thousand years ago, the largest ice-age floods in geological history scoured the landscape in a few days time. Almost two hundred years ago, the Lewis and Clark expedition camped here. And during World War II, a huge community sprung up in the middle of the desert to support the development of plutonium for the atom bomb.

Pasco, Washington is the physical setting of THE WATERMASTER. It is one of the three cities making up the "Tri-Cities" the other two being Richland and Kennewick. I have taken liberties with the geographic locations of some familiar landmarks. The Horse Heaven Hills, White Bluffs, Rattlesnake Mountain and the rolling hills of the Palouse are all real places, but a reader familiar with this area might not find them where expected. That's the fun of writing fiction. I get to change stuff up!

The Zion Nuclear Power Plant, in Zion, Illinois is real, but the timing of the decommissioning of the plant is not.

The neighborhood where Susan lives exists only in my imagination, as do the characters in my story.

I hope you enjoy THE WATERMASTER as much as I enjoyed writing it.

❧❦

To my dad, Oliver Dickinson.
You stand at my shoulder daily.
I finally did it.

❧❦

THE WICCAN CALENDAR

Sabbat	Alt. Name	Associated Holiday	Date	Occasion
Samhain		Halloween	Oct 31	Pagan New Year, Honoring the dead, Cleansing and releasing
Yule	Winter Equinox	Christmas	Dec 21	Rebirth, Life triumphs over death
Imbolg		Candlemas	Feb 2	Purification, Initiation, Dedication
Eostara	Lady Day, Spring Solstice	Easter	Mar 21	Conception, Regeneration, New Beginnings
Beltane	May Day	May Day	May 1	Passion that fuels Life, Joy, Fertility
Litha	Midsummer, Summer Equinox		Jun 21	Transition, Planning
Lammas	Lughnasadh	First Harvest	Aug 1	Gratitude, Abundance, Fruition
Mabon	Fall Solstice	Thanksgiving (Second Harvest)	Sep 21	Giving thanks, Reflection

CHARGE OF THE GODDESS

Whenever you have need of anything, once in a month, and better it be when the moon is full, then shall ye assemble in some place and adore the spirit of me, who am Queen of all witches. There shall ye assemble, ye who are fain to learn all sorcery, yet have not won its deepest secrets; to these will I teach things that are yet unknown. And ye shall be free from slavery; and as a sign that ye be really free, ye shall be naked in your rites; and ye shall dance, sing, feast, make music and love, all in my praise. For mine is the ecstasy of the spirit, and mine also is joy on earth; for my law is love unto all beings.

Keep pure your highest ideal; strive ever toward it; let naught stop you or turn you aside. For mine is the secret door which opens upon the Land of Youth, and mine is the cup of the wine of life, and the Cauldron of Cerridwen, which is the Holy Grail of immortality. I am the gracious Goddess, who gives the gift of joy unto the heart of man. Upon earth, I give the knowledge of the spirit eternal and beyond death, I give peace, and freedom, and reunion with those who have gone before. Nor do I demand sacrifice; for behold, I am the Mother of all living, and my love is poured out upon the earth.

I who am the beauty of the green earth, and the white Moon among the stars, and the mystery of the waters, and the desire in the heart of man, call unto thy soul. Arise, and come unto me. For I am the soul of nature, who gives life to the universe. From me all things proceed, and unto me all things must return; and before my face, beloved of Gods and of men, let thine innermost divine self be enfolded in the rapture of the infinite. Let my wor-

ship be within the heart that rejoiceth; for behold, all acts of love and pleasure are my rituals. And therefore let there be beauty and strength, power and compassion, honor and humility, mirth and reverence within you. And thou who thinkest to seek for me, know thy seeking and yearning shall avail thee not unless thou knowest the mystery; that if that which thou seekest thou findest not within thee, thou wilt never find it without thee. For behold, I have been with thee from the beginning; and I am that which is attained at the end of desire.

Doreen Valiente, (1950's)

CHARGE OF THE GOD

(Song of Amergen by Robert Graves)

I am a Stag: of seven tines
I am a Flood: across a plain
I am a Wind: upon the waves
I am a Tear: the sun lets fall
I am a Hawk: above the cliff
I am a Thorn: beneath the nail
I am a Wonder: among flowers
I am a Wizard: who but I
sets the cool head aflame?

I am a Spear: that roars for blood
I am a Salmon: in a pool
I am a Lure: from Paradise
I am a Hill: where poets walk
I am a Boar: ruthless and red
I am a Breaker: threatening doom
I am a Tide: that drags to death
I am an Infant: who but I
peeps from the unhewn dolmen arch?

I am the Womb: of every holt
I am the Blaze: on every hill
I am the Queen: of every hive
I am the Shield: for every head
I am the tomb: of every hope

The Charge of the Goddess is reprinted with the permission of the Doreen Valiente Foundation. The Charge of the God is from the book THE WHITE GODDESS, by Robert Graves.

PROLOGUE

Charlie Gottschalk woke in the dusty dawn and cracked open one crusted eye to view the wind-up alarm clock next to the couch. 6:32. He rubbed the gunk out of his eyes and sat up. Today they were coming. Finally. He'd had enough of the suspicious looks of that damned Freeman nosing around. It'd been almost a year for fuck's sake. Now someone he could trust would finally be living in that house and everyone would leave him alone.

Charlie pushed himself back and maneuvered his legs around the piles of newspapers and trash cocooning the couch. He struggled to stand up and held onto the old lawnmower handle to get his balance. He'd have to get that fixed one of these days. He yawned loudly, scratched his stubbly face and hitched up his boxer shorts. Even though the chair she died in was covered with newspapers, old rags and a few dirty dishes, he still couldn't look at it. All he could see was the accusation in her eyes as she took her last breath.

Aw, fuck. It was all her fault. All of it.

It was all going to be behind him soon. He limped along the trail leading to the bathroom, where he pissed into the bathtub. Today would be a good day.

❧❦

BELTANE – NEW LIFE

"I am a lure: from Paradise…"

❧❦

Chapter One

೭∘೯

Struggling to keep my car on the road in the rising wind, I follow behind the lurching U-Haul. The end of our cross-country journey is a few miles ahead. The last few hours, I've been dodging herds of tumbleweeds galloping across the highway. The first one sent my adrenaline into overdrive. Once I slammed into it, sending pieces flying into the wind, I realized they were benign. But the wind steadily pushes my car toward the shoulder while sudden gusts make me swerve like I am drunk. My shoulders and arms ache. I try to relax my vise grip on the steering wheel when another gust pushes me to the side of the road. I worried the wind might flip the high profile U-Haul weaving back and forth ahead of me, and I might become a widow as quickly as I became a wife.

Suddenly the emergency lights on the truck blink on. I barely see them through the thickening dust. Jay slows down and pulls off to the shoulder. I pull in behind him as my cell phone rings.

"What's the problem?" I ask.

"The goddamned truck stopped! It just quit!" Jay screams.

"Hold on, I'm coming up."

I shove my shoulder against the door to open it against the wind, and a gust slams it shut behind me. Too late, I realized I should have exited the car on the other side. A semi whips past me blowing dust into my mouth and eyes. I yelp and scuttle over to the side of the road, finding some relief from the wind on the lee side of the U-Haul.

As I drag myself into the cab and slam the door, Jay bangs on the steering wheel in frustration.

"What the hell?" he yells. "First the goddamned thing won't go over fifty and now it stops? Jesus H!"

The trip had already taken two days longer than expected—and now this!

"Calm down, Jay! We're just outside of town. Let's call and get some help."

I grab my cell phone from my sweatshirt pocket and search for U-Haul dealers. We'd just passed a sign announcing upcoming exits to Kennewick a little way back, so I call the first dealer I find in Kennewick.

"Hi! Yeah, um. I'm Susan Bradley...um, I mean Glasser.

Will I ever get used to my new name?

We rented a U-Haul in Illinois and we broke down right outside Kennewick. I squint into the dim brown light of the growing dust storm.

"I see an exit sign just ahead of us. I think it says 'Coffin Road.' Yeah, thanks."

Coffin Road? Really? Even as I contemplate sitting stalled at the side of the road in a brown cloud, my imagination takes over as I wonder how Coffin Road earned its name. I see a coffin sliding off a truck, body and bones skipping down the road...

The Water Master

৯৯৯

We had dreaded the work it would take to pack two homes for our move, but we finished quickly. First we packed up Jay's little house. He asked some guys from work to help with the heavy things, and his stuff was in the truck in no time. Jay is a minimalist. He had a few framed awards from work, some sports memorabilia, and his favorite painting that hung over his bed: a modern piece with big squares of bright yellow, green and red, with black slashes of paint cutting through it. I saw nothing beautiful in it, but it seemed to be the one thing he valued, so I kept my mouth shut.

I had completed most of my packing prior to our wedding, fully expecting to move a few belongings to Jay's house after selling my furniture. But Jay's job offer and our decision to move to the Northwest required a quick change of plans. I kept my furniture for our new house in Pasco, Washington. Jay's description made it sound like a castle compared to our former homes.

My load held boxes of family photos, framed photographic landscapes taken by my dad, two sets of antique china inherited from my mother and my grandmother, boxes of seasonal placemats, a load of tablecloths and two sets of silver that had been passed down over the years—much of it still packed in the old original boxes. I had never lived where I had room to display or use my cherished belongings, but I was excited about the future possibilities of acquiring an antique hutch to display my treasures. Jay rolled his eyes when I shoved four boxes of Christmas decorations into the truck. I couldn't wait to have a real home to decorate!

We decided to take Interstate 80 to Washington in hopes of avoiding the hours of traffic through Milwaukee and Madison. Leaving Chicago, I followed the U-Haul through the bumper-to-bumper traffic of the western suburbs and then…finally the cornfields of Illinois and we were on our way.

At the first rest stop, Jay informed me the truck was slow-moving.

"I'm afraid the trip is going to take longer than planned," he said.

I couldn't hide my disappointment. We'd discussed stopping along the way to visit historic sites and take a few brief photo hikes.

"That's okay, Suze. You don't need to be behind me all the way. Pull off where you want to and enjoy the sights. Just give me a call and let me know what you're doing, okay?" he said as he hugged me and kissed the top of my head. "Besides, you need to get out and stretch that back of yours. And at the rate this truck is going, it'll be easy for you to catch up to me!"

The first day was a push to make it to the Nebraska border, and it didn't happen. We kept each other awake the last few miles by talking on the cell phones until we could find the next motel, grab dinner and go to bed. We were road-weary, but Jay took the time to give me a back rub. Too tired to make love, we cuddled together and quickly fell asleep.

By the middle of the second day, I was bored out of my mind. Would Nebraska never end? I wanted to see the mountains! Jay entertained me by calling on the cell phone and telling bad knock-knock jokes, pointing out misspellings on road signs and talking sexy.

I should be holding him up. He was the one driving that horrible truck!

Blue skies and puffy clouds made a picturesque backdrop for the wildflowers beginning their spring bloom. When something caught my eye, I pulled off the road to take pictures or read historical markers out loud to Jay over the cell phone as he soldiered on.

By the time the mountains appeared in the distance, my excitement had waned. We were already hours late arriving at our destination. Jay remained upbeat and had already called his new boss to tell him he'd have to put off his start date. I felt like a slug. Jay's never-ending supply of energy held me together, and he encouraged me to enjoy the scenic overviews and tell him all about them the next time we actually had cell service.

Dirty snow still hugged the steep mountainsides. I had plenty of time to view the scenery as I followed behind the limping truck, straining to the tops of steep inclines. Since Jay had encouraged me at the beginning of the trip, I was happy to do the same for him now. He was a little frayed around the edges. I felt sorry for his struggles with the damned truck. Pulling over to take in the views was a relief for me, but I felt guilty doing it. My back was stiff and sore, and each time I left the car, pain shot down my right leg. Jay checked with me each time I stopped to make sure I was all right, continuing to assure me he would enjoy the view later, when I could show him my pictures. We pushed each day of driving longer than was comfortable, trying to make up some miles.

We hoped to be able to stop in Salt Lake City, but decided against it for the sake of time. The Mormon exodus from Illinois in the 1800s and their settlement in Salt Lake City were testament to the lengths people will endure for religious freedom. While our beliefs were far from those of the Mormons, the history was fascinating. As I snuggled against Jay's chest in our motel room after another long day of driving, he gave me a soft kiss and assured me it would be our first vacation. I fell asleep spooned against him and woke in the dark to his gentle caress. We made sleepy love and fell back to sleep, sticky and satisfied.

Interstate 84 out of Salt Lake snaked northwest across desolate lands. This was our last day on the road. The teasing phone calls back and forth dwindled to reporting the need to pull off to make a pit stop, buy gas, or stretch. I lost the desire to photograph everything in sight and just wanted to get there. I hoped never to see another mountain pass again. I couldn't imagine making the same trip in a covered wagon. Throughout the trip I'd been touched that Jay remained so thoughtful toward me, despite his own misery.

⤳⤵

But today he is short with me, distracted and grouchy. I feel desperate to cheer him up.

"At least we're not lost in the mountains of winter, like the Lewis and Clark expedition, or dragging oxen through the mountains and hunting for food."

"But we've been dragging this Fuckin' Oxen through the mountains," he says, which temporarily lightened his mood.

"The tow truck is on its way."

"And then what?" he says.

"Jay, Honey! Really, it's going to be all right. I'm sure they can tow the truck to the house. We'll figure it out."

"Fucking U-Haul!" Jay pounds the steering wheel and lets out a shriek. I back into the door until the handle digs into my back.

Jay's normally sparkling blue eyes turn black with anger and his white knuckles grip the steering wheel. This is a first. I've never experienced any moodiness or even frustration from Jay. Rage isn't even on the radar.

A sudden gust of wind rocks the truck, startling both of us.

"Holy shit," I say. "What is this?"

"It's a fuckin' dust storm! What do you think it is?"

I squint through the windshield, trying to see into the brown cloud swirling around us. Visibility is nearing zero and I hope no one plows into us.

"I've never seen one before. I wonder how long it'll last?"

Jay hesitates. Calmer now, he says, "How would I know? Look it up."

I squeeze my shoulders to my neck, trying to release some of the tension, wincing as the small of my back reminds me of the painful days behind us. I ease off the door and bend my head to the cell phone to research dust storms in Southeastern Washington. I learn that we could be eating dust for minutes or hours. Radar shows a front moving through the area causing this mess and it will probably last the night.

Great.

Chittering like an idiot, I rattle on about the weather as we wait for the tow truck. The combination of the dust storm and Jay's explosive anger keep me on edge. I revert to counseling mode. When my clients went off the emotional deep end, it was better to focus on facts rather than feelings. It usually worked, and to my relief, it is working now. The more I talk, the more Jay relaxes until eventually he lets out a deep sigh, rubs his hands on his thighs and lays his head against the back of the seat.

"Thanks for talking me down, Suze," he says.

I smile and lean over to kiss his cheek.

"No problem," I say. "In sickness and health, dust storms and dead fuckin' oxen and all that." I give the dashboard a playful kick. "Fuckin' Oxen."

Jay laughs a little and shakes his head. He pulls me in as close as he can to kiss me.

"You're the best."

By the time the tow truck pulls up, Jay is his usual amiable self.

The U-Haul guy takes the dust storm in stride, quickly hooking up the U-Haul to the tow truck. We follow him to the Coffin Road exit and head for our new home.

ॐॐॐ

Blah blah blah. This trip has been a nightmare. She's been chattering like a magpie and I'm doing my best to be a support-

ive husband. But the truck's breaking down put me over the edge. I'm pissed and just about done. If she doesn't shut up.... But then I saw the fear in her eyes and I'm going to have to hold it together for a while. I need her and I don't want to blow it.

࿇

"Is this house ever going to cool down?" I ask as I wipe my forehead, startled that I'm not sweating.

"Babe, this house has been closed up for months. Everything is hot in here. It's going to take days to cool down," says Jay. "I don't want to turn on the AC until we're done moving stuff, okay?"

I look out through the open door toward the gravel driveway where a group of three high school boys, strong and still energetic after four hours of moving our belongings, sit on the curb drinking Gatorade and relaxing for the moment.

"How do they do it? I don't think we could have completed this move without their help."

"If it weren't for my new boss, we'd be doing it ourselves."

"They're nice kids."

"I guess they're from Dan's youth group at his church."

"Tell him how much we appreciate it when you start work. They've done a great job."

"For sure," Jay agrees. "Let's get back at it. We're almost done."

We walk back into the burning sun. The membranes in my nose pucker in the dry air. I sneeze. My mouth is

24

dry as chalk despite the bottles of water I am sucking down, and I'm not sweating. My ponytail remains straight and the stray hairs around my face fail to curl into tangled wisps, as they would in the humidity of Chicago.

Ha, Evergreen State, my ass.

I'm relieved the dust storm ended during the night. Who knew that most of Washington is a desert? And here we are in the middle of it, moving into a shabby rent-to-own house on two acres of hobby farmland north of Pasco. Jay's description of a huge and spacious house is all wrong!

Did he really see this place at all? Or did he just want me to believe him to get me out here? Maybe he was so focused on the great deal he'd landed, or maybe he was just a guy and had no idea of the picture he had painted in my head.

I try to shake off my disappointment. I see the potential in the house with some upgrades and remodeling. Right now I just want a shower and a glass of wine, but it's still going to be awhile. How could it be this impossibly hot in May? The neighbors who walked over to greet us said that this heat is out of the norm this early in the spring, but the nights are deliciously cool.

"It was a dry winter," they said. "No snow and little rain."

For a Chicago girl like me, the dry heat feels, well… dry. I still feel grit in my teeth from the dust storm. Today, however, the air is calm and clear. Jay's new boss has willingly given him a few more days before starting work, relieving both of us and giving us more time to settle in.

The Water Master

We round up the boys for the last of the furniture and boxes. Between the two of us we have enough to make a household. Finally.

☙❧

A few hours later, after paying our helpers enough to buy pizza, we're sitting on the couch, feet up on boxes, cooling down in the air-conditioned house.

"Well, whatdya think?" asks Jay, grinning as though he has just conquered Mt. Everest.

I think he is feeling awfully proud of himself. I hate the house but try not to let it show.

"I think I need elves and a shower."

Jay grins. "Well, I think the shower works, but the elves are hiding in cool caves somewhere."

"What is it? Like 105?"

"It's not that hot...maybe 95."

"Ah, but it's a dry heat," I say.

Jay nods. "That's what they say."

"How about I track down a grocery store and buy some basics and some dinner while you find the bathroom stuff? When I get back we can eat, shower and go to bed."

"Sounds good. Especially the bed part," he says with his sexy grin.

"Don't even get your hopes up. Not happenin'."

Jay looks disappointed. "You're kidding, right?"

"No, I'm not kidding! I'm exhausted and my back is killing me. I need a shower, food, a heating pad and some sleep. Tomorrow I'm looking for a massage therapist. It's going to take weeks to recover from this!"

"Fine." He gets up abruptly and stalks out of the room.

What the hell?

కాండ్

I grab my purse and walk out the front door, stiff and moving slow. The sun scalds my face as it hangs over the western horizon. I look at the front yard with dismay. The dead grass and tumbleweeds resting in mounds against the west side of the house mean the owner has done nothing to keep up the property while it waited for its new inhabitants. My disappointment is profound. I'd left it to Jay to make all the arrangements. It was his new job, his move. He was the one who had come out to look for a place for us. His little house in Zion had been so cute, and we had talked at length about what kind of house we wanted. It looked nothing like this one, which is ugly—a basic ranch house with no frills. The front entry opens right into the living room. From the front door you can see through the eat-in kitchen to the back sliding door and back yard. A little hallway off the living room to the left leads to the master bedroom and bath, two other bedrooms and one bathroom. The only positives are the huge property and the ready-to-go raised bed gardens in the back.

Green lawns and colorful flowers surround the houses on our road. Horses graze in the fields and a few of our neighbors raise cattle. Our closest neighbors, Rosie and Russ, stopped by to stay hello as we unpacked the truck. Their garden is well on its way already. I can't wait to plant my own garden, and hope it isn't too late in the growing season. I'll figure it all out later. Jay has no interest in gardening or landscaping, so it will all be up to me. There will be lots of sweat equity going into our new house. I hope that he will eventually enjoy the fruits of my labors when he bites into a sweet tomato from our own garden.

It's so dry! Settling here in the days before air conditioning must have been torture. I can see why the Feds chose to make this area part of the Manhattan Project, where plutonium for the atom bombs was manufactured for the eventual destruction of Japan. The middle of the desert is a great place for the top secret work. Generations later, the government employs thousands of people to clean up the radioactive mess left behind. My husband is one of them.

Even though I am discouraged and bone-tired, I grin all the way to the grocery store. I love Jay and I'm excited to be starting a new adventure. I consider whether or not I want to work. Should I find a counseling job, or do something completely different? I've listened to people's problems for a long time: drugs, alcohol, domestic violence, marital problems, mismanaged adolescents, gambling. I've heard it all. I'd become a counselor because I was curious about people, maybe even nosey. I wasn't afraid to ask hard questions and speak the unspoken. I was so good at picking up on behavior patterns and feeling cues that some of my clients accused me of telepathy, but I am burned out. It's always better to leave at the top of your game.

The Water Master

As I fiddle with the small pearl earring in my earlobe I think maybe I should do something more practical, something that allows me to see progress every day instead of wondering if I'm really helping my clients. Luckily, this new job of Jay's pays very well and I don't have to worry about work immediately. I really don't have to worry about work at all. The money left to me by my parents makes me wealthy, but that is my secret. They raised me to be self-sufficient, and I have never touched that money. It was socked away for the proverbial rainy day. I live on what I make and still shop at thrift stores. I can't help it. That's the way I'm made. I'll get the house in order and try to coax the yard and garden up to snuff before I go back to work.

I park the car at the store and pull down the visor. I look pale and my bloodshot eyes are pocketed in dark circles. After the long days on the road, I move like an old lady and my back is killing me. It is a constant effort to keep the pain under control with regular exercise and yoga. Moving across country with the constant bending, lifting and driving will take weeks to mend. I'll have to work in small bursts to unpack and decorate our new home.

I blink my gritty eyes, rub them and re-tie my shoulder length reddish-brown hair into a messy ponytail, ignoring the few gray strands showing up here and there. Gently slapping my high cheekbones to regain some color, I take a deep breath, smile at my image, flip the visor into place, and gingerly exit the car to limp into the grocery store. I buy a roasted chicken and some prepared salads, milk, eggs, bacon and orange juice and head home.

Home. Nice.

ॐ०॰६

The next morning, the house has cooled to a reasonable temperature. I wake up dehydrated and stiff, with a headache and a mother of a back spasm. I shuffle to the master bathroom and root around in my makeup bag for ibuprofen. No luck. I took the last of it before bed.

"Shit," I mumble. "I should have bought some at the store last night."

The thought of bending over to unpack boxes makes me queasy. Jay is still sleeping, so I sneak out of the bedroom to find my softball.

"I know I put that thing where I could find it," I say to myself. After searching through a few boxes, I remember it's in the pot of my beloved ficus, the only place I was sure I could access easily.

As I lie on the floor with the ball under my lower back, I consider my options for the day. Jay is scheduled to go in to work in the afternoon to finish the hiring paperwork and pick up his security badge.

"Whatcha doin'?" Jay says as he shuffles out of the bedroom.

"I'm hurting pretty bad this morning. I think I'm going to call around for a massage if that's okay with you."

"Sure. Are you up for making some bacon and eggs?"

I sigh. Just once I'd like him to cook. "Okay."

Jay leans over and kisses me. He has that look in his eye.

"Really? Now? Honey, for real there's no way. I'm dyin' here."

Jay frowns. "I miss you!"

"I miss you too, but I can barely move! Give it a few days, ok?"

Jay scowls as he looks down on me. "That massage better work."

I hear the screen door open and someone knocks on the door.

"Who the hell could that be this early?" I ask.

I roll over, rise from the floor and gimp into the bedroom. No sense showing the neighbors my early morning look!

Jay answers the door and I hear him talking to someone. I throw on some shorts and an oversized shirt and walk back out to the living room to see who it is. I stop short at the size of our visitor. Standing on the doorstep is a very corpulent, very tall, scroungy old guy. He is at least six-foot-four. His filthy white t-shirt barely covers a massive belly that hangs over a pair of brown-stained blue jeans held up by greasy, frayed suspenders. It looks as though he uses his whole front side—chest, belly and legs—to wipe his filthy hands. His unshaven cheeks hang in wrinkles around his chin, and the few uneven tobacco-stained teeth produce a smile that looks more like a grimace.

"Hi," I say, taking a step back from the smell wafting from his body into the livingroom.

"Hi, yerself, young lady!" the man slurs, as a thin drool of tobacco juice flows along the frown line on his chin. "I'm Charlie Gottschalk. Wanted to welcome y' folks to the house and see what I can do ya for and how ya like the house and such."

I look at his fat, unshaven face and try to quell the quiver rising up my spine. This must be our landlord.

"I'm Susan, and I guess you've met Jay already."

"Yep. I sure have. How'd the move from Chicaga go?"

"Long drive, but we made it," Jay says with an unfamiliar polite tone.

"Yep. Well, I don't get why anyone would live in the city like that."

I decide against a complicated explanation of why we never truly lived in the city.

"We think we'll really like it here. We like the open space and the rural environment better," I say in an attempt to be friendly.

"Yep. It's rural all right. But too many folks have moved in ova' the years. Down there in the Tri-Cities it's pretty fulla folks. Too many for my taste. We can do without all them stores and franchises. Brings in too many outa-towners and gangs and stuff. I like to keep it real simple."

"Tri-Cities?"

"Yep, we call it that. It's Richland, Pasco and Kennewick. Kinda like one big town now."

"So—where do you live?" I ask.

"Oh, just down the road there. I got myself a little place. My wife died here a few years ago. Just me by m'self now. Kids moved away. Don't see 'em much. They don't like it here and I don't like ta leave home, so there ya are."

Charlie peered into our living room. "Looks like ya got a lot of unpackin' to do, eh?"

"Yeah, we probably need to get started," Jay says, backing into the living room as if to close the door.

I watch the man move his chewing tobacco from one side of his mouth to the other and wonder if he uses the space where his two bottom teeth are missing to spit out the juice—and then worry he will spit right there. I still feel nauseous from the back pain, but watching him makes it worse.

Charlie scans my body, his eyes lingering on my bra-less chest and finally looks me in the eye.

"So, I'm also the Watah Mastah for yeh."

"The what?" I asked.

"The Watah Mastah!" says Charlie, raising his voice.

"What's a Water Master?"

"Whaddya mean what's a Watah Mastah? Ya never heard of a Watah Mastah?"

"Umm, no.".

"Well, well." Charlie grins. "I guess you don't got those in Chicaga, eh, little girl?"

I bristle. I do not like this man. Did Jay meet him when he was out here, or did he make this deal some other way? I never thought to ask.

"I'm the one that's in charge of yer irrigation here!"

"What do you mean—in charge of?" Jay remains quiet.

"I make sure the water is regulated so no one uses too much and everyone gets some."

"I'm sorry? I don't understand." I cross my arms over

my chest.

Charlie leans back, turns his head and spits into the flower bed.

"It's kinda like a volunteer job. I used ta work for the Irrigation District and then I retired. But I get bored and no one else wants ta do it, so I do. I don't care what people say about me, so it's a good job fer me. Keeps me busy. Lets me be the kinda unofficial neighborhood watch guy, too!"

Who watches the neighborhood watch guy?

"So, how do you define 'neighborhood?'" I ask.

"Are ya being smart, missy, or don'tcha know what a neighborhood is?" he snarls.

I'm getting the creeps. Jay's continued silence isn't helping.

"I didn't mean to offend you. We aren't used to all this space between neighbors. I really don't know how big the neighborhood is."

"Oh. Well, I kinda take care'a everythin' between th' highway to th' south down there and th' river along over th'other side there. Them hills off to the north and the main road into town on th' other side kinda wrap it up."

"That's a big neighborhood." *Why is Jay so quiet?*

"Yeah, well, I know most of them folks all along in there. Most of 'em been here for years, though some of 'em are gettin' on and sellin' out to the likes'a y'folks. The couple that rented this here house from me left las' spring. I hadn't found a good renter till the two'a ya showed up."

"So, are you the guy we talk to about starting up the irrigation?" I ask.

"Yep. I kin help ya with that. I'm bettin' there's a few repairs needed and I know the pump needs replacin', but I can get someone out here for ya to take care of it. Y'need to stop by the irrigation office and settle up the bill, y'know. That's not part'a yer rent."

"I'll do that. Thanks for letting me know."

"I'll call 'em for ya and get 'em out soon's possible. How's that?"

"Great!" Jay says finally piping up. "We appreciate you stopping by." He seems in a rush to get him off the front porch.

"Okay, then. I'll talk to y'folks soon."

Charlie Gottschalk turns and walks down the steps to his beat-up pickup truck. He leans a little to the right and has a slight limp. The toe of his right boot turns up, like he is missing toes. Yikes! He is weird.

"Well, he's interesting, huh?"

"You could say that," says Jay.

I feel a strong urge to shower. "Did you meet him when you signed the papers for the house?"

"No. It was all done through a realtor. "

"Well, I hope he leaves us alone. He gave me the creeps."

"Oh, Honey, he's just a local. He can't be all that bad if he's able to maintain his house and this one."

I sigh heavily, considering the next thing I want to say. "It doesn't look to me like he maintains this one much at all! This place is pretty shabby and it's going to take some work to get it looking nice."

Jay's face hardens. "Do you have a problem?"

"I'm a...a little surprised is all," I stutter. "Your description sounded like the house was a...um...a bit bigger, and maybe had a little, ah...more style."

Jay pulls me toward him. "I think that was your imagination...wishful thinking on your part," he says, as he leans down and kisses me.

I'm confused. "Maybe. The yard's a mess, though. It's going to take hours of work to get it where I want it."

Jay laughs. "Not my problem."

I roll my eyes at him. "I know. You've told me a million times. You don't want calluses on your tender little hands!" I say, trying to smile.

"You got it!" Jay says as he walks off to shower.

"I'll start breakfast," I say, as I shake off a prickle of unease.

☜☞

Charlie squeezes into his truck and starts the motor. He stares at the house, spits tobacco juice on the floor of the truck and moves his chaw to the other cheek. *That woman is going to be trouble. I could see it in her eyes. The boy is pussy-whipped. This isn't going to go well.*

☜☞

Jay bangs around in the bedroom, constructing the bed and unpacking sheets, pillows, and quilts. I work in the kitchen. The cabinets are older built-ins, in need of a paint job to cover the ugly yellowed wood. I stack the hodgepodge of everyday dishes into the cupboard and think that two professional people in their early thirties should have nicer stuff than this! My good china will remain packed away…again. A hutch is out of the question. There is no room for it in the kitchen.

While the house is small, it is still bigger than either of our former homes. I lean against the door jamb of the kitchen and look into the living room. It is big enough to hold a couch, coffee and end tables, a few chairs, and our TV and stereo. The beige carpet is nothing special, but appears to be new and clean. A large picture window provides a panoramic view of a cloudless blue sky and the Saddle Mountains in the distance. The front door opens directly into the living room. I imagine building a half-wall to set it off from the living room. Three bedrooms include our master bedroom and bath. The guest room will double as an office/ritual room. Who will our first guests be? With my sister's obsessive focus on her passel of kids and Jay with no family to speak of, it is unlikely we will entertain any guests soon. I mentally shrug and return to my chores.

Around noon, Jay comes into the kitchen. "Got time to make me a sandwich before I go?"

"Oh, geez, I forgot to get sandwich meat at the store last night. Can you pick up something on your way to work? I'll just eat breakfast cereal. Can you stop at the grocery store on your way home? I've started a list."

Jay gives me a hard stare and then sighs with a shrug.

"If I have to. I should be home about four. We've got a long weekend before I start work and we can get some of this stuff wrapped up. I need some time with my baby." Jay wraps me in a bear hug and pats my butt. I hug him back and we share a long kiss.

"Can't wait!" I say. And I mean it. The move has been hard on both of us. We need some cuddle time to reconnect.

࿐

Jay shakes his head as he leaves the house. *I can't count on her for anything. No sex for days, no lunch. What good is she? Patience. Patience.*

He drives south, to Pendleton, Oregon to sign the lease for his studio apartment.

࿐

I spend the afternoon applying the finishing touches on the kitchen. As I start on the bathroom, someone knocks on the front door. Afraid Charlie has returned, I answer the door with trepidation to find our friendly neighbor who had welcomed us on moving day. She is a petite woman with short brown hair shot with gray, a small sunburned nose, and big brown eyes with dark long eyelashes that draw envy from those of us who have to wear mascara to look presentable. She and her husband live across the road and "down a ways."

"Hi! It's Rosie, right?"

"Yeah, Rosie Sharone. Hey, I'm sure you're busy with unpacking, but I wanted you to know we're available if you need anything. Out here it's nice to know who your neighbors are."

"I'm so glad you came over. Jay's out at Hanford getting badged this afternoon and I'm waiting for him to bring home some groceries. I'm getting really hungry!"

"Tell you what. Why don't you let me bring over some snacks right now?"

"Really? Thanks!"

"I'll be back in a few minutes. Is there anything you need?"

"Do you have any Coke?"

"I do. I'll be right back."

I leave the door open for her return and head to the bathroom to empty the final box. In a few minutes Rosie is back with two boxes of crackers, spread cheese and a six-pack of Coke in hand, along with two glasses with ice.

"Wow! This is perfect!" I say.

I clear a spot on a chair for Rosie and make space on the coffee table for the cheese and crackers.

"How long have you lived here?" I ask as I sink back on the couch with my Coke.

"Russ and I moved here when we married about twenty years ago. This is the first house we bought and we've never wanted to move."

"I can see why. Your landscaping is beautiful and your flowers are gorgeous! I can't wait to get this place looking that good."

"Your place is a little rough, being empty this last year," says Rosie as she takes a bite of cracker, "but it shouldn't take too long to get it back into shape."

"I can't wait to dig my hands in the dirt and plant the garden. Did you know the people that lived here before us?"

"Not very well," says Rosie through a mouth full of crackers. "Amanda Clement, the wife, would wave when she took her walks. Her husband Andy hung out with Charlie a lot."

"Charlie, our landlord?"

"Uh-huh," says Rosie as she put another cracker in her mouth. "I have no idea what the attraction was. Andy seemed to be a pretty normal guy, but I don't think Charlie's right in the head. Andy helped Charlie around his house some. Over time, we didn't see Andy and Amanda as much, and then they were gone. They weren't in this house more than a year. No one knows what happened to them. We joked about how they could have changed their identity and escaped to South America or something."

"Did anybody ever look into it?" I ask.

"The police investigated, but I never heard much about it. Charlie would probably know more, since it's his house."

We munch crackers without talking for a moment. Then Rosie asks, "What about you? How'd you end up moving out here?"

"Actually, I was in the process of moving out of the city and in with Jay when a headhunter called about this job. We'd been planning on buying a house at some point near his work at Zion Nuclear Power Plant, but he was laid off. After that, everything happened so fast. We were married and moved out here in the same month!"

"What does Jay do?"

"He's an electrical engineer. He was hired at Zion to work on decommissioning the plant. The company ran into some financial problems and had to lay off most of the employees. Jay was one of them. Hanford Nuclear Assets hired him to work in the Public Relations department. He translates technical language into press releases and documents the general public can understand."

"Wow! An engineer who can speak our language? That's rare!"

I laugh. "He's really good at it."

"He sounds like an interesting guy," says Rosie. "Russ and I look forward getting to know you two."

"That'll be great. We'll get together after we settle in." I grab another cracker. "I really appreciate the cheese and crackers. I feel better already!"

"Good. I'm glad I could help."

"To be honest, I was nervous when I heard you at the door. Charlie stopped by this morning…"

"Now that's an ugly way to start your morning!" laughs Rosie. "He may be your landlord, but be aware he's like a bloodhound, sniffing out stuff that's none of his business."

"He gives off a bad vibe."

"Yeah. He's irritating but mostly harmless. When he was the Watermaster, he was pretty stingy with the irrigation."

"What's the story with that?" I ask as I reach for more crackers.

"Are you familiar with irrigation and all the politics that surround it?"

"Not really. Where I come from we just count on rain and house water during the dry times."

"Yeah, well this area wouldn't survive with just rain. Irrigation followed the railroads. Various entrepreneurs developed their own private systems. Then, in the early 1900's, the Feds took over and started to regulate water usage. That's when the regional irrigation districts formed."

"Where does the water come from?" I ask.

"From reservoirs up in the Cascade Mountains and the Grand Coulee Dam. Years with lots of snow, we get lots of water. Less snow, less water. There's competition for the water between the serious farmers with thousands of acres and homeowners like us. If you don't pay your bill, your water gets shut off. Unfortunately, everyone on that pump is also without water. Nothing like a little peer pressure from the neighbors to encourage you to pay your bill!"

"What does any of that have to do with Charlie?"

"He worked for the Irrigation District for years as the Watermaster. His job was to manage the competing interests. He controlled the pumps and turned users on or off depending on who needed water and how much was available..."

"I'm confused. You're speaking in past tense."

"Well, Charlie used to be the Watermaster. He isn't anymore, although he tells everyone he is. The irrigation district got rid of him a few years ago."

"Got rid of him?"

"Nobody really knows what happened. You know how personnel issues are. One day he was driving his own truck instead of the District's and that was that. But he still acts like he's the guy."

"He told us he was in charge of the irrigation," I say.

"Not really. He knows people and still tries to throw his weight around, but he's pretty ineffective. No one pays much attention to him."

"It seems a little...antiquated, to have a person doing that," I say.

"Nowadays we don't need a neighborhood Watermaster, since the flow is regulated by technology. Years ago, when Charlie started his job, the Watermaster had a lot of power, and he loved it. I think he lives in a bit of a fantasy world where he still controls the neighborhood."

"Charlie told me he could get the irrigation people out here to start us up. Is that true?"

"Oh, yeah, but you'll pay for it!"

"How much will it cost?"

"Oh, I'm not talking money. I'm talking favors."

"What kind of favors?"

"Whatever he decides he needs. He'll coerce you into paying somehow, and when you least expect it."

"How does he get away with that?"

"He's so hard to deal with that most people avoid confronting him."

"So he just walks all over you?"

"Well, not me. He seems to target people. Like the folks who lived in your house, the Clements. First they had a good relationship with him, and then something happened to sour the relationship, and then they left."

"That makes me really uncomfortable. I think I need to call the irrigation repair shop before he does."

Rosie looks out the window. "Too late!"

I watch three trucks pull up to the house and a crew of men pour out, tools in hand.

"Oh, shit."

The Water Master

We step out to the front porch to greet the irrigation crew.

"Ma'am? Hello! Charlie gave us a call. We'll figure out what's up and give you some idea about what to do, okay?" I note the man talking is tan and handsome under his Seattle Mariners baseball hat and the scrub of beard on his face.

"Thanks," I say. "What are you going to do exactly?"

"We'll see what it's going to take to get the irrigation up and running. We'll check the pumps, the electrical hookups, and check for leaks in the pipes. Charlie says it's been down for about a year. We'll give you an estimate of what needs to get done."

"Ooohkay," I say. I'm out of my comfort zone with irrigation, water, pumps...what will this cost?

Where is Jay? I wish he were home to deal with this.

It is almost five.

And why didn't Charlie make all these repairs before I had to deal with it?

"It'll take a few hours. We'll get the list to you before we go."

Just then Jay turns into the driveway. He scowls as he gets out of the car and then gives me a 'what's going on?' look.

"Hey! What's up?" he asks as he slams the car door. He pulls two bags of groceries out of the back seat.

We climb down the stairs to meet him.

"Charlie arranged for the irrigation guys to see what we need."

"Hi," says Jay, as he greets the Mariners Hat Guy.

44

Rosie turns to me. "It looks like you have your hands full," she says. "I'll get out of your hair. Keep the Coke and snacks. Please stop by if you need anything, okay?" She trots down the steps and down the street. Jay's lips press together as he stares after Rosie.

"Jay, can you talk to these guys? I'm in the middle of a few things inside," I say.

I reach for the groceries in his hands and notice his tension. "Yeah," he says and turns and walks around the side of the house with the crew.

Inside the cool house again, I put groceries away and watch the men talking and gesturing as they walk the property. At the far end of the lot, they all hover over something in the ground for long enough that I lose interest and go out to the car to get what I hope are more groceries. The car is full of bags.

Ah. Great job!

Back in the house, I discover steaks, baking potatoes and salad makings, and start dinner.

He bought charcoal, bless his heart!

I walk out to the patio to start the charcoal, grateful that we'd decided to pack the old Weber grill after all.

A few minutes later, Jay enters through the back slider, still scowling.

"I told you I wanted nothing to do with dealing with all the crap in the yard!"

Surprised at his tone, I back away from him.

"I thought since you're much better at mechanical things than I am, you might be able to understand what they were talking about. It's all over my head."

"I don't know crap about this shit!" he yells. "I had no idea what they were talking about and felt like an idiot."

"I'm sorry! I had no idea—" I say trying to soothe his anger.

"This is your problem and you deal with it!"

"Okay. Okay. There's no reason to be so upset! At least tell me what they said."

"They can tell you themselves! And it's a good thing Charlie took care of it for us since you're so stupid!"

My mouth drops open in shock. He admits to knowing nothing about irrigation, but I'm the stupid one? He really means it when he says he isn't going to be the least bit of help. But calling me names is new. Defensive, I say, "Charlie's involvement may be more trouble than it's worth."

"What?"

I relay what Rosie shared with me earlier. Jay growls.

"Susan, he's just helping out. There's nothing wrong with him."

"It's not just that he's a slob. There was something about the way he looked at me."

"You women and your intuition. I think you're a little overly sensitive. He's our landlord, so you better get over it," say Jay. "I'm going to change into some shorts."

⁂

During dinner we discuss our plans for the next few days. I decide it is best not to talk about the yard or the irrigation repair costs. Perhaps worry about his new job is making him unusually irritable. I'm not used to walking on eggshells, but two angry outbursts out of Jay within a few days makes me cautious. I'm certain it is due to all the adjustments of marriage and the move, and it will pass.

As Jay slices into his steak, he shares his first impressions of work, which are positive and upbeat. He likes his boss, despite feeling like he's been asked a few inappropriate questions, such as what church he attends and if he has kids. He hasn't felt safe discussing his Wiccan practices, and wants a better handle on the work culture before sharing too much.

I understand. I was relieved that the topic of religion hadn't been part of my conversation with Rosie.

About the time we finish dinner, the Mariners Hat Guy knocks on the back door. Jay reaches over to slide open the door and take the list of irrigation items that we need to address. He is relaxed now, and the men talk sports for a few minutes. After the crew leaves, we put aside the list to deal with later. Jay's earlier moodiness is gone.

After cleaning up the kitchen together, we finally put our feet up and share a bottle of wine. Later, we enjoy the lovemaking we've put off for days.

That night I slept like the dead.

Chapter Two

❧❧

By Sunday night the house is in order. Now Jay can return to a clean and functioning household after his first day of work. I like taking care of him. My mom and dad had such a great marriage and we had a supportive, peaceful household. I hope to provide that for Jay. Sometimes he seems a little needy. I feel certain he will eventually relax once he gets started in his new job and we settle in.

Before bed, I review the irrigation list. First I need to find the Irrigation District office and "settle the bill."

How much will it cost? I also want to schedule a massage, but with whom?

The latest buzz on the news is about a local massage business that the police shut down. The therapists were unlicensed, and oh-by-the-way were also performing sex acts on their customers.

I need a good recommendation.

Monday morning, Jay takes off at four-thirty and I decide to get up about the same time. By eight, I have completed some detailed unpacking, showered, applied my makeup, and I feel ready to face humans again. As I walk out to the car, I see Rosie walking her golden retriever.

"Hi!" I call, waving as Rosie walks up.

The dog sniffs my feet and wags its tail. "This is Walker," says Rosie. "And he does."

I laugh. "I love dogs. Can't wait to get settled in enough to adopt one!"

"There are a lot of rescue organizations around here, but it's likely a dog will find you. Out here, people tend to dump their animals. Just be patient!" says Rosie.

"I'll keep that in mind."

"Hey," I say. "I'm looking for a massage therapist and was wondering if you happen to know anyone?"

"Yeah, I do. There's a doctor's office not too far from here that has a massage therapist a few days a week. I can't remember her name, but the office is called Three Rivers General Practice. Dr. Elwin is the doc. He's one of those guys that got part of his schooling paid for if he practiced in a rural area. He could have moved into the Tri-Cities years ago, but chose to stay out here. He's a great guy and someone to consider if you need a GP."

"Thanks. I'll give them a call."

"You could probably just stop by. They're at the intersection of Road 202 and the highway."

"I'll stop by on my way to town," I say as I get into my car.

"Have a good day!" says Rosie as Walker tugs her down the street.

৵৹৹৵

I easily find the doctor's office and walk inside to make an appointment.

"Can I help you?" asks the surly gray-haired woman at the reception desk.

"Hi. I'm new in town and understand you have a

49

massage therapist here?"

"Yes, we do. Would you like to set up an appointment?"

"I would! Thanks!"

The receptionist, sticks her nose in the air as she looks through the bottom of her trifocals to locate the appointment calendar on the computer.

"I hate this computerized appointment system," she says. "I much prefer paper."

"It can be hard to get used to," I say, in an attempt to mollify her.

The woman shoves a form at me. I complete it with my name, address and phone number and hand it back to her.

"Marisa can see you on Wednesday at three. Will that work?"

"Yes, thanks."

The receptionist writes out the appointment on a card. I read the names. *Marisa Ramirez, Massage Therapist. Thomas Elwin, MD. Karen Elwin, ARNP.* It is a real family practice. I wonder if the receptionist is related, and hope the rest of the practice isn't as grumpy as she is.

The next stop is the credit union to set up our joint checking account. I'm not entirely comfortable with combining our money, but Jay insisted and promised to leave the money management in my hands. We agreed to not charge more on credit cards than we could pay off the next month, and to discuss large purchases prior to buying anything. However, the one area that Jay vehemently rejected was electronic banking. My own accounts had been electronic since that option was available, but Jay is paranoid about account hackers. I appreciate the ease of viewing my account status whenever I want to. To me, the risk is negligible. Now I'll be stuck waiting for a monthly statement. I agreed to try this method, but I'm not convinced it will work.

A half hour later, I finish at the credit union. Accounts are in place, temporary checks are in hand, and as I sit down in my car, I let out a deep breath. Combining our money feels more married than standing before the judge and saying "I do." However, my inheritance, which is managed by my financial advisor in Illinois, will stay right where it is. Jay has no idea how much money I have, and I prefer to keep it that way. All I told him was that I had a small inheritance tied up in investments, and my sister and children will remain the beneficiaries if something happens to me. I intend for the money to stay with my family. At the time Jay shrugged his shoulders as if it didn't bother him, but I noticed the muscles working in his jaw as he changed the subject. He'll just have to deal with it.

After a few more hours of trying to find my way around town to set up phones, television, gas and electric, I locate the Irrigation District office just off Main Street in Pasco. I enter the cool office and feel like I'm stepping back in time to the 1940's. It smells of old wood and older carpets, and years of brewed coffee and stale cigarette smoke. Built-in desks and cabinets of dark walnut contrast with cream-colored walls. The hushed voices and paper shuffling make me think of the library of my childhood. Sunshine angles through a row of windows above the door and feels hot on my back.

The lady at the front desk squints into the ray of sunlight. She looks as old as the building. She is dressed in a beautiful red belted shirt-waist dress. Her gray hair, pulled up in a bun, looks old-fashioned but attractive.

"Can I help you?"

"Yes. I have a list of things I need to take care of to start up our irrigation. We just rented our house, and apparently I'm supposed to settle the bill," I say as I point out the statement on the list.

"Okay. Let me go pull the records."

The woman disappears. After a few minutes, I sit down in one of the old leather chairs by the front window. Through the wooden blinds I observe a busy downtown, cars angle-parked up and down the street, a hardware store across the street, a shoe store next door to that.

The receptionist returns with a folder.

"Okay, let's see what we have," she says. She shuffles some papers and looks confused.

After a long pause she says, "Well, it looks like Charlie paid what the old owners owed...hmm. I'm surprised he did that. Even though it's his house, the renter is usually responsible for the costs of the irrigation. I guess he figured he better pay it since we were unable to find the past renters to collect. You actually owe one hundred twenty-five dollars and sixty-seven cents for your first payment this year."

"How far back did the old owners owe?" I ask.

"I can't really share that with you. I'm sorry," says the woman.

"Oh, of course," I say, embarrassed. I should have known better.

I write out the check and she gives me a receipt. I ask about the billing process and she tells me we will have two bills per year, one in April and one in October. Failure to pay the bill will allow the county to put a lien on the property.

I don't want Charlie mad at me for that! I'll make sure that bill gets paid!

I leave the office relieved that irrigation wasn't as expensive as I thought it would be. I hope the repairs won't cost too much. I'm anxious to plant my garden!

❧

The next few days are a whirlwind of organizing, filling cupboards with staples, unpacking more boxes, and making sure Jay gets up and out every morning. He comes home tired, but enthused about his job duties and his co-workers. Driving out to his office in the middle of the desert requires leaving by four-thirty and arriving home around six. He works 'eight-nines'—eight nine-hour days, with every other Friday off. Jay wonders if three-day weekends make the long work days worth it.

I can't wait for my massage appointment. My muscle spasm keeps nagging, but at least I can bend over if I'm careful. Lifting heavy boxes is out of the question. Jay stacked them so I can unload each one, break it down and then unload the one underneath it.

The Water Master

Wednesday afternoon I drive to my appointment. Entering the office, I find no one at the front desk. I wait a moment and finally ring the bell situated on the counter in front of me.

I hear movement in the back of the office and an attractive woman in a white lab coat appears.

"Hi. Sorry about that. Do you have an appointment?"

"Yes. With Marisa."

"She's finishing up with a client. She'll be out to meet you in a minute."

"Shall I pay now?"

"Actually, you can pay her. She takes care of her own billing."

"Thanks." I sit down.

I watch the woman as she moves around the reception area. I assume she is Karen Elwin. Her forehead is knotted in worry lines. Her thick red hair is pulled back in a scrunchy and tucked back under, like she'd been in a hurry to pull her hair out of the way. Freckles stand out on her pale face. Her skin is clear and it's hard for me to tell how old she is. Thirty? Forty?

The music in the office is soothing, but the vibe is off. Something is wrong here. I sit quietly and close my eyes. I hear Karen walk down the hall, her footsteps muffled on the deep carpet. I become aware of voices in the back of the office—Karen and a man's deep voice speaking in a low but intense tone. I hear "billing," "computer," and finally a hissed "Shit!" and a door slamming. Everything goes quiet, then a door opens down the other hall. I open my eyes to see a short, chunky woman I assume to be Marisa walk out with her client.

"Wow. That was great. I can actually turn my neck now. Thanks so much and I'll see you next month," says the woman.

"Okay then," says Marisa.

I like Marisa immediately. Her Hispanic heritage is evident in her dark complexion, brown eyes and black hair pulled up in a knot on the top of her head. She looks like she has just finished an exercise workout.

She must put intense physical effort into her massage!

She is wearing yoga capris and a tank top, and her bare feet whisper across the carpet as she walks toward me. Her face is open and friendly, her smile of welcome, genuine.

"Hi. I'm Marisa. I'm sorry, I don't know your name. We had a little glitch in the system this morning. I know I have appointments, but I'm not sure who they're with!"

"I'm Susan Br...Glasser."

"Nice to meet you. I have some paperwork for you to fill out, if you don't mind."

She hands me a clipboard and busies herself behind the counter while I answer the usual medical questions. It takes a few minutes for me to finish, and by that time Marisa has prepared the massage room and returns to walk me back.

I follow Marisa down the short hallway to the tiny room. Pleasant new age music plays and the lights are low.

"So, tell me about what's going on with you," says Marisa.

"I've spent the last two weeks packing, moving from Illinois and unpacking, and my lower back is killing me."

"Anything else?"

"I need some all-over TLC."

"You got it. Remove your clothes and lay under the covers face up and I'll be back."

I am used to the drill. I take off my clothes and hide my underwear under my shorts and shirt on the bench. Earrings and necklace removed and rings off, I crawl under the covers. A heating pad warms me from head to toe, and despite the heat outside, it is welcome in the air-conditioned office.

Marisa knocks. I say, "I'm ready."

She rustles into the room. I hear her pull her stool around to the head of the table. Marisa adjusts the little pillow under my head and starts working on my neck. Every touch feels painful, but oh, so good!

As Marisa works my head and neck, I finally begin to relax. We chat a little here and there, but it is a relief not to be expected to talk. Halfway through the hour, I roll onto my stomach for Marisa to work on my back.

As she begins to knead my lower back, Marisa grunts in concern. "You are really knotted up back here. When was the last time you had a massage?"

"It's been months. The wedding and move took up all my time."

"Wedding?"

"I married my husband about a month before we moved."

"Where'd you meet your husband?"

I had noticed some goddess statues in the room when I came in, so I take a chance.

"At the Midwest Pagan Festival."

"Oh, how cool!"

With relief, I go on. "We met there last summer. He just sauntered up to me like we were old friends and introduced himself."

I smile to myself remembering the moment. Pagans as a whole are a mish-mash of quirky, but he stood out as a yuppie among hippies, except for the dragon tattoo on his arm and his long, almost black hair pulled into a ponytail. He towered over the other men at six feet five. Being taller than average myself, I was immediately attracted to him. He wore a long-sleeved cotton shirt, sleeves rolled up to just below his elbows and unbuttoned top to bottom. His hairless bare chest was well-sculpted, but not too muscular. I found the veins on his arms and well-shaped hands just plain sexy. He wore cutoffs, as opposed to the other men who wore saris or loincloths or nothing at all. His shorts showed off long tan legs and narrow feet with perfectly-shaped toenails. Beneath his high forehead, warm brown eyes sparkled with intelligence and interest in me, and within minutes we were discussing our favorite authors, trips we had taken, and all the things we still wanted to do. It was love at first sight, and though we lived two hours apart, we managed to meet almost every weekend, sometimes at my apartment in Chicago but mostly at his little rental house near the Wisconsin border.

"We had a long-distance relationship for awhile, but were able to see each other practically every weekend. And then he proposed."

"Tell me about the proposal. I love proposals!"

"Well, we were walking on the beach along the shore of

Lake Michigan. It was just a few blocks from his house. Suddenly he knelt down in the sand and said, "You and I are just alike. We love to learn, we're on the same spiritual path and we want the same things out of life. Will you marry me?"

"Oooh, that sounds so romantic," says Marisa.

"It was. We had a lot of fun in a short period of time. But all the change…new town, new job, I'm not working. I feel a little unsettled."

"I'm sure it will all work out," says Marisa in her soothing voice.

We are quiet for awhile. Finally, I get up the nerve to ask, "Can I ask you if something bad happened here today?"

Marisa hesitates. "Why do you ask?"

"I noticed some tension when I walked in the office. Generally, my intuition is pretty good."

"You're right. Our receptionist just up and quit."

"I'm sorry. "That must be causing some problems for you!"

"I'm not sure what Tom is going to do. It's hard enough running a small practice without this issue."

"Is this going to affect you at all?"

"Not really. I rent space from them and they refer to me. I do my own billing."

"I noticed when I made my appointment to see you that the receptionist was not a happy camper."

"She hated the new computer system and just wasn't adjusting to modernizing the office. She made sure everyone knew that!"

"It's probably best that she's gone, then."

"We'll have to wait and see. In the meantime, Tom's

wife is trying to figure things out up front. But she'd much rather focus on her patients. She's a little lost."

We are quiet again while Marisa digs her elbows into my lower back.

Thank the gods! The pain is exquisite. She is awesome!

After the massage, I dress and examine myself in the mirror. At a little over five foot eight, I've maintained my athletic build for the most part. I'm starting to get a little gut on me, and will have to work on that. I keep my shoulder-length hair in a ponytail most of the time. It's easier to deal with that way. My make-up is minimal—usually a dash of mascara and lip gloss—and I hate to fuss with my clothes. I'm happiest in sweats and tennis shoes, but can dress up well in a pinch. After my massage I look a little lax around the eyes, and notice the laugh lines around my mouth more than usual. I pull my hair back in its usual style and go up front. The woman in the lab coat is shuffling papers at the desk.

"Are you Mrs. Elwin?" I ask.

"Yeah. You can call me Karen. Everyone does."

"I'm Susan Glasser."

"Did you want to set up another appointment with Marisa?"

"Definitely."

We work out my next appointment and Karen hands me the appointment card.

Taking a chance, I ask with some hesitation, "Do you need some help?"

"What?"

"Well, I noticed your receptionist is gone and I sense

the office is a little out of control. I'm new in town and, um…maybe I can help you."

"Do you know computers?"

"I'm a licensed counselor. Not here…in Illinois…ah, and in my last job I had to enter all billing, insurance and case notes into a software program. I should be able to find my way around whatever you have."

Karen hesitates. "Can you give me a minute?"

"Sure."

I sit down in the waiting room.

What am I thinking? It felt right to make that offer. I wasn't going to work for awhile, but it won't do any harm, will it? Although Jay and I agreed to pool our money, I'm still not comfortable with the idea, particularly if I'm not earning any of it. A job, even if it doesn't pay much, will help with that problem and I can put my earnings toward the landscaping and other yard projects. I'll have to hire out the physical labor, since Jay isn't going to help me and I can't do it myself. I won't be bored. I can even ride my bike here if I want to. I wonder what Dr. Elwin's medical philosophy is. Is he open to alternative healing practices? He has a massage therapist in his office, so that's positive.

Thoughts bubble through my head as I second-guess myself. A few minutes later, Karen comes back. "Do you have a minute to talk with me and my husband?" she asks.

I lick my dry lips. "Sure," I say, with more confidence than I feel.

I follow Karen to the back of the office.

Karen offers me a seat at a round table in the small break room. She pulls a bottle of water out of the refrigerator and offers it to me.

"You'll need to hydrate. I talked to Marisa and she really worked your back. You'll feel a little sick unless you drink enough water."

"Thanks," I say, grateful for her thoughtfulness.

I hear footsteps in the hall and a man enters the room looking like he has just stepped out of the pages of GQ. My jaw drops. Dr. Elwin is six feet of athlete. It is obvious he takes very good care of himself. His face is framed in curly, thick dark hair with a touch of gray at the temples. His blue eyes look tired and worried, but I believe they can sparkle under the right circumstances. His long nose profiles the strong features of a Roman gladiator. His self-confidence and charisma are immediately clear.

I am embarrassed at my reaction to his astonishing good looks and am momentarily unable to speak. Karen laughs.

"He has that effect on everybody," says Karen. "The old ladies love him. They call us 'Ken and Barbie.'"

I take a breath. "Sorry! How embarrassing!"

Dr. Elwin chuckles as he takes a seat and leans back on the rear legs of the chair. He rocks back and forth as he speaks.

"I was just talking to Marisa about you."

I wait.

"She said you feel right."

"What?"

"She said she liked how you felt. I trust her. She's worked here for three years and she's good people. If she says you're good, you're good."

I don't know what to say.

"Sooo…"

"So, tell me what you think you can do for us?"

"Well, I'm not sure what's going on exactly…"

"Neither are we."

"I'm good with people, or at least that's what my clients thought. Well…most of them, anyhow."

Tom smiles and nods.

"I know computers and actually like setting up and organizing anything. I live about two miles from here and I can be flexible with hours and salary…well, I…"

"We can talk about that later," says Tom.

Karen and Tom look at each other and Karen gives him a slight nod.

"Okay," says Tom.

"Okay?"

"Yep. You're hired. I don't have time to do anything but see patients. Silvia was a good receptionist until she got pissed off. I may be wrong, but I think she screwed us. Maybe even stole money from us, and I need to figure it out. Show me what you got."

"Um. Okay. When do you want me to start?"

"Tomorrow. Seven-thirty. You and Karen work out the details."

Stunned, I stand up and shake his hand. He gives me a strong handshake and looks right into my eyes. "I'm putting my trust in you," he says. "It's not a commitment I take lightly and I hope you're worthy."

I hope I am too.

৵৽৶

The Water Master

Once home, I slump on the couch with a cold glass of water and review my mental to-do list. The massage has worked wonders, but there are still boxes to unpack and a household to arrange.

I need to get the irrigation taken care of. I call the number Mariners Hat Guy has provided, and make arrangements for Premier Irrigation to come out to the house late in the week. I read off all the parts on the list, and the man on the phone assures me I'll be well taken care of.

Whatever happened to the good old garden hose and sprinkler? I'll just relax for a little bit.

As I slide my water glass onto the coffee table, I close my eyes and let my mind wander. I drift off.

ॐ

"Hey!" Jay says as he walks in the front door. My eyes fly open. Startled, I look at my watch. So much for productive activity!

"Hi," I say as I sit up, wiping the sleep from my face.

"Busy day, eh?" Jay asks with a grin.

"Wow. I had no idea I was that tired!"

"Me too. Why don't we just eat out and call it a day."

"Sounds good. Give me a few minutes to wake up."

Not knowing a good local restaurant, we decide on the franchise near the highway. It is less crowded than we expect. Over salads, we discuss our day. I share my news about the new job and my experience with Dr. Elwin.

"How much will you be paid?" Jay asks.

"I don't know. Does it really matter?"

"Oh, that's right. I forgot. You don't need money

since you have a bunch stashed away," he teases.

I don't find it funny.

"That's a low blow," I say. "I told you. That's my emergency fund. I've depended on myself for a long time, Jay. I need to know that money is there in case something bad happens."

"Well, now that we're married, that should be *our* money."

"Please, Jay. Give it some time. I'm not ready to do that yet."

"Okay, okay," he says as he distractedly reaches over and squeezes my hand.

My stomach tightens. This is not the first time he has brought the subject up. All he knows is I have a little money tucked away for a rainy day. I have yet to tell him that I have a few million dollars in various accounts and CDs. I have never touched it, and never will unless I become sick or can't support myself for some reason.

I know it looks a little crazy, living such a frugal life-style with all that money just sitting there. But my parents gained their wealth when I was in high school and never flaunted it. We lived simply. Ruthie and I were expected to work for our spending money. Mom and Dad viewed their wealth as an unexpected windfall, the result of a fluke invention patented by my dad and his boss. It took off like a shot, and money poured in. Mom and Dad had dreams of a perfect early retirement in their perfect house, but the dreams turned to the nightmare of Mom's stroke and early death, and Dad's unending grief and drinking, leading to his demise a few years later. That left me and

Ruthie with all that money. It felt like dust to me. Ruthie had used some of hers to build a house to fit her large family, putting the rest away for future college expenses. I'd already started my career, and living by myself, never saw a need to spend wildly on material things.

I like knowing I have the security of my investments for the future, but prefer to make my own way. Every time I think of that money I get sick to my stomach. I really want my parents back. I miss them every day. They had been my rock and had supported me as much as they could before the money poured in. They didn't even know what to do with all of it! But everything changed so fast then. Dad was gone more, mom was distant. I floundered around until I found that helping others kept my mind off my own problems. Then mom died and it all went to hell. I'd been a shell until Jay came along. He had a way about him that made me feel like I belonged somewhere again. While it appeared that Jay managed his finances perfectly well, I had seen too many marriages founder when it came to money management, particularly when there was a lot of it. I need time to see how we worked together before adding him to those accounts.

We eat in uncomfortable silence. I decide to try again.

"It sounds like the receptionist was upset about something and she took it out on the doc. I have no idea what it was. I'm looking forward to figuring it out."

Jay looks concerned. "Be careful. If she was into anything illegal, they may need to press charges. Then you'd be called as a witness."

"How is that a problem?"

"The personal lives of witnesses are always called into question," says Jay.

"So?"

"So you're a Wiccan in Christian territory. How do you think that will play out?"

"I don't see that my beliefs make any difference. It's my personal ethics that matter," I say. I hate it when he gets paranoid and suspicious. I sound grouchy.

"I'm just saying it's best to stay out of the spotlight."

"We'll cross that road when we get there," I say, tamping down my spiking frustration.

"I really don't think you get it, Suze. I work with people who make it pretty clear that if you aren't with them regarding their religious beliefs, then you are against them."

"Aren't you doing the same thing? Sometimes you wear your righteousness about Wicca on your sleeve. It can be just as offensive. Just keep it to yourself and focus on your work. It shouldn't be about who is right and wrong. You don't like it when the holy-roller types do that."

"Wicca is who I am!" says Jay, his voice rising.

I notice the couple at the next table giving us a strange look.

What's up with him?

"Wicca doesn't define you, Honey. It defines how you live. If you live your spiritual beliefs then people just see a good person. It doesn't matter if you're Christian or Wiccan. Your kindness, service to others…all that stuff is what matters, not your religion."

"What about all those crooked politicians touting

their Christian values?" he says. "The general population agrees with them."

"The general population? That's what the news and the talking heads would have us believe. We know there are thousands, if not millions of people that believe it doesn't matter what religion you are, as long as you don't hurt others and strive not to do damage...that's what it takes to be a good human."

"That's naïve. You should take the readings I've assigned you more seriously. The more I teach you, the more you'll understand how careful we have to be."

I feel a chill. When Jay asked me if I wanted to be his student, our relationship was just starting. I was thrilled to have a mentor and jumped at the chance. At the time, I felt I could learn a new view from him, and I had. Jay is a scholar of all religions, well read and able to discuss anything from Hinduism to Catholicism.

Jay introduced me to new authors, particularly Dagan Moore, a noted scholar among Wiccans and also Jay's teacher and High Priest. Once back to my grind in Chicago, I read everything I could find. Jay and I talked on the phone every night before bed and studied together on the weekends. He was a great teacher, but now he is less focused on spirituality and the metaphysical. He seems almost obsessed with learning about leading groups, directing people and the politics of religion. I don't want him directing my spiritual life. Nobody should do that. But I don't want to be contentious about it either. I just want to find a spiritual path that is fulfilling and peaceful.

The Water Master

"We'll see," I say. "Let's go home. I have a new job in the morning."

Jay shoves his chair back and marches out of the restaurant.

❧

I don't want her working at that goddamned doctor's office. Whatever is going on there is none of her business. She should be home with me, maybe have a few harmless hobbies, maybe she can make some home improvements or garden. But work? No way! That's not going to last long. I'll make sure of that!

Chapter Three

࿔

As the sun pokes through the slats of the blinds in the bedroom, I crawl out of bed. Jay has already left for the day. It's very early but I want to relax a little before starting my new job. After showering and munching on a toasted bagel, I enter our meditation/ritual/office room. We have yet to set up the altar. I pull out my meditation pillow and fold into the meditation posture: legs crossed, back straight. I close my eyes and take a few deep breaths. My meditation practice has suffered since I met Jay. Our weekends have been busy and I spend more time reading than meditating. I shift my focus to slow my breathing. My mind wanders to the conversation with Jay last night. I'm disturbed.

Something's off. What is it exactly? I quiet my breath again and let my mind relax a little.

A scene from a movie comes to mind. In it, a woman is hanging up a bathroom towel. A man comes up behind her and trapping her between his arms, adjusts the towel. He smiles coldly and says to the woman, "Remember how I taught you?" The woman looks down meekly and says, "Yes. I'm sorry."

My eyes fly open and my stomach lurches. "What the hell was that?" I say out loud. I look at my watch and realize I need to leave—soon. I gather my things together feeling troubled, but quickly turn my mind to the new job and questions about what I will find at Dr. Elwin's office.

࿐

I arrive at the office just as the doctor and his wife pull up and park. They both welcome me with smiles and handshakes. They're so friendly. I hope they aren't in too much trouble.

Karen gives me a tour of the office, showing me the exam rooms, the file room and the now-familiar conference/lunchroom. Next is a brief overview of the appointment and billing software. The program is similar to the one I used in Chicago and I feel like I can get a handle on it fairly quickly. By the time my orientation is complete, it is almost nine and patients are due soon.

I review the appointments for the day and pull the patient files. I decide to review the billing history for each of them, looking for anomalies. Perhaps I will have time to talk with each one, and see if they have noticed any discrepancies on bills or insurance.

As I unlock the front doors, the first patient is already waiting. I log him in and place his file in the holding bin for Karen.

The morning continues in this fashion. I briefly interview the patients about any billing concerns. Only one woman indicated that she had never received any information from the insurance regarding an office surgical procedure. She'd paid her co-pay to Silvia, but hadn't seen the insurance billing. I agree to look into it and set her file aside.

Just before lunch, Marisa arrives. She welcomes me with a bear hug and a big grin.

"We're so glad you're here," she says.

"Well, I have you to thank!"

"I just have a feeling you're going to be great for us!" says Marisa.

"We'll see. There are some problems to figure out."

"Maybe we should all sit down at the end of the day and put our heads together."

"Good idea. I'll make it happen."

On my first day, I find an easy rhythm that surprises me. The process is similar to the various counseling offices I've worked in, only now I am on the other side of the desk. The patients seem to adore Dr. Elwin and Karen, who genuinely care about each patient. Their medical philosophy is holistic and includes the patient's input and level of motivation when prescribing a therapy.

Marisa's clients float out of her office massage drunk, with glazed eyes, mussed hair, and eager to set up their next appointments. Between patients, I manage to talk with Karen and Dr. Elwin—*"Call me Tom for God's sake!"*—and they agree to order dinner in and discuss the billing situation.

I call Jay.

"Hey, Jay, do you mind fixing your own dinner tonight? I'm going to be late."

"Whatever!" He slams down the phone.

Oh, jeez!

Eventually, the pizza and salad arrive, Tom locks the office doors, and we assemble in the conference room. I look at the salad in dismay.

Salad? that leaves less room for pizza—I'll try not to eat like a pig in front of my new bosses.

"Where do you want to start?" Tom asks.

"On the pizza!" I say, smiling.

"I'm right there with ya!" says Tom as he shoves the salad aside. Everyone laughs.

"So much for eating healthy," says Marisa.

After a few moments of chomping in silence, I ask, "Why don't you tell me what happened?"

Karen and Tom exchange looks.

Tom says, "Before we do that, can you tell us more about you?"

"Sure. I'm from Chicago, for starters..." I tell them about my professional past: earning my Master's degree in counseling with a focus on addictions, my frustration with insurance companies driving treatment plans, my decision to enter private practice, and my eventual mental exhaustion after years of dealing with the emotional pain of others. I went on to describe my ambivalent feelings about living in the city. I loved the food and entertainment options but felt cut off from nature. I talked about meeting Jay, our brief courtship and marriage, and our move to Washington. I made them laugh a few times, and they asked questions here and there while finishing up the pizza.

"Is anyone going to eat this salad?" asks Karen. The room goes silent. "Okay, then. I think I'll just put this in the fridge for tomorrow's lunch."

Tom leans forward. "Susan, here's what we know,"

he says.

I sit back and take a sip of water. "Okay."

"Silvia has worked for us since we opened the practice over twenty years ago. She became like family to us. She set up the billing system from scratch and developed her own way of running the office. For the first year I kept a close eye on the books, and made sure everything was done to our standards.

"Karen and I were newly married, and she was finishing up her ARNP. It was a busy time and a difficult practice to build. My medical degree was financed by a group that required I work at least four years in a rural environment, with the focus of our clinical practice on itinerant agricultural workers. I chose Pasco. Back then all the docs were in town, and I was the only one out here in the sticks. And it was much more rural then. Now we have restaurants and a grocery store on this side of the river. As time went by, some of the farmers sold their land, and the investors bought it up and divided it into the hobby farms like the area where you live.

"We built our practice and kept our whole-person philosophy despite the fights with the insurance companies to see more patients and take less time. It's been hard to hold on, but here we are.

"Silvia began to bog down a few years ago. All the insurance was going electronic and there was too much paper. She wouldn't discuss making changes until we had a serious talk. We realized if the practice was going to remain viable into the future that we had to learn this stuff.

"The three of us reviewed software and picked the

one we have now. We spent a week attending classes in Seattle to learn the software and all the other computer programs we needed to electronify the office. We thought Silvia was on board, but soon her demeanor changed. She was short with the patients and surly most of the time. We thought her mood would improve, and it did, for awhile. Then we started receiving letters from the insurance companies that things weren't matching up. Payments and appointments didn't make sense. A few patients complained that they weren't receiving insurance forms. Their explanation of benefits was confusing. Some had made their copays but insurance wasn't being billed. Medicare became involved, and they've been sending us inquiry letters about patients who were billed for appointments that we have no record of. It's a huge mess."

"Have you contacted a lawyer or the police?"

"No. Not yet."

"You already may be under investigation if Medicare suspects fraud."

"Yeah. But this disaster didn't come to a head until last week."

"What happened last week?" I ask.

"Silvia was having one of her 'grump attacks,' as we called them. She was slamming stuff around the front desk and muttering to herself about working for a bunch of idiots. That put me over the edge. I lost it. I yelled at her and told her we were in deep trouble because of her incompetence, and she walked out. We haven't seen her since."

"You're better off without her," I say.

"I think we are," says Karen. "But it's disturbing to

us, too. We put our trust in her. We were close friends and colleagues—or at least we thought we were. I'm afraid she may have really done some damage."

"The first thing we need to do is write letters to Medicare and the other insurance companies and let them know you're investigating wrongdoing in your office. You have to be proactive to let them know it's not you that is responsible for this. And you need to at least alert the police department to let them know you suspect theft or fraud on Silvia's part. You also need advice from your attorney on the best way to proceed. You shouldn't do this without someone backing you up."

"Wow!" exclaims Marisa. "You seem to know what you're doing!"

"I worked for an office that had a similar problem, and while I wasn't actively involved in all the details, I was deposed and understood the process that they went through. It was a grim experience."

"I'll contact our attorney and the police department. We can set up a meeting and go from there," says Karen.

"I'll write the letters to the insurance companies. I'll need a list of patients who have complained about billing," I say.

"I can get that done for you," says Karen. "I think we all may be working extra hours to figure this out."

"Yep," says Tom as he yawns. "Let's wrap it up."

"One more question," I say. "What is Silvia's last name? I need it for the letters."

"Gottschalk," says Karen.

The image of Charlie Gottschalk walking down the

sidewalk with the funny, leaning limp pops into my mind. "Any relation to Charlie?" I ask.

"Her brother," says Karen as she leaves the room.

శ్రోడ

I sleep poorly and wake frequently, forgetting my dreams except for the feeling of despair or fear each one left behind. My nightmares disappeared when I met Jay. I hope this is a fluke. Returning to the sleepless nights and terrifying dreams after my mom's death isn't an option. It must be all the change, the move...

Frustrated, I get up before sunrise. Jay's already out of the house—earlier than usual—and left without saying goodbye.

As the coffeepot gurgles, I open the slider and step out to the patio. It's going to be another warm day. I try to shake off my low mood. I want it to be leftovers from my sleepless night, but it's more than that.

When I arrived home the night before, Jay was angry. The quick phone call to him explaining I would be late should have been a no-never-mind, but it wasn't. Not by a long shot. When I came through the front door he had a beer in his hand and glared at me, obviously angry.

"Is this how it's going to be?" he shouted. "Late nights with your doctor friend?"

"I told you about it. Why are you so upset?"

"Because when we got married I expected you to be home. You don't care about me! I'm in a new job, it's beyond stressful, and right away you're off and running in another direction," he yelled.

Confused, I said, "I don't understand. You took care of yourself for years! Fixing your own dinner so I can attend a late meeting has nothing to do with whether or not I care about you."

The argument went on with no resolution. I finally apologized—for what, I'm not sure. I needed it to end it so I could retreat to my bed. Jay, of course, wanted to make love. I told him in no uncertain terms to leave me alone. The tension pinging off of Jay's body felt as if I were sleeping with a cougar on the hunt. I had hoped things would be better this morning, but Jay had left without a word.

Jay had never shown any evidence of this angry streak when we were dating. Most of our weekends together had been spent at his place, because we'd enjoyed the quiet woods around his house. My apartment on the North Side never had felt like home, so I didn't mind. And Jay was so easygoing about the few weekends I was on call and couldn't get away to spend time with him.

He never used to complain. Maybe it's just the stress of the new job...

As I sip my coffee, I make a mental list of chores for the weekend.

I'll concentrate on whatever has to be done for the moment, because if I think about the mountain of work required to improve the house and yard, I'll just cry. What was Jay thinking? Couldn't he have found a better place than this? Did he feel rushed about finding a place to live, or was he trying to save money by going cheap? Starting my new job gives me less time to work on the house. Have I made a mistake? My offer to work for the Elwins came out of nowhere, like an unseen hand shoving

me in an impulsive direction. Of all the changes I face, working
for the doctor and his wife excites me the most.

I glance at the clock and realize if I don't speed up, I'll
be late for work. I quickly rinse my coffee cup in the sink,
grab my purse and leave.

ॐ

It's a busy day. I enjoy the light conversation with
the patients. People with medical problems are similar to
those with mental health issues. Some manage their own
care. Others want someone else to do it for them. I'd had
difficulty managing my frustration with my clients who
bitterly complained about their lot in life, but did nothing
to change it. Karen and Tom appear to manage their patients with empathy, but I am pretty sure a bit of eye-roll-
ing occurs behind closed doors.

Karen moves some patients around to give her time
to compile her list of patients with billing complaints. At
the end of the day she reviews it with me.

"Can I take some of the patient files home with me?"
I ask.

"Our policy requires that all files remain in the office. If something happens to the file—it burns up in a car
wreck, is eaten by the dog or is stolen, we're sunk. Not
only do we lose the file but the patient's confidentiality as
well," says Karen.

"Ahh," I say. This news means I will have to do my investigation at the office, not at home. Given Jay's reaction
to my first late night, this strategy will certainly irritate
him. "Okay. Is it all right if I work here on the weekends

and at night?"

"Sure. We'll probably be here too, since we need to get to the bottom of this."

"So, I think what I'll do this weekend is write the letters to the insurance companies, and I'll start on the files next week."

"Sounds good. Keep track of your hours. And get some rest and finish unpacking!"

I sigh as I open the front door. I 'm not sure I'll get it all done.

☙❦❧

Jay and I put our argument behind us over the weekend. I was up by five on Saturday and had the letters finished by eight. Jay didn't get up until later, so my project didn't interfere with our time working together on the house. We finished setting up all the rooms, broke down the boxes, and stocked the cabinets. I wrote out a menu for the week and bought all of the ingredients. I cooked a few meals and froze them in individual servings, so Jay would have food if I was working. It felt ridiculous to take care of a grown man this way, but if he needed home cooking to feel cared for, then I would do it. He would have food on the nights I worked late.

Sunday afternoon, Jay drove over to Charlie's house to ask him some questions about the house. I miss having trees, so I asked him to check with Charlie to see if we could plant some. He was gone about two hours. When he came back he poured wine for both of us, and we sat in our newly unpacked and clean living room to relax.

"You were gone an awfully long time, just to ask Charlie a few questions," I say.

Jay rolls his eyes.

"What's the problem? I visited with him for awhile."

"What's his house like?"

"We didn't go in. He brought me a beer from inside and we sat on his front porch. Thank God it was in the shade. Sitting outside in this heat sucks."

"So, what'd you find out?"

"I got a name and number for a landscaping guy." He hands me a piece of paper.

"I'll call him tomorrow," I say. "I need my trees."

"Maybe we can plant some fast-growing trees, put in your garden and decide where we want the kennel."

"Kennel?"

Jay smiles. "You said you wanted dogs, right?"

I laugh. "You're kidding! I thought you didn't want to go there yet."

"Well, it won't be right away, but I can see us adopting some dogs. The back yard is fenced and will be a great place for them."

I feel a surge of joy.

Everything is going to be fine.

"So, tell me what you found out about Charlie," I say. I'm thinking about his sister Silvia and wonder what their story is.

"He spent the whole time gossiping about our various neighbors."

"Like what?" I ask, disgusted with my willingness to partake in gossip.

"Hmm. Let's see. Take your little neighbor friend that was here the other day…"

"Rosie?"

"Yeah. She and her husband separated a few years back and then got back together. She rules the roost, as he says, and he's a big wimp and lets her make all the decisions."

"How would he know that?"

"I didn't get a good feeling from her either. She seemed nosey."

"All she did was bring me snacks and we had some neighborly conversation. That's not nosey."

"Anyhow, Charlie told me a little about your Dr. Elwin too."

"He's not 'my' Dr. Elwin, Jay. He's my boss."

"Apparently he didn't treat his last receptionist very well. Charlie gave me an earful about how he might be sued for age discrimination and how he made her work late hours, embarrassed her in front of patients and criticized her work."

"Did he mention that the receptionist is also his sister?" I ask.

"Yeah. What difference does that make?"

"Well, his opinion is rather one-sided. I think there's another side to the story."

"So what is it?"

"I don't know yet, but we'll figure it out eventually."

"It sounds like you're all out to get her," says Jay.

Why is he so defensive?

"I wouldn't say that, but she did leave some billing problems behind."

"What do you mean?"

"I probably shouldn't talk about it."

"You can tell me," says Jay as he teasingly pulls my hair.

I smile at him and kiss him on the cheek.

"Sorry, Honey. I love you, but this is work."

Jay pulls away from me and stares at me with hard eyes.

"I don't like secrets," he says.

My heart beats a little faster.

"I'm not keeping secrets. It's work stuff. Confidentiality and all that—"

"So, you're not going to talk about work with me?"

"Of course I will. You know, the usual 'how was your day' stuff—but I'll probably have to work some late nights to help them catch up. That's why I did all that cooking this weekend, so you'll have a good meal if I can't get home for dinner."

I'm nervous and talking too fast.

Jay is silent. He takes a quick sip of wine. "I don't like it. I want you home. And from what Charlie tells me, you're working at a crappy place, for crappy money. And I don't trust you with that Elwin guy. I hear he's a player!"

"From who, Charlie?" Now I'm pissed. I yell, "And when have I ever given you a reason not to trust me, for God's sake?" I jump off the couch and take my wine glass to the kitchen for a refill.

Silence from the living room.

I stand at the counter, not daring to drink the wine because I want to slug it down.

The Water Master

Jay stands in the doorway to the living room. "I'm sorry, Suze," he says, calmer now. "I don't know why I said that. Of course I trust you. I'm just...I don't know. I don't feel right when you're not here."

What do you say to that?

"Jay, can we just clear this up? We're both adults. We both lived alone for a long time. There's no reason why you can't take care of yourself if I'm not here. It doesn't mean I've ditched you. And you, of all people, should understand confidential work stuff. You've got your secret squirrel clearance at your own job and I don't ask you to reveal confidential information, right? Can you deal with that?"

"Yes, I can deal with that." He comes toward me looking for a hug. "I'm sorry."

Reluctantly I let him hug me. My confident, cocky husband is needier than I ever imagined.

Who is keeping secrets from whom?

I pull away and begin to clean up the kitchen. I change the subject.

"Full moon next week. When do you want to do ritual?"

"Let's do it on Wednesday. Are you ready? Have you memorized your parts yet?"

"Yeah, I worked on them while you were out here interviewing, remember?"

Jay reaches for me again. I let myself lean into him and try to let go of my anger. Jay kisses the top of my head and says softly, "We'll be all right, Honey. Just follow my lead."

❧❧

The Water Master

I have to control myself better. Susan's job is screwing everything up. I don't want her to work and I certainly don't want her keeping secrets from me. Whatever happened at Dr. Elwin's office must be a big deal. Charlie told me that Silvia walked out with no explanation. There has to be something wrong with that doctor. How am I going to make Susan see she is making a big mistake? I'll have to think about this. There has to be a way...

☙❧

I'm too busy with patients coming and going to focus on the billing research during regular office hours. Working through lunch and an hour or so after the office closes might not complete the job as quickly as I'd like, but at least Jay will see I am taking his concerns seriously, and he can count on me to be home by the time he arrives from work.

I'm able to thoroughly review four or five files a day. Eventually, Silvia's MO becomes apparent. Sometimes she charged the patient their co-pay, but wouldn't record the appointment. She'd probably pocketed the co-pays. The deceit was easy to see once chart notes were compared to charges, but it also required a detailed and time-consuming review of the chart notes. Silvia also charged insurance for non-existent appointments. This was most noticeable with the few Medicare and Medicaid patient charts I was able to review. For Silvia to take the insurance payments when they came in, she had to keep track of the fake charges and move money from the office account to her own, or forge Dr. Elwin's signature. Discrepancies were evident in almost every chart I touched.

Tom, Karen and I had decided to research only the

84

last two years, just to get started. Going back ten or twenty years will take forever.

Late one afternoon, I find a few minutes to talk with Karen and Tom about my initial findings.

As we gather around the table in the lunch room, Karen says, "By the way, I contacted our attorney. He's going to talk to a detective and will be in touch."

"So where do you think this is all headed?" Tom asks me.

"Not only did she steal from the patients and the insurance, but she stole from you. So far I can document a few thousand dollars in losses, and that's just on ten or fifteen patients. I think she forged checks, modified the appointment book, and pocketed co-pays, depending on the patient. I have no idea if or how she may have transferred money out of your accounts to her own."

Tom sighs and chews his cheek in thought.

"I guess we just keep at it, hmm?" he says. Karen takes his hand and squeezes it. Tom's face is etched with worry lines that seem to have appeared overnight. Karen's lips are chapped from nervous chewing. Even if I could magically produce the stolen money, the deeper damage done by Silvia's deceit and disloyalty will never be healed.

"I'll do whatever I can to get the info we need," I say. "Do you guys mind if I leave on time tomorrow? We have plans tomorrow night."

"Not a problem! Doing anything fun?" asks Karen.

"Date night. If we don't plan them, they never happen!"

The Water Master

౷

Wednesday evening, the orange full moon rises above the horizon while the western sky fills with the pinks and purples of the desert sunset. Much as we would both like to be outdoors for the full moon ritual, Jay feels it is safer to be indoors. He is too uncomfortable to risk being seen and having our actions misunderstood.

Tonight the spare bedroom becomes our ritual space. A small altar sits in the center of the room, with the ritual implements of sword, broom, salt, water, wand, scourge, candle, pentacle and athame, along with cakes and ale. Dagan Moore had built the altar as a gift to Jay when he raised him to third degree High Priest. While I appreciate Dagan's time and effort, I think the work looks amateurish. I would never tell Jay, though! He is very proud of it. I scan the altar to make sure we have everything. Jay is very particular about his altar, making it a rule that all things on it be treated with the sacred respect they deserve. In everyday life, the athame is just a hunting knife, the goblet is just a glass, the salt is just seasoning and the wand is just a stick. To Wiccans, these all have symbolic significance.

I spend a few minutes in silence, tamping down my irritation with all the froo-froo. To sit on the back patio and silently watch the full moon rise, while listening to the sounds of the night, is enough for me. But once I decided to walk this path, I had to accept that the froo-froo is part of it.

Jay enters the room in his black robe and red stole, which have the symbols of his Third Degree High Priest embroidered throughout. My robe is black as well and my stole is white with pentagrams embroidered along the bottom. Making the stoles had been one of my "assignments" and much as I hate sewing, I managed to make the stoles look good enough for Jay's critical eye.

"You ready?" he says.

"Yes."

Jay stands in the doorway as I begin cleansing the circle. Taking the broom, I walk around the altar clockwise or 'deosil' three times, quietly reciting the words that consecrate the circle. Next, I close the circle, using the sword.

I lay down the sword and walk to the entrance of the circle where Jay stands.

I ask, "How do you enter?"

He replies, "With an open heart and an open mind."

I twirl him clockwise and take up the sword once more to close the entrance to the circle.

Jay approaches the altar to perform the blessing of the salt and water, which he then sprinkles around the boundary of the circle and sprinkles me as well. I take the goblet and sprinkle him in kind. We then bless the circle using incense and the candle, and Jay places the wards in the four directions.

After completing that, together we raise the circle, drawing our arms skyward. Jay then performs the ceremony of drawing down the moon.

I begin to feel nervous at this point. Jay is such a stickler on memorization. I stand in front of him, and with my athame draw a pentagram in the air in front of him and say:

The Water Master

Of the Mother darksome and divine
Mine the scourge, and mine the kiss;
The five point star of love and bliss—
Here I charge you, in this sign.

After completing the drawing-down, I have my final long memorization to recite. The *Charge of the Goddess* is beautiful prose and I savor the sound of some of the phrases, but not all of it makes sense to me and it is *long!*

After completing the first half I take a deep breath. My heart pounds.

Did I say it right?

I look at Jay for encouragement, but his face is rigid and serious. I let out a sigh and Jay gives me a dirty look. A few minutes later, I'm done with the *Charge* and Jay recites the *Charge of the God*.

The full moon ritual recognizes the cycle of the moon that is represented by the Goddess. For this ritual, our meditation focuses on releasing the past and embracing our future together in this new place. I have difficulty focusing on the future. My neck prickles as if some unseen force has brushed against it. I shrug my shoulders and rub my neck. Jay senses my movement and opens his eyes at the same time I do. He raises his eyebrow in quiet reprimand. I try to calm myself by thinking of the comforting imagery of the full moon representing the female: the Goddess. The powerful force of the moon pushes and pulls at the earth, affecting the tides, people's moods, and women's natural cycles. The God is represented by the sun: hot and strong in summer, weaker in winter, but always returning.

I was raised in a Christian church, but had never really believed what I was taught. I liked being part of something bigger than myself and the feeling of belonging and acceptance. But it all ended when my parents died. My grief made everyone, including the pastor, too uncomfortable. The most they could offer was to pray for me, but I needed to talk and to share and to cry with someone. After I moved away, I never went back to church, but wandered from book to book, author to author, looking for the spiritual answer. The closest I had come was Wicca. I was willing to give it a try, and Jay's instruction had helped me understand the deeper meaning behind the ritual.

Wiccan imagery helps me visualize that, while all things are not equal, they all have their time. If Jay is the sun and I am the moon, this difference does not mean one is better than the other. It means we have opposite strengths and can balance each other. I hope it isn't bullshit.

I snap out of my thoughts when Jay gently rings the bell, ending our meditation.

The ritual ends with the blessing and sharing of cakes and ale. I had stopped at the grocery store and bought a small carrot cake. The 'ale' is our favorite wine. We close the circle and remain silent as we leave the room.

I remove my robe and walk out onto the patio. The moon is high in the sky and looks smaller than it did earlier in the evening. Jay walks out beside me and puts his arm around me.

"I like the big sky out here," I say.

"Me, too." He pauses. "What was going on with you during meditation? You weren't focused. You need to work harder at that."

"Oh, I was just thinking about the imagery of the ritual and how it really does help me see things in a different way."

"You were supposed to be meditating on letting go of the past and focusing on our future."

"I couldn't settle down with those thoughts. But isn't it supposed to be a spiritual experience? My spirit led me to a different place."

"That's lack of discipline on your part. I thought you were better than that! And you were hesitating during the *Charge*. You should have that fully memorized by now."

Unwilling to allow Jay to alter my mood, I say, "I love the words. It's hard to concentrate and say the words the way I want to."

"When you have the ritual memorized and can perform it without a hitch, you'll be able to complete it without thinking, and then you can fully realize the spiritual significance of the words you're speaking," says Jay.

I deflate. I don't want to argue but I don't agree with Jay.

"Okay. I guess I should work on that, huh?" I turn to go inside, the beauty of the evening lost for now. Spiritual experiences are supposed to make you feel happy and light. I felt that tonight until Jay burst my bubble. I know in my heart that I am on the right track. How can I get Jay to see that, when he is so intent on teaching me the right way to be Wiccan? Wicca might become a burden I don't want to bear.

When is that bitch going to learn there's a right way and a wrong way to do things?

Jay tried to put aside his frustration with Susan.

Dagan never would have allowed me to get away with that

kind of laziness. But there are more important things than ritual right now. The late nights she spends at work must have something to do with that damned doctor. Damned good thing I told that story about a doctor appointment today so I could get out of work to check out that Elwin guy. He sure is all caught up in himself and being a doctor and all—and way too good looking. I know she's attracted to him. How long will it be before she tells her first lie? Hell, she's already refusing to answer my questions—and she's certainly less interested in fucking. She looks like shit in her sweats. And she won't dress up for me like she did in the beginning.

Jay ripped open the dresser drawer to get out a clean tee-shirt, slammed it shut and stared at himself in the mirror on the wall above the dresser.

I gotta get myself under control. I don't want her to know how pissed I am.

He stalked into the bathroom, stepped into the shower and as the hot water beat against his shoulders, he jacked-off. That always helped.

ॐ

During the next few weeks Jay and I fell into a pattern of work, sharing a late pre-prepared dinner and falling into bed. Jay complained that our sex life was disappointing. We were both tired, but he insisted we have sex as often as possible. I tried to comply, talking to myself about giving and loving and caring, but his demands left me feeling used. Saying *"Not tonight, honey"* didn't go over well. Jay pouted and made me feel like I was responsible for his happiness. It was easier to give him what he wanted.

When we'd lived apart, our weekends had been passionate. Jay spent time with me, learning my body, finding his way to my favorite spots and patiently bringing me pleasure I had never experienced before. Now it seemed he was less attentive, more interested in his own pleasure than mine.

I need time to build the mood. So, I would gently guide Jay, trying to slow him down, but he lost patience with me and gruffly told me what to do for him. I tried talking to him at dinner, the only time we were always together other than when we went to bed. He insisted he was fine, but didn't seem to realize that I wasn't. I found that the more I tried to be heard, the less Jay heard me. Our conversations turned into arguments of who needed what more than the other and I knew, with all of my counseling experience, that I was falling into a negative cycle of interacting that I felt powerless to stop. So, I gave up.

After work and on weekends I tended the garden. I planted tomatoes, cucumbers, squash, carrots, peppers, red leaf lettuce, and one bed of my favorite herbs: basil, oregano, parsley and mint. Pots around the patio held petunias, stephanotis and geraniums. I threw some wildflower seed along the fence for good measure. The landscapers had planted fast-growing shade trees on the west side of the yard. It will be years before they will provide shade, but at least it is a start. Charlie told us that any improvements we make on the property will eventually be deducted from the final sale price when we are ready to buy. I keep close accounts of each expenditure.

Thankfully, the Clements had constructed four raised

garden beds with irrigation spouts sprouting out of each one. The irrigation guys had connected a large hose to each spout, and then smaller hoses to each planting area. This system prevents weed growth where no plants grow, and also slows water loss from evaporation. The irrigation is on a timer, but I have trouble figuring out how much water I should run. Some days the garden is soaked and others it's completely dry. Since the water runs during the night, I'm not awake to see what's going on. I already had to start over with the over-watered cucumbers that rotted before they barely broke the soil. My new name for the irrigation is "the irritation."

I called Premier Irrigation a couple of times to see if they could figure out the problem, and they assured me the irrigation was set correctly. On the weekends, I tested the system and it seemed like everything should be working, but my plants looked stressed as they rose out of the dirt. I spot-water the dry spots and continue making adjustments. All of the fiddling has made me more comfortable with the irrigation, and I now feel somewhat expert at setting the timer.

Despite my late start planting the garden, my plants grow quickly in the heat of the long days. During the week, I get up early to wander back to the garden with my coffee and enjoy the early morning coolness as I review the progress of my plants. The fragrances emanating from the herbs make me eager to prepare salads with fresh basil and tomatoes. I'll have to wait for that, though. The plants have a ways to go before I can start harvesting, and work is keeping me too busy to cook the meals I'd like during the week.

Jay's attitude about the yard work remains unchanged. The most he is willing to do is mow the lawn with the used riding mower we purchased from the local yard and feed store. He listens to music or books through his headphones while I tend my plants and the flower beds along the front of the house.

Dagan Moore's new book is now published, and Jay can't stop talking about it. The theme of this book is less spiritual and more about coven management and teaching. I find it boring and have difficulty reading it.

During my workday, I focus on taking good care of the patients and finishing the initial audits of the charts. I delved deeper into the billing history, and discovered that there was a reason Silvia had become so irritated with her job after the computer billing was put into place.

Without the computer, Silvia was able to easily pursue her fraudulent behavior by entering non-existent appointments on the calendar after the day was done. Then she billed them out to the insurance company or Medicare and must have confiscated and forged checks as they arrived at the office. She had actually forged some case notes! My research took me to the local banks in an effort to track down Silvia's account information, but I was unsuccessful. The banks would only talk to the police.

Once the computer system was set up, Silvia had difficulty faking appointments. When a patient was seen in the office, the entry couldn't be changed and all the billing occurred off that entry. At that point, I was able to see that Silvia had begun pocketing co-pays—small potatoes compared to the insurance payments, but still money. I also found appointments entered without corresponding case notes.

After pulling all this information together for Tom and Karen, I asked for some time at the end of one of our lighter days, knowing we all would have a little energy left to discuss the ramifications. I lock up after the last patient, grab files and walk back to the conference room.

Tom is already there sitting with his feet up on the conference table while Karen rummages in the refrigerator for some snacks. We settle ourselves at the table as Karen lays out some cups of yogurt and spoons.

"So with the patients we discussed, how much money did Silvia steal?" asks Tom.

"Right now, I'm estimating it's in the tens of thousands of dollars."

Karen puts her head in her hands and Tom looks stunned.

"That's… ..shit!" he says.

Karen looks stricken. "Why would she do this to us?"

"I don't have a clue," says Tom. "She was fine until we got the computer. But she was so private…never discussed her personal life at all. Everything I knew about her I heard from other people."

"What *do* you know about her?" I ask.

"She's worked her whole life, never married, lives way out of town on her own, and her only living relatives are Charlie and his kids."

"That's it?"

"Pretty much. Various patients would mention seeing her at the grocery store or at church."

"And when Charlie lost his toes, she helped him out for awhile," says Karen.

"Yeah, what's up with Charlie and his toes?" I ask.

Tom grunts. "Hmm. That was pretty ugly. His wife lost her foot at the same time."

"His wife? It's hard to imagine anyone marrying Charlie!"

"That's a story in itself. His wife was a real beauty. Tall, slim, long black hair. Gorgeous, big brown eyes. Really smart. She was part Native American—her mother was a member of the Yakama Nation. They were a mismatched pair."

"How did they get together? Do you know?"

"Not for sure. It may have been one of those young love stories. I think she got pregnant before they married. Both families were Catholic. You know the story."

"And she stayed with him all those years because she believed it would be a sin to divorce him?"

"I have to think so," says Tom. "Charlie had to be miserable to live with. She did her duty, that's for sure."

"So back to the foot story," I prompt.

"Yeah. Charlie and his wife were cleaning up behind their house about ten years ago. They had managed to move some of the junk off the property, and he was trying to start an old mower so they could mow down the weeds. She was helping him remove some debris out from under the blade, but he hadn't turned off the mower. When it let loose, she fell backwards and the mower lurched forward and took off her foot right at the ankle. Charlie jumped off the mower and tripped into the blade somehow. The whole thing was a bloody mess. Thank goodness someone heard them yelling and called for help. Margaret lost so much blood she almost died."

"Where does Silvia fit into all of this?" I ask.

"She stayed out at their house while they healed up," says Karen. "She cooked, cleaned, got them back on their feet…well, not exactly." We all laugh at that.

"What about his kids? Where are they?"

"All I know is that he has a son who moved away years ago after getting into a little trouble right out of high school. He's never been back. He has two daughters that live in Seattle. I don't know much about them," said Karen.

"Charlie mentioned that he lost his wife a few years ago," I say.

"She wasn't right after that accident. She didn't leave the house at all. I heard she was mostly bedridden and wouldn't make the effort to get up. Charlie never talked about it," says Tom. "It didn't slow him down any, though. Once his toes healed up he was back at it, nosing around everyone's business and doing his irrigation thing."

"I wonder if Silvia's stealing money had anything to do with taking care of them."

"Charlie qualified for disability and he had a little money from his own family. I'm not sure why she would have needed to do that."

"When people do illegal things, usually their reasoning makes perfect sense to them, but not to anyone else," I say. "How did Charlie's wife die?"

"Heart attack. Died in her sleep," says Tom.

"How was Charlie after that? Did Silvia's demeanor

change at all?"

"Silvia was the same private person she always was. The only reason we knew she was helping them out was because Charlie told us. Charlie, on the other hand, seemed to have more time on his hands and seemed pretty chipper after Margaret died," says Tom.

"Where does Silvia live?"

"Out on the old highway toward Prosser," says Karen.

"Have either of you been out to see if she's still there?" I ask.

"No. I'm too pissed off. I'm not sure what I'd do!" says Tom. "I gave all the pertinent information to the detective and I'm leaving it up to him. He told me not to do or say anything to her. I'd like to go rip her face off…"

Tom abruptly stops himself from saying more, but his anger is palpable. He rubs his forehead as his knee bounces up and down. Karen reaches over to touch his shoulder, but he shrugs her off. I give her a sympathetic look.

"I think I might take a ride out there this weekend and see if she'll talk to me," I say.

"What are you going to do?" says Tom. "Ask her for our money back?"

"She doesn't have to know I'm on to her. I can talk with her about the job and ask some questions about how to do some things, see what she says."

"Good luck," says Karen. "She might greet you at the door with a shotgun for all I know."

"I'll take Jay. He can be scary when he wants to!"

Chapter Four

❧❧

Saturday morning, I rise early to weed the garden. I crave a BLT with tomatoes from my own garden, but it will be late summer before they are ready to harvest. Last night I bought tomatoes from the store, which aren't going to be nearly good enough. But on rye toast with crunchy head lettuce, I'll have to make do. Carrying my steaming coffee, I wade through the unmown grass, thinking Jay is behind on that chore. The wet grass clings to my shoes, but the further I walk, the wetter the grass gets until water rises up around my feet with each step. I stop to stare in dismay as water pools around my ankles. My garden has disappeared under a huge puddle! Looking back toward the house, I can see the slight incline that caused all the water to pool at this point in the yard.

Have I been watering too much? Maybe a pipe has broken!

I squish back to the garage to check the irrigation timer. It is set accurately. I turn the whole thing off. Typical to every household emergency, it is Saturday. I have no idea what to do next, and Jay will be no help. Rather than wake him, I walk down to Rosie's house to see if Russ can help me.

The couple is sitting on their wide veranda porch, enjoying their morning coffee.

"Hi! You're up early!" says Rosie.

"I got up to work in the garden and discovered a little problem."

Russ puts down his paper. "What's up?"

"The whole back yard is flooded. I turned off my controls but I'm pretty sure that's not all I need to do."

"Yep. I'll show you," says Russ as he gets up from the table.

We walk back down the road to my house. Russ wades through the flood and leads me to the main irrigation spigot in the corner of the yard.

"You have to turn it off here, too," he says.

"I should have known that," I reply.

"It's all new. Don't worry about it." Russ cranks on the rusty handle and turns it a few times. It squeaks in protest.

"You just need a little WD-40 on this and it'll be easier to turn."

"I guess I need to have someone come out and repair whatever's broken, huh?"

"Yep. My guess is it's a main line, given the amount of water sitting here."

"Great."

Just what I need, another problem. It'll take days for everything to dry out. Mold will set in by that time.

After we slosh back through the water and up to the front of the house, I give Russ a quick hug. "Thanks for your help. I really appreciate it."

"No prob. That's what neighbors are for!"

I wave at Rosie, still sitting on their front porch and

mouth *"Thank you!"*

Rosie waves back.

As I turn to walk up the front steps, I let out a startled yip. Jay is standing behind the screen door, arms crossed, hands under his armpits, and a dark look on his face as he stares at me with black eyes.

"Morning, Honey!" I say. "You scared me!"

"What are you doing?"

"The back yard flooded. I asked Russ to help me figure out what I need to do to stop it."

I'm talking too fast and I hear the tremor in my voice.

"I didn't know I had to turn off the irrigation at the back, and I'm going to have to—"

"I'm sure he helped you, too," interrupts Jay in a flat voice. I know what he's implying but pretend not to. It's too absurd.

"Yeah. He showed me where to turn off the main valve. Looks like I'll need to call those *irritation* guys again!"

Jay opens the front door for me. The hair on the back of my neck stands up as I brush past him.

Jay snaps the front door shut and pulls me to him, gripping my chin in his hand.

"I don't want you turning to the neighbors for help. You should have asked me!" Jay hisses.

"Jay, let go of me! You're hurting me!" I shrug him off and back up. "I didn't want to wake you and you've made it very clear that you won't help with the garden or the irrigation. That's why I asked Russ!"

"Is that the only reason?"

"Jesus! You're disgusting! His wife was right there. I did nothing to deserve this!"

"We'll just see about that," he says as he stares me down. "And don't bother with those idiots at Premier. Charlie can fix it, or he'll figure out who can!"

"I don't want Charlie in our business!" I scream, as Jay stalks back to the bathroom. He puffs out his chest and walks with the rolling gait of a professional wrestler, arms held out to the side.

His swagger would be laughable if he hadn't just manhandled me. Is he trying to make himself appear more threatening? Jay has never shown a bit of jealousy until we moved here. Did I really do something wrong? I don't want him to feel threatened, but I thought I was doing the right thing by not bothering him with this problem. If I didn't have the garden, would this be such a big deal? He warned me I was on my own with it. Could I have handled it differently?

The voices in my head bat questions back and forth. He had told me not to bother him about the garden, so I didn't. Now he's pissed about it. What is the right answer?

Shaken, I cook breakfast for the two of us. Jay acts like nothing happened, but my hands don't stop shaking until much later.

৵৹৵

Charlie slept a little later than usual. He's not used to getting up in the middle of the night, but he had to do something. He felt sorry for Jay, having that bitch of a wife who doesn't take orders. Jay had gone on and on about all of her "interests" and she was supposed to be taking care of him. Charlie knew exactly how to distract her but felt a little sore after punching that hole. It was sheer pleasure watching the water bubble out of the ground. He felt like he'd discovered oil. And in fact, he was getting closer to the payoff. He limped to the kitchen, ignoring the rat that scuttled in front of him. Time for coffee and another day of keeping an eye on things for Jay.

ॐ

After a hearty breakfast of sausage and eggs on Sunday morning, I suggest we drive the back road along the Yakima River to scout out places for kayaking and to enjoy lunch in Prosser. Then I tell Jay I want to stop at Silvia's to ask a few quick questions about office procedures. Jay hesitates and then agrees. He shows no sign of the temper I'd witnessed the day before and is his usual relaxed self, affectionate and funny. Rather than talk about what happened, I decide to enjoy his good mood, and hope he won't have another jealous fit.

Following Karen's directions, we find Silvia's house along the Old Inland Empire Highway at the base of a basalt cliff. It is a square, white, two-story house with black shutters—probably built in the 1940s—with a large screened-in front porch. Maple and oak trees shade the house and yard, and the grass sparkles with droplets left from recent watering. Perennials growing along the driveway and across the front of the house look leggy and unkempt, but the few pots at the base of the steps overflow with well-tended petunias in reds and purples.

Jay steers the car up the gravel drive in front of the

house. I can hear a dog barking in back of the house. It sounds big and mean, but remains behind the fence. I breath a small sigh of relief. The last thing I need is Cujo chomping on my arm.

The front door opens as we get out of the car, and there stands Silvia, dressed in khakis and a denim shirt, tucked and belted at the waist. Her short gray hair is neat and perfectly done, curling around her forehead in a somewhat old-fashioned 'do.'

"Silvia? Hi. Remember me? I'm Susan Glasser. I met you at Dr. Elwin's office when I set up my first appointment for a massage?"

"Oh...yes. How can I help you?" Silvia steps onto the screened-in front porch and stands at the door without bothering to open it, her arms crossed over her chest. I mentally groan.

This is not going to be easy.

"This is my husband Jay," I say as he walks up beside me. Her eyes flick in his direction, but she doesn't acknowledge him. "Sorry to bother you, but I started working at Dr. Elwin's office and I'm struggling with a few things that I think you can help me with. I know this is a little awkward, but I could really use your help."

Silvia's eyebrows lower in a scowl. "What do you mean? You're the receptionist now?"

"Yeah. It's kinda funny how that all worked out, but yes. I'm the receptionist."

Silvia makes a spitting sound of disgust. "I'm not interested in helping you. They can all go to hell as far as I'm concerned!"

"Look, I know you left kind of suddenly—"

"You're damned right I left suddenly! That office is hell! Computers be damned. If he wanted a computer specialist he should have hired one!"

"I realize that it was frustrating for you—"

"Not frustrating. Infuriating! What do you want from me?" yells Silvia as she throws open the screen door and marches down the steps.

The dog barks furiously.

"I just need help understanding how you managed the billing. It's all a little overwhelming—"

"Well, isn't that just tough for you!" spits Silvia, her voice rising. "Figure it out yourself. I didn't get any help from those two. They were so high and mighty, making decisions that I didn't want anything to do with. They can help you. Not me!"

"I had no idea," I say, backing away a little. Jay puts his arm around me. I can feel the pressure of his hand on my arm saying *let's go!*

"Of course you didn't. You'll find out just how miserable those two are. I feel sorry for you!"

"I'm sorry I bothered you," I say, raising my voice over the now frantically barking dog. I open the door to the car.

As I look up at Silvia, I see a look in her eyes that screams *"crazy."*

"Thanks for your time," I say as I close the door. Jay, already in the driver's seat, starts the car. I'm sure I saw Silvia's mouth say *Fuck you!* I'm floored. Silvia seemed so put-together when I first met her and now she just seems like a crazy lady with a bad attitude. There is no dealing with her.

"Phew," I say as I blow out the breath I didn't know I was holding. "That was freaky!"

"Wow!" says Jay as he drives away. "Sounds like you're working for a real asshole!"

"You're kidding me!" I say. "Can't you see how crazy she is? She up and quits with no notice, leaves a mess behind and…that attitude! Give me a break!"

"It's your fault you decided to work there. It's not her problem!"

"Really? You're going there again? You have no idea what this woman has done!"

"Of course I don't, because you won't tell me."

I sigh.

"You know when I can, I will."

"All I know is that you're working late every night for a pittance and leaving me to fend for myself. I didn't sign on for this!"

"Why are we back on this subject again? I thought we were doing fine! You're turning everything around! And besides, I'm cooking all weekend to make sure you can eat. Is there any reason why YOU can't help me?" I start to cry. I'm so mad I can't speak.

Jay drives faster. The two-lane road twists along the river and he is driving too fast.

"Slow down!" I sob. I scrabble for tissues in my purse and try to calm myself. Everything hits me all at once… the arguments, Jay's sudden neediness, his anger, the garden…I am furious!

The Water Master

Jay slows down, but his breath hisses through gritted teeth. His face is red. His knuckles blanch in a death grip on the steering wheel. If I don't get the situation under control, his rage will explode. I keep my voice as calm as I can.

"I'm sorry, Honey, really. I know all of this change is hard on you. I never should have stopped to see Silvia. It was a stupid idea. I had no idea she would behave the way she did, and I'm so glad you were with me. If you hadn't been right next to me, well…she was scary and who knows what she would have done."

Play to his strengths. Talk him up.

"You're not thinking, Susan. What did you expect?" Jay hits the steering wheel with the heel of his hand, making me jump. "You knew she left on a bad note. Why would you think she would want to help you?"

I bite my thumbnail, trying to think of what to say.

"I guess I expect the best in people, not the worst," I mumble.

"Lesson learned, then," says Jay.

I try to hold back my tears, blowing my nose now and then as we drive in tense silence. Jay was the perfect boyfriend, kind and generous, giving me space when I needed it. Now that we are married, he is being a controlling jerk and completely unsupportive.

Am I a good enough wife to him? He doesn't think so. Our relationship was effortless until we moved out here. What am I doing wrong? I've got to try harder. Jay just needs more time to adjust to everything. I can do more to make him feel good about our marriage and about me.

107

The Water Master

But as we continue our outing to Prosser, I can't shake the heaviness settling on my soul. Once again, Jay acts as if nothing has happened. I am devastated, but he appears to be unconcerned...or unaware? I struggle to carry on my end of the conversation. Jay points out an interesting house or a cute store that I can barely see through the film of tears. Jay finds a restaurant for lunch. I want to be at home, but do my best to get through lunch without another argument. I'm silent on the ride back. Jay hums along with the radio.

As we enter Pasco, Jay notices a store in a strip mall and pulls into a parking place in front of 'Star's Place—New Age Bookstore and Healing Herbs.'

"Maybe we'll find some people here with similar spiritual interests," says Jay.

I drag myself out of the car, craving a pillow to bury my head in rather than attempt a social outing.

As we enter the store, the smell of incense and herbs surround us. A friendly woman greets us with: "Blessed Be. Take a look around and let me know if you need help."

One side of the store is lined with floor-to-ceiling shelves filled with a hundred or more large jars of herbs, each artfully labeled with its contents. The rest of the store is packed with racks of jewelry, tie-dyed clothing, incense, and oils. Shelves along the back of the store contain New Age books on herbal and natural healing, alternative spirituality, meditation and yoga. A couch, chairs, and a round coffee table in the corner invite customers to sit and read and sip tea. The turmoil I felt moments before evaporates. A relieving sense of peace settles over me.

"Is there anything in particular you are looking for?" asks the woman. She is dressed in a long broomstick skirt in a pattern of red and orange and a flowing red blouse that sets off her long blonde hair, caught up in a loose ponytail that flows over her shoulder.

"Hi. We're new in town and I saw the store so thought we'd check it out," says Jay.

"Welcome! You won't find another store like this in the area. I can order anything you need, so let me know if you don't find what you're looking for."

"I'm Jay and this is my wife Susan."

"I'm Star."

"Is that your real name?" I burst out, immediately realizing how rude I sound.

"Oddly enough, yes! My parents had me during their hippie stage and named me Star. My last name is Knight with a K. Lucky me!" She gives a rueful grin. "It just so happens that my name seems to work well in this environment!"

I laugh. "I'm sorry I sounded so rude."

"No problem. I hear that a lot. People think it's my Wiccan name."

"You're Wiccan? So are we," says Jay as he rushes the counter. Jay and Star chat as I browse. I hear Star mention her coven and notice Jay writing down the information. Apparently, she's inviting us to a ritual. Good. Maybe that will help Jay feel better. I find some catnip and chamomile to make myself a calming tea, and hope it will help me relax.

As I circle back to the counter, Star says, "About ten

people are in our coven and we'd love to have more. Please come next weekend." She draws a map to the location and Jay stuffs it in his jeans pocket. Star smiles as I set the jars on the counter.

"I'll take an ounce of each," I say.

Star weighs out the herbs and puts them in sandwich bags. "There you go," she says, "Enjoy!"

I smile at her. "Thanks! I'm sure we'll be back!"

After we get home, I head to the bedroom for a nap. I feel drained and confused. Jay follows me in.

"Another nap?" he asks.

"Yeah. I need a little break," I say.

"Why? You've hardly done anything today!" says Jay.

As I crawl under the covers I say, "Enough, Jay. I've had enough today."

Jay stares at me for a long moment and leaves the room. I close my eyes in relief and sink into blessed sleep.

෧ං෧

Jay grins to himself as he replays the incident with Silvia.

She's a firecracker, that one. Susan has no idea who she's dealing with.

෧ං෧

I wake up sucking air. The nightmare of being strangled by a hand with no body begins to fade, but I rub my neck as I get my breathing under control. The room is dark. I look at the clock. The dinner hour is long gone. Something isn't right. I listen to the house, trying to figure out what it is. The house feels empty.

The Water Master

I walk into the living room. The room is dark. Jay isn't home. I turn on the kitchen light and pull salad fixings out of the fridge for a light dinner.

Maybe he's gone out for a hamburger or a beer.

I peruse the free health magazine from Star's store as I munch my salad. Jay waltzes in about the time I finish cleaning the kitchen and gives me a beer-laden kiss.

"Where've you been?" I ask.

"I walked over to Charlie's and had a beer with him."

"Did he invite you in this time?"

"No. Front porch drinking again."

"It's going to get pretty cold this winter."

Jay laughs and holds my head against his chest. It feels good.

"Look," he says, "I'm sorry I'm giving you a hard time. My new job, your new job, moving here...everything is so different than before. You seem to be off doing your own thing...I don't know. I just feel kinda crummy."

I pull away from him to gather my thoughts. To buy time, I fill the tea kettle with water, place it on the stove and turn on the burner. We need to talk but I don't want another argument.

"Jay, you're doing your own thing too, you know. You're gone from 4:30 in the morning till 6:00 at night. I have no idea what you do with your time at work. You rarely talk about it."

Jay sits at the counter and rubs his hands through his hair. It's the first time I notice the circles under his eyes. He looks wiped.

"You want to know about work? Meetings, meetings,

lunch and more meetings. It's going all right, I guess. My boss seems to appreciate me and I think I've helped out with some long-term problems. The days are pretty long, though."

I reach over and rub his back.

"What exactly is your job?" I ask.

I'll never understand his work—too technical for me. But at least he's talking to me!

"If I told ya, I'd have to kill ya," says Jay with a tired grin.

"No, really, Jay, what are you doing?" I take his hand and lead him to the living room couch. I pat the place next to me, inviting him to sit. Instead, he moves to the other end of the couch, slips off his shoes and puts his feet up on the coffee table.

"I'm like the go-between for the brainy science guys and the public relations people. I guess you could say I'm a translator. I have to know everything about what they're doing, but can only translate a very little bit so that no operation secrets leak out."

"I guess that makes sense. Is it hard to do?"

"Not really. It's just being aware—like, all the time—about who you can say what to."

"Sounds a little challenging. Do you like it?"

"Yeah. It's okay. Sometimes it's a little slow and I get bored, but overall it's pretty good."

I relax and reach for his hand. He rubs my knuckles with his thumb and lays his head against the couch.

"What about your work, Suze? How's it going?"

"I love it. It's busy. The days go by really fast. Tom

and Karen are fun to work with. I give it a ten. I'm not counseling and I don't miss it!"

"But you're still solving other people's problems, right?" asks Jay.

"What do you mean?"

"You know. Whatever it is you're helping them with."

"Oh, that. Yeah, I guess. It's like solving a mystery though. It intrigues me."

"Sometimes…well, sometimes it seems like your mind is at work and not here with me."

"It is on my mind a lot, but I try not to let it interfere with us."

"But it does, Suze."

"What makes you say that?"

"You don't seem as invested in your studies with me. You're home late most nights."

"I know I'm behind on my reading. I guess right now I'm more interested in my job."

"Nothing should take precedence over your spiritual life, though."

"Nothing does. I try to live my spiritual life everyday by doing the right thing. It has nothing to do with a certain dogma or what someone has written. I want to keep a balanced perspective, and even though this seems trite, I try to be kind. That's my spiritual life right there. If I read something that gives me insight, so be it. But all the ritual, the rules, the right and wrong way to do things…that doesn't seem as important to me."

"But that's what you agreed to as my student!" whines Jay.

"I thought I was just going to learn about writings on spirituality, and you would introduce me to Wiccan concepts. I didn't realize I would be on timelines and your expectations of the right way to be spiritual!"

"What are you trying to say?"

"I just need you to back off a little, okay?"

Jay sighs and scratches his head. "I'll give you some space, but you're not giving up completely, right?"

"I'm not giving up at all."

Jay reaches for me. I move over and lean into him. As he kisses the top of my head, he says, "Okay. All right. I'll back off. You set the pace."

Relieved, I look up at him. "Thank you. I love you, Jay."

Honest conversation is the best foreplay. Much later that evening we fix sandwiches for dinner and eat sitting next to each other at the counter, discussing future improvements we want to make to the house and yard.

I begin to give Jay an update on our finances when he cuts me off and says, "By the way, I told Charlie we were up at Silvia's."

"What?"

"Yeah, I told Charlie about our little visit. He was none too happy. Wondered why you were sticking your nose where it didn't belong. He said he's gonna have a little talk with you and that doc of yours."

"Why did you do that?"

"That's what you get for not thinking things through," says Jay with a self-satisfied grin.

Speechless at his cruel tone, I just stare at him, jolted

to my core by the quick-change artist sitting in front of me. Jay grins at me with flat eyes and saunters out of the kitchen.

As I slip under the covers that night I feel like Scarlet O'Hara in *Gone with the Wind. "Tomorrow is another day."* I hope I 'll wake up to some sort of enlightenment, but it is doubtful. Jay rolls over to spoon me and immediately falls asleep. I slip away from him to sleep on the edge of the bed.

వ∞ఓ

After that damned trip to Prosser, I needed to get away from her. Hanging with Charlie really did the trick. It felt good to relax with a few beers, we didn't have to talk much and it got me away from the house. A few hours of 21 and roulette gave me the hit I needed to keep going. It's good to be back in the saddle again. The hookers love me. I'm finally getting laid the way I want. It's a shame I have to use rubbers, but I don't want some stupid disease to get in the way of my plans. Susan had better get with it pretty quick.

Chapter Five

੭੦ত

For the next few days I'm careful around Jay. I finish Dagan Moore's book, just to please Jay and get him off my back. I try to talk about it with him, but he answers in grunts, his mouth in a tight line and his eyes avoiding mine. Most nights he comes home long after dinner. When I ask where he's been, he'll say he was at Charlie's. He smells of beer and cigarettes, like he's been at a bar.

The harder I try to make things better, the worse I feel. Every time I do something nice for Jay, he finds fault with it. I'll come home early enough to cook a good dinner, and he will tell me I'd made a mess. I'll arrive home a little late with a knot in my stomach, afraid he'll be angry and he won't be home. When he asks me when I'll be back from an errand, he's furious if I'm a few minutes late.

Our shared spiritual path should be the cement in the marriage, but it's actually a wall. Jay focuses on the intellectual nuances and takes pleasure in flaunting his knowledge in a smug and superior way. He's been a solitary practitioner, but all he talks about is starting his own coven. He treats my need for spiritual simplicity like it is naïveté and ignorance. I quit talking about it. He talks over me anyway.

Star's ritual is tonight. It's my first New Moon ritual.

The Water Master

My only other group experience was the full moon ritual at the Midwest Pagan Festival. Jay invited me to go with him, and I accepted with trepidation. I read about rituals, but the Wiccan stereotypes niggled in the back of my mind. I know Wiccans don't eat babies and kill goats, but still! Jay seemed trustworthy and was so excited to take me to my first ritual, I decided to go. And in the familiar hills of Wisconsin, with the light of the full moon filtering through the shadows of the trees, I felt something I'd been longing for: a way to connect with nature again. And I wasn't alone. Jay shared it with me.

Now Jay's recent behavior makes me wary, and I hope the evening will be without incident.

Fridays at the office are slower than the rest of the week, with appointments ending around 12:30. This schedule gives us time to catch up on paperwork during the afternoon, so we can start the following week fresh. With my initial investigation completed and compiled, Tom and his attorney met with me to review the details, and then they contacted a detective with the police department who will join us this afternoon. All the affected insurance companies, along with Medicare and Medicaid, are now involved and we are waiting for their information requests. I feel anxious about how this situation is going to play out. Jay and Charlie's developing friendship unnerves me. Eventually Charlie's anger at discovering that I am playing a key role in the investigation against Silvia might rub off on Jay. Who knows how he will react?

❦

"Good morning," says Tom as I walk in the door. "Happy Friday!"

"Yay," I say with little enthusiasm.

"What's up with you?" says Tom.

"Long week, glad it's Friday, tired and cranky. You?"

"Long week, tired, not cranky but ready to relax," says Tom. He smiles at me. "Why cranky?"

I blow out a sigh and make a face. "You know what they say about the first year of marriage."

"Oh, that! Anything I can do to help?"

"Not really. I'm just a little frustrated with our lack of time together. I'm hoping tonight we can reconnect."

"What are you doing tonight? Something fun?"

I hesitate, but decide to chance it.

"We're going to a Wiccan ritual tonight."

"Oh! Did Star finally reel you in?"

My head snaps up in surprise. Tom is very matter of fact. No funny look.

I laugh. "Yes, she did. We met her at her store."

"Are you and Jay Wiccan?"

"Jay more than me. I'm playing around the edges."

"Star's great. She's rock solid, despite all the new age-y stuff she sells."

"How do you know her?"

"We met a few years back. Karen and I dropped by her store to buy some tea and got to know her from there."

"Have you been to her rituals?"

"No. Not our thing, exactly. It seems to attract a few more nuts than we're comfortable with."

"I know what you mean, but it's outdoors, and I'm

hoping by connecting with a group of like-minded people we won't feel so spiritually isolated."

"Well, I hope it works for you."

I'm quiet for a moment.

"Tom, can I ask you something?"

"Sure."

I pause, not even really sure what I want to ask.

"Is it okay if I talk with you and Karen about some of this spiritual stuff and...other stuff?"

"Sure! No problem!"

"I just don't...I mean, I... We have this professional relationship, and—"

"Say no more, Susan. Please believe me when I say you are fitting right in and we welcome more personal conversations."

Sighing with relief, I reply, "Thanks. I need that. I'm really feeling at loose ends everywhere but here. This first-year marriage adjustment crap is a pain. I'm sure it will get better, but right now, work seems to be my favorite place!"

"Fine with me. Just know that I don't keep secrets from Karen and she doesn't keep secrets from me."

"I would never put the two of you in an awkward position," I say. "I really like both of you and love how you work together. You seem to have a real partnership."

"We've had our bumps and bruises, believe me. In the end it seems that mutual respect and letting each other be the best we can be works best," says Tom. "That's it."

"Simple," I say. "I like that."

Our first patient walks in, and our conversation ends

with Tom giving me a squeeze of my shoulder. I feel tears well up and choke them down, turning to smile and welcome Mrs. Hanson.

After lunch, Dale Freeman, the detective from Pasco PD, arrives for our meeting. He's tall—over six feet—built like a linebacker with broad shoulders tapering to a surprisingly slim waist for a man his size. A sandy brown mustache droops down the sides of his mouth and his light brown hair is brushed back, exposing a high freckled forehead. He looks uncomfortable in his sport coat and tie and I can picture him sitting in his recliner, watching football, beer in hand, comfortable in jeans and a T-shirt. Today, however, he is all business.

"Dale, I don't think you've met Susan. She's put in hard hours working on the initial investigation."

"Tom tells me you've done a great job starting the investigation and putting the information into a format that will be easy to follow. Thanks!" says Dale.

"You're welcome. Glad I can help."

Karen sits back, Coke in hand. "Well? What's the news?" she says.

"Here's what we have so far," says Dale. "We've subpoenaed the banks where Silvia has accounts and we've received all the records. She has shoveled a significant amount of money in and out of her accounts and checks for large sums have been written to Charlie Gottschalk."

"Why would Charlie need money from Silvia?" asks Karen.

"We don't have an answer for that, unfortunately. Charlie hasn't changed his lifestyle at all. He's still driving that nasty truck and wearing the same pants every day!" replies Dale.

"How much are we talkin'?" asks Tom.

"So far it's around $345,000 and change."

Tom goes pale. "How much of that is out of my pocket?"

"Most of it is directly from the insurance companies and Medicare. But I think you are out around $100,000 so far."

"So far?" asks Karen.

"We've only gone back a few years. I think the research needs to go back to the day you hired her."

The room goes dead silent. Karen's pale cheeks flush and she tears up. "How could this happen? Why did this happen?"

Tom's jaw muscles work as he reaches over and takes her hand. His knee bounces up and down as he tries to contain his anger.

"That bitch!" he says. "We got totally screwed. We never should have trusted her the way we did!" He stands up and leans against the counter, chewing his cheek.

Dale uncrosses his legs and sits forward. "Here's what I need from you. Since this is definitely a criminal investigation, absolute confidentiality is required. This case is not to be discussed—at all—outside of this room. Got it?"

I shift in my chair. "Then you probably need to know that my husband has become friends with Silvia's brother, Charlie. I don't know why or what the attraction is, but he's regularly drinking with Charlie on his front porch."

Karen looks up in surprise. "Really? Charlie is such an ignorant kind of man. We haven't met Jay yet, but I'm assuming he's more of an intellectual type. I hope I'm not offending you."

"No offense taken. I don't get it either!" I turn to Dale. "How do you suggest I handle this?"

Dale looks down at the floor and makes a sucking sound. He is quiet too long. "Well?"

Dale looks at me with concern. "Charlie's not one of the good guys, Susan. He's been on our radar for a while for various reasons. None of which we have ever been able to pin down."

"He's given me the willies since I first met him," I say.

"He gives anyone with any people smarts the willies," says Dale.

Tom looks worried. "What else do you have on him Dale?"

"Nothing specific. He was questioned when that couple disappeared near here last year—"

"The couple that lived in my house?" I ask.

Dale's eyebrows shoot up. "You live in that house?"

"Yeah…"

"Now, isn't that interesting!" says Dale in a quiet voice.

"Okay, now I'm seriously freaked out," I say. "What happened to those people?"

"We don't know. It's still an open file."

Tom asks, "What do you suspect happened to them?"

"They were behind in their house payments, their taxes and bills. We initially thought they just skipped town.

They had no family to speak of. But there were some clues that made us think they had come to some harm."

"Like what?" I ask.

"Something didn't add up. They'd been retired for a few years and were seen puttering around. They took pride in the house and yard. After a while, the house deteriorated and they were seen less and less. They kept to themselves more, but there was no evidence of any serious health problems, or money problems for that matter. We investigated everything about them: assets, debts, bank activity. Nothing stood out. With their retirement they should have easily been able to pay their bills..."

"The Irrigation District told me they were behind on the bills and Charlie paid the bill right before we got here," I say.

"Sounds like they were trying to avoid something or someone," says Karen.

"That was our thought. When we questioned the neighbors, they said Charlie and the husband spent time together and then suddenly their friendship ended. About then, the Clements kept more to themselves and the house went downhill."

"Hmm, I wonder what Charlie had on them," I say.

"What do you mean by that?" asks Karen.

"Something my neighbor, Rosie, said. She said that Charlie would make people pay whenever he did favors. She made it sound innocent. Like 'you scratch my back and I'll scratch yours.' Charlie made the first calls for us to get our irrigation fixed and running, and she said he would probably make us pay him back somehow."

"That's one of the directions we went with the investigation. We thought maybe Charlie was involved. We never did find any real evidence," says Dale.

"Jay is spending too much time with that man," I say.

"I don't know what to say about that, except be careful and keep your ears open," says Dale.

"Gee.....thanks," I say.

Tom stirs. "So what's next?" he asks.

Dale sits back. "We need you to go through all of your files since Silvia started to work for you."

Karen and Tom groan. I put my head in my hands. "You've got to be kidding!" says Tom.

"No, I'm not. You have to help us gather all the information we can get. We don't have the manpower to put someone in here. It's going to be up to you. Even if you find she wasn't embezzling money early on, you may be able to pinpoint when it started."

"When can you arrest her?" I ask.

"When we have enough evidence to give to the DA. They're going to ask for it all anyhow, and we will need to show beyond a reasonable doubt that she's guilty. The more evidence, the better. Our investigation is separate from investigations by the insurance companies. I have no idea when they will pounce and frankly, I'd like us to be first. This is a serious theft and embezzlement charge against Silvia. We want it to stick. And we want to get as much of your money back as possible!" says Dale.

"How much time do we have?" asks Tom.

"I would say we have at least six to eight months. I'll stay in touch with the insurance investigators to check their progress with the case and try to coordinate. But I can't promise anything."

"In the meantime, Silvia is enjoying her freedom!" says Karen, raising her voice.

"I'm afraid so," says Dale. "It's the nature of the beast."

"Do you think she knows we're on to her?" I ask.

"It's hard to know, but since she's still living in her home and going about life as usual, I have to surmise that she thinks she got away with it, or that she's smarter than everyone else and she doesn't believe we will ever have the balls to arrest her. Excuse my language."

"Typical sociopath," I say.

Dale looks at me with interest. "Sounds like you've run across them before?"

"Yeah. I was a counselor for years and saw my share. The only way to win with one is to get out of their way or outsmart them at their own game."

"You got that right," says Dale.

I sigh, my thoughts suddenly elsewhere, worrying about the time it will take to get this audit finished. At least I can spread out some of the late nights over the next few months. I want to wrap up this investigation so I can move on.

"Okay," I look at Tom and Karen. "I'm in."

"It's hours of work, Susan," says Tom, concern in his voice, knowing what I am up against at home.

"Yep, it is," I say, smiling. Then I have an idea. "What do you think about asking Marisa if she can help with the files?"

"That's a good idea," says Karen. "She's trustworthy and might appreciate making a little extra money."

"Can you afford it?" I ask.

"We either pay you or her. We need to get the job done."

I sigh with relief.

Chapter Six

꘎

As we drive out to the property where Star's coven holds their rituals, the sun shines bright in the western sky and the fields along the Yakima River are blanketed in light green as young plants sprout from the earth. The Yakima River, swollen with melting snows from the mountains, floods the lowlands. I sit with the written directions in my lap, thinking through the best way to approach Jay about the next few months of extra hours at work. I can't tell him any specific information, and he will feel betrayed, as if I am hiding an affair from him. I feel a loyalty to Tom and Karen that he won't accept. They trust me and it feels good. They don't question or test me like he does. While I realize a marriage requires a higher level of trust and loyalty, I have never done anything to make Jay distrust me.

The more time Jay spends with Charlie, the less he trusts me. I can't tell Jay not to see him, because that would just make matters worse. On the other hand, if I express any dislike toward Charlie, Jay becomes defensive and argumentative. I will leave it alone until this investigation is done.

"You're deep in thought," says Jay.

"Hmm? Oh, just enjoying the evening. It's so different here than Illinois, isn't it?"

"Yeah."

We are on the Old Inland Empire Highway, winding around basalt cliffs. Passing Silvia's house, I notice her outside with a huge black dog, working among the flowers. She looks so innocent. I sigh. I don't understand why some people are so mean. Why would Silvia steal all that money? I make a mental shift, trying to banish negative thoughts from my mind so I can enjoy the evening. The land below us is lush with irrigated fields. Cows and horses graze, and old barns and newer houses dot the landscape. I muse about the early settlers and how difficult it must have been to hand-dig irrigation ditches that kept their crops alive. How did they stand it? Such hot summers.

"You went away again," says Jay.

"Oh, sorry. Just thinking about the early settlers. Wondering what brought them here, how they managed to eke out a living on this land before the irrigation was developed."

"It couldn't have been easy. Charlie was telling me about his grandparents who moved here from Kansas years ago. His grandfather worked on building the irrigation canals. I guess irrigation is in his blood."

"Has he ever talked about the rest of his family?"

"Not really. Why?"

"Oh, you know me, ever the nosey counselor. Trying to learn the family history so I can better understand my client," I say, trying to add a little humor to my answer. It doesn't work.

Jay's face gets that all-too-familiar hard look. "You

don't have any business with him, do you?"

"Business? No! What do you mean?"

"You and that doctor friend of yours are prying into Silvia. I know that much. You'd better leave her alone!"

"Jay, I'm just having a conversation! What happened to talking and joking about people we know without it becoming an argument? And what do you mean we are prying into Silvia?"

"Charlie told me you're nosing around where you don't belong when it comes to her."

I don't know what to say, and can't say anything anyhow.

Jay sighs and glances over at me as I lean further away from him. "I'm sorry, Honey. I guess I'm feeling left out of your life right now. It just seems like everything you do has an ulterior motive. I think if you cared enough about me you would just, I don't know…just be there more, I guess. And you wouldn't be helping out people you barely know and working for almost nothing."

I can only think of how unavailable Jay has been lately. *Where does he get off?*

"Oh, crap!" I say. "We just missed the turnoff." I look down at the directions. "See if you can turn around up here."

"You were supposed to be giving me directions!" Jay snaps.

"Sorry! Geez. So we go a block out of our way!" I snap back.

We put our argument on hold as we drive up the dirt road to the small ranch where we will meet Star's coven.

As we pull up next to the barn, Jay puts the car in park and takes my hand. "Hey," he says. "We need to go into the circle with perfect love and perfect trust. Can you do that?"

I sigh, "Yeah. I can," I lie.

We walk into a large room with high ceilings. The concrete walls keep the room cool. Tables set up in a U-shape are arranged with tablecloths and vases of fresh flowers. Candles burn in tall sconces along the far wall. A great deal of work has gone into making this a special night.

"I'm so glad you could come!" says Star as she greets us. She introduces us to a small group of people. Most of them look normal, although a few are wearing the usual Pagan garb of flowing skirts, tie-dye shirts and Goddess tattoos.

Star takes our potluck food of salad and my favorite rice dish of pulao that I made the night before. We visit with a few of the coven members. Once Jay shares that he had been raised to third degree High Priest by the one and only Dagan Moore, he becomes the rock star. Everyone gathers around him and one of the women gushes all over him. It's obvious Jay loves the attention and is in his element when he's with people who share his beliefs. He's happier than I've seen him in a long time. My heart softens a little as I realize that he might be lonely.

Can that be why he spends so much time with Charlie? We need to get out more, meet new friends.

When Dagan Moore's name is mentioned among Wiccans anywhere, the conversation always turns to his amazing charisma and intelligence. He's written three books that are Pagan/Wiccan Bibles. It wasn't until I read Dagan's second book that I realized that Wicca was a modern spiritual practice with no historical basis. So much of the early European religious practice was stamped out by Christianity that no one really knows what the true practices of the pre-Christian religions were like. Wicca evolved in Europe and America in the early twentieth century. Since then, various writers have put their personal spins on it, so there are a tremendous variety of practices within a loose structure of ritual practice.

Dagan hadn't taken on many students, but he and Jay had hit it off at a festival in Seattle, and Dagan had asked Jay to be his student. Jay is lucky to have the experience and relationship he's had with Dagan.

I wander into the kitchen where Star is putting food in the refrigerator.

"This is a great place," I say. "How'd you find it?"

"It's rented for lots of different functions…weddings, family reunions. Sara gave us the lead. Her sister was married here. We're lucky to be able to schedule our rituals here."

"How long have you all been together?" I ask.

"This group has had a steady core of about six people for three years. You know Pagans, they come and go depending on what the newest, coolest thing is."

I laugh. "I know what you mean, although I'm fairly new to all of this and still finding my way."

"So, what's your story? How'd you get into Wicca?" asks Star.

"I spent most of my adult life focused on my career—"

"Which is?"

"I'm a counselor. Or at least I was."

"So anyway...?" says Star.

"So anyway, I was starting to feel empty. I'd walked away from my church after my parents died. It just didn't make any sense to me. After they died I tried talking to my minister a few times. He just wanted to pray with me. That wasn't what I needed. I was drifting and really sad. And really lonely."

Without warning, tears well up. I blink a few times and notice Star doesn't try to change the subject or make me feel better. She just smiles and nods her head.

"Go on," she says.

"So...I lost myself in my career, helping people with their problems. I tried to spend more time outdoors, closer to nature and all that. That's where I'm happiest. Anyhow, I wandered the book stores and read books on Wicca, along with a few on Buddhism and Hinduism. The Native American stuff really interested me, but I couldn't see myself intruding into a culture that isn't mine. Eventually, I heard about the Midwest Pagan Festival and decided to go."

"You went alone?"

I grin. "I did!"

"That took some guts!"

"Not really. I decided to attend as an observer. I wasn't going to do anything that made me uncomfortable. I'd read about skyclad rituals and I wasn't about to run around naked!"

"Good for you! It's totally unnecessary," says Star.

"I also didn't know how I'd feel in a ritual, so I was biding my time, deciding what to do, when I met Jay. He walked right up to me like he knew me. We started talking and I was just so...*taken* with him!"

Star smiles. "Ah, love!"

"He seemed really grounded. I mean there were some weird people at this place, so open-minded their brains were falling out. Jay just exuded intelligence and interest. He looked conservative compared to some of those wackos!"

"Oh, I know all about those people!" Star laughs.

"So, he invited me to a workshop on Goddess energy, and when the workshop was over we talked about female energy and how male and female balanced each other. I finally began to understand that the God and Goddess is just a representation of male and female—that I didn't have to worship or pray to a deity, but I could identify with the strengths and characteristics of various gods and goddesses. It was a huge eye-opener!"

"Yeah, and what else did he open up?"

I laugh at Star's earthy humor. "Well, I was...smitten, as they say!"

"I bet you were! How long after that did you get married?"

"First he asked me to be his student. I learned so much from him just hanging around at the festival. He took me to a full moon ritual, and that's where everything seemed to click for me. It meant so much to celebrate the full moon outdoors. I just loved it. So, anyhow, a few months later he proposed. I was shocked at how quickly it all happened, but it just felt so right!"

"Have you been married before?"

"No. I had a few boyfriends over the years but I never wanted to share my space. With Jay, I just wanted to be with him all the time. I love sharing space with him!"

"So, tell me all about the wedding! Was it beautiful?"

"Actually, it was very simple. It was just my sister and her husband and Dagan Moore. And, of course, the Justice of the Peace."

"Dagan Moore?" asks Star, her face scrunched in concern.

"Yeah. He was Jay's teacher. Raised him to third degree."

"That man is so full of himself..." Star pops a nacho chip into her mouth, which muffles the end of her sentence.

I am a little surprised. "He's supposed to be the end-all and be-all of Wiccans! What makes you say that?"

"Oh, well, I..."

"Oh, don't worry, I don't care about him one way or the other," I say.

"Phew. I thought I'd made a faux pas. I really don't like the guy. He's arrogant as hell and mean to people who disagree with him. Like, I mean, mean! Despite all the talk of equality between the sexes, he really doesn't like women. Look how the guys flock to him. The men stand next to him, the women worship at his feet. He's one of those guys that charms everyone and smiles a lot. But watch his eyes. They don't smile."

I remember his smile at our wedding dinner when

The Water Master

Ruthie tried to bring Jay and Dagan out of their private conversation to focus on our future as a married couple. Star is right. His eyes hadn't smiled at me that night.

"Where did you meet Dagan?" I ask.

"Oh, at a Seattle bookstore, years ago," Star replies. "So, does Jay buy into all his teachings?"

"Yeah, he does. He's a bit of a...perfectionist," I say.

"What's Jay's story? Where's he from?"

"He's from Wisconsin. Grew up there, went to school there."

"Have you met his family?"

"He had a falling-out sometime back. He doesn't talk about them, and I haven't met them."

"That doesn't bother you?" asks Star.

"Not really. I've counseled a lot of people who walked away from a dysfunctional family to stay sane. Usually they're the healthiest ones!"

Star looks at me with interest. "Hmm. So, listen..."

Jay strides into the kitchen and puts his arm around me.

"What are you girls talking about?"

"Oh, the usual girl-talk," I say. "How we met, how much I love you, all that stuff."

Jay hugs me tight. "She's great, isn't she?" he says to Star.

"Yes, she is!" says Star. "I'm glad you guys came."

Jay keeps his arm around me and guides me out of the room.

Star says, "Susan, anytime you want to talk, stop by the store."

The Water Master

"I will! Thanks!" I say over my shoulder, feeling certain I had just made a friend.

As the sun sinks to the horizon, the coven wanders out to the field where the ritual altar is arranged. I feel comfortable with the group. Everyone is easygoing, although a few are a little dodgy. The Maiden cleanses the circle and the Warder sets the protections in the four quarters. He looks like Worf from Star Trek. Worf the Warden. I giggle. I have to take this more seriously or Jay will notice! I mentally slap myself on the back of the head to prepare myself for ritual.

Each person is drawn into the circle with the question, "How do you enter?" and the answer, "With an open heart and an open mind." The High Priest is a small man with dark hair and a neatly-trimmed beard and moustache. I like him right away and wonder about his relationship with Star. Is she just his High Priestess, or is she more than that?

As I enter the circle, I feel an immediate change in the air. Calm and still within the circle, the light breeze I felt before is absent in the sacred space.

The ritual proceeds with Drawing Down the Moon. The recitation of the Charge of the Goddess and God is shared among all, with each person reading a line, going round and round the circle until finished. I wonder how Jay will react to the coven members bringing a script into the circle.

The mystery play is a brief skit about the significance of the season for this New Moon. The High Priest and Priestess make a show of flirting with each other and eventually join in a brief kiss. A flower springs up between them and everyone laughs. I am impressed with the costuming of the players. Simple masks represent the God and Goddess, and unlike some of the more evangelical Wiccans, there is no nudity or wild sex, thank the gods! At the end of the skit, coyotes begin to howl along the edge of the basalt cliffs to the west of the circle. I feel a thrill as more coyotes answer to the east and am grateful for the opportunity to share this time with these people in the outdoors below a darkening sky. I breath easier than I have in a long time, although I notice Jay watching the High Priest with great intensity. I wonder what he is thinking, but part of me really doesn't want to know.

Cakes and ale are shared all around to end the ritual. The 'cake' is moist rosemary bread and the 'ale' is a home-made beer, too sour for my taste. But I am touched by the personal effort these people put forth to make a meaningful ritual.

The circle breaks and everyone heads back to the building for potluck and celebration.

As we sit around the table eating dinner, the talk and laughter flow around me. Jay sits next to Ronny, the High Priest. They are deep in conversation. I sit next to the woman who was obviously flirting with Jay earlier. She calls herself "Flower."

"Did you hear the coyotes?" she asks like a small child. "I called them, you know."

"You called them?"

"Yes. That's why they came and spoke to us."

"You don't think that perhaps they do that every night?"

"Oh, no. We're special so they came to join us. At my call, of course."

"I see," I say with feigned interest.

Geesh. I wonder if I'm being too judgmental. Nope.

Discernment is different than being judgmental, and I discern that this woman is loopy. It still amazes me that in one room you can have brilliant intellectuals and dopey, new-age-y weirdos, and they all get along.

The potluck consists of a wide variety of foods, from vegetarian to hearty meat dishes. I serve myself some moist and tender pulled pork piled high on a large bun, along with a few side salads. I am enjoying the heck out of the food I didn't have to cook. As I munch with gusto, my ears prick up at Jay's voice. It has that edge that puts me on high alert.

"Dagan says that all Wiccans need to know the ritual by heart," says Jay.

"If people want to do that, it's fine. We've found that once you do ritual a few times, you tend to know what you need to know and it all comes out fine in the end," says Ronny. He's trying to remain congenial, but is having trouble pulling it off.

"But then it's different every time. It's supposed to be the same," says Jay with indignation ringing louder now.

"Sorry. I disagree with you and Dagan. This is our coven and this is how we do it."

Ronny's polite disagreement with Jay worries me. How will Jay respond? Jay glances at me, notices my warning stare, and looks around the room. Everyone else has just gone silent. His face changes when he realizes he has made a scene. He smiles at Ronny. "I'm sorry. Sometimes I get carried away. The ritual was great. You guys do a fine job."

Jay's eyes aren't smiling.

৵৽

What a bunch of idiots! It's like being with third graders when you're in a Ph.D. program. They completely fucked up the Charge of the God and no one had memorized any part of the Drawing Down ritual. It's a good thing I'm here. I'll get them straightened up and start my own coven. That Star is a piece of work. Now that Susan is telling her everything about our relationship, I have to get her away. This being polite business is starting to wear on me. I'll show Susan how much better it will be if we start our own coven. Now that I've found this group, I'll just siphon off a few folks for myself...

৵৽

I nod off on the drive home and our earlier argument is forgotten. We fall into bed and wake up the next morning unusually late.

I start the coffee and open the back slider to a perfect sunny day. The air is filled with the wet smell of new-mown grass and warm dirt. I start the bacon frying and Jay comes up behind me, naked after his shower and ready for action.

I laugh as he rubs up behind me. He kisses my neck and takes my hands. "Turn off the bacon...let's go."

An hour later, I stretch like a cat. Jay is back in the shower and I definitely need one. I feel sated like I haven't felt in some time. We certainly celebrated the new moon in our own way! Last night's ritual relieved some of my tension and distracted Jay enough from our issues to make this lovemaking session a release and relief for both of us. I decide to take the rest of the day off from everything. We can enjoy a stress-free day in each other's company and maybe work in the yard a little. I don't want to tell Jay about more long days at work just yet.

Jay comes out of the shower with a big grin on his face.

"That was awesome, Babe."

I smile back. "Yes, it was!"

"Now what?"

"I say we eat a huge, greasy breakfast, read the paper and relax today. Let's just do what we want to do!"

"Sounds good. Although I promised Charlie I would help him cut down a tree."

Why is he willing to work in Charlie's yard but not in ours?

"What time?"

"Whenever I feel like getting there."

"Okay. Maybe while you're there, I'll go over to Rosie's and see if she wants to ride bikes or something."

Jay hesitates. "I suppose."

I let it pass.

After a relaxing morning with little conversation and much reading, Jay leaves for Charlie's. I walk down the street to see if Rosie is home. I carry a plate of cookies left over from last night's ritual potluck as a token of neighborliness. My knock on the door initiates frantic dog barking. Feet shuffle behind the door. There's a brief moment of silence while I am viewed through the peephole and the door opens. Russ is still in his pajama bottoms and T-shirt, his hair rumpled as if he's just gotten out of bed.

"Hi, Susan. Come on in."

"I'm not interrupting, am I?"

"Yeah. You're interrupting our day of doing nothing."

"We had a morning like that. It was heaven," I laugh as I enter their house.

I find Rosie in the kitchen, which smells of bacon and maple syrup. The Sunday paper is scattered across the counter and pans and dirty dishes are piled around the sink.

"Hi, Susan. Welcome to our Sunday abode!"

"Smells like heaven," I say as I give Rosie a brief hug.

I hand over the plate of cookies. "I've been really bad about paying you back for helping me out with the irrigation. I didn't bake these, but some friends of mine did and they're yummy!"

"Thanks!" says Russ as he plies the plastic wrap off the top and grabs a huge chocolate chip cookie. "Did you find out what caused the leak?"

"Premier said to wait a few days and give things time to dry out and they'll come out and take a look. I hope it gets figured out soon. My garden's a mess!"

"I'm sure they'll fix it," he says. "What are you up to?"

"Just wondering if Rosie is up for a bike ride," I say.

"Yeah. I'd love to go. Let me get dressed and I'll come down and meet you in a few minutes."

"Sounds good!" I say as I open the front door to leave. Just then Charlie's beat-up truck drives by. Jay sits in the passenger seat and both of them stare at the house as the truck slows down. My heart flips. Jay doesn't acknowledge us.

"Um. What's that about?" asks Russ.

"I have no idea," I say, trying to cover my embarrassment. "Charlie asked Jay to help him take down a tree. Maybe they're on their way to buy something from the hardware store."

"No, they're not," says Rosie. "They wanted to know what we were doing. That guy is weird."

I hope she is referring to Charlie.

"Does Charlie drive by here often?" I ask.

"Our house isn't on the way to anything for him," says Russ, scratching his head.

I don't know what to say, so I say nothing.

Rosie takes a deep breath. "Well, I'll see you in a few minutes, okay?"

"Sure," I say without looking at them. I walk down their steps and onto the road, my neck prickling with the sense I am being watched, although by this time Charlie and Jay are long gone.

Fifteen minutes later Rosie and I meander through the neighborhood on our bikes, chatting about the neighbors and commenting on landscaping highlights as we ride side by side. Most of the houses are large, with bikes, balls and toys littering the front lawns. Retirees likely live in the smaller homes with well-manicured lawns. Some lots have been divided into smaller properties of prefab starter homes.

Few cars drive past, but every time I hear one draw

near me I wobble to the side, as I look over my shoulder to see who it is. To my relief, Rosie doesn't bring up Jay's weird drive-by. But I worry he'll show himself again, and I have no explanation for his behavior.

As we leave the neighborhood, Rosie leads me onto the gravel road winding along next to the irrigation canal.

"Is it all right for us to ride here?" I ask. "I saw a 'No Trespassing' sign!"

"It's fine. Locals use the access road for walking, bike riding, walking their dogs. Sometimes even riding horses!" she says as she swerves around a pile of dog poop that looks like a souvenir a horse would leave behind.

"Watch out for that!" Rosie yelps.

Pushing my mountain bike through the basalt gravel is hard work. In no time I am out of breath and sweat tickles the side of my face, but quickly evaporates in the rising heat of the day.

"How far does this go?"

"I don't know, really," puffs Rosie as she lifts herself off the bike seat through a particularly bumpy patch of road. "The canals go on for miles and miles out here. In the city, the irrigation is routed under bridges and you can come and go off of them pretty easily. Here, once you're on it, the only way to get off is to turn around or ride through an orchard or someone's farm."

The irrigation canal appears as a pretty little river in places, with tall grasses growing along the sides and patches of little yellow wildflowers here and there. A momma duck quacks loudly, warning us away from her babies who squeak along the edge of the canal. Biking past a cherry orchard bordered by towering cottonwood trees provides a pocket of cool moist air, a brief respite from the heat.

As we ride by a flattened area of grass littered with beer cans I say, "Great place to party, I guess!"

"Yeah, the old-timers tell some pretty hair-raising tales of their adventures out here in the middle of the night. I'm pretty sure their kids do the same thing!"

We ride in silence for a few more minutes until Rosie pulls off onto a side path.

"Where are you taking me?" I laugh as I wobble around a large pothole.

"You'll see!"

The gravel changes to a sandy car track. We leave behind the cool air of the irrigated orchards for the heat of the desert and the sagebrush and rabbitweed. As we round a curve, I catch my breath.

"This is my favorite place," says Rosie.

In the distance, the White Bluffs of the Columbia River stand stark against the hot blue sky. The curve of the river sparkles in the sun. The dot of a bright yellow kayak floats beneath the bluffs. I can imagine the swallows flitting out of their nests on the cliff. A slight breeze lifts the hair off my neck. I let out a deep sigh.

"Oh, Rosie! This is beautiful! It's so peaceful!"

We sip on water bottles. A flock of pelicans glide along the river and a raptor hunts overhead. I see the flash of its white head.

"It's an eagle!"

"There are lots of eagles here. More than most people

realize. It's pretty wild out here. Coyotes, elk, deer. Sometimes even cougars!"

"Thanks so much for bringing me out here, Rosie. I haven't taken the time to see the desert this way. All I saw when I got here was a monotonous landscape."

"You just have to work a little harder to find places like this."

My eyes scan the horizon. The Horse Heaven Hills roll along the south end of the landscape, still green from spring rains, except for one hill blackened along the side.

"What happened there?" I ask, as I point with my water bottle.

"Brush fire. They spring up fairly frequently out here."

"What causes them?"

"Lightning, someone driving their car in the grass, stupid people lighting fireworks. The big Hanford fire a few years back was caused by a car accident. That one was scary. By the end of August the air is usually pretty hazy. If it's not local fires, the smoke drifts in from other places. It's a relief when the rains start in the fall!"

"So, we have a fire season and a rainy season?"

"Pretty much!" laughs Rosie.

After a short rest we ride back to civilization. As we get closer to home, I ask, "Where is Charlie's house exactly?"

"It's down the road and around the corner, the opposite way from our first turn out of the neighborhood."

"On the way to town?"

"Yeah, if you're taking the back road."

"Can we ride by there? I'd like to see the place. Maybe we could stop and see what he and Jay are up to."

"If you want to," says Rosie. She hesitates. "What's Jay's fascination with him, if you don't mind my asking?"

"I don't really know," I admit. "I'm sorry about how that looked when they drove by your house."

"Well, Jay's behavior is certainly not your responsibility!" claims Rosie as she swerves to miss another pothole.

We huff harder as we pedal up an incline where we stop for another water break. Our neighborhood spreads out before us. I can clearly see the layout of one and two-acre lots with fences surrounding small pastures for horses or cows. Our house looks lonely and gray compared to some of our neighbors' houses, but I resolve to see the beauty in the small things. Like Rosie says, "*You just have to look a little harder.*"

The road to Charlie's is downhill and then flat. My butt hurts and my hands and shoulders feel bruised and stiff. I am using muscles that have been in hiding for awhile.

As we glide back to familiar territory, Rosie leads me down the road to Charlie's house. The sound of a chain saw leads us to an older brick ranch house with peeling trim and a well-manicured but empty front yard. A porch runs across the front of the house with a sagging swing and a few dirty white Adirondack chairs. Rosebushes of all colors grow wild across the front of the house on both sides of the door. The mature trees in the front yard provide deep shade for the west-facing house.

We park our bikes and walk around the side of the

house to the back yard, following the racket of the chainsaw. We stop in mid-stride as we come upon the chaos that is Charlie's back yard. Rusting farm machinery and old cars are barely recognizable under the piles of trash and tumbleweeds that cover them. Weeds grow tall in every available spot, adding to the tangled mess. Jay bends over a felled tree, running the saw, shirt off and sweating, his back to us. Charlie stands with a foot on the trunk, stabilizing it, and sees us when he turns his head to spit tobacco. He sticks his toeless foot in Jay's side to get his attention. Jay shuts down the chainsaw and turns to see what Charlie is looking at. His face goes rigid.

"Hi!" I say, swallowing my sudden discomfort. "We were bike riding and thought we'd come by to see how things are going."

Jay straightens up, wipes his forehead and sits on the tree. "We're doing fine," he says in a clipped tone.

I guess we aren't welcome at this party!

Charlie spits and grins. "How y'girls doin' this fine day?"

"Oh, good," says Rosie. "It's getting hot though."

"Sure enough is," says Charlie. "How 'bout one'a'ya gals gettin' us some ice tea?"

"Is there some inside we can get for you?" I ask.

"Naw! Not in my house!" yells Charlie. "Go make us some and bring it over!"

I open my mouth and close it. Rosie grunts in surprise.

"Sure," I say, not feeling sure at all. "I'll go home and make some."

I'll have to go home, brew the tea and drive it back. How stupid is that?

Jay starts up the chainsaw and turns back to his work.

"That was weird," says Rosie.

"I don't even know what to say. What are we, his maids or something? That guy has a horrible attitude."

"I don't think he likes women very much," says Rosie.

"You think?"

"And I've never been in his backyard," says Rosie. "What's up with the Jekyll and Hyde house?"

We pedal back to my house and Rosie leaves me with the promise to visit again soon.

I don't believe she meant it. Why would she want to spend time with the neighbor with the weird husband? And how do you defend your husband's behavior when it isn't something you understand?

I set the teapot on to boil and lay out Jay's favorite teas. I chew on my thumbnail, waiting for the water to boil.

Once the tea steeps, I dig around the back of the cupboard for my old Tupperware pitcher, fill it with ice and pour the tea over it. Covering it with the watertight lid, I go to the car and am about ready to leave when I realize I will need cups. If Charlie isn't going to let me in his house, he probably expects that, too. I sigh in frustration and go back into the house to get three plastic cups and fill them with ice. All this for a man I can't stand. The heat and the bike ride have taken it out of me. I just want to be done.

I pull into Charlie's driveway and leave the car, balancing the pitcher and glasses. The chainsaw is still buzzing, so they won't notice if I snoop a little. I walk up the steps to the front porch and peek in the filthy window next to the front door. Mountains of newspapers and trash fill the room. What floor I can see is thick with grime. A narrow path leads through the garbage to what must be the kitchen where the counter is covered in more trash. Goosebumps rise on my arms. Charlie is a hoarder! I once had a client who hoarded cats. Having no idea how to help her, I referred her to a psychiatrist and called animal control, relieved at being done with her.

Charlie has serious issues! I wonder if Jay knows that's why he's never been invited into the house.

I rush back down the steps and around to the back of the house.

How does Charlie manage to hold it together enough to keep the front of the house looking so nice?

The men stop their work when they see me. Jay looks beat.

"Here you go!" I say as cheerfully as I can.

I set the cups down on the stump and pour for the three of us. Jay chugs his down. Charlie picks his up and smells it.

"This don't smell like any tea I ever drunk!" he says.

"Oh?" I say.

He takes a sip and spits it out, spraying my sandaled feet. I step back.

"It's Jay's favorite," I say, looking for help from Jay.

"What are ya? A sissy boy?" jeers Charlie.

"It's a combination of black tea with lavender and raspberry...it's refreshing," I add.

"Not to me it ain't," says Charlie. Jay looks everywhere

except at me.

"Sorry about that, Charlie," he says. "I should have told Susan to make us some plain old Lipton tea."

I am fuming.

He should have told me?

"Sorry, it didn't work out," I say. "I guess you'll just have to get some water on your own." I turn and walk away without looking back.

I'll be damned if I'll be treated that way! Jay didn't even stand up for me! What was that about? 'Sissy boy?' He puts up with that?

I get in my car, slam the door and leave Charlie's, spewing gravel in my wake. I spend the rest of the afternoon cleaning the house, working off the adrenaline and dreading Jay's return. He will be hot, tired and grouchy, and probably mad at me for going to Charlie's in the first place. This isn't going to be a good night.

❧

Jay arrives home after our usual dinner hour. I have made spaghetti, but didn't put much effort into it. A jar of Ragu, a little extra oregano, and Romano cheese are about all I could muster. Jay strides into the house, whistling under his breath, covered in sweat and wood dust.

"I'm gonna grab a shower," he says as he walks by the kitchen.

I put his spaghetti in the microwave and make myself a cup of tea while I wait for him. Ten minutes later he is in the kitchen, toweling off his hair with a big grin on his face.

"Smells great! I'm starving!"

"I ate earlier. I didn't think you'd be gone this long," I say.

"Yeah. Once Charlie gets going, he doesn't stop. He had me doing all sorts of stuff to help him clean that backyard up. What a mess!"

I don't respond. Jay finally looks at me. "What's up with you?" he asks.

"I'm really upset about how Charlie treated me this afternoon and want to know why you didn't stick up for me." I say, sounding calmer than I feel.

"The tea thing? That was no big deal."

"It was to me!"

"That's just Charlie's way, Hon. He's a little bit of a bully."

"So, why in the world did you tell Charlie you should have told me to make plain tea? That sounded like you are the master of the house or something!"

"I'm sorry he was such an ass."

"Jay, I've seen you in plenty of situations where you don't let people walk all over you. But you let Charlie wear you out doing work around his house while he yelled and treated your wife like shit!"

"I don't let anyone walk all over me, and I was trying to be neighborly."

"Well, he's doing it and you can't see it. No one I know likes him or wants to be around him. Why do you hang out there? What's the attraction?"

"He's lonely. I feel kinda sorry for him."

"Well, maybe you need to ask yourself why he has no friends or family. Why his kids aren't anywhere near here and why in the hell he's such a pig! He's a hoarder, you know."

"Suze! Knock it off, all right?"

"Just tell me you'll never let anything like that happen again. I can easily stand up for myself, but without your backing, he's going to continue to treat me like crap."

"Fine! I'll try harder next time."

"And I don't think you should spend so much time with him. He's not a good person and you don't need him."

"Well, if you were home more—"

"Just stop, Jay. Stop! Just because I'm not home when you want me to be doesn't mean you have to seek out a lowlife like him! And why is it okay to help him with yard work but not me?"

"Hey, I told you from the start I'm not into that stuff. I'm just helping out a neighbor, but don't think I'm going to get in the habit, because I'm not!"

"Jay, if you think it's okay with me that you will spend an afternoon in someone else's yard before ours is fixed up, it's not. It's definitely not! Why don't you make friends with some of the normal neighbors? Rosie's husband is a nice guy. Call some guys from work or something!"

"I'm not hanging out with Rosie's husband. Charlie says he's a huge wimp, letting Rosie get away with all kinds of stuff—"

"There it is again! Charlie telling you how to feel or what to believe about Russ, and you've barely talked to the guy. And why the hell were you driving by like a stalker when I was over there?"

The Water Master

Jay stares at me. His eyes turn black and cold and the muscle in his jaw twitches. "I don't trust you with them."

"You don't trust me? Where the hell is that coming from? What have I done that you don't trust me with them?"

"Frankly, Susan, I don't trust you with any of these people here. They're victimizing Silvia and bad-mouthing Charlie. Maybe they're influencing you too much!"

"Jay, I can trust my own instincts. I didn't like Charlie the moment I met him."

"Well, I think your instincts are crap!" Jay grabs his cooling spaghetti and stalks to the living room.

I hear him turn on the TV and can tell by how his fork hits his plate that he is furious. I put the dishes in the sink and walk through the living room to the bedroom without looking at Jay. I can feel his hateful stare on the back of my neck. As I undress for bed I blink back angry tears. I cry when I am mad and I am really mad! And scared. My marriage is in trouble.

I wake in the middle of the night with the light on and my book on my chest. The other side of the bed is empty. I tiptoe across the floor and open the bedroom door. The light of the TV flickers in the dark as Jay snores on the couch. I am relieved he didn't come to bed.

What did I do to destroy his trust in me? He is jealous. Insanely jealous. He doesn't want me to be friends with anybody. Anybody but him.

When we first met, we couldn't keep our hands off each other and wanted to spend every spare moment together. We lived two hours apart, and could only get together on weekends. I'd put my friends aside, and while they understood, I realized now that isolating myself might have been a mistake. We never spent time with friends. Jay promised me we would socialize later. Whenever I tried to talk about getting together with my sister or friends, he'd change the subject, usually by nipping me on the ear and planting a deep, sexy kiss on my lips. When I had planned our wedding, we'd wanted to keep it simple since we really didn't have time to invite anyone. He barely knew my sister and never talked about his own family.

Why didn't I see all these warning signs? Clearly, he wants me all to himself.

Jay never discusses his past loves and doesn't want to hear about mine. At our age, we have to assume we've been intimate with others.

I slide back into bed and turn the light out. In the morning, I'll inform Jay not to expect me home till late—and he can make his own dinner. I haven't had time to cook for the week, and I'm not doing that again. I dread his reaction. I hate to fight. As a counselor, I'd chronically found myself managing conflict, but it was not mine. Living with it is a different experience.

I sleep badly the rest of the night—anxious and headachy, stomach in knots. Jay marches into the bedroom at his usual time and enters the bathroom, closing the door hard—not quite a slam.

Waiting for Jay to finish his shower feels like an eternity. I chew my thumbnail to the quick. Finally, Jay comes out of the bathroom.

"Jay, can we talk for a minute?"

"Not sure why. Until you learn to care more about me than everyone else, I have nothing to say to you."

I sigh. "Jay, I love you. I don't know how many more ways I can show you. I care about you and our marriage. And I also care about friends, having good people in our lives, and accomplishing things at work."

"You can have your friends and your work. I'm not stopping you!" Jay jerks on his jeans and begins to button his shirt.

"Jay, I don't want to argue. And I don't need your permission. I've needed to tell you something all weekend but it's never been the right time."

Jay rolls his eyes and frowns at me. "Great. Now what?"

"The project I'm working on at the office is becoming more…intense than I expected." I am trying not to trip over my words. "The next few months will require serious overtime. I asked for help, and Marisa is going to work with me too, so that should help us finish sooner…"

Jay's back is to me as he picks up his keys off the dresser. Suddenly he turns and flings them across the room. They hit the window and a chip of glass flies onto the floor. I freeze, shocked into silence.

"Fuck you, Susan! Fuck you! You are such a bitch with your high and mighty talk of friends and work. You have no idea who you are dealing with. No idea!"

I can't move. My heart pounds so hard that my t-shirt vibrates, tickling my skin.

In two quick strides, Jay rushes the bed and towers over me, his face flushed and angry, fists clenched by his side.

"I could so hurt you right now," he hisses. "But I won't. Not yet. The last thing I need is your doctor friend asking you about the bruises. But you need to clearly understand that this is not what I bargained for and you will not work late. I expect you home! And I am sick and tired of your turning me down every night. You know how much I like fucking, so you damn well better be ready."

I take a deep breath. "I don't fuck. I make love."

Jay's eyebrows shoot up.

"We'll just see about that," he says in a menacing voice.

Jay turns and stalks out of the room. My body shakes uncontrollably. Tears pour out as a deep groan emerges from my lips. I curl up into a ball of despair.

I have really, really made a big mistake. I'm such an idiot! How did I miss this?

※

LITHA – TRANSITION

"I am a breaker: threatening doom..."

※

Chapter Seven

࿇

I cry myself dry and then drag myself to the bathroom, feeling heavy as wet cement. Once in the shower, I let the water pound my shoulders as I stare at nothing, knowing I have to pull it together so I can work. I hug myself with a towel to dry off, patting every droplet of water. I squirt Visine into my puffy, red-rimmed eyes, hoping it will 'get the red out,' and apply a little more makeup than usual. Breakfast is out of the question. I can barely swallow my own spit, much less food. I feel beat up. And I'm late for work.

Karen sits at the front desk reviewing the files for the day as I come through the door.

"Sorry, I'm late," I say. "Rough morning."

Karen glances up with a smile that quickly turns to one of concern. "What happened?"

"Um. Argument with Jay. Nothing to worry about."

Karen just looks at me. I want to cry, but I take a deep breath to calm myself.

"Well...let me know if I can help," says Karen. "Been there and done that. Hopefully it will blow over."

I doubt that Tom has ever raised a hand to Karen.

"Thanks," I say.

"We've scheduled some time out of the office today so we can drive over to the file storage and gather all of the charts. I think we can fit them in the break room and wade through them in some kind of order."

"Sounds good. Did you get a chance to ask for Marisa's help?"

"Yeah. She's good to go. She agreed to work a few hours a week, after she's done with clients and her case notes."

"Okay. I'll do the same, and hopefully we can finish this by the time Dale needs all of the evidence."

"How about the weekends?" asks Karen. "If you can work a few weekends, Tom and I can help."

"No problem," I lie.

My cell phone rings mid-morning, setting me into a mini-panic. It isn't Jay. I raise my elbows to air out the sudden dampness in my armpits.

"This is Susan."

"Hi, Mrs. Glasser. This is Mike from Premier Irrigation."

"Hi, Mike. What did you find out about my leak?"

"Well, it's a funny thing. We turned on your water and it started bubbling right up out of the ground. After we turned it off we found a hole in the ground. It looks like someone jabbed a hole right into the irrigation pipe. We dug it up and sure enough, the pipe was broke through."

"Are you telling me someone vandalized my irrigation?"

"Yes, ma'am."

"Who would do that? Have you ever seen anything like this?"

"We've never seen anything like it before."

I open my mouth to speak, but nothing comes out.

"Ma'am? You still there?"

"Yeah. Sorry. Were you able to fix it?"

"Yes ma'am. We just had to dig up a few feet of pipe and replace it. It's all working now. Just turn your timer back on."

"Thanks. What's this going to cost me?"

"I left the bill on your door."

"I'll send a check right away. Thanks for your help."

I slump in my chair. I can't wrap my head around it. Why would anyone go to the trouble of pounding a sharp object into the ground hard enough to put a hole in my irrigation? Watering problems have been chronic since I planted the garden. The flood has ruined my herbs and drowned the vegetables. Could Jay or Charlie be this crazy...to do what? Prevent me from gardening? It makes no sense.

My mind is still whirling when Tom and Karen close the office at lunch and we drive over to the storage facility in Tom's pickup truck. Tom pulls up to the locker and unlocks the door. Inside, neatly stacked and labeled, are at least forty file boxes. My stomach sinks.

"Wow! All these? You've seen a lot of patients in twenty years!" I say.

"Yes, we have," says Tom. "There's a lot of life in these boxes."

As we pack the truck, I ask, "Do you have copies of the appointment books in here too?"

"We filed the appointment books in one box," says Karen. She shuffles around the boxes in the back of the truck. "Here they are."

I open the box, and there in perfect chronological order are appointment books dating back to the beginning of their practice.

"This will make our job so much easier," I say.

After stopping for sandwiches, we head back to the office. Marisa has just finished with her lunch client and takes a break to help us unload the boxes. Once all of them are stacked in the conference room, there is barely enough room to sit at the table and open the refrigerator. We squeeze in around the table, eating lunch and discussing the game plan.

"Susan, since you've already started this process, maybe you can suggest the best way to go about this," says Tom.

"If we work in pairs, you and Karen and Marisa and me, one person can review the patient file and read off each appointment date while the other person types it into the spreadsheet. One person can do the job, but two will make it more efficient. We can record the information from the charts first, then as we go through the appointment books day by day, we can confirm or deny every appointment against the case notes and make other notes regarding any other discrepancies."

"Sounds good," says Tom. "Karen and I can start our own spreadsheet, and when we finish, we'll put the two of them together and we'll have our data for Dale."

Now that we have a plan, I hope it will keep my mind off my troubles with Jay—and the stupid irrigation.

The rest of the day goes smoothly. Late in the afternoon I answer a call from Star. If she hadn't identified herself, I wouldn't have recognized her voice. It is barely a whisper.

"What's up?" I ask.

"I need to make an appointment," croaks Star. "My herbs aren't working. I'm really sick."

I make arrangements for Star to come in right away and twenty minutes later, she walks in looking pale and feverish. I have prepared some hot tea for her which she accepts with a weak smile.

"Have a seat. Doctor will be with you in a few minutes," I say.

Star sits with her eyes closed. Tom eventually finishes with his last patient and Karen comes out to get Star. By the time Tom is finished, Marisa and I have started on our first box of files. I stop long enough to set up a follow-up appointment with Star and wish her well.

Star notices the stack of files. "Looks like you're working on a big project."

"Yeah. We're doing an audit." I think that is a generic enough answer to satisfy anyone who asks.

"It doesn't look like much fun. Good luck!"

"I hope you feel better," I say.

"It's hard to keep the store open when I feel this bad. Thank the gods I have my friends to help. Ronny can work at the store a little, and a few others are filling in during the day."

"I wish I could help too, but I'm going to be busy here for awhile."

"Thanks. See you soon?"

"I'll stop by when I can," I say as I turn back to my work.

"Bye and Blessed Be!"

"Blessed Be," I say without thought.

Marisa and I complete the logging and documentation of a few files during our first hours together. At this rate it is going to take months to complete the entire audit! Will I still be married when we finish?

When I arrive home, Jay is gone but has left evidence he's been home long enough to eat a dinner of scrambled eggs and bacon. Dirty dishes are scattered throughout the kitchen. It looks as though a bomb has exploded. I clean up after him and try to settle down with a book, but can't relax.

What kind of mood will Jay be in when he comes home? Will he come home?

I decide to call Star to see how she's feeling.

"Hello?" Star answers with a weak voice.

"Hi. It's Susan. I thought I better check up on you."

"It's strep throat. I let it go too long. I slept for awhile after I picked up my prescription and feel a little better."

"Is there anything I can do for you? I don't even know if you live with anyone who can take care of you."

"I'm by myself, but a few of the coven members brought over some soup and ginger ale."

"Okay. Just thought I'd ask."

"I appreciate it. When I'm feeling better, let's get together, okay?"

"Great. Rest well."

"G'nite," says Star in a tired voice.

The short conversation with Star grounds me a little—a brief reprieve from thinking about my own problems.

Where is Jay? I crawl into bed with my book and soon

turn out the light to sleep. Sometime during the night, Jay slips into bed beside me and wraps his arm around me, to spoon me as if nothing had happened. I stiffen against his touch, but soon relax in the warmth of his body. This is the Jay I married, not the monster that was in our bedroom early this morning. I know he loves me.

We can make it work. I finally fall asleep.

৵৽৶

But Jay remains absent most of the time. Every day is the same. He leaves before me in the morning and returns home after I'm in bed, stinking of beer and cigars. I pretend to sleep and hide my nose under the pillow to avoid his reek. Jay sleeps like a rock for a few hours, but is up and out on time each morning. He is silent and hurries to leave the house, or is tired and a little drunk when he arrives home. Once he's in bed with me, my nerves buzz and I can't sleep. I need to address his late nights, coming and going as if he doesn't have a responsibility to me, his wife. But I'm scared. He is cold and distant, but at least he isn't threatening. I choose to keep my mouth shut.

Work helps. It's a relief to handle solid information, even though the billing discrepancies are piling up as Marisa and I work late reviewing file after file. I work, eat and sleep. Rosie called me to go for a walk one night and I begged off. On another night Star left a message to call her and I was too tired to pick up the phone.

Today is Friday, the end of a long and tiring week. At about three o'clock Tom walks into the reception area where Marisa and I are slaving over more files.

"I think we've all had enough for the week. I think you two should leave at the normal time tonight," Tom says.

"Oh, that's okay. I'd like to get through this stack before I go home," I say.

"Do you mind if I go? I have things to do," Marisa says.

"No problem."

Jay won't be home anyhow. What's the sense of going home to an empty house and a confusing marriage?

After everyone leaves, I complete a few more files.

I open a new chart and see my own address. It's Amanda Clement's file, the woman that lived at my house before me!

I quickly type the dates of her appointments into the spreadsheet and study the chart to see if the appointments add up. Every appointment where Amanda Clement was seen by Tom matches the case notes. I color-code the cleared appointments with the designated highlighter color, so if her name shows up elsewhere in the appointment books, we will know there are no case notes to match. Then I settle down to read the file.

Tom's first appointment with her had been about fifteen years ago. She'd had a rash on her arms and abdomen. He treated her with antihistamines. Tom found no specific allergies. I notice that Amanda had two or three appointments a year with various ailments that were easily treated. As the years went on, Tom's notes indicated that Amanda was appearing depressed and she had alluded to marital problems. The last few appointments she was joined by her husband, Andy. At that time, she had digestive problems.

I check her age at the time of the last appointment. *Sixty-seven years old.*

Emotional problems frequently show themselves physically. Women tend toward digestive problems, aches and pains and sleep disruption. I wonder if Amanda's marital problems were the basis of her visits to see Tom. Maybe her husband's presence at the doctor's office was his effort to remain in control of her rather than to support her.

I go back through the file and notice a few changes of address until about a year before they disappeared, when they moved into my house. Charlie's house.

I call Tom and Karen. Tom picks up the phone.

"Hello?"

"Hi, it's me, I'm still at the office. Hey. What do you guys remember about Amanda and Andy Clement? I was just reviewing Amanda's file and noticed there were no billing problems. That's unusual in itself, since almost all the files have had at least one billing discrepancy."

"Hold on. Let me get Karen and we'll both talk with you."

Karen picks up the extension. "What's up?" asks Karen.

"As I was telling Tom, I was just reviewing Amanda's file and noticed there were no billing problems. Isn't that strange since almost all the files have had at least one billing discrepancy?"

"I'd have to read the notes to remember," Karen says.

"When she and Andy disappeared, the police questioned us about them, but nothing stood out."

"Did you read the file?" Tom asks.

"Yes. Maybe I shouldn't have..."

"I don't blame you. The whole thing is such a mystery. What's your take on it?"

"Sounds like she had vague physical complaints that I would associate with depression or stress."

"I remember thinking that at the time," says Tom.

"Were they into herbal remedies at all?" I ask.

"Not to my knowledge," responds Tom. "Why?"

"Some of the symptoms she had could be related to side effects of too many herbs or the wrong kinds of herbs."

"I never thought of that," says Tom. "I was always looking at food sensitivities or bacterial infections."

"Any clue why her husband would come in with her?"

"It got to the point where she couldn't drive sometimes. She'd get shaky or nervous or something. He would drive her everywhere."

"I wonder if something else was going on?"

"If you think she had a serious illness, you can see we ran all kinds of labs. Nothing showed up."

"I mean that something else...like her husband, or even Charlie...was doing something to her."

"Like what?" Karen says, her tone changing to concern.

"I don't know. It's just a feeling I have. You know, the whole thing with how Charlie was a suspect, they lived in our house, the change in Jay since he's been hanging around with Charlie…"

I'm saying too much.

At the same time, Tom and Karen both say, "What about Jay?"

I sigh, sit back and hug myself. "I, um…"

Karen's voice softens. "It's okay. What's going on?"

"I'm so embarrassed. I don't even know what to say."

"Look. We're friends here. You can say anything."

I feel the tears behind my eyes, rub them away and take a breath to keep my voice from shaking.

"He's out late and rarely home. I assume he's with Charlie, but I don't know for sure. I really don't know what's going on! He says I'm working too much and he wants me home more, but he's not there as it is. I just don't know."

"Look, the situation at work is really our problem, not yours," says Tom. "You've been more than generous with your time. If being home more will help, we can handle this without you."

"I appreciate that but I don't think that's the real problem. I don't know what it is, but that's not it."

I blink back tears. "I'm so sorry. I'm your employee. I shouldn't have said anything."

"Too late!" says Tom as he laughs. "You're our problem and we'll help however we can."

"For now I'm just glad I told you," I say. "Thanks."

We say good-bye. Later that evening I realize we never finished discussing the Clements.

The Water Master

❧

When I arrive home, Jay is slouched on the couch, beer in hand, watching TV with an unfinished pizza, still in the box on the coffee table in front of him.

"Hi. Long time, no see," says Jay.

"Hi," I say. I try to remain as neutral as I can, despite the lurch of fear and anger that makes me want to scream at him.

"Want some pizza?" he asks.

"Yeah. I'll stick a few pieces in the microwave. Thanks."

He makes no move to kiss me or take my hand, so in an attempt at conciliation, I lean down to kiss him. He turns his face so I kiss his cheek.

Okay. That's how it's going to be.

While the microwave heats up the pizza, I wash up a few dishes and clean the counters. The microwave beeps and I open it. The pizza smells bad. I'm hungry enough to eat it anyhow. Carrying my pizza and a Coke to the living room, I sit at the far end of the couch, put my feet on the coffee table and take a bite. The crust is mushy, but it's food. Jay sits silently at the other end of the couch watching a sci-fi movie. I'm done after one piece.

"That pizza was awful," I say.

"Yeah, I didn't like it either," says Jay. "I'm still trying to find the best pizza in town. So far, there isn't any."

"I'm going to have a bowl of cereal."

I walk into the kitchen and toss the pizza into the garbage, pull down a box of Frosted Flakes, pour cold milk over the cereal and carry it back to the living room.

The Water Master

"How ya doin'?" I ask Jay as I sit down again. *We have to get past this silence!*

"Tired."

"Me, too."

"Are you working tomorrow?" asks Jay.

"Umm, I'm planning on it."

Jay pull his feet off the coffee table, sits up and turns toward me.

"Look, I...I'm sorry I've been such an ass about all this. I've been thinking about us a lot lately. Since your late nights aren't going to go on forever, I'm willing to take over more. Do some cooking, so we aren't eating this crap every night. Help more around here. We'll make it through this, and then when it's over, we can regroup. What do you say?"

Relief washes over me. "Really?"

"Really," says Jay.

"Oh, Jay! That means so much to me. I've hated the tension between us!"

"I don't like it either," says Jay. "We'll get through it."

That night we fall asleep in our favorite spoon position, and sometime during the night, make love like we mean it. I drift back into a contented slumber.

෯෧

Jay stares into space with a big grin on his face.

Wow, that was easy. If the stuff I put on the pizza works, I'll find a way to get some more. Charlie said it worked great on that Clement lady.

෯෧

171

The Water Master

I wake up Saturday morning. My stomach gurgles. It must be the pizza I ate last night. I feel so tired. My eyes are scratchy and my throat feels raw. I'm emotionally exhausted.

Why did I eat that crap?

I make some peppermint tea to settle my stomach and add some ginger for good measure. It's all I can swallow before I go to work. I leave Jay sleeping in, knowing it will be past noon before he gets up. I'll come home for lunch. Maybe I can plan some crockpot recipes for the week. If he is willing to try harder, I can, too.

The four of us finish off another box after working all morning at the office. We decide to call it a day and to return on Sunday afternoon. My nausea continues through the morning, and finally eases off about the time I leave for home. Pulling into the driveway, I see Charlie's truck parked in front of our house. My stomach sinks.

Jay and Charlie are at the counter in the kitchen. The men snap their heads up and give me the deer-in-the-headlight stare. I obviously interrupted a conversation they didn't want me to hear. Half-finished bacon and eggs lay on greasy plates. Jay glares at me.

"What are you doing home?" he asks.

"We knocked off for the day," I reply.

"They gotcha workin' some long hours over there, Missy!" says Charlie through a mouth full of food. My stomach turns at the sight of bacon grease on his stubbly chin.

"Nothing I can't handle," I say.

"I figured since you weren't home I'd have Charlie

172

over for company," Jay says, forcing cheerfulness into his voice.

"Oh. Okay. I didn't realize I'd be off this afternoon. I thought maybe we could plan the menu and do some shopping together," I say to Jay.

Jay huffs. "I told you I'd take care of the meals. What didn't you get about that?"

Jay's snotty tone embarrasses me. I say, "I know. I just thought since I had time, we could do it together."

"It would have been nice for you to give me some warning, you know!"

I bristle. "Excuse me for making myself available! I am only trying to help!"

"No need. I've got it under control," he says as he dismisses me.

Charlie smirks. "Looks like he told you!" he says.

"That's okay," I say, trying not to let them get the best of me. "I'll work in the yard this afternoon."

I open the refrigerator and pull out sandwich meat, mayonnaise and lettuce. Charlie and Jay are silent as I make my lunch. Charlie looks at Jay as if he expects him to banish me. I deliberately take my time making my sandwich, while chatting about the weather, the neighborhood, and the work to be done in the yard.

When I'm sure the men are fed up with me, I say, "I'll leave you guys to it and go watch TV while I eat my lunch."

Charlie rolls his eyes and wipes his chin with his shirtsleeve. "Y'go watch your girlie shows," he says. His tone of voice and his evil smile make me want to take a shower. It isn't worth the trouble to try to one-up him. I leave the kitchen, plop down on the couch and use the remote to turn on the TV. As I scan the choices, I find my favorite movie, the classic, *Gaslight*. I eat my sandwich and become involved enough in the movie that I'm able to tune out Charlie and Jay's conversation. Soon Jay yells from the kitchen to say they're leaving for awhile.

"Okay. Will you be home for dinner?" I call out.

"Maybe," he says.

So much for his meal planning.

After the movie, I walk out back to see what needs to be done in the yard.

The garden has dried out from the flood. I loosen the packed dirt, preparing it for the new plants I picked up at the lawn and garden store. In one raised bed I dig holes and plant tomatoes, peppers and squash, sprinkling fertilizer around each plant. I replant the other bed with herbs. I'd bought mature plants this time around in hopes I will have a harvest by August.

Next, I turn my attention to the weeds along the fence lines and then clear tumbleweed from the side of the house. Using the flat of my shovel, I beat the tumbleweed into piles that can be shoveled into trash bags. It feels good to beat the hell out of something! Most people burn tumbleweed, but fire scares me. I've heard frightening stories about homeowners paying the costs of extinguishing a devastating but unintended brush fire.

Eventually, an impending back spasm reminds me I'm overdoing it. So, I put my shovel and gloves in their place in the garage and drag myself into the house. I lie down on the living room floor to stretch out my sore muscles. My mind wanders back to the Amanda and Andy mystery.

Maybe Star will know something about the former owners of our house. She might be familiar with herbs that can cause the physical symptoms that Amanda experienced. I know I'm working on a hunch, but I need to play it out.

Grabbing a granola bar on my way out of the kitchen, I shuffle to the car and crawl into the driver's seat like an old lady.

Damned back!

My mood shifts as soon as I walk in the door of the herb store.

Star must burn magic incense!

I take a deep breath of the exotic odor. Star is on her knees behind the counter, rummaging around for something on a lower shelf. "I'll be right with you," she says.

"Okay. It's just me."

"Oh, good! I'm glad you stopped by." Star pops up from behind the counter, blowing the hair away from her face and breathing hard. "Those stupid plastic bags slip and slide all the way to the back of the shelf. Every once in a while I have to dig."

"Are you over your strep throat?"

"Getting there. Not a hundred percent by any means. The antibiotics helped. I hate the side effects of those things. That's why I got so sick, though. I waited way too long and my herbs wouldn't do the trick."

"Sometimes modern medicine actually works," I say, laughing. "However, I prefer herbal remedies myself."

"I'm eating a lot of yogurt. It's helping with the lovely

side effects," says Star.

"Well, I'm glad you're doing better."

"Are you done with that big job at Dr. Elwin's office yet?"

"No. Just taking the afternoon off."

"I'm about ready to close. Is there anything you need?"

"Not really. I just wanted to ask you some questions about herbs."

"Ask away," says Star as she comes around the counter. "Let's sit for awhile."

We sit in the corner of the store where two comfortable chairs and a loveseat are arranged around a large round coffee table. Herbal magazines and books are scattered across the tabletop, along with various essential oil testers and spray bottles of rose and lavender waters. Tea tree oil simmers in a censer.

As I sink into one of the chairs, I stuff a pillow behind my aching back. "This is where that wonderful smell is coming from," I say.

"Yeah. My customers make it smell good when they spray the samplers and test the oils. I don't really plan on any certain aroma. It's just what happens here."

"It certainly adds to the great energy. I really like it!" I say.

"Thanks. Now what can I help you with?"

"Did you know the people that lived in our house? The Clements?"

"No more than I knew any other irregular customer. Why?"

All too aware of the confidential nature of medical records, I hesitate.

"Um. My neighbor mentioned they'd gone missing awhile back. I'm curious about what happened to them. Were they customers of yours?"

"Mr. Clement was. He bought herbs to sprinkle around the base of his house to keep the bugs out. That's about it."

I know about those herbs, but none of them would cause a human to become ill, despite how well they work to keep the bugs away.

"Thanks. Maybe I'm going down a dead end."

Star is thoughtful for a minute. Finally she says, "I do remember Mrs. Clement coming in once. I really didn't know who she was until I saw her picture in the paper a few months later, when she and her husband went missing."

I perk up. "What did she buy?"

"She was looking for information about protection."

"Protection? From what?"

"She didn't say. But I sold her a book on protection rituals. I probably sold her some herbs or something to help her with that, but I don't remember. I try not to ask too many questions. Half the time, my customers believe some pretty unbelievable things that I'd rather not know about."

"Did either of the Clements ever refer to Charlie Gottschalk when they were here?"

"No. I would have remembered that. Charlie was on everyone's radar—still is. He's a creepy guy and the few people who did befriend him figured him out pretty fast and kept their distance."

I shake my head. "Jay's radar must be off then. He and Charlie are very friendly."

Star shifts in her chair. "How do you feel about that?"

"I don't like it. Charlie is so demeaning to me. He was in my house this afternoon and I felt like I wanted to sanitize the whole place."

"Take some sage home with you. Some say it rids a house of negative energy."

"I will. Thanks. I just don't understand what Jay sees in him. I thought Jay had good intuition about people. Charlie's energy urges me to run away, but seems to suck Jay in."

"Has this changed Jay in some way?"

"Oh, yeah. It's either a change, or it's a part of him I was unaware of when I married him."

"Charlie brings out the worst in him?"

"Or I am. We didn't plan for me to work. Starting this job so quickly and then choosing to work more hours on this project...maybe he's changed because I'm not around as much as we thought I'd be. I took time off this afternoon and tomorrow morning just to spend with him, but he didn't know I was going to be home, so he'd already made plans with Charlie. He was pissy about it."

"Maybe it's you, but I doubt it. He didn't acknowledge that you tried to spend time with him?"

"No. He didn't know I was coming home. I don't think he likes surprises."

"Does he know you'll be around in the morning?"

"No, but I'll tell him, and—"

"—and we'll see what he does with it."

"Yeah. We'll see what he does with it. In the meantime, let me know if you think of anything that could help me solve the mystery around the Clements," I say.

"Will do. Here's your sage."

I breath in the sweet tangy sage smell. I'm not sure I believe it will help, but I am willing to try anything.

☙❧

Charlie and Jay are driving to the Casino in Charlie's pickup truck.

Jay shoves aside the trash at his feet as he says to Charlie, "The pizza didn't work, Man."

"Ya must have screwed something up, Boy."

"I think she just didn't eat enough of it. It was bad pizza already, and then I put that crap on it."

"Well, Boy, you'll have to come up with a different plan."

☙❧

I stop at the grocery store and buy a roast chicken and some salads—my fallbacks when I don't feel like cooking. The chicken smells marvelous and I realize how hungry I am for home cooking. This will have to be good enough tonight.

It is after six o'clock when I get home. I set the food on the counter and decide to cleanse the house right away. I light the end of the sage and let it burn for a moment before blowing out the flame. Smoke curls up from the glowing tips. I walk around each room in a clockwise direction, waving the smoke into the corners. I spend more time in the kitchen, where Charlie's energy lingers like a grease spot suspended above the counter. I chant "peaceful home, peaceful home" in a whisper as I perform this simple ritual.

When I finish, I go outside and rub the burnt ends of the sage on the cement patio until they are out. I place it in a flower pot sitting next to the house to cool before bringing it into the house to add to our ritual collection. As I open the door to the kitchen, Jay comes through the front door.

"Hi, Hon," I say. "I've got some dinner here if you're hungry."

Jay strides into the kitchen with a beer in hand.

"Not hungry. Charlie and I had dinner down by the highway."

I hold my feelings in check, including my frustration that Jay did not cook dinner as promised.

"Do you want to sit with me while I eat?" I ask.

"Okay. Any ice cream?"

"Your favorite. It's in the freezer."

Jay pulls out a pint of Haagen-Dazs Chocolate and sits at the counter next to me.

"And what did you do this afternoon?" he asks.

"Worked in the yard, went to the grocery store."

He sniffs the air. "And burned some sage?"

"I thought it would be nice to cleanse the house a little."

"You should have waited for me and let me do it."

"I wanted to do it myself. It felt right."

My hands are sweating.

Is this another fight?

"Suze, you don't just do things when they feel right. You do them when it is right. You have to prepare for a cleansing ritual just like any other ritual."

"It wasn't a ritual. I just burned some sage," I say, trying to keep the defensiveness out of my voice.

I wait for the bomb to fall and it doesn't.

After a few minutes of eating in silence, I say, "I'll be home all morning tomorrow. We're not going to work until after lunch."

"Mmm."

"I thought we could spend some time together."

"Sorry. I've made plans."

"On Sunday morning?"

"Yeah. I'm going out with Charlie."

"Where are you going on a Sunday morning?"

"The Casino. Charlie says Sunday morning is the best time. We can score a cheap breakfast and gamble for a while before all the old ladies limp in after church."

"Since when do you gamble?"

"Not often, but it's fun every now and then."

I'm speechless. In all our time together, Jay never mentioned gambling!

"Um," I say, "Can we talk about budgeting some money for this?"

This is the wrong tack. Jay's head whips around and he glares at me.

"Are you saying I can't control myself?"

"No, Jay. I'm not comfortable with the idea of gambling with our money. We've never discussed this before, and —"

"I'm gambling with my money and I can do whatever the hell I want with it!" Jay's voice gets louder and he clutches his spoon with white knuckles.

"You've never gambled since we've been together! Why now? Why Charlie?"

"How would you know I never gambled before? And why not and why not Charlie?" say Jay, his tone sarcastic.

"I just don't understand. One minute you're telling me how I should follow certain rules to do a proper cleansing ritual and the next you want to gamble with Charlie but won't follow any rules for how to spend our money!"

"Because you've got no business telling me what I can and can't do!" yells Jay as he pushes away from the counter and stands over me.

I will myself to continue as my heart hammers in my ears. "I'm not telling you what to do. I just want to discuss it and plan. I've seen the worst of how gambling ruins people. I don't mind your doing it for fun! I just don't know how much you plan to spend!"

Jay smiles his cold smile. "Everything I do is just for fun. Didn't you know that?" he says.

"That's not funny, Jay. Just take it easy, okay?"

I want to end the argument to prevent a possible fist in the ribs. He's trying to remain in control of himself, but his hand shakes as he gulps down his last bite of ice cream and throws his spoon into the bowl with a loud clang.

Without another word, Jay tosses his beer bottle into

the recycling bin and leaves the room. A few seconds later I hear the TV go on, and he switches the channel to a science fiction movie that he's seen a hundred times. I put the food away and shut myself in the bedroom. Jay never comes to bed. I sleep alone.

☙❧

Jay picks Charlie up at dawn, mulling over the fight with Susan the night before.

There's no way that bitch is going to tell me how to spend my money! She better loosen up pretty damn quick, or there'll be hell to pay. The whores are cheaper this time of day. I feel sorry for the women who take care of Charlie. How do they do that without gagging? Not my problem. Charlie's got the money and he tips well. Whatever he wins gambling is spent on sex... or whatever you call what he does. I can't decide what I like better—whoring or gambling. I like winning big. And, I like fucking whatever bitch I'm with as long as she's submissive the way I like it. The last one put up a fight when I wanted to tie her up—like she was afraid I'd kill her or something...huh.

Jay licks his lips. *Today will be a good day. I can feel it in my hard-on—exactly where I want to feel it.*

He adjusted himself as he pulled into Charlie's driveway.

☙❧

The next morning I wake to a quiet house. I throw off the blanket and tiptoe to the bedroom door. The living room is empty. I look out the window. Jay's car is gone. I have the house to myself.

As the coffee pot gurgles, I stare out the back door

183

at my newly planted garden and wonder if I will ever see it produce. The coffee pot beeps and I pour the steaming brew into a mug, adding peppermint and chocolate syrups and half and half—my weekend vice—and cheaper than Starbucks. I carry my treat back to the bedroom and crawl back under the covers with my book and read for awhile before showering for work and making an egg sandwich for lunch. I don't want to think about my marriage or Jay.

The afternoon at the office is quiet and productive. We complete another box of charts and find fraudulent billing in many files. Silvia is very clever. Her victims were older patients who had difficulty understanding and tracking insurance billing, or patients who had undergone major surgery, had injuries from accidents, or had to deal with multiple insurance companies and payouts. Tracking bills and insurance payments is difficult enough for an organized person, so it's typical for the patient to assume if something is missing in the billing record, it's because he or she made the error, not the biller or the insurance company.

The files of young patients or some of the better-educated patients showed no discrepancies at all. Clearly, Silvia had picked her victims with precision. She knew who might potentially cause her harm and who would not.

I get home around 5:30 and open the door to a glorious smell of home-cooked food. Jay is pulling a roast out of the oven.

"Oh, boy, that smells good!" I say.

"I thought you'd like this. Roast beef, mashed potatoes and real gravy, peas and carrots and chocolate pie. The pie was made at the grocery store…hope you don't mind."

"It smells fantastic!"

Is he Jekyll or Hyde tonight? I am too hungry to care.

"Put your purse down and let's eat!" says Jay.

The table is set with my brightest place mats.

"Oh, Jay. The table! It's beautiful."

Jay stops long enough to give me a deep kiss.

"This is so nice! Thanks for cooking dinner."

"I said I would and I did."

"Yes, you did!"

"I figured we could eat leftovers for a few days. Between the chicken you bought and the roast beef, we're good for sandwiches for the rest of the week."

"I'll make some chicken salad."

"Don't forget to put celery in it. I love the crunch."

I laugh. "I know, honey, I know."

We eat together and chat easily until our plates are clean. I'm not about to ask about his gambling outing. I don't want to ruin a good thing. I sit back, my stomach extended.

"Oh my gosh, I ate too much!"

"Me too. Let's clean up and go to bed."

We scrape the dishes and put them in the dishwasher. I bend down to get the dishwasher soap under the sink and a back spasm suddenly drops me to the floor. I moan.

"Jay, help me up!"

Jay rushes to my side and helps me off the floor. Bent over, I limp to the couch.

"Crap, crap crap! This damned back!"

Jay looks disgusted.

"What do you need?" he asks, with no enthusiasm.

"Heating pad and softball," I gasp. "Ibuprofen too."

"So much for our romantic evening," says Jay under his breath.

Jay's feelings are the least of my concerns. This hurts more than it has in a long time.

Jay brings the items to me, along with a glass of water. He helps plug in the heating pad and hands me the softball, which I place under the worst of the spasm. He sets the remote where I can reach it.

"Guess you're the one sleeping on the couch tonight," he says as he covers me with a blanket.

"Not by choice," I say with a weak smile. "Not by choice."

Will I ever get a break?

I barely sleep. Each time I change position, the pain takes my breath away. After a long night of wishing the pain away, while worrying about my marriage, my job, and my future, I feel like I have run a marathon. As the sun rises, I am still in agony. About the time I should have been at work, I reach for the phone and call Karen to tell her I am taking a sick day to nurse my back. Marisa gets on the phone and tells me to come over at 9:00 and she will give me a free massage. I agree, hoping I can get moving again.

Despite believing I hadn't slept all night, I must have, because I didn't hear Jay leave for work. I need the bathroom. I roll off the couch onto my hands and knees and use my hands to walk up my legs until I am standing as straight as I can. My back has been my weakest point ever since I was in high school. Sledding with friends, I had an unfortunate and painful introduction to a tree. My back hasn't been the same since. My parents took little notice because I didn't complain. When it hurt, I dealt with it, and when it didn't, I forgot about it.

With a jolt, I realize I am dealing with my marriage the same way. Every time Jay is nice to me, it makes me forget the fight we had just hours before and I live as if the nice Jay is the real Jay. There is an uncomfortable pattern emerging. I don't want to think about it. My back might be easier to fix. I'll talk to Tom and get a referral from him. For now, I'll count on Marisa.

I limp to the bathroom and take a long, hot shower. The more I move, the better I feel. By the time I leave for the office I discover I can get in and out of the car without hydraulic assistance from a crane.

Marisa's healing touch provides me with some relief. I stay at work for the rest of the day.

Tom stops by my desk on his way out.

"How's your back doing?"

"It's manageable."

"Do you know what's wrong with it?"

"Not really. I've been nursing it since I was a kid. I thought maybe you could refer me to someone to take a look at it."

"Remind me tomorrow and I'll give you the name of a guy I know."

Tom starts to leave and then turns around and asks, "Would you and Jay like to come over for dinner this weekend?"

"That would be nice! I'll ask Jay."

"I think it's time we meet him."

I smile.

Dinner would be nice.

Then my smile fades.

Will Jay behave?

I want to believe that every time I walk in my front door, Jay will be the loving and supportive man I first met. Now intimate or easy conversations flip to tension or an outright argument with no warning. Past boyfriends had their quirks, but never left me feeling off-balance and uncertain.

I'll try harder to provide Jay with the extra attention he seems to crave.

Feeling more hopeful than I have in awhile, I prepare steak, salad, and baked potatoes for dinner. Jay arrives home in time for me to pour our ritual glass of wine. The patio is hot in the early evening sun, so Jay pulls chairs around to the front of the house, which provides the only shade on the property at this time of day.

"I'd love to build a covered porch on the back of the house," I say. "The patio bakes in the sun."

"Why don't you contact a contractor and do that?" says Jay.

"Really?"

"Yeah, I think we should do it. If we're going to make this place ours, that's a good place to start."

"I'll work on that," I say.

"Charlie may know someone. I'll ask him."

Trying not to let my annoyance show, I agree.

The Water Master

"Tom and Karen invited us for dinner next weekend."

Jay stares off into the distance.

"That's fine. Let me know when."

"Great!"

"It's not great. I'll go because you work for them. That's it."

My stomach clutches. *Damn him! What is his problem?* Trying to keep the peace, I say, "Thanks. I know it's not your first choice."

Jay looks away again. "Yeah. Support. What are you going to do to support me?"

"What?"

"If I go, what are you going to do for me?"

Confused, I reply, "I don't know what you mean."

"Simple question, Suze. Tit for tat. I want something in return."

"What?"

"I've told you what I need. Let's start with sex. I need it more often than you do, apparently. Or do your interests lay elsewhere?"

I don't take the bait.

"You have a point. I've been pretty distracted. I miss our little lovefests, too."

Jay softens. *Maybe I can really do this!* He reaches for my hand and kisses it.

"I love you, Suze. Making love is when I really feel you loving me."

"I know. I can be there for you, Jay. I can."

"Thanks, baby. Let's schedule some date nights. That way we can promise some time for each other."

"Sounds good."

"Let's start now," says Jay with a wicked smile.

"I'll try. Just be gentle." I mentally wince as I realize what this could do to my back.

We kiss long and hard, just as Russ and Rosie drive by. They honk and wave. I giggle and go inside, with Jay following close behind.

Chapter Eight

࿇

The heat of the summer days intensify as the sun moves toward Solstice. I wake early on Saturday to tend to the garden. The herbs and vegetables grow quickly in the long sunny days. The irrigation works perfectly now. I pick at what few weeds are growing and putter around the yard, enjoying my coffee and the cool, clear morning air.

Tonight is our dinner at the Elwins's house. I am nervous. While my marriage seems on the upswing with our newfound time for each other, I feel Jay's tension whenever I talk about work or my friends with him. Just the other day, I stopped at the herb store to visit with Star and he was upset that I didn't come straight home after work. After that, I agreed to call and let him know if I was going anywhere after work. This stifles me, but he is so anxious. I hope it will calm him and he will begin to trust me. At least he is pleased that we were invited to the Solstice ritual next weekend.

The Elwins's neighborhood contains large houses with expensive landscaping. They live on a ridge overlooking the Columbia River with a view of a large island and the desert of the Hanford site beyond. I immediately fall in love with the white and yellow patterned cushions that decorate the white wicker chairs which are arranged in an inviting style on the beautiful wrap-around porch. It reminds me of the old homes along the main street of the Wisconsin town where I grew up. As we pull into the driveway, Karen steps around the corner of the porch and waves at us.

Jay sighs heavily. "Here we go."

I ignore him and grab the wine and flowers.

"Hi, you two! Welcome to our home!"

"I love it already!" I say. "Karen, this is my husband, Jay."

"Hi, Jay. I'm so glad to meet you."

"Same here," says Jay.

"Tom's inside. Come on in."

I step into a foyer with a sleek granite floor and soaring ceilings. The soft grays and yellows provide a backdrop for bright patches of crimson red and indigo blue decorating the open design. Karen leads us to the sunny kitchen where Tom is preparing hamburgers on a huge island in the middle of the kitchen.

"Tom, this is Jay," I say.

"Jay! Nice to meet you. I'd shake your hand but I'm a little greasy."

"No problem. Thanks for inviting us," says Jay.

We make small talk as we sit at the counter, drinking wine and munching on sliced cheese and apples. Karen pulls homemade potato salad and coleslaw out of the refrigerator. Tom is in and out, grilling the hamburgers. My mouth waters every time he opens the door, allowing the smoky smell to waft into the kitchen.

The Water Master

Dinner is set on a glass table on the east side of the porch, out of the sun. I begin to relax as Tom and Jay discuss Hanford and the history of the area. Jay knows more about Hanford than I realized. He and Tom seem to hit it off. Karen and I clear the table after dinner and bring coffee and apple pie out to the guys.

"That was the best hamburger I've had in a long time," I say as I sit down.

"Probably because you didn't have to cook it," says Tom.

"Yeah. Dinners at our house have been a little hit and miss," says Jay.

Uh-oh.

"Ours are too," says Tom. "It's hard to keep up when both people work. Especially on the Hanford schedule… or a doctor's schedule, for that matter."

"So when are you going to release my wife at a decent hour?" banters Jay.

Karen groans. "We'd all like that. Believe me."

Tom glances over at me. I give a slight shake of my head. In an effort to change the subject, Tom says, "Karen, why don't you give Susan a tour of the house."

"Suze would love that, wouldn't you, Suze?" Jay is staring at me. *What is he up to?*

We leave the men at the table. Once inside, I let out a little sigh.

"You all right?" asks Karen.

"Yeah. I'm fine." I smile. "I can't wait to see the rest of the house."

The Elwins's home is designed with relaxation and

beauty in mind. Karen tells me about their interest in supporting local artists as she shows me the beautiful paintings they have collected over the years.

"I've never asked. Do you guys have kids?" I ask.

"No. That's never been in the cards for us," Karen answers with no discomfort. "But we have lots of nieces and nephews who visit. We love to have guests stay with us, so we designed the house with that in mind."

"It's amazing. Thanks so much for showing me."

We walk back downstairs and out to the deck. In an instant my Jay-radar is on. He is wearing his barely polite face with a rigid set to his lips as he listens to Tom.

"—up to Susan."

"What's up to me?" I ask Tom.

"Jay was saying that he's unhappy with the long hours you're working. I was telling him that working late is up to you."

I flush in embarrassment.

"Jay, you and I can talk about this later."

"Well, he's your boss, Suze. I just thought he should know he's causing some problems at home."

"Jay. Let's not talk about this now," I whisper as I take his hand.

Jay pulls his hand away. "Whatever."

I can't believe it!

Where does he get off talking to my boss like that?

I have no idea how to save the evening.

And just like that, Jay turns his charm back on. "I'm sorry. That was rude of me. Forget it happened."

Tom relaxes a little. "More wine?"

"No, thanks. I think we should head home. You ready?" he asks me.

"Yeah. I was up early this morning and am a little worn out. Thanks for the wonderful evening. I'm so glad we came."

I want to bite Jay's head off.

"Oh, I forgot to ask you, Susan. Did you call Dr. Amarov?" asks Tom.

"I did. I have an appointment next week. I made it close to the lunch hour. Can we work out the schedule on Monday?"

"Sure," says Karen. "I hope he has some answers for you."

"Thanks for the referral and for the wonderful burgers. See you Monday."

᷇ᴥ᷇

We drive home in silence. I am seething. Jay seems relaxed, as if he's gotten his digs in and is ready to move on.

What is wrong with him? How do I talk to him about this intrusion without starting a fight? I have to let it go or let it happen.

As we pull into the driveway, Jay turns to me and asks, "When were you going to tell me about your doctor appointment?"

I shake my head in confusion. "What?"

"So now you're keeping secrets from me?"

"No! I just hadn't gotten around to telling you about it. I wasn't hiding anything from you!"

"Why did I have to hear it from Tom?"

"Um. Because he was the first to mention it?" I an-

195

swer sarcastically. "Jesus, Jay! What's wrong with you! You have no right to interfere with my job!"

"Yes! I do! When it interferes with my life, I do."

"How would you like it if I went to your boss and said you need to be home earlier?"

Jay laughs. "That will never happen."

Frustrated and furious, I jump out of the car and slam the door shut. He follows close behind. Once inside, he kicks the front door shut and grabs my arm.

"I know what's going on here. He knows more about your life than I do! I can tell by how he looks at you that you two are up to something!"

"Bullshit. Get your hands off of me!" I jerk away from Jay and rub my arm.

"Quit your job! You don't need it! You've got your money stashed away and should use it! You were drooling over their house, and we could have all that and more if you weren't so damned selfish! You're not going back there!"

"I'm not quitting," I say through gritted teeth. "Deal with it!"

I back away and run into the bathroom, locking the door behind me. Hands shaking, I begin to sob as Jay pounds on the bathroom door.

"You better not be fucking him!" he yells.

"I'm not!" I scream in fury.

With one final pound on the door, I hear Jay slam the front door shut and the house is silent.

I sink to the floor in shock.

❧

Sunday morning I wake up alone yet again. Jay is asleep

on the couch and looks bad. As I walk past him to the kitchen, he wakes up and reaches out his hand to me.

"Hi, baby."

"Hi," I say curtly, backing away from him.

"I'm sorry about last night." He stretches and yawns. "Forgive me?"

"Whatever." I do not feel forgiving.

He follows me into the kitchen.

"Really, Suze. I'm sorry. I don't know why I got so mad."

"I hope you figure it out because I don't want to go through that again."

"I will. I promise. Tom's just so…intimidating."

"Intimidating? He's just a nice guy."

"He's got everything we don't."

"What do you mean?"

"Beautiful house, money, you know…"

"Envy doesn't become you, Jay. We've made our choices and here we are. We can have a good life."

"With you in my life, I know we will." He hugs me and kisses my neck. "Let me cook breakfast."

I sigh. "Okay." I kiss him back. Silly me.

ༀ

That evening as we prepare for the Solstice ritual with Star's coven, I am a little less on guard. We had a good day as we did chores together and Jay was his usual funny, conversational self. We discussed Dagan Moore's book as we dusted and vacuumed in the house and tidied up the yard. Jay didn't complain once about helping me outside, and I hoped he was past his refusal to help me.

The Water Master

The longest day of the year passed a few days ago. Dusk lasts till past 10:00 at this time of year. Driving to the ritual through the Yakima Valley, I note the changes since spring. Trees and fields are green and lush where irrigation or the river provide water, but the desert grasses are drying out from lack of rain. Sagebrush paints a smattering of dusky green across the desert and among the basalt cliffs. It is hot, and the evening sun glares through the windshield. Jay has the air conditioning on high and I feel chilled. The heat feels good when I get out of the car and greet coven members sitting at picnic tables outside the hall.

Jay steps out of the car. Everyone stands to greet him, surrounding him with the attention he craves and leaving me in the dust. I walk away from him and his groupies, in search of Star and find her in the kitchen once more.

"Are you doing all the work while everyone else sits around?" I ask as we hug in greeting.

"I love putting all the food together. No problem," says Star.

"Can I do anything?"

Star gives me instructions for setting fresh flowers into vases and placing them on the table.

"Where did you get these flowers? They're beautiful!" I say.

"My house. I love flowers. I'm overgrown!"

"Wow! You really have a green thumb."

"It doesn't take much around here—frequent watering and infrequent weeding."

We chat about our work and the coven for awhile until Star decides it is time to start ritual.

"If we wait until it's completely dark, we'll be here all night," she says.

The Solstice—or Litha—ritual represents the Sun God at his strongest, providing long warm days and the promise of a life-sustaining harvest in the future. After the cleansing of the circle and the warding of the quarters, the coven members enter the circle. The significance of the season plays out with a romantic interaction between the High Priest and Priestess acting as the God and Goddess. Their actions are accompanied by much laughter and joking. By the time the ritual ends, the eastern sky is dark and the western horizon glows pink and orange. An owl hoots from a tree at the edge of the field.

I let the others walk ahead and spend a few moments in the quiet of the night. The temperature is perfect. My skin tingles. I feel so alive and in the moment. The owl hoots again. I lie down on the grass and look into the dark night, picking out the constellations as the stars peek out. In this moment I feel the peace I have been yearning for since I moved to the desert.

Voices rouse me from my meditation and I hear Jay yell, "Suze! You out there?"

"Yeah. Coming!" I respond.

He just can't stand it if I'm not within eyesight.

Candlelight flickers on the walls of the meeting hall. A large banquet table along one wall holds a variety of foods. Everyone helps themselves. I try to sit next to Jay, but Flower beats me to it. On the other side of Jay sits a skinny little man that I don't remember from the last ritual. Another young woman sits next to him, and they are deeply engrossed as Jay shares a story about Dagan Moore. I sit next to Star and Ronny, glad to avoid the same stories about Dagan that I've heard hundreds of times before. At least Jay has a fresh audience.

After dinner, I join the cleanup committee, wrapping food and washing dishes. I laugh at the easygoing banter and join in with the joking and teasing. I am in a great mood when we finish and go in search of Jay. I find him sitting on a bench outside, Flower right next to him, gazing at him in rapt attention. The skinny guy and other girl sit on the ground. As I walk up to them, conversation stops.

"Hi. Jay, are you ready to go?"

"Sure. Just give me a minute."

I sit next to him and he says, "Suze, give me a minute."

He's shutting me out! Really?

I walk back into the meeting hall, gather our things and take them to the car. Star and Ronny stand talking next to his bright red Mustang.

"Susan, I'm glad you and Jay could come. I hope you make it a regular thing," says Ronny.

"I think we will. I loved the ritual tonight. And what a gorgeous evening!"

Star gives me a hug goodnight before getting into her car.

"Give me a call. Let's get together," she says.

"I will."

Star drives off, leaving me and Ronny to say goodnight.

"Star really likes you," says Ronny. "I think she's been lonely for a good friend. I'm really glad you guys moved here."

"Me, too," I say.

Ronny gives me a long hug, just as Jay walks up.

"Hey! What's going on?" he says in an angry tone.

"I was just telling your wife how glad we are that you came," says Ronny as he pulls away from me.

"Yeah. Right," says Jay as he grabs my arm. "That's not what it looked like to me."

"Sorry, Man. No offense intended," says Ronny as he gets into his car.

"Jay! Let go of me! That was so rude!" I say as I jerk away from him.

"What's going on between you two?"

"Nothing! I was thanking him for inviting us and he hugged me goodnight. Star just left!"

"Whatever. Just watch out for that guy."

"Watch out for what? Hugs?"

"Men never just want a hug, Suze. They always have something else in mind."

"Bullshit! Besides, he's gay."

"So?"

"So, you're being ridiculous. There's nothing there but friendship, Jay. Get over it."

By this time we are sitting in the car. Jay is getting ready to back out. He puts his arm around me and roughly pulls me toward him.

"I don't care if he's gay or not. He better keep his hands off you."

I turn cold, and it isn't the air conditioning blowing on me. I can't think.

Finally, he lets go and I can sit up again. I say, "I'll take care of it."

"I already did. We're not going to any more of their stupid rituals. I'm starting my own coven."

"What?"

"Yep," he says proud of himself. "We've already got three members."

"Is that what you were talking about when I walked up?"

"Yep. I'll be High Priest, Flower will be High Priestess. You can be the Maiden and the other guy, Billy, will be Warder. Jenny can be your trainee."

I shake my head. "I wish you would have discussed this with me first."

"I told you I wanted to start my own coven, so I did."

"You're stealing from another coven, though."

"It's not stealing if someone begs you to lead a new coven!" says Jay with a grin.

"They begged you?"

"Yeah. It'll be great. You'll see."

"I should be High Priestess, Jay."

"Flower's been in Wicca longer than you have. She already has her First Degree initiation. You're still a novice."

"And I'm also your wife. I don't think it's a good idea."

"Too bad for you, then," says Jay, dismissing me yet again.

We drive home in silence, my thoughts a jumbled mess.

The Water Master

I like Star's coven. I don't want be forced be into a coven with him and his little groupies. Flower is a flighty, stupid woman. Billy has no backbone. I don't even know that Jenny girl. Both those gals are young, in their twenties — and full-bodied. No, this is not good at all.

❧

I wake up in the middle of the night and replay the hug with Ronny.

Jay is insanely jealous. I'll have to be more careful.

LAMMAS – FRUITION

"I am a thorn: beneath a nail…"

Chapter Nine

≈◆≈

I am on fire from the inside out in the desert heat. The weather prediction indicates the intense heat will continue for weeks. This is summer in the Tri-Cities. Stepping barefoot onto the cement patio burns like hot coals. In Chicago, the heat could suffocate you, as if you were wrapped in a wet blanket while sitting in a sauna. Desert heat burns hot on the skin and the sun is white-hot to the eyes. Fires in Oregon, Ellensburg, and east of Walla Walla dump smoke into the Columbia Basin, where it remains trapped by the high pressure cell hovering over the area. The hills surrounding the Tri-Cities are ghostly shapes in the haze. Any work in the garden has to be done at dawn and dusk.

I feel claustrophobic having to stay inside where it is cool. Keeping the shades drawn leaves the house in perpetual dusk, and I am suffering the winter blues in the middle of summer. Jay's unpredictable mood swings toss me like a boat without oars on a stormy sea. Every time I think I am meeting his needs, he throws me off again with some other requirement that I can't predict.

First he wants me to tell him where I am every minute. Then I have to come home right after work, even though he isn't home yet. If I say something like, "I'm going to the grocery store. I'll be home in an hour or so," and happen to run into a patient and chat at the store, he's furious with me for being late. He accuses me of lying to him. The accusations occur often, and the more I defend myself, the more he claims I protest too much. I am tempted to lie to prevent the fights, but there is really nothing to lie about. How can I change a perfectly innocent response into another perfectly innocent response?

Jay, however, lives by his own set of rules—coming and going as he pleases. I assume he is with Charlie most of the time. When he is home, he is happy and participates in helping around the house, or he is morose and mean. Anything can set him off.

My confusion causes me to feel like I have late-onset Attention Deficit Disorder. I leave my keys in the refrigerator, put the bread in the linen closet, and forget to lock the house when I leave. And each time I space out, it gives Jay more ammunition to point out my deficiencies, leaving me feeling stupid and nervous. Chronic anxiety takes the place of thinking, planning and problem solving. The more Jay demands of me, the more I look like the airhead, uncaring wife he complains about.

Date nights are a joke. Thursday night and Sunday morning are our "dates," but Jay is the only one receiving any pleasure from it…if that's what you call it. He mostly ignores me while he pleases himself and I feel used. He shows no love or affection toward me. He never kisses me anymore. And if I refuse him or tried to avoid a "date," he pouts, accuses me of not caring enough about his needs, and we will have yet another argument. I take the path of least resistance and go through the motions.

The Water Master

My job is the only functional part of my life. After Jay's rude behavior at Tom and Karen's, they treat me no differently than they did before, and they don't ask about Jay or absolve me of my embarrassment. Their mutual respect for each other is a daily reminder that I'm not crazy for wanting what they have. In fact, I had that when I first met Jay. I hope I can get it back again. I never suspected that Jay's kind and thoughtful attention toward me when we were dating would end once we married.

The file audit is more than half done. It is clear that for years, Silvia had been stealing from the practice, the patients, and the insurance companies to the tune of thousands of dollars. The Elwins are upset that they'd put their trust into someone who brought such ruin to them. Karen monitors my billing practices closely, and I can't blame her. They aren't going to make the same mistake twice.

Every time I walk into the office I feel safe. Each night as I walk out the door, I am surprised black storm clouds aren't forming on the western horizon, because I am sure a tornado is approaching.

ॐ∾ॐ

Saturday morning I wake up early, slide out of bed so as not to awaken Jay, pull on shorts and a t-shirt, and head for the coffee. I checked the garden the night before, and some of the cherry tomatoes are ready for harvest, as are the first cuttings of basil, oregano and thyme. I am anxious to start before the heat of the day and am looking forward to a fresh salad for lunch with homemade herbal dressing.

I pour coffee, grab my gloves, shears, and a large bowl

off the counter, and walk out into the early summer morning. The temperature is perfect. A little breeze cleared the air of some of the smoke, but the sun is still hazy. Halfway to the garden, I stop. Something's wrong. I let out a little yelp and run to the garden. Plants are pulled up by the roots and thrown onto the grass. Dirt is scattered everywhere and the irrigation tubing is pulled up and cut into little pieces. I sit down hard in the grass and stare at the mess, too stunned even to cry.

What the hell?

I can't breathe, and feel as if someone has just reached into my heart and pulled it out by the roots, too. I pick myself up and begin collecting the edible tomatoes from the wilted plants, and cut the stems from the roots of the destroyed herbs. I study the damage.

This is purposeful and evil. Gardening for the season is ruined. There will be no big juicy tomatoes, no squash. I might start some new pumpkins, but why bother?

Dejected, I drag myself back to the house, leave my sad harvest on the counter and go out to the garage to adjust the irrigation so it will no longer water the garden. I check the front of the house, relieved to find my flowers still intact.

Jay is up and pouring coffee when I come in the house.

"Mornin'," he grunts.

"Hi."

"You don't sound very cheery. Looks like you got a lot of stuff out of the garden."

"The garden was vandalized last night. This is what I saved."

"What do you mean, it was vandalized?"

"Someone pulled up all my plants. That wouldn't have been you, would it?" I say with ice in my voice.

"No! I would never do that! I know how much it means to you."

"That's what I'm afraid of. You know exactly what it means to me," I say.

"Maybe it was a kid. Did you check with Rosie? How's her garden?"

"It's too early. Maybe I'll go down there later."

I doubt anyone else's garden has been hit, but it is worth a shot. I don't believe Jay, but I'm not going to argue with him about it. I've learned by now that he will lie to me with no compunction. I go back to bed and sleep the rest of the morning.

I'm depressed. The saying that depression is anger turned inward is true. I have no energy for anger. After my shower, I gather up a bouquet of the cut herbs to take down to Rosie. Rosie and Russ are enjoying lunch on their front porch. They wave and pull out a chair for me as I walk up the front steps.

"Want some coffee?" asks Rosie.

"Yes. Thanks. I need something to help me wake up!"

"What's up? You look like you just lost your best friend!" says Russ.

"My garden was vandalized last night. All the plants were pulled up by the roots and the irrigation was cut up into little tiny pieces. I was wondering if you got hit too."

"That's terrible!" says Rosie.

Russ takes my hand. "I'm so sorry!"

"Your garden is fine, isn't it," I say.

"Russ, go take a look," says Rosie.

Russ leaves the table and we sit in silence, sipping our coffee. Russ comes back shaking his head. "Everything's fine."

"It was a personal attack. I know it," I say.

"Who would do such a thing?" asks Rosie.

"I have my suspicions."

Russ shakes his head. "You haven't lived here long enough to make enemies. I'm sure it was a fluke."

"I don't think so." I sigh. "It's not the first time it's happened, you know. First the flood and now this. It's just so stupid!" I slam down my empty coffee cup in frustration.

"Do you think you should call the police?" asks Russ.

I think about it. "Yeah. I do. I know exactly who I'm going to call." I stand up. "Thanks. For everything. I'll let you know if I find out anything."

With more energy than I've had in days, I rush back to the house and into the living room where Jay is eating breakfast in front of the TV.

"Rosie's garden is fine. I'm calling the police."

"No, you're not! That's ridiculous!" says Jay as he slams down his plate and stands up.

"No, it's not. There've been too many odd incidents with the garden. Someone is targeting us."

"You're paranoid. It's just a kid or something. You're not calling the police!"

Breathing hard, adrenaline pulsing, I lean toward my husband and said clearly and with determination, "Watch me."

Jay sits down and picks up his breakfast, looks back at the television and says in a menacing tone, "You'll regret it."

෨෴

I call Dale Freeman. I don't want to talk with anyone else. Of course, it is Saturday and I feel bad interrupting his time off, but I have to tell someone who won't think I'm crazy. With Jay listening, I leave a message for Dale, telling him briefly what happened and asking him to call me. I wait for the third degree from Jay. It never comes.

When Jay finishes breakfast he showers and leaves the house without a word. I wonder if he vandalized the garden. It has to be him or Charlie—or maybe even Silvia.

With Jay out of the house, I push a CD into the player and crank up the volume in hopes that the beat of the music will uplift me. I spend the rest of the day futzing around the house, cleaning, organizing, and trying to think my way out of the fog that engulfs me.

Late in the afternoon, Dale calls me back.

"Hi, Dale. Thanks for calling back. I'm sorry to bother you on a weekend."

"What's up?"

I tell him about the garden and my belief that I am being targeted.

"I sound like a crazy paranoid person," I say. "Maybe it's nothing."

"Given the situation at Dr. Elwin's office and your concerns about Charlie, I don't think you're being paranoid at all. Do you mind if I drive over and take a look?"

"No. Please do."

"Give me twenty minutes or so. I'm not far away."

"Thanks, Dale. I really appreciate it."

My nerves are on edge. I hope Dale can come and go before Jay shows up—if he shows up. Jay's chronic absences are beginning to feel normal. It is just too hard to argue. And I am relieved when he isn't home. At least I can work around the house without his critical reminders to do things his way.

It is too hot to sit on the front porch to wait for Dale, so I watch for him out the front window. He pulls into the driveway a few minutes later, and as he unfolds out of the car, I am struck by his presence. He may be built like a linebacker, but he moves with agility and walks with a quick and easy stride to the front door. Before he can knock, I open the door.

"Hi. Come on in."

"Thanks."

Dale is dressed in cutoffs, a Seattle Seahawks T-shirt and a pair of flip-flops.

"This really is a day off, isn't it?" I ask with a laugh.

"Yeah. I try. My job is 24-7, but I figured you wouldn't mind if I didn't put on a tie today."

"No problem. I'm sorry I had to call, but I'm pretty upset."

"Show me the garden."

As I take him out the back door I can sense Dale taking in the details of the house, storing them away in his memory for later retrieval.

We walk to the back of the yard and Dale surveys the damage.

"It's definitely vandalism." He looks around. "There's a few footprints here."

He points to the ground around the withering roots of my tomato plants. Dale crouches down and brushes debris away from three clear prints. I bend over his shoulder. One print clearly shows a right footprint that sinks into the dirt further on the right side of the foot than the left.

"That's Charlie's print, isn't it?"

"Why do you say that?"

"See how it sinks like the weight is on the outside of the foot? Charlie walks that way."

"Very observant of you!" Dale smiles up at me.

"So, you agree?"

"Well, it's my first thought. What do you want to do about it?"

I like how he is matter-of-fact and leaves the choice to me.

"I don't understand why he doesn't like me. Why would he do this?"

"You said he and Jay spend a lot of time together. Is he jealous of you for some reason?"

"I have no idea. Since we got here, Jay's behavior has changed for the worse and I'd like to blame it on their friendship. But I know enough about human nature to know that Jay wouldn't be acting like a jerk if he didn't have it in him already. Maybe Charlie is jealous. I just don't get it."

"Do you want to file a complaint?"

Dale stands up. I step back, cross my arms and bite my cheek in thought.

"I'm a little afraid to."

"Why?"

I think about what I want to say and just decide to say it.

"Jay told me I would regret calling the police."

Dale gives me a puzzled look.

"Maybe there's more to this than I realized," he says, more to himself than to me.

"What do you mean?"

"I don't know exactly. But I think something's really wrong in your world."

I open my mouth to protest and then close it.

"Dale, you're right. Something is really wrong in my world. I married a wonderful guy who treated me like a queen. A month later we move out here to this shitty little house, and he spends his nights with a low-life like Charlie, who is just supposed to be our landlord, not his best friend!"

I start to cry.

"I'm so embarrassed. Everyone's been so nice to me and my life is a wreck. I've always been able to take care of myself, and here I am complaining about a stupid garden being torn up. What's wrong with me?"

Now I'm sobbing. Dale starts to reach for me and stops.

"Susan. Let me look into some things, okay? I don't think you're crazy, but I do think either Jay or Charlie or both of them are trying to make you feel that way."

"You do?" I sniffle.

"Yes. I do," Dale says with conviction.

I wipe my eyes and take a deep, relieved breath.

"Do you think I should file a complaint?"

"If it's going to make you feel threatened, then let's not do anything formal. I'll write up my own notes and look into a few things. You, however, need to be careful. Something's going on and I want to keep an eye on it."

"What do I tell Jay?"

"At the risk of sounding like a marriage-wrecker, I'm pretty concerned about Jay's behavior. Make a decision that's safe for you, okay?"

"You don't know the half of it. I agree with you completely," I say, almost to myself.

"Looks like you're done gardening for the season."

"Yep."

We walk back to the house, into the welcome chill of the air conditioning.

"Can I get you something to drink?" I ask.

"A quick glass of water and then I have to go," says Dale.

I reach for two glasses from the cabinet, drop ice into them, and fill them with water from the refrigerator. I lean against the counter, grateful for a few quiet moments as we sip from our glasses. I notice Dale looking around the kitchen. His eyes wander along the kitchen floor and stop a few times. He is trying to look casual, but I notice he is very interested in whatever caught his attention.

"What are you looking at?" I ask.

"Hmm? Oh, nothing."

"I see you're a football fan," I say, pointing to his T-shirt.

"You have to be a Seahawks fan around here. Besides, it gives me something to talk about at work. What about you?"

"I could care less about football, but I used to follow the Bears a little."

"I'll tell you a secret." says Dale. "I watch the highlights when the games are over. I have better things to do with my time!"

I laugh. "That's good to hear. I'm sure your family appreciates it."

Dale looks at the floor. "No. No family living with me."

"Really?"

"I've been divorced for years. It's hard to be married to a cop. I decided a long time ago I wasn't going to put a woman through that again. My ex and I are friendly. We have a daughter and she's married and lives over in Portland. She and I are close. She's awesome. Smart, pretty. I'm not happy about the guy she married, but what can I say? They married too young, but they're doing all right. It's just me and my dogs."

"More than one?"

"Two. Big ones. They're great company. They just roll over and go back to sleep when I have to leave in the middle of the night and wag their tails when I get home. No complaints. It's great."

"I miss having a dog. I grew up with one. She was my best friend."

"What about you?" Dale asks. "Is this your first marriage?"

"Yeah," I say, blinking back tears again. "I never thought I'd marry, to tell you the truth. My parents died a couple of years apart when I was in my early twenties. They had an amazing relationship. My dad worked hard and my mom loved taking care of him, but she didn't lose herself. She was a brilliant artist in her own right. My dad was a scientist, an inventor. One of his tinkerings, as he called them, made him a millionaire. And then... poof! Mom dies, he's devastated and he never gets over it. Watching him go through that, I...well, it changed me. I finished college and went to grad school after that. Nose to the grindstone, you might say. I dated a few guys, but nothing clicked. I gave up after awhile. My sister, on the other hand, got married right out of high school and has a bunch of kids. I get my kid fix when I see my nieces and nephews, and that cures me for quite some time!"

"So, if your dad was a millionaire," says Dale as he waves his glass around the kitchen, "why this?"

"It's hard to explain."

"You got your money stashed under a mattress?" asks Dale, looking concerned.

"No. It's invested. I only use what I need. I don't like depending on it, or anyone else for that matter. I like to make my own way. When I was a kid, we didn't have a lot of money. My parents taught us to be frugal and work hard. I can't seem to stop."

Why am I telling him all of this? What is it about him that makes me comfortable enough to share this personal stuff?

Dale sets his glass on the counter.

"Thanks for the water. It's way too hot out there."

"Thanks for stopping by. I really appreciate it and I'm sorry for the meltdown."

"You needed to let it out." Dale smiles. "Hang in there. I think you'll be fine. We'll get to the bottom of this thing. Don't worry, okay?"

"Thanks, Dale."

As I close the door behind him, I hope he's right.

I go to bed alone that night. Jay never comes home.

ॐ∘ॐ

Dale chews his thumbnail as he drives away from Susan's house.

She is in trouble. Something isn't right.

He has a hard time juggling his feelings. From the moment he saw her, something shifted in him. It is hard to remain professional around her.

She is smart…really smart. And she's pretty. Not the way some women try to make themselves pretty. Just naturally pretty.

He noticed that she tugs on her earlobe when she is nervous and she tugged a lot when he was at her house. He smiles.

The way she jumped in and started that embezzlement investigation was brilliant. Quick. Simple. This guy, Jay. Who is he? Something is bugging me about this. I have to make some calls.

Chapter Ten

༄༅

Monday begins with my appointment with Dr. Amarov. I am distracted already and nervous about seeing him, thinking of all the worst possible outcomes—back surgery, paralysis and an early death. But the appointment goes well, and I walk out with a prescription for physical therapy and pain meds for the worst of the pain.

Jay hasn't mentioned preparing for the Lammas ritual. I want nothing to do with it. Lammas is the celebration of the harvest, and I have nothing to show for my work in the garden other than a few drying herbs.

Should I go to Star's ritual? No. I'd rather not have another fight with Jay. It's easier to keep the peace—for now.

It's Friday night, the end of July. I take a glass of wine and wander out to the front porch to sit in the late dusk and wait for Jay to come home. The heat has kept everyone inside for weeks and it looks like days of excessive heat will continue for awhile. Evenings give a brief reprieve, and tonight a slight breeze from the South, though warm, helps me relax.

The phone rings inside the house. I get up to answer it.

"Hey! It's me," says Jay.

"Hi! I thought you'd be home by now," I say.

"No. I'm still at work. It's going to be a late night."

I can tell by the tone of his voice that he is distracted. "What time do you think you'll be home, then?" I ask. "I don't know, I gotta go."

Click.

I hang up the phone.

I don't believe him. Wonder what he's up to. I'm not going to worry about this now. It's been a long week.

I walk back to my chair on the porch, lift the wine to my lips and I stretch out the kinks in my neck. I've been working late almost every night, both to stay away from home and to try to finish up the audit. We still have a few boxes to go, but Dale is satisfied with our progress and is working closely with the DA to build a case against Silvia. He hasn't talked to me any further about the garden incident or my meltdown. He showed up at the office a few times since his visit to my house and only asked a few questions about our progress on the audit. I am disappointed that he wasn't friendlier, but he was on duty, after all.

Something moves off to the side of the porch. My stomach jumps.

Is it a coyote? No, it's too small. It's a dog!

It is snuffling and digging around the bushes along the edge of the house. I put my wineglass down and use caution as I walk toward the dog. It growls softly and then whines.

"Hi, doggie. Nice doggie," I say in a hushed voice. I sit down about six feet away from the dog. It is lying in the dirt and panting hard.

"What's wrong?" I ask. The dog growls again. I watch

it for a few minutes and realize it is a she, and is in labor.

"Oh, crap," I say out loud. "Puppies."

I rise from the ground and go back to the house for a bowl of water for the poor thing. I find a stainless steel mixing bowl, fill it from the tap and walk back to the panting animal.

"Here you go, sweetie," I say as I lower the bowl of water and place it near the dog so she can drink. The dog looks at me with wary eyes. I dip my fingers in the water and hold them out to the dog. She begins to lick my fingers. I dip my hand again, making a bowl of my palm and the dog drinks again and wags her tail. I push the water closer to the dog and she stands up, drinks it dry and lays down with a thump and a groan.

The dog is skinny and obviously worn out.

She is going to give birth soon. I don't know the first thing about taking care of a pregnant dog. I can't leave her out here by herself.

I hurry to the garage and find a box. I dig around in the tool drawer for a box cutter and cut out one side. Carrying the makeshift nest into the kitchen, I line it with old towels and rags.

I rummage through the refrigerator and find some leftover steak. I cut it up into little pieces to bait the dog inside. I also find a lightweight rope to slip around the dog's neck. I figure the dog won't fight me too much, being in labor and in pain.

As I approach the dog, she is lying on her side and thumps her tail a few times. She doesn't object as I slip the rope around her neck. I pat the dog's head while giving her a piece of steak. The dog takes it in her mouth and spits it out.

I tug gently on the rope and the dog resists.

"Come on. Good doggie!"

The dog groans and sits up. It is dark now and it's difficult to see the animal under the bush. She won't budge. I decide to carry her into the house. She is a mutt, maybe twenty-five pounds. I reach under the bush, wrap my arms around the dog and scoot her out to the grass.

I have to be careful lifting her. I don't want to hurt myself in the process.

She doesn't protest, but her eyes look frightened.

I engage my core muscles and using my leg to lift her weight, I carry her into the house and place her in the box, petting her as I say, "Oh, I'm sorry doggie. You'll be fine."

In the light, the dog looks disheveled and dirty. I can't even tell what color she is. She is malnourished and missing patches of fur. Her neck is worn raw, like she's been tied up for a long time.

I bring more water and put it next to her head and then call Rosie.

"Hello?"

"Hi, Rosie. I have a pet emergency."

"What's up?"

I tell her about the dog.

"I have no idea what to do. Do you?"

"It sounds like you can't do much of anything until she gives birth."

"I've never done this before."

"Neither have I. But I bet you can look it up on the Internet!"

"I thought you knew everything about dogs!" I say. "But Internet it is."

"Let me know how it goes. And when you're ready, we'll call the dog rescue group to help you out."

"Thanks. I think."

It's late and I'm tired. The dog is in heavy labor. I bring a pillow and blanket to the kitchen and lay down next to the box to rest. I assume Jay won't be coming home tonight, which is fine with me.

I awaken to a squeak. The dog is licking the first puppy clean and another one is emerging from the birth canal. I sit up and rub down the first pup with a clean towel and place it near momma's teat. The dog licks the second puppy as it squirms and squeaks. The process repeats two more times and the stray falls into a deep sleep while the puppies feed and sleep and squirm. I am pleased. I feel like a new mother myself. I leave the new family and fall into bed.

అఇఅ

I wake up with the sun streaming through my bedroom window. I can't wait to see how the puppies are doing. When I enter the kitchen the new mother wags her tail, but growls as I reach for her. I sit down next to the bed until the dog relaxes, licks water from my fingers again, and then finally allows me to pet her.

I open the sliding door and encourage her to go outside by lifting her up and putting her down by the door.

"Go outside," I say as I push her from the rear. The dog hesitates, looks back at her puppies and steps outside, relieves herself, and rushes back in to settle down next to her pups. I cut up some more steak and open a can of tuna. The dog eats it all up in one gulp.

"I gotta get you some food!" I say.

After a search on the Internet, I decide what to buy for momma doggie and leave for the store.

"What am I getting myself into?" I say out loud as I back out of the driveway. I feel happy and excited for the first time in months.

I want to keep the dog and maybe a puppy, but I'll have to make sure no one else claims her. Maybe no one will, given the poor state of the dog, she was probably dumped. What am I thinking? I can't keep dogs right now. Not with all the uncertainty in my life!

I finish my shopping and drive home. My stomach sinks when I see Jay's car in the driveway. I hurry into the house to find Jay sitting at the counter with a cup of coffee. He frowns at me.

"What's going on with the dogs?"

"It's a stray. She was getting ready to give birth under the bush in the front yard. I couldn't leave her there."

"Do whatever you have to do to get rid of her, or I will," says Jay in a threatening tone.

I ignore him as I fill a bowl with dog food. The dog won't get out of her box. She eyes Jay.

Jay leaves the kitchen. I hear the shower. The stray walks to the bowl and eats with gusto. She finishes quickly and trots to the door. I let her out.

It's amazing how fast she's learning how to trust me and knows what to do.

I leave the door open for her and put the rest of the groceries away. The dog walks back in and curls up with the puppies, looking relaxed and satisfied.

When Jay comes back to the kitchen, the dog growls. I glance at her and notice the wary look again. Jay laughs.

"Stupid dog. Don't bite the hand that feeds you!"

"I fed her and she didn't bite me!" I say. The anger in my voice surprises me.

Jay walks over to the dog and she growls again, showing her teeth.

"Jay, stay away from her. She's really nervous."

Jay backs up a little.

"What's her problem?"

"She's obviously been mistreated. Sometimes dogs distrust the gender of the person who owned her. Maybe she doesn't like men."

"Typical woman, huh," says Jay, sarcasm dripping from his lips.

I'm not in the mood to argue, so I ignore him.

"What are your plans today?" I ask.

"We need to practice for next week's ritual soon," he says.

That is the last thing I want to do.

"Okay," I say without enthusiasm.

"What's your problem?" asks Jay.

"Let's see. You're never home and I don't know where you are. You make threats and you want me to participate in a spiritual ceremony with you and your new High Priestess," I respond.

Jay glares at me. "Are you saying you're not going to do it?"

I sigh. "I'll do it. But I'm not happy about it."

"I don't care."

"I know you don't. And that's oh-so-spiritual of you."

"Whatever."

Jay leaves the house yet again, leaving me alone with my new family of dogs. I look down at the satisfied mother and smile.

"I don't think I care anymore either, little puppies."

৵৽

I don't believe it. This woman won't stop. Dogs and puppies? What the fuck? Maybe the stuff I put on the pizza will work better on dogs. Yeah. That's the ticket.

৵৽

I spend the rest of the weekend caring for the puppies. I call the Humane Society and the dog rescue organizations to see if the dog has been reported as lost. It is no surprise to learn that no one is looking for her, but I leave information about her, just in case.

Sunday night after another dinner by myself, I tackle the doggie bath. She submits to it with reluctance. As I wash off the dirt, I can finally see her markings clearly. She is reddish brown with flecks of white and gray. Her face looks like a Corgi, but her legs are long and her tail curls up at the end. A true mutt if I ever saw one. I clean her neck wounds as best I can. She is in pain, but doesn't resist. I rinse her off and take a towel to her before allowing her down on the floor, where she shakes water everywhere and does a crazy dog run into the living room to rub along the carpet. She returns to the box and licks her paws.

"I need to give you a name," I say. This dog brings out my own mothering instincts and I am grateful for the distraction from the grim reality of my marriage, just like some of my clients who have children in hopes the marriage can be saved.

"I'm going to call you Brighid," I say out loud. "She's the Goddess of healing and wisdom."

The puppies tangle themselves up as they nurse and Brighid does not notice that she has taken the form of a goddess. To continue the theme, I name the three females Diana, Venus and Artemis, and the one male I name Zeus.

కింక

My new dog family distracts me from my very real problems. No one claims my pup, so she's my dog, puppies and all! I read everything I can find on the Internet about raising puppies. I take the new family to the local vet, where everyone is de-wormed and the vet schedules all the puppy shots. He gives me high fives on how well Brighid is doing, despite being malnourished and mistreated. He tends her neck wounds and gives me a large bottle of antibiotics, which I am to give her four times a day. When Brighid isn't with her pups, she lays her head on my leg or whatever other part of my body she can touch. She worships me and it feels good!

Jay never pulls off the ritual practice. We aren't home at the same time, or he comes home so late I am already asleep. I have the maiden's part memorized and am not worried about it, but dread having Jay's new friends to the house for ritual. He leaves a note for me on Friday morning that says we will gather at 7:00 pm and I am to have the house clean and ready for company.

"Give me a break," I say out loud. "The house is always clean. Bastard!"

I have no idea what food to prepare, so I make a list of salad makings to buy on my way home from work. I hope the others will bring pot-luck food. I wish I didn't care how the evening will play out. It's Jay's problem that he failed to tell me the plan, but I know he will make it my problem if things don't go well, despite my well-meaning efforts.

After work, I run by the grocery store, arriving home at the same time Jay pulls up.

"You ready for tonight?" he asks as he gets out of the car.

"I guess."

"You don't sound like it!"

"Yeah, well. I have no information to go on and we never practiced. I'm not sure what you're expecting tonight—"

"I expect you to be the perfect maiden that you are," he says, in a sticky, sweet voice.

His attitude throws me. I expect him to be demanding, but instead he helps me with the groceries, makes salads and prepares the robes for ritual. By the time the guests arrive, I am less on edge. Brighid and her puppies are in the bedroom, alleviating my worry of how she will react around strangers.

Flower arrives and re-introduces the new coven members, Steve, Jerry, and Jenny. Steve is the mousy little man. He is quiet and follows Flower with his eyes at all times. Jerry is somewhat aloof but it's clear he's enamored with Jay because he hangs on his every word. And Jenny is a pale young woman with a lost look in her eyes.

Jay sits us down in the living room with some appetizers that Steve brought and reviews the meaning of the ritual with us. Once again, I fall under Jay's spell as he weaves history and mythology together to form a picture in my mind of the true meaning of our celebration. His lesson makes me more conscious of the significance of the harvest in the larger world. I just take it for granted that food will always be available. I was able to stop by the store to buy fresh vegetables from local farmers and the trip took only ten minutes. I didn't have to grow and harvest what I'm eating tonight. My ruined garden is a miniscule blip compared to the devastation that could occur if regional or worldwide crops fail. At this moment I feel grateful to my husband for reminding me that I am part of a larger world. I've had no warm feelings toward him for some time but now I look forward to sharing time alone later in the evening.

We head out to the back yard for ritual. Jay set up a small altar but chose not to surround the circle with candles, still not sure that the neighbors would take kindly to pagan practices. The night is very dark, no moon. The air smells of smoke from distant fires.

I cleanse the circle and Steve wards the four directions. He stumbles through his lines and I see a look of disgust cross Jay's face. I am glad I haven't screwed up my part, though it feels hollow to me, knowing Flower is the

High Priestess. I do a mental shake of my head to return to the right frame of mind to participate in ritual in perfect love and perfect trust. I'm not feeling it.

It's obvious that Flower and Jay have practiced together. Her lines are perfect and they are the only two people involved in the ritual skit. Jerry and Jenny don't need to do anything, and they watch Jay, hanging on every movement, every word.

At the end of the ritual, we share ritual kisses with each other, and I don't miss the lingering kiss between Flower and Jay.

Jay has not been spending his nights with Charlie.

As the ritual ends, I realize that I think I knew of his affair with Flower all along. That's why I'm so calm. It's not a surprise.

I smile my way through the meal and send everyone home with polite mumblings about *"Come again"* and *"See you at Mabon."*

Jay and I are silent as we clean up. My earlier loving feelings toward him are replaced by sad resignation.

I thought I had married a strong, self-possessed man, but now I know I was wrong. When things are normal it fosters hope that Jay will be more loving and appreciative. But just like Pavlov's dogs, the intermittent caring and attentive behavior—helping out, compliments, spooning me at night—just keep me drooling for more. I'm in a trap! I dismiss his anger and insane behaviors every time he shows love or kindness toward me.

I know from my counseling experience that an abused woman believes her man will never hit, choke, beat, or kill her. I'm in that same cycle of denial. My own husband has threatened to hit me. So he will hit me someday. He cares nothing for me. He's having an affair. The bright and happy future with Jay is out of the question. But I can't reject him outright. It feels too dangerous right now. Leaving the marriage requires careful planning. I need some time. I'll use Jay's current distraction with Flower to my own advantage.

After we finished cleaning up the kitchen, Jay turns to me and says, "I'm going out for a beer with Charlie."

He's lying, of course.

He gives me a peck on the cheek.

"Have a good time."

❧◦❧

MABON - REFLECTION

"I am a tear: the sun lets fall..."

❧◦❧

Chapter Eleven

ॐ⊸ॐ

Taking on my new dog family is probably something I don't need right now. I am most likely facing a divorce. I have to go to physical therapy on a regular basis. And, the audit is still a high priority at work. But Brighid is a great watchdog. When not tending to her puppies, she keeps an eye out for cats, blowing leaves, and squirrels. Her mellow bark lets me know she is on top of things. It comforts me to have her with me.

I have decided that when the time is right, I will buy the house and land outright from Charlie. It isn't the best house, but I want to stay in the area. I have good friends and a job. I need a little stability. Maybe it is time to use some of my money for me.

I am beginning to dream about starting a small dog kennel or dog rescue. The property is perfect for it. While that is probably far in the future, I can fix up the house, and if I find a better place to live later, I'll sell it. We have a rent-to-own contract with Charlie, so I don't see any roadblocks to my plan, other than Jay. I'm not sure how or when to proceed.

The late August days are too hot to keep the dogs outside all day, so I come home at lunch to let them out and eat a quick bite before returning to work. Today I plan to buy an outdoor kennel and a doggie door for the back slider, and I'm not asking Jay for help. Although he is home most nights, he often smells of beer and cigarettes and isn't speaking to me. It's obvious that he has checked out.

Rosie offers her husband for the shopping trip to buy the kennel. Russ agrees to help me set it up. Although the yard is fenced in, there are too many holes for puppies to escape through, and hawks and coyotes are always looking for a good meal. I need a sturdy enclosure.

Russ knocks on the front door, setting Brighid to frantic barking. I stand over the dog until she sits and quits barking. Then I open the door for Russ.

"Good morning!"

"Hi, Russ. Thanks for helping me out."

"No problem. I've put together a few kennels in my life."

Brighid wags her tail and dances when Russ bends to pet her.

"She likes you. She's not that friendly with everyone."

"I'm a dog guy. They know a friend when they see one. Let's go!"

An hour later we're back at the house with a box of kennel parts in the back of his truck, an igloo dog house and a dog door that fits onto the sliding door while keeping the house secure. It takes about a minute for Brighid to understand how to leave and enter the house. By the time the kennel is done, all the puppies are following her.

Russ covers the top of the kennel with a tarp to keep the sun and the hawks out. I prepared the dog house with old towels. The dogs have a new home. Brighid, panting with excitement, checks out her new digs and the puppies mill around, yipping and jumping.

"Are you going to want one of these puppies when they're weaned?" I ask.

Russ laughs. "I'm so glad you asked. Rosie's been bugging me to ask you, but I wasn't sure what your plans were. The answer is yes!"

"We'll sort it out later," I say. "And please take two if you want. Thanks for all your help. Jay should have been the one helping me with this. He, ah, he hasn't been home much."

"I'm glad to help. But what's up with Jay? Is he all right?"

I blow my hair away from my forehead and wipe my chin with my forearm.

"Well, without going into a lot of detail, I'm probably going to be filing for divorce."

Russ looks surprised. "It's kind of early in your marriage for that kind of problem, isn't it?"

"Yeah, but when you know it's wrong, then it's just wrong and I have to move on."

"Well, I'm glad to help. Let me know if you need anything," says Russ as he squeezes my shoulder.

Jay shows up later in the afternoon, energetic and friendly. I steel myself against his charm, but it is like Christmas to see the Jay I knew when we first met.

"Looks like you got the dogs settled. Who helped you with the kennel?"

"Russ."

"That was nice of him. Sorry I couldn't be here."

I expect a fight.

"Want to go to a movie?" Jay asks.

An image pops into my head of a comic strip. My character has a bubble over her head filled with exclamation points and question marks.

"Uh. Sure," I reply.

"Great! Then let's have dinner somewhere."

I situate the dogs and follow him out the door, off balance and uncertain again.

The movie is a new Sci-Fi that doesn't interest me, but Jay wants to see it.

Why is he being so nice all of a sudden?

Dinner is the same. He is chatty and friendly and his interest in my plans for the dogs appears to be genuine. The small talk comes easy.

As we sip coffee over dessert, I can't stand it anymore. "Jay, what's going on? Why the sudden change?"

Jay sighs and shifts in his seat. "I've been thinking— about us."

I'm silent.

"I...don't think I've been treating you very well."

"That's an understatement," I say.

"Suze, give me a minute here. I want to explain."

I sit back and cross my arms.

"I'm listening."

"I've been confused. Getting married was such a change in lifestyle for me. I wasn't used to being home every night and sharing and having to consider someone else all the time. Charlie...well, Charlie didn't like you from the start, and—"

"What does Charlie have to do with it?"

"I don't know. He and I hit it off right away. We can just talk, you know?"

"No. I don't know. He's a pig. He's hateful. I'm really hurt that you let him get in the way of us."

"I know. I'm sorry. He's just a guy. Guys talk."

"So do girls, just so you know. Which takes me to the next and more important question."

"Flower, right?" asks Jay.

"Yeah. Flower." I spit out her name.

Jay shifts forward in his chair and looks right at me. "I can promise you, I've never had sex with her."

"Define sex, please." My voice is hard.

"I've never done anything but kiss her."

"And that's not enough? Jesus, Jay! Do you have any idea what you've done to us?"

"I know, Suze, and I'm so, so sorry. Is there any way you can forgive me?"

"What about your anger, Jay? What do you intend to do about that?"

He looks at me in surprise.

"What do you mean?"

"You've threatened me, pushed me. It's unacceptable."

He looks defensive for a brief moment and then softens.

"I'll try harder to stay calm," he says.

"So what now?" I ask.

"So, I'm asking if we can try again. I know you're on your way out. I wouldn't be surprised if you've contacted a lawyer. Are you willing to forgive me and let me try to make it up to you?"

"I don't know if I can trust you, Jay. There's too much I don't trust right now. You're gone all the time—"

"I've been gambling. I'll quit."

"Great. One more thing for me to worry about? Gambling, infidelity and anger. What's in it for me, Jay? Really! And what made you decide you wanted to try again?"

"It was Lammas. You were so indifferent. You didn't argue with me, you were a little automaton. I realized how much you had shut me out, and I missed you."

I am seething and blinking back tears. I grab my purse and stalk out. Jay scrambles to pay the check and follows me out to the car where I lean against the door, chest heaving in great sobs.

Jay wraps his arms around me.

"I'm so sorry, babe. So, so sorry. I can make it up to you."

"I don't know if you can, Jay. You've hurt me and I don't trust you."

"Will you at least try?"

I sniffle, feeling good in the warmth of his arms. I turn my head so I can breathe and look out over the valley in the setting sun.

I want to stay. Can I make it work? Wait. Will he make it work? I'll find out, one way or another.

"Okay, Jay," I sigh. "I'll give it one more try, but it's all up to you now. Got it?"

Jay sets his chin on top of my head and says, "Got it. Thank you."

The Water Master

∾

I had to do something, she was slipping away. When Charlie and I talked it over, he said that Silvia thought it best to admit to everything and ask for forgiveness. I had to soften her up. I need that money bad.

∾

Jay makes amends by allowing me set the tone and pace of our relationship. I can't bring myself to make love to him. I am still too angry. He backs off and just sits with me, holding my hand as we watch TV or rubbing my back. I want to spend time with Star's coven and he agrees to continue with me and drop his coven for now. He still wants to be my Wiccan teacher, but I refuse. I like studying at my own pace and want more information from other people like Star. He bristles a little but lets it go.

Brighid still doesn't allow Jay near her, but Jay has softened toward the dogs and he and Zeus are buddies, so we decide to keep the pup and Brighid. Tom and Karen take Venus, while Diana and Artemis go with Russ and Rosie. I envision doggie family reunions in the future when our friends come to visit.

Rosie and I spend time together training the puppies, and soon all the dogs are trotting next to us as we walk the neighborhood each evening. Walker, Rosie's old dog, plods along beside us, giving sideways looks to the puppies as they nip at his legs.

The days shorten as the sun moves toward Fall Equinox. The grass on the surrounding hills dries to brown in the late summer heat. Now and then I notice white smoke rising in the still air behind a hill or out in the desert, but the fires never come close to town. The air remains hazy, and I wake every morning with itchy eyes and a scratchy throat.

At last, I can concentrate on work. We are nearing the end of the file boxes and have pages of documentation to refine for Dale. He stops by the office one evening to check on our progress.

"Hi, Susan. How's it going?" he asks as he walks through the door.

"Hi. It's going!"

He leans on the counter and I am struck once again by his calm presence and genuine kindness.

He looks around to make sure no one is listening and whispers, "Any more issues with the garden?"

"No. Actually things are going well. Jay had some sort of epiphany and is...um, behaving as a proper husband should."

I don't miss Dale's brief look of surprise and then disappointment, despite his effort to remain professional. "Good. I'm glad to hear that. No more issues, then?"

"Nope. Maybe next year I can try the garden thing again."

"Maybe," says Dale. "Can you gather the gang so we can talk?"

"Sure."

Tom, Karen and Marisa are finishing their day and the last patient is out the door. We gather in the lunch room.

"Are you guys about done with the research?" he asks.

Tom dips his head toward the last few file boxes sitting on the floor. "Once those are done, we'll be able to give you a final result."

"Good. With the info you've given me so far, we'll put together a case to present to the DA. We hope to make an arrest before too long. Any more odd behavior from Charlie?" Dale asks me.

"Not to my knowledge. Jay rarely sees him now."

"Good. Get me the final spreadsheets as soon as possible and we'll move forward."

Dale is very businesslike but I feel like a light switches off when he leaves.

৯৯৯

Dale walks to his car, gets in and sits down to think about what he knows so far.

Jay's playing Susan. I don't know why. Charlie's never kept a friend for long. His relationship with Jay is odd, to say the least. What's the connection? It's time for a trip to Chicago. My old buddy is a private detective there. He can help me out. Hell, I'll pay for it myself if I can just see Susan smile.

৯৯৯

Star invited Jay and me to her full moon ritual, which was much less formal and held in her back yard with whomever felt like coming.

Flower will be there, and I don't want Jay to see her. I don't really want to see her either.

This is our first visit to Star's house. Following the directions, we turn into a subdivision with smallish homes and pull into the driveway of a little ranch-style house painted a deep maroon with a white door and shutters. Petunias and stephanotis grow out of hanging pots along the front of the house. Roses bloom in the side yard and pots of herbs sit strategically among the stones that landscape the front yard. It is beautiful–and very much like what I wish I could have. I feel sad again about my troubled garden.

As if Jay is reading my mind, he says, "Next spring at our house will be different. I'll get it looking real good for you, honey."

I enjoy the smell of blooming lavender as we walk up the front steps. I ring the doorbell and Star answers the door almost before the bell stops ringing.

"Hi! Come on in!"

The living room is a step down to the left and blooms with colorful pillows. A couple of beanbag chairs slouch in a corner and a blue corduroy couch reclines along the wall next to the fireplace. A cat, sleeping along the top of the couch, jumps down to greet us.

"This is Sweetums. Hi Sweetie-Sweetums. How's my favorite kitty?" says Star, in the voice reserved for babies and favored pets.

I reach down to pet Sweetums and the cat arches her back along my legs. Sweetums is a hybrid cat of many colors—gray, orange, and white on her body, with a pure white head and a big black spot on her forehead.

"Having a pet to greet you when you come home. Nothing quite like it," I said.

"She's my rescue kitty. I found her at the store. I should have named her 'Catnip' or something more apropos, but 'Sweetums' came out of my mouth. She was starving, skinny, and ragged, and now look at her. She's fat and sassy."

The Water Master

I give the cat a scratch on the head and follow Star into the kitchen as Jay visits with the arriving guests.

When Flower arrives, I can hear a change in Jay's voice as his conversation becomes more forced. Flower stays away from him. She looks morose and avoids looking at me. However, after the ritual, I find myself nose to nose with her as we pass through the back door at the same time.

"Can I talk to you?" asks Flower.

"What about?"

"I think you know."

"I have nothing to say to you."

"I just want you to know I'm not giving up," says Flower with honey in her voice.

"What?"

"I love him. He doesn't love you. He's lying to you. Are you an idiot or what?"

I stand paralyzed.

"And if he told you we didn't sleep together, he's lying."

Flower walks away. I still can't move. Star notices the interaction and steps over to me. Jay is talking to the guys and doesn't notice.

My hands shake as Star reaches for me.

"What was that about?" she asks.

"Nothing. Nothing."

"Bullshit, nothing!"

"I can't talk about it now, Star. Later, okay?"

"Okay. But promise me…"

"Yeah. All right." I swallow, but my throat is dry. I reach for a bottle of wine, pour a big glass and gulp it down. Jay's groupies are still distracting him. I want to leave, but the food is sitting on the table, hot and ready to eat. I don't want to make a scene.

Somehow, I endure the rest of the evening. As we drive home, Jay natters on about his gushing groupies and doesn't notice my mood until we arrive home, when I slam the car door shut and run into the house. He finds me sobbing on the couch.

"What the hell, Hon? What's wrong?"

"That bitch Flower! That's what's wrong!"

I tell him what happened. He holds me and says all the right things, including telling me that Flower is jealous of me and he has no intention of continuing the relationship, blah, blah, blah. Some time passes before I calm down. When we go to bed, he wraps his arms around me until I fall asleep.

The emotional hangover the next morning is painful. I ache from head to toe, and my mouth feels like I've sucked cotton all night. The whining dogs goad me out of bed. Jay has already left for work. I feed the dogs, take a shower, eat a little breakfast and drag myself to the office.

※

Labor Day weekend arrives with high winds that keep everyone indoors. Tumbleweeds hop across the yard. Dust blows down the road in brown waves. Whistling winds vibrate the house and rattle the windows. Through the dirty haze I can barely see Rosie's house crouched against the wind. Brighid whines and paces while Zeus watches. His forehead wrinkles in worry. Walking outside leaves grit between my teeth and dust in my hair. The wind blows for days. Toward the end of the week, sudden silence wakes me in the middle of the night. The windstorm ceased and in the morning I lift the shades. The sun is shining bright in a clear blue sky. Brighid and Zeus prance at my feet while I prepare their food. I look out to the back yard to piles of tumbleweed crowding against the fence.

"Crap! More cleanup," I say aloud to myself.

That night, Jay pulls into the driveway with a contraption hooked to the back of his car.

"What's that?" I ask as he comes in the door.

"I borrowed it from Charlie. It's a burn trailer. We can burn all those tumbleweeds in the backyard without worrying about starting a fire."

Surprised that he is thinking ahead—surprised he is helping at all—I say, "Fire scares me, honey. I'd rather not burn them."

"No problem. Charlie is on his way over, and he and I will do it."

Yuck. Charlie. "Okay. Thanks."

After our quick dinner of salad and grilled chicken, Charlie shows up at the door. Brighid and Zeus both bark, bristle and back away from him. He ignores them.

The men pull the trailer around to the back and begin burning the tumbleweeds. The smoke rises like an earthly spirit in the cooling night air. There isn't a breath of wind. I keep the dogs in and they sit by the back door, alert and whining off and on.

As I carry out the trash, I overhear the men talking. I stop to listen.

"—money to be made, boy!"

"I know. I just need to get things calmed down around here first."

"Well, don' wait too long, boy."

"I know what I'm doing. Let it rest, will ya?"

"Pussywhipped, that's what ye are."

Jay laughs. "Not on your life. No way."

"Yeeeah. We'll jus' see about that, boy."

What the hell is that about? What money is he talking about? Is Jay setting me up?

I go back inside. By the time Jay and Charlie are done with their fiery task, it is dark. I'm in bed, reading a novel with the dogs cuddling close to me. Jay saunters in, smelling of smoke.

"Well, that job is done."

"I'm glad nothing burned but the tumbleweeds!"

"I've done that job enough to know how to manage it," says Jay.

Puzzled, I ask, "What do you mean? You've never burned tumbleweed before, unless there's some in Wisconsin!"

"Oh, I meant that Charlie's done it a lot."

"Ooookay," I say, certain he's not telling me the truth. "So, I overheard you guys saying something about making money?"

Jay busies himself stripping for his shower.

"Hmm? Oh, Charlie just wants me to gamble with him. He hates going by himself. I told him no."

That is not at all what I heard. I need some time to figure our what they're up to.

250

The Water Master

By the time Jay is out of the shower, I pretend to be asleep and he has to shove growling dogs out of the way to join me.

❧

Fall Equinox foretells the cold days of winter. I meet the shorter hours of daylight with dread. The dogs help. They greet me joyously every morning with licks on the face and doggie smiles. I try to relax under Jay's attention and good mood, which remains consistent.

The changing colors of the desert are subtle compared to the wild reds and deep golds of the Midwest fall. Instead, the sagebrush, grasses, and trees become paler versions of themselves—soft browns, golds and tans blend together in a mosaic against the neutral pallette in the hills. The only spot of color in the latté landscape is the deep green of winter sage. My friends promise me that winter snow is rare but the days will be gray and chilly. It has to be better than the deep snow and bone-chilling winds off Lake Michigan.

I have been planning the Mabon ritual with Star. I enjoy her friendship and guidance as I read books by and about Hindus, Buddhists and Christian mystics. Inspired, I've written a poem and Star suggests I read it at ritual. I feel honored to be more than an observer this time, and decide to surprise Jay.

Today, our drive through the Yakima valley is peaceful. Jay and I chat about the differences between the Midwest and the desert Northwest, both admitting the area is growing on us. We drive by Silvia's house without noticing or mentioning her. Content, I allow myself hope for our future.

Once we arrive, the groupies surround Jay like piranha on bait. I leave him discussing the mythologies surrounding the Equinox and search for Star, finding her in her usual place in the kitchen.

"Wow! Something smells wonderful!"

"I didn't have time to bake my rosemary bread, so I brought it here to finish," says Star.

We hug and I set out the plates and silverware. We chat for a few minutes as the group gathers in the large room, waiting for ritual to begin.

I'm nervous. But I've participated in enough of Star's rituals to know that no one will judge me.

We walk out to the field. Star and Ronny perform final preparations to the altar, step out of the circle and the ritual begins.

The slow beating of a drum sets the solemn mood of the ritual as each person enters the circle. It reminds us that before modern times, the oncoming winter could mean death without the harvest to sustain the population through the dark days of winter.

The warder casts the protections in each direction, the High Priest and Priestess purify the water, and the ritual skit begins. It portrays the story of the Sun God leaving the Goddess for hidden lands. The Goddess is bereft, but the growing child in her womb gives promise of new life in the spring. I take a deep breath to try to calm my nerves as it is time to read my poem.

The Water Master

I let go of Jay's hand, step into the middle of the circle, and walk around once, clockwise, building energy.

In a shaky voice I say:

The Sun God grieves his loss of strength
As the dark of night extends its length
The Goddess Moon sheds her light
On the darkness of her night.

He watches as her beauty grows
The hope of spring within her glows
His seed is planted, yet he must wait
The future within her is his fate.

Balance of the light and dark
Goddess and God does life embark
Locked in love, the ebb and flow
Of power, passion, stag and doe.

He flexes muscle, slowly waning
Goddess smiles, belly gaining
He lays to sleep in grasses dry
She waits while life quickens by.

Back and forth the life blood flows
God and Goddess in the throes
Of stronger, weaker, in the duel
Each ensured of their time of rule.

All is equal at this time
They repose as one sublime
Not caring that as darkness grows
And winter comes, the cold wind blows

The Water Master

The Sun God's embers will slowly cool
He'll rest in silence, a peaceful jewel
Moon Goddess rises as life within
Springs forth, months hence, to begin again.

I walk back to Jay and reach for his hand again. He pulls away from me. In the light of the candles I can see his jaw working.

He's pissed! But why?

I feel kicked in the stomach.

Ceremonial kissing ends the ritual. I notice that Jay kisses Flower like he would kiss his grandmother. But he then kisses me the same way. We go inside for the feast.

Even the glorious smell of baked rosemary bread does not relieve my anxiety. Everyone sings my praises for my part in the ritual...except for Jay. I sit, numb and squeeze back my tears.

Star bumps my elbow. "Hey, what's wrong?"

I whisper, "I think Jay's mad at me for reading my poem."

Star looks at me with concern. "Really? I thought he would be proud of you."

"I don't know what's wrong. I feel horrible."

"Don't let him get to you. Even though he's been working harder on your marriage, you and I both know he has a fragile ego."

I look over at Jay holding court with his usual groupies, Flower among them. He doesn't look fragile right now.

"Maybe." I sigh. It is going to be a long drive home.

❦

The Water Master

Tension emanates from Jay as we walk to the car. We begin a silent drive home. I try to make light conversation.

"Wasn't that rosemary bread good?" I ask.

"Uh-huh."

More silence.

I can't stand it anymore. "Jay, what's up with you?"

"You're an idiot if you don't know."

"Jay, don't play games with me. What's the problem?"

"You have completely left the reservation, Susan! What right do you have to participate in a ritual like that?" he yells.

"What do you mean?"

"You refuse to take part in my coven, but you waltz right in like you own the place as long as you're with your little friend Star. She is not the be-all and end-all of High Priestesses, you know!"

"You're overreacting," I say, trying to steady my voice. "I thought you'd be proud of me. That poem meant a lot to me. Can't you just be happy that I did something meaningful for me?"

"Right. You're a piece of work, you know that? You're selfish and stupid. I don't want any part of you right now, so just shut up!" he screams.

I shrink back from Jay as far as I can and stare out the window. His jealousy and cruelty are irrational.

All of his positive efforts to make things better—what are they? Fake? Who is the real Jay?

I know the answer. I just don't want to accept it.

SAMHAIN - RELEASE

*"And ye shall be free from slavery…
and ye shall dance, sing, feast…"*

Chapter Twelve

❧❦

Jay gets up early. He usually sleeps in on Sundays.

"How come you're getting up?" I ask.

"Can't sleep," he responds like a door slamming shut.

I sigh. "Are you still mad?"

"You don't get it and you never will," Jay says.

"Nope, I guess I won't. And I don't want to, either. You're the one that's selfish."

"Whatever."

Jay dresses and leaves the room. A short time later, I hear the front door open and slam shut. We are on another downward spiral. This time I'm not going to stop it. I am done trying.

I roll over and the dogs snuggle on either side of me, cocooning me in the blankets. I sleep in the warm embrace of my dogs until almost mid-morning. With coffee in hand, I grab the newspaper off the front porch. The dogs stand at their food bowls until I fill them. While they crunch their nuggets, I peruse the paper. My cell phone rings. Star's name pops up on caller ID.

"Hi, how are you this morning?" I ask.

"Good. Just checking on you. Can you talk?"

"Yep. Jay left early this morning."

"Where does he go this early?"

"I can only guess," I say. "I'm sure it's somewhere

with his old buddy, Charlie."

"Are you all right?"

"Oddly, yes. He's been playing me. I have no idea why, but it's pretty obvious he's not the kind and loving husband he wants me to think he is. He's selfish and a narcissist, and I really don't care right now."

"I just wanted to make sure you were safe. He looked a little scary last night."

"He's distant and cold. That's about it."

"Okay. Take care, will you?"

"I will. Thanks for calling."

A little later, Rosie knocks on the door for our Sunday morning walk. Walker and the two pups run into the house to see Brighid and Zeus. Chaos reigns until we let all the dogs out into the back yard. We pour coffee and sit on the back patio in the cool fall morning.

"Where's Jay this morning?"

I sigh. "We had a fight. Well, really he had a fight. I don't think I did anything wrong, but he left this morning. I don't know where he is or when he'll be back. I feel like the freakin' drama queen with all these ups and downs with him."

Rosie remains quiet for a moment.

"I don't want to take sides or make you uncomfortable, but I don't think it's you, Susan. I think it's him. Ever since he drove by the house that day with Charlie I've had a bad feeling. What are you going to do?"

"Wait and see for now."

"Don't wait too long. Are you keeping a handle on your money? Is he gambling? I know Charlie gambles a lot."

"If he is, it's not with our money. The accounts look pretty good right now."

"Keep an eye on it. I'm a little worried about you."

"I will. I appreciate your help. You guys have been great."

"It's no problem. Besides, you gave us two awesome dogs!"

We watch the dogs running around the yard. I am thrilled at the change in Brighid. She is happy and healthy and friendly to everyone—except Jay.

Jay's behavior continues to confuse me. Most nights, he is home, and we get along fine. But every now and then he disappears, stays out late and comes home with no explanation. I learn not to ask, because an argument will ensue and somehow I am to blame for the problem of the moment. Tonight, we eat without conversation as we sit at opposite ends of the counter. I read a book and Jay stares into space. The dogs beg at my feet.

Out of the blue, Jay says, "I've been thinking that I really am going to start my own coven. You and I need to refocus on at least initiating you to your First Degree. Where are you in your studies?"

"You're kidding! Jay, we've talked about this. I don't want to be your student right now. Our marriage is still fragile and I think it's a really bad idea. It just sets us up for power struggles. And I have my own point of view on some issues, which you don't seem to appreciate."

"You don't know enough to have a point of view," says Jay.

I can hear the arrogance in his voice and try to ignore

it. "I have my opinions, but you don't want to hear them."

Jay snorts. "For what they're worth!"

I just look at him, keeping my gaze neutral. "Do you have any idea how much it hurts when you say things like that to me? It's demeaning."

"Don't pull that counseling crap and your big words on me!"

Expressing my feelings is counseling crap? Geez.

I sip my tea. Jay is agitated but I can see he is trying to keep his emotions under control. I keep my mouth shut.

"So, you're still not ready for me to be your teacher?" asks Jay.

"Nope!"

"I don't think you really know what's right for you, Susan," Jay says. The threat in his voice puts me on high alert.

"And you do?"

"When it comes to spiritual training, I know what I'm doing. I've had plenty of students in the past who thought I was a great teacher."

"You weren't married to any of them, I presume?"

"No. I wasn't. But I could have been!"

"Count me out. I'm done." I'm amazed I can play at being strong when I have to grip my mug to prevent him from seeing my hands shake. I am terrified.

"So be it," says Jay, not looking at me. "We'll just see what happens."

We sit in stoney silence for a few minutes. Then Jay says, "I'm sorry I get so pissed off, Suze. I know I get a little intense. Let's talk about this later, okay?" He is turning on the charm. I don't believe it for a second.

"No. I'm done discussing this subject."

My heart is in my mouth.

Jay looks at me with contempt. "Oh, yeeeahh. I get it."

He stands up and towers over me. Suddenly he pulls me toward him and gives me a kiss that melts my belly and practically takes me to my knees, leaving me breathless and confused.

"I still got it," he says. He grabs his jacket and saunters out of the house. I sit very still, and the dogs do, too.

❧

At work, I push my marital problems to the back of my mind. Our team works together like a well-oiled machine. My expertise using the computer program simplifies the medical end of things. I'm able to triage patients and arrange the schedule so Tom and Karen aren't overwhelmed with too many difficult cases at once. I've figured out a way to simplify the billing, and try to keep my interactions with the insurance companies professional, though they often try my patience.

The audit is done. Now our job is to organize the information into useful data for Dale and the District Attorney.

Silvia has done extensive damage. She's over-billed or stolen money from more than half of the patients we've audited. It ranges from a co-pay here and there to large sums billed to insurance for appointments that never happened. Silvia must have forged signatures on checks and set up separate accounts in other banks. Now the insurance companies are aware that Karen and Tom had nothing to do with the crime, and they are legally off the hook.

I meet with Star and her coven one night a week for discussions on books and essays from many different spiritual paths. Jay has taught me many things, but his style is to criticize. Star's method is to encourage open discussions on our thoughts related to the readings. On the nights I come home and Jay happens to be there, he doesn't speak to me about where I have been and when I try to share something new I've learned, he is cold and disinterested. Some nights he has his own group at our house—all of them ignore me. I feel like a stranger in my own home. I feel more and more at home at Star's house, and often stay after everyone leaves to have a few moments of girl talk.

One night, after a meaningful spiritual discussion on the writings of Carl Jung and spirituality, Star asks me to stay.

We settle on the couch with a special blend of tea made from chamomile and comfrey as the cat sleeps on the top of the couch.

Star gives me a long look and asks, "What are you waiting for?"

I blink. "What do you mean?"

"What are you waiting for? Your husband is rarely home, he's doing his own thing, he's mean to you or ignores you completely. What are you hoping is going to happen, and why aren't you making things happen?"

"I...I don't know."

Star gives me a few moments to think.

"Look, really it's none of my business, but things aren't right with him," she continues. "Slogging on day to day hoping Jay will change isn't working."

I grin. "You sound exactly like me when I was a counselor. When you're in it you can't see the patterns that are obvious to someone else. I'm living on hope, I guess."

"Susan, you're a strong and smart person. You have the ability to take care of yourself. You did it for years."

"I know." I sigh and look away as tears spring to my eyes. "I had a good life in Chicago, but it blossomed when I met Jay. Change is so hard for me since my parents died. I trusted Jay. Moving out here was a big change I would never have attempted by myself. It was a risk, but I was so in love, none of that mattered. Now that I'm here and my life has gone to shit, I just feel paralyzed. I want my dream life to come true and I guess I'm kinda stuck."

"I understand, but you have to start paying attention to what's real, not what you hope is real."

I know Star is right. My dream and my reality are so far apart. I am putting myself at risk financially and maybe even physically. Jay never keeps a promise. His default is to be a single, irresponsible guy—if not worse. I have to do something.

"You sound like a wise old crone. You practicing?" I say, trying to lighten the discussion.

Star laughs. "I've been accused of worse! Will you at least think about what I said?"

"Of course, I will. You're right. I know it. I just need a little time to get my head in the right place, and figure out what to do."

"Do you want to go back to Chicago?"

"No!" I say without hesitation. That answer, at least, I

am sure of. Except for Jay, I like living here, love my job and enjoy my friends. I don't want to walk away from that.

"Then at least you know that. If you need a place to stay, you know you can stay here, right?"

"Thanks. I don't want to put anyone out. But I'll consider it in an emergency, okay?"

"Good." Star leans over and gives me a hug, upsetting Sweetums, who gives a quick angry meow and jumps off the couch in a huff.

We both laugh at the cat. I ask, "Does Sweetums like dogs?"

"Not really," says Star.

But what would I do with the dogs?

Chapter Thirteen

❧

A cold front blew through for a day and a half. Cold fronts in the Midwest were blustery and brought rain and thunderstorms. Here, they just bring high winds, blowing dust, eventually a little rain, and then clear skies, still air, and a killing frost that hit with a vengeance on a Saturday in early October.

By afternoon, the sun is shining brightly and the day is glorious. I work in the yard as the dogs cavort at my feet. I pull up the last of the dying flowers, empty the few remaining pots, and close down the yard for the season. Jay's been gone since Thursday night. His absence makes it easier for me to avoid thinking about the future. I bask in the peace of being by myself, but still fail to make a firm decision about moving forward.

The counselor in me is slapping me upside the head. But I remain stuck. When I fell for Jay, I fell hard. I'd never been so loved and cared for. What happened to that? I want it back. I was over thirty before I felt like I was finally living. Would I ever fall in love like that again? It has all been a lie. I kick myself for reading all those romance novels when I was a kid. Life isn't like that. I thought I had pretty good radar for the bad guys, but it failed me when it was most important. Now I don't trust my own judgment and feel doomed to a lonely life, with only my pets for company.

I sit on my haunches, pulling the last of the weeds and feeling miserable despite the warm sun on my back. I know nice guys are out there. Dale seems like a great guy, but his marriage had failed. Tom and Russ are both happily married. The good ones always are. Rosie and Karen are lucky to have them. I sigh in frustration and stand up, stretching my back. I whistle for the dogs and we troop into the house to finish the chores for the day.

Samhain, or Halloween, is fast approaching. In the Wiccan calendar, Samhain is halfway between the Fall Equinox and Winter Solstice and is a time of great celebration. It's the Wiccan New Year, the time when the veil is thinnest between the two worlds of life and death. In ancient days, this was the time of year when difficult decisions were made regarding what food to save and what animals to kill, or to feed during the winter in hopes more stock would be produced in the spring. At the same time, there was great celebration and fun to be had as each person gave their lives over to fate—clearly unable to control whatever the future held.

Each member of Star's coven will prepare for this ritual individually. Star tasked us to journal our thoughts and beliefs about life and death and memories of loved ones who have passed, so our minds will be open to the meditation during ritual.

Those who have passed might make themselves known during the meditation by appearing in the smoke of the ritual fire, or leaving behind a symbol of some kind.

The Water Master

Since my parents' deaths, I have been avoiding thinking about them, but the memories flood in now. I feel the bittersweet memories of my life with my family like an open wound on my skin. It seems like anyone can see into my heart, which I want to protect. But I can't.

Journaling a little every night brings me dreams about my parents and also distracts me from dealing with Jay, who is gone now more than he is home. When he is home I felt transparent, and am helpless and needy when he turns on the charm. I have fallen into his arms a few times and later regretted letting him make love to me. His attention confuses me even more, and his smug grin makes me feel used rather than loved.

Jay and his three groupies have met at the house a few times. I don't know what he is planning for Samhain ritual and we don't discuss it. All I know is they will be at the house while I am gone. I worry about the dogs. Samhain has nothing to do with ritual killing of animals. Only the sickest people perform that evil under the guise of some sort of Satanic practice. That is not Wicca. However, given Jay's unpredictable behavior, and Brighid's obvious dislike for him, I decide to take the dogs elsewhere. Star's house is out. Sweetums would eat them alive.

On Friday, Dale stops by the office to give us an update on Silvia's case. Without thinking, I ask if he would mind taking care of my dogs for the weekend.

"Sure! I'd love to. My guys would love the company! Are you going out of town for the weekend?"

"No. It's Halloween and I won't be home. I'm a little

worried. I don't know what people are like around here on Halloween."

"Yeah. We've had animals disappear this time of year—mostly cats. But I'll be around and they'll be safe. No problem."

"Thanks, Dale. Can I bring them over Saturday morning?"

"Sure."

Dale writes down his address to confirm the arrangement. I feel safer knowing the dogs will be under his care.

༒

Samhain is on a Saturday—convenient—given that the coven planned rituals for the weekend. Jay is again up and out before I wake up. I promised Dale I'd bring the dogs over before eleven in the morning. I have a few hours to kill, time enough to enjoy my coffee and the newspaper and review my journaling for tonight.

After my shower, I go to the bedside table to retrieve my journal. It isn't there! I search through the drawers, look under the bed, search my purse, the office and anywhere else I can find. It is gone. I sink down on the bed to think about when I saw it last. I was writing in it before bed. I had set it down on my nightstand and didn't put it away like I usually did.

Jay must have taken it.

With a sinking heart, I realize that Jay is going to use my journal—my private thoughts—to hurt me. Maybe the hurt is in the taking. He's taken too much from me lately.

I wrack my brain to remember what I had written in my journal.

The Water Master

Is there anything that will make Jay angry? Probably.

Anything could set him off. I'd never dream of snooping into Jay's private things.

What is he looking for?

Tonight's ritual is important to me. I have avoided dealing with unhappy memories of the death of my parents for too long. I never realized until now I had also avoided dealing with the happy memories: what it felt like to be part of a family, the jokes, the laughter. I had shut all of those memories out. Now that some of the good feelings are back, I am looking forward to a ritual where I can accept the totality of that experience and perhaps connect with the spirit of my parents.

My private thoughts are now in the hands of a man I don't trust. Will he use them in his ritual tonight? I've never been in a Samhain ritual with him and am not sure what he has planned. Knowing him, he'll follow the rules. I search for Dagan Moore's book on ritual instruction and review the Samhain ritual. Nothing is out of the ordinary. Maybe Jay took it just to be cruel.

There isn't much I can do about it. I work with the dogs, training them in their basic commands and throwing the ball for them until they are worn out by the time I drive them over to Dale's house.

Following his directions, I drive to an unfamiliar part of Pasco. The neat little bungalows along the street were probably built in the 1950s. The yards are in various states of autumn disarray, some still colorful with mums and marigolds, others prepared for winter, some shabby and unkempt. Once I find Dale's address, I am relieved to see a neat, manicured lawn, and a house looking freshly painted a pale blue with white trim.

Dogs bark inside as Dale opens his front door. Two furry monsters bound out to greet me. I laugh, patting their heads while Dale's repeated calls to "Come!" and "Down!" are completely ignored. I pick up little Zeus so he won't bolt. Brighid is big enough to hold her own. We all crowd into the house and Dale shoos the pack into the back yard, which is clearly owned by his dogs.

We stand on his patio watching the dogs sniff each other's backsides.

"I gave up on the back yard. These guys dig and make trails. The back yard is theirs and the front yard is mine."

I laugh. "With dogs that big, you have to let them have some space of their own! What kind are they?"

"Arlie is a lab/mastiff mix and Joe is some kind of retriever/Springer/St. Bernard mix."

"My gosh, they're big!" I say as Arlie nudges my elbow with his snout.

Brighid races around the back yard, alternately smelling the ground and running from the bigger dogs. She looks happy, so we leave the dogs to their butt-smelling and go inside. Zeus struggles out of my arms and scampers to the door to watch and whine.

"Will Zeus be all right with these guys?" I ask.

"Let's give him time to adjust. If he's bowled over by them, I have a small kennel for him."

"I really appreciate your doing this for me. I don't know why I'm so nervous about them."

Dale is quiet while he pours coffee.

The Water Master

I sit down at the kitchen table and look around. While the house doesn't have any womanly touches to speak of, it is neat and clean. Seattle Seahawks hot pads hang from the cupboard over his stove, and the mug he hands me across the table sports a Mariners logo.

"I'll pick them up tomorrow, if that works for you."

"I'll be here, unless I'm called out to work for some reason."

"Does that happen often?"

"It depends. Some weekends are quiet, but most weekends there's some sort of excitement. Drive-by shootings, domestics..."

"Does your job ever wear you out?" I ask.

"It's my life. I guess I see so much ugliness that I notice the little things, the good things, as much as I can. Like the dogs, for instance. Playing with them is a great way to regroup after a rough day."

"I know what you mean," I say as I sip my coffee.

"Susan, it's none of my business, but how are things with Jay?"

"I really don't know," I reply.

We are silent for a minute. I shift under Dale's gaze. He isn't going to let up.

"What do you want to know?"

"I don't really know. I just feel like something's not right. I'm a little confused. My detective antennae are up, but I'm not sure they're accurate."

"Do you usually trust your instincts?" I ask.

"Yes!"

"Why don't you trust them now?"

273

"Because I'm…." Dale stops and looks away.

"What?"

"I'm…ah, well…you're on my mind. I don't know why. You've impressed me with the investigation at the Elwins' office, and…it just seems odd that you're with a guy like Jay."

I am at once confused, flattered and offended.

"Um. Thank you and fuck you," I say in a flat voice.

Dale laughs out loud. "Wow. You put me in my place."

"Well, it pisses me off that you would assume that Jay has always been this way and that I would just accept it! When I met him, he was an amazing, charming, caring guy. He treated me like a queen. What you see now is not the man I married. The new Jay is a jerk I don't want to be around."

"Then why are you?"

"I'm working on it, okay?" I say. The chair scrapes the floor as I jump up and take my cup to the sink.

"Look, I'm sorry," says Dale as he stands up and follows me. "I'm worried about you, that's all."

"You and everybody else," I reply.

I turn around and lean against the counter. Dale, stands next to me, close enough for me to smell his aftershave. I want his nearness to be uncomfortable, but it isn't.

"Dale, I really appreciate your caring. My marriage sucks and I'm trying to find my way. I'm drained. Can you leave it alone?"

"Sure. I'm sorry if I intruded. Just let me know if you need anything, okay?"

"Okay." I reach out and touch his arm. "Thanks."

Dale reaches for my hand and squeezes it. I look in his eyes, shocked by the desire that overcomes me. I step back, I take a deep breath and say, "I gotta go."

ॐ

Dogs safe with Dale for the weekend, I go by the herb store to help Star prepare for the evening. The store is full of customers, so I sit at the couch and pour a cup of tea.

Star's customers celebrate Halloween in different ways, buying ritual tools, incense, and certain herbs that are purported to have magical properties. Many come in costume. I giggle and shake my head at some of the outrageous and odd customers that Star takes in stride.

"How do you stand it?" I ask when we have a quiet moment.

"Stand what?"

"The crazy people who come in here?"

Star laughs. "Those crazies are my bread and butter!"

"I know, but geez. It seems like most of them are a little kooky!"

"Like I said, bread and butter. And I have normal customers, too. Today is just a very weird day!"

Star sinks into the couch next to me. "You ready for ritual?"

I sigh. "I guess. I wanted to review my journal this morning, but it's gone. I think Jay took it."

Star rubs her forehead in frustration. "For god sakes, Susan!"

Startled, I ask, "Are you mad at me?"

"No! I'm mad at the situation! If your private things aren't safe, then you aren't either! I just wish you'd get out."

"Okay! I promise next week I will find a lawyer," I say, surprised I can state that so easily.

"Really?"

I look into the dregs of tea at the bottom of my cup, wishing I could read my future in them.

"Really."

"Finally!" says Star, reaching over and play-slapping me on my shoulder. "Let's get ready to go."

Tonight's ritual will be solemn. Just a quiet entry into the circle, a short description of the meaning of the day, and while Star quietly beats a rhythm on the drum, the ritual fire will be lit in a huge cauldron and all will meditate on those who have passed before.

The evening is chilly. I wear a heavy coat under my robe. After raising the circle, the air becomes very still. The fire warms the air. Although I can see the trees in the distance swaying in a gentle breeze, the smoke from the fire rises straight into the dark night.

I sit cross-legged on the ground. Taking a deep breath, I settle into my meditation, and with eyes half open, let my gaze fall on the fire in front of me. The wood cracks and the flames dance, entwined in orange, red, blue and green. I watch the play of colors and relax with each breath.

A picture of my father forms in front of me. He stands at the top of the stairs in the house where I grew up. He looks down on me at the bottom of the stairs, worry etched on his face. My mother stands behind him.

The Water Master

"Climb out of it, Sis! You need to hurry!"

The sudden end of the drumming shakes me back to the present. I feel weak and dizzy as I stand up. The cakes and ale help ground me, but I am emotionally spent.

My dad is the only person that ever called me "Sis," and that was only when he was really mad or really serious.

We eat a subdued dinner, each absorbed in his or her thoughts, and no one sharing, as we were instructed. It is important not to dilute the experience.

I am deep in thought as I drive home. Turning onto our street, I expect to see more cars in front of the house. Instead, I see two people entwined in a passionate embrace, leaning against Jay's car. It's Jay and Flower.

Furious, I pull up behind the car, jump out, slam the door and rush them.

"Jesus, Jay! What's the matter with you?"

Jay smiles his slow smile while Flower snuggles deeper into his arms.

"What's the matter with you?" he says.

"Nothing a lawyer can't handle!" I scream.

Jay's smile disappears immediately and he shoves Flower out of the way.

"You're not getting a divorce!" he yells after me. "I'm not done with you yet!"

I slam the door, lock it and hope like hell he doesn't have his keys. I hear a door slam, and look out the window in time to see Flower's car backing onto the front lawn to get around my car. He is gone for now.

I sink to the floor and cry. It takes awhile, but eventually my crying jag ends and I call Star.

"Hello?"

"Star? It's Susan. Sorry to call so late."

"Hi. Oh, you don't sound so good."

"I'm not. I need to talk with you. Can we get together for breakfast?"

ॐ

Jay tucks Flower under his arm as he speeds off. She grins, enjoying the thrill of winning.

I can't hold this together any longer. Being married to her sucks. She and her high and mighty expectations. I'm not getting anything I want, including her money. She's probably going to file for divorce and that's the last thing I'm gonna let her do. She should have given me her money a long time ago and I'm tired of waiting.

Jay steers with his knees while he dials his cell phone.

"Charlie? It's Jay. We need to talk."

ॐ

Sunday morning dawns rainy and cold. I take a quick shower, dress, and grab a few pieces of fresh fruit to take to Star's house. I feel as raw as the weather.

I step into her front hall and the odors of bacon, fresh herbs and onions make my mouth water. My appetite returns.

"Mmm. Breakfast smells delicious!"

The breakfast nook next to the window overlooking the back yard is set for two with the red Cottage Rose pattern dishes that are reminiscent of those at the family cottage where I spent my summers as a child. Red napkins and a vase of red roses complete the theme.

278

"You like red?" I ask.

"How'd you guess?" laughs Star.

"It's beautiful. Thanks for making it so nice."

I cut up my oranges and pour coffee for us while Star pulls an egg casserole out of the oven and prepares the plates.

Sweetums jumps up on the windowsill while we settle at the table.

"So—what's going on?"

I take a deep breath.

"Jay's with Flower again. I caught them at my house last night."

"And this surprised you?" asks Star.

"No, it didn't. But it still feels like shit."

I unload the whole story. I tell her about Jay's moodiness, jealousy, threats, sideways comments about getting to my money, and his absences from home. I steer away from our sex life. That is too personal. Star lets me keep talking, asking a few clarifying questions now and then. By the time I am done, the coffee pot is empty and Sweetums is snoring in her spot next to the window.

Star says nothing as I blow my nose and wipe away the last tears. By saying things out loud, I can hear my own weak excuses for Jay's behavior. When I speak of my efforts to try to please him, I sound just like the voices of so many of my past clients. I remember my frustration at their inability to see that their actions are futile in the face of an irrational partner. I sound like an idiot.

"It really bugs me that Jay raided your coven," I say.

"That should be the least of your worries, and it

doesn't bother me in the least," says Star.

"Really? Why?"

"Because people make choices. I don't own them and they don't owe me anything. Besides, of all the people he could have chosen, he took the three weakest links in our group."

"I noticed! What's up with that?"

"He needs to be in control. He chooses people who are needy."

I squirm. I never thought anyone could control me.

"Please don't take offense, Susan. I wasn't necessarily referring to your marriage."

"I think it does translate to my marriage. How did this happen?"

"From what you tell me, you haven't been close to anyone since your parents died. I don't think it takes years of counseling to figure out you were waiting for a white knight to make you feel special."

"I didn't know it. I wasn't conscious of it."

"Are you now?" asks Star.

"I'm all too aware of it now. I fell right into it. I really don't know anything about him, other than what he told me. The only person I met that had anything to do with his history was Dagan Moore, and I didn't like him from the start."

"You mentioned he comments about your money. What's that about?"

"All I ever told him was that I'd inherited some money from my parents. I never told him how much, and I've made it clear that I'm not ready to put any of it in his name. But he brings it up now and then, hinting that he should have equal access to it. Once he asked me if I'd made him beneficiary yet."

Star is thoughtful for a minute.

"Have you ever Googled yourself?"

"What?"

"You know. Have you ever looked up your name up on the Internet?"

"No. Why?"

"Let's see what's out there," says Star as she stands up to look for her laptop. She finds it on the kitchen counter and returns to the table. "What's your maiden name?"

"Bradley."

Star types for a few seconds. Her eyebrows shoot up. "Is your dad's name Cooper Bradley?"

"Yeah," I say. *Crap.*

Star turns the computer to me.

"Look. There must be twenty articles about your dad, and here's his obituary."

I scan the page. Articles about my dad, his patent, selling his patent for millions—it is all there. I scan the obituary and of course, my name is in print, along with the rest of my family. And there is the rags-to-riches story from the *Chicago Tribune.* I remember how upset my parents were about that article. They preferred anonymity and tried to keep us away from the limelight. At the time, Ruthie and I enjoyed the attention, but now I understand how worried my parents must have been about someone hurting us to get to their money.

I slap my hand over my mouth as everything becomes clear.

"Jay...he...he..."

"He knows you're rich," says Star as she completes my thought.

"Oh shit, oh shit! How stupid could I be? It never occurred to me that he would research me! Oh my God," I moan. "He doesn't love me. He wants my money."

Star snaps her computer closed and sits back, allowing this horrible insight to sink in.

"So what now?" asks Star.

"I need to get my feet back under me. He's demoralized me to the point I can't think. It's like the movie *Gaslight*. He's making me think I'm the crazy one, but he's had an ulterior motive all along. And I wonder what Charlie has to do with all of this?"

"It is what it is. All you have to do is make a decision about what to do next. I'm worried now. You need to take some steps to protect yourself."

"I do. Oh, how do I start?"

"Let's make a list of things to do," says Star.

We put our heads together and come up with six items I need to address. I write as I speak out load.

"One. Lawyer – get referral from Dale. Two. Change the locks. Three. Tell Elwins what's going on. Four. Call Ruthie with update. Five. Call Nancy about protecting investments. Six. Dogs-give them up?"

We hug and I leave the house feeling—well—awake. But now I'm scared. I drive home in a fog, feeling hung over. Once home, I examine my swollen eyes and pale face in the bathroom mirror and think again of my father's warning during ritual last night. I slap on a little make up and drive to Dale's house to pick up the dogs.

When I ring the doorbell, I hear a cacophony of barking along with Zeus's high pitched yip. Dale opens the door wearing jeans and a Seahawks sweatshirt, cup of coffee in hand.

"Hi," he says. "Come on in."

Brighid jumps up and down until I kneel and scratch behind her ears. Then she runs off with the other dogs as Dale opens the back door. Zeus yips and circles in the kennel until I free him. He covers me in licks and scrambles out of my arms to run puppy circles throughout the house. Dale lets him out as well, leaving the dogs to their own devices.

"Zeus and the big dogs were great together. They're protective of him."

"Did you get any sleep?"

"Oh, yeah. Zeus cuddled up with me in bed and the three big dogs slept on the floor. We had no problems."

I put the thought of cuddling with Dale aside.

"You don't look so good. What happened last night?" Dale asks.

"Let's just say I had a decisive moment. Can you recommend a good divorce lawyer?"

Dale reaches over and squeezes my shoulder. "I can. Good for you."

I feel the weight and heat of his hand on my shoulder and all I want to do is lay my head on his chest and feel his arms around me. I guard myself against wishing for his comfort, realizing all I want is someone to comfort me. The image of my father trying to protect me is my only comfort for now — that, and the support of my friends.

I move away from Dale as he goes to the counter and digs around in a drawer for a pen and paper. He writes something down and gives it to me.

"Diane Reeves is the best divorce attorney around. She's a little pricey, but well worth it. You know, Susan, I'll do whatever I can to help you."

"I'll probably take you up on that, but I'm not quite sure what I need. This might have been a test for keeping my dogs again at some point — probably sooner rather than later."

"I'll do whatever it takes to help you stay safe."

"Thanks. I'll call Diane tomorrow. And thanks for taking care of the dogs last night."

I gather up my pups and leave.

꩜

Dale watches Susan leave his house.

It is too quiet with all the dogs gone. Or maybe...oh never mind.

He calls a buddy who likes to make a few extra bucks doing surveillance and asks a big favor.

꩜

How is it possible I could I have fallen in love with a sociopath? I should know better, given what I've seen my clients go through. He wrapped me around his little finger and other parts of his body. I have to get rid of these thoughts about what the marriage could have been like and deal with the truth. It's hard to fathom that he researched me and decided to seduce me into marrying him so he could get to my money. I don't want him to know I'm on to his plot and will act as if nothing has changed. I need to talk with the lawyer and clear the path to exit my marriage.

෨෧

Monday morning I call a locksmith, and by noon the locks are changed. I drag Jay's belongings to the front yard and heap them in a pile. I call and leave a message that he'll have to pick up his stuff today. After that it's going to the dump—or maybe I'll set fire to it.

Jay never responds to my message. But, even now, knowing my marriage is over, I feel an obligation to remain faithful and to carry on as if I were still married, including paying bills and making payments on the credit cards, as I wait for the divorce wheels to start turning.

෨෧

Jay's belongings disappeared from my front lawn, soon after I dumped them there. He made no effort to contact me, which was a relief. The next few weeks fly by as I try to reorganize my life. I meet with the attorney, I go to work, and I cuddle with my dogs at night. I feel like I'm taking back control of my life and realize how far out of control it had become.

In the meantime, the Elwins, Rosie and Star each invite me to Thanksgiving dinner. I decide to celebrate with Star and whatever 'orphans' show up at her house. Thanksgiving celebrations with my family were boring events when I was young, full of old people and adult conversations. But this Thanksgiving, I find myself excited about spending the holiday with people I really like.

The Water Master

Star loves to entertain, and I catch her festive mood as she and I cook and prepare a feast for her guests. We play silly games before dinner and during the meal each person shares a funny Thanksgiving story that has all of us in stitches. By the time it was my turn, I say,"Well, the only story I can think of is that every Thanksgiving my mother would slide the rolls into the oven while she did the last minute preparations for dinner. About halfway through the meal, the smell of burning bread wafted into the dining room. My mother would stand up and yell. 'The rolls!' She'd run to the kitchen and pull out a pan of blackened bread. Fans on and windows open, we'd finish our dessert with the taste of charcoal in the back of our throats."

Everyone chuckles and Star says, "I think we're safe to eat pumpkin pie without that smell in the room."

As we sip coffee and munch on our pumpkin pie, I hear my cell phone ring in the other room. Expecting my sister to call, I excuse myself from the table to search out my phone. I catch it on the fourth ring. The number is not familiar.

"Hello?"

"Hello, Suze, it's me."

My stomach jerks. It has been weeks since I've heard Jay's voice.

"What do you want?"

"Just want you to know I was thinking of you today, enjoying Thanksgiving with all of your friends." He laughs a low, threatening laugh.

The phone goes dead.

Frozen, I stare at the phone. In two seconds, he ruined

everything. I run to the living room window and look out in time to see receding taillights. He's been watching the house. I bite my lip with worry. I don't want to ruin everyone's good time, but I don't trust him.

Star, as usual, notices something is wrong. She gives me a questioning look.

I say, "Jay's been here. I need to go home."

Star says, "What do you mean he's been here."

"He just called. He sounded threatening. He was outside your house."

Ronny stands and says, "Let's go outside and make sure everything's okay."

The three of us go outside and Ronny shouts, "My tires are flat! All four of them!"

My heart sinks. All the cars parked in front of Star's house sits on four flat tires.

Star look at me. "Jay?" she asks.

"Jay."

We trudge back into the house and Star calls the police. I call Dale and tell him what happened. He insists on going to my house to make sure the dogs are okay. He promises to tell the officer what to look for, but we all know that Jay's phone call alone doesn't provide any proof that he is the vandal.

Hours later, all the guests and cars are gone. Thankfully, the tires were only deflated, not destroyed. One tow truck driver put everyone back on the road—for a fee, of course. I paid for it.

Star and I clean up the kitchen, packing leftovers into an already stuffed refrigerator. Sweetums comes out from her hiding place and I gave her a few bites of turkey.

My phone rings again. It's Dale.

"I'm sitting outside your house. There's no sign of Jay. I'll hang around till you get home. Take your time," he says.

"I'm sorry you had to do this, but thank you. I'll be home soon."

"No problem," says Dale. "I'll talk to you in a little bit."

We hang up.

"Do you want to stay here tonight?" asks Star.

"No. I need to get home."

"I'd rather you didn't. The sleeping giant is awake again."

"He's done his damage for the night. He just wants me to know he's not going away easily. I already knew that," I say.

Why am I not scared. I should be. I guess that's what comes with living in fear every day. It becomes the norm.

I drive home on my now inflated tires. I pull into the driveway and park next to Dale's car.

He steps out of his car and says, "Are you okay?"

"I'm fine. I'm just tired."

"Susan, I don't think you should stay here anymore."

"I'm beginning to see that, too. But what do I do with the dogs?"

"I can take them."

"That could work. Let me think about it a little bit, and I'll get back to you. Thank you so much, Dale. I don't know what I would have done without your help tonight."

"Susan, I need to get a little more information, but some time soon I will need to talk with you about what I think has been going on."

"Great. Just what I need. I'm going to bed. Thanks again. Good-night."

ॐॐ

Dale stares after her. He shakes his head a little and gets back in his car. As he drives down the road, he waves at his friend that he hired to do surveillance.

ॐॐ

I enter the house as the dogs greet me with snuffles and licks. I sink to the floor and let loose the sobs that I've been holding back all night. The dogs lick my face and then lay with their heads on my legs, looking at me with worried eyes. I get up and let them out for their nightly routine. Then we all pile into bed. I fall asleep knowing the slightest noise will start them barking.

❧❦

YULE - REBIRTH

"I am a boar: ruthless and red..."

❧❦

Chapter Fourteen

❧

As winter solstice draws near, chilly winds blow in on one cold front after another with rainy, cloudy days. Twilight descends at three in the afternoon, and despite the loss of my precious sunlight and the impending end of my marriage, I feel hopeful. It has taken a couple of weeks to meet with Diane, my attorney. I trust her and I'm assured the divorce should be fairly simple, since Jay and I share little community property and have no children.

Given Jay's threat that he would never divorce me, I'll wait for the paperwork to be completed before deciding how to proceed. I'm not in the mood for more confrontations. He wants my money and isn't going to let go easily. At least he's temporarily distracted by Flower. I will use that to my advantage.

I never ask him about my journals. I don't want to know if he has read them, nor do I want to listen to him make some cutting remark. I have already gathered all of my private things and put them in a locked box that I took to the office and locked in my desk drawer. I also put together a 'to go' bag of toiletries and clean underwear, just in case I have to flee. Jay might be locked out, but I'd rather be on the safe side. I never thought I'd be in this position.

I wish I could go back in time and tell my former clients how sorry I am that I didn't understand how hard it is to leave a marriage, no matter how bad. Now I'm living it. You want your home and you want to leave. You want to trust, and each day you discover why you shouldn't. You long to be held, and when you let him hold you, you feel used. You want to give, and you discover he's taking. You let him stay because you worry what he's doing when he's gone. You trust, and he steals the things most precious to you.

On a December evening after the patients are gone, I'm wrapping up some billing when I hear a knock on the office door. I look up to see Dale beckoning to be let in. I call for Tom and Karen as I walk to the door.

"Hi, Dale. What brings you here tonight?" I ask. Tom and Karen appear.

"Can we sit down?" Dale asks.

"Sure," says Tom as he motions Dale to one of the waiting room chairs. "What's up?"

"Well, it's Susan I really want to talk to," says Dale.

My heart pounds in my chest. "What's wrong?" I ask.

"Nothing's wrong. I've been thinking about this for awhile and now I'm going to ask you. Since you live in the house where the Clements lived, you could let me in to do some forensics. Charlie wouldn't allow it after the Clements disappeared, and we didn't have enough evidence to get a search warrant. Now, all I need is your permission."

Goose bumps tickle my arms and I rub them. I hadn't thought about this terrible possibility until now.

Something bad could have happened in the house, in my bedroom or kitchen!

294

"Do I need to sign something?" I ask.

Dale reaches into his briefcase for some papers. "This gives us permission to search your house. Fingerprints are probably long gone by now, but it's possible we could find blood evidence."

My stomach turns. *Blood!* I swallow, but my throat is dry. "I don't see why not. What will this do to the house? Will you be tearing it up? Moving stuff?"

"Our investigators try to be polite when it comes to moving things around. They'll do their best to put everything back where it belongs. If we have to tear up anything, we'll discuss options with you, but I doubt it will come to that."

"I can't imagine Charlie would be happy about this," I say. "Can it be done in one day?"

"I don't know the answer to that," says Dale. "It depends."

I have watched enough true crime dramas to know that forensics take more than a half hour with ten minutes of commercials.

"When do you want to do it?"

"Whenever it's convenient for you."

"Let me think about this a little, will you?" As I say it, I feel ridiculous.

The whole thing gives me the willies.

"Call me when you decide," says Dale. "In the meantime, we're preparing a warrant for Silvia Gottschalk and will be serving her when the time is right. I wanted to warn you that it's likely bail will be set and she will be able to leave jail within hours of her arrest. She'll be furious. We plan on keeping an eye on her and all of you, but you will have to be extra vigilant."

"That's just great," says Tom with disgust. "We're the victims yet again."

Karen says, "Do you think she's dangerous?"

"I think she's diabolical," says Dale. "She's not likely to come at you directly."

"Just like her brother, Charlie," I say.

"Let us know what's going on, okay?" says Tom.

"Will do," says Dale as he rises to leave. He looks at me. "Are Jay and Charlie still hanging out together?"

"I assume so," I respond.

"Keep your ear to the ground. You may hear information that could be helpful."

"Jay's not talking to me much these days," I say. "Maybe we could arrange the search after he gets the divorce papers."

The conversation stops as everyone stares at me. At last, Karen says, "Please call or come to the house anytime you need to, Susan."

Dale says, "Take her up on that."

"I will."

&

After Dale leaves, Tom, Karen and I head home. As I eat dinner, I think about what it might be like to have a bunch of investigators in the house. After cleaning up, I stretch out on the living room floor and wonder when this carpet was put down. I stand up, look around the house and realize the living room carpet matches the wall-to-wall carpet throughout the house. But as I look closer I see it is newer. All the rooms have a coat of fresh paint.

How will they do blood spatter testing when the walls have been painted?

Christmas is coming, but I'm too distracted to decorate the house. I have already completed the shopping and mailing for Ruthie's family. I hug myself as I stare at the one place in the living room a Christmas tree might fit. Now that I 'm aware a murder could have occurred here, nothing is going to make me feel better about this house—not even Christmas decorations.

I walk out into the dark night and cross the road to the mailbox, pull a stack of mail out of the box and carry it back to the house. Sitting at the counter, I rifle through the usual junk mail and fliers. In the middle of the stack, an envelope with IMPORTANT NOTICE! OPEN IMMEDIATELY! catches my attention. It's a letter from the irrigation district. I tear open the envelope and dismayed, I see a returned check with INSUFFICIENT FUNDS stamped across it. I stare at the check in disbelief. It's the October payment for the irrigation. That stupid irrigation! How could we have insufficient funds? And why did it take so long to be notified? I mailed the check in early October. Turning the check over, I notice that the received date stamp was just before Thanksgiving.

What is going on?

Jay must have removed it from the mailbox and held onto it for some reason. Or maybe the culprit is Charlie.

I just checked the accounts the other day. Everything looked fine.

The Water Master

Oddly enough, Jay is still depositing his checks from work to help with the joint bills for the house. Without telling him, I opened a checking and savings account in my name where I deposited my last few paychecks. Today is Friday and I promised to work tomorrow. I'll have to wait until Monday to straighten this out at the bank.

I take the checkbook from the letter holder on the kitchen counter and check the balance.

That looks right.

I review the copies of the checks that have been written.

I have paid a few bills since I wrote the irrigation check. That means all the checks will bounce. What in the hell happened?

As I flip through the checkbook, I count at least six checks that were torn out, along with the paper copy behind each check. No one could have removed them except Jay. We both know the checkbook resides in the letter holder. We stuff it behind other papers so it isn't immediately visible.

No one else walking through the kitchen would see it, would they? When did he take them? How did he get in?

I swallow my simmering anger.

I never wanted to pool our funds. I'm good at managing my money. Jay seemed responsible in the beginning. I'm the one who proposed that we open a joint account for bills, and still keep separate accounts for personal spending money. Jay wanted nothing to do with it. 'We're married and your money is mine and mine is yours,' he'd said. Now he's taken all our money? My credit is on the line! What does he need it for?

I talk myself down.

Maybe there is another explanation.

I dial his cell phone and leave a message, asking him to call me back right away. A half hour later I hear his car in the driveway.

Crap. Why didn't it occur to me that he would just show up? I meet him at the door.

"Hi, Suze," says Jay. He gives me a kiss on the forehead, which I ignore. "Give me a minute. I need to use the head." He brushes past me as he goes toward the bathroom and I return to the kitchen.

A few minutes later he yells, "I left my lights on. I'll be right back."

When he returns, he says, "What's up?"

"This!" And, I shove the bounced check toward him.

Jay's expression doesn't change. "What's this?"

"It's the check I wrote to pay the irrigation in October. It bounced."

"How could it bounce? Did you make a math mistake in the checkbook?"

"No. Checks are missing. Do you know anything about that?"

Jay's anger is immediate. "Are you accusing me of stealing checks?"

"I'm just trying to figure out what happened. Do you know?"

Jay grabs the checkbook out of my hands and rifles through the pages, pretending to be concerned.

"I think you screwed up. How come it took you so long to notice this?"

"Jay, that's not the point. They're gone. Our balance is zero, according to the bank. What happened to the money?"

"How should I know?"

"I can't keep track of checks I don't know about! Did you write checks on the account?"

"Did you?" Jay asks stepping toward me and tossing the checkbook across the counter.

"Yeah! Our bills!"

Jay is quiet, preparing to lie to me—again.

"Someone must have broken in the house and taken the checks," he says.

"I don't think that's what happened."

"There you go accusing me again!" yells Jay.

"I think you took the checks. I'm not sure why. Gambling, maybe? Expensive jewelry for your girlfriend?" I can't help myself.

"Knock it off, Susan. You don't know what you're talking about."

"I want to know why you did this!" *I want to scream.* I squeeze my eyes shut to keep the angry tears at bay.

"I'll go to the bank and figure out what happened."

I don't trust him. "We'll both go," I say.

"Oh, so now I can't even do that right?" whines Jay.

"Get off it, Jay. I know you did this."

"Fuck you!" he yells, storming out of the house. The dogs cower at my feet.

The next morning the ringing phone wakes me up. I glance at the clock on the wall. "Eight o'clock! Damn it! I forgot to set the alarm. I was supposed to be at the office at seven thirty to finish up the audit. Today is supposed to be our last Saturday of work. Hello?"

"Susan, are you all right?" It's Tom.

"Yeah. Sorry. I overslept. I'm fine. I'm so sorry. I'll be there as soon as I get ready."

"Okay. We were worried. See you soon." Tom hangs up.

I've never been late for work a day in my life! This is ridiculous.

I feel drugged as I get out of bed.

I'm so tired!

Although I feel like I'm slogging through mud, I hurry to leave. But something's not right. I stop for a moment to get my bearings. The dresser draws my gaze. My jewelry box is slightly askew. I open each drawer, performing an inventory. Opening the ring drawer, I see two rings are missing.

"Mom's rings are gone!"

My memory shoots back to the day my dad gave me her diamond wedding rings. They are very special to me, although I rarely wear them.

Jay must have taken them when he was here last night.

I search my dresser drawers and find my panty drawer in disarray.

Jay had been digging around in my underwear! How could he?

The hair on the back of my neck bristles. My skin crawls. I feel raped. I'm furious at Jay and enraged at myself.

Why didn't I think about him doing something like this? Stupid! Stupid! Stupid!

The Water Master

Adrenaline kicks my brain into high gear. I gather the few pieces of jewelry that are left and load them into a makeup bag to add to my box at the office.

❧

We finish the audit spreadsheet by the end of the day and email it to Dale. I don't feel like airing more of my problems, so I keep the latest news to myself. After work, I make a quick salad as I try to get my racing thoughts under control. From Jay's thieving behavior, to Dale's request to search the house, to Silvia's pending arrest, my life is spinning out of control.

The dogs bark a warning. A car pulls up to the house. I look out the window. Jay is back.

I open the door and step onto the porch. I have no intention of letting him in the house.

"What do you want?" I yell as he gets out of the car.

"I just want to talk to you."

"I have nothing to say to you. You stole my rings!"

"You're crazy!" he says as he stomps up to the porch. "First you accuse me of stealing checks, and now this?"

"Give me a break, Jay! I know you did it!"

Jay grabs my neck with one hand as he pushes me back into the house. The pressure make me dizzy.

"Let go!" I can barely get the words out.

He shoves me and I tumble backwards. Sharp pain shoots through my arm and shoulder. I lie on the floor in shock and suck air as Jay stalks to the ritual room. I hear him rifling through the desk. By the time he comes back to the living room, I am sitting up, rubbing my neck and sweating in fear.

I can't fight him. Brighid stands guard in front of me, growling with teeth bared. Zeus cowers behind the couch.

"What do you want?" I croak.

"Wouldn't you like to know?" he snarls as he saunters to the front door. Brighid snaps at his heels. Jay turns and growls at her. She stops and glares at him with teeth bared, willing him to leave. Jay laughs and walks out, slamming the door behind him.

Zeus comes out from hiding and sits on my leg, shaking and looking for comfort. Brighid, returned from her duty, looks at me with worried eyes. I stand up, wincing as I try to put weight on my arm for leverage. My shoulder and arm hurt like hell.

I'm on auto-pilot. I go to the freezer and pull out an ice pack to slide under my collar. The dogs whine and paw at my legs. I walk back to the living room and ease into the recliner. Brighid and Zeus jump into my lap and stare at my face. I sob. Brighid licks my hand.

"You guys know when something's wrong, don't you?" They wag their tails in reply.

A sad calm overcomes me as I think about next steps. Jay stole from me and attacked me. I have to protect myself. Now that he knows I am aware of the bounced checks, he will need to find money elsewhere.

Oh crap! The credit cards!

Wiping my tears, I shuffle to the desk in the ritual room. Jay had rifled through the drawers, scattering papers everywhere.

The Water Master

What was he looking for?

I paw through the pile until I find the credit card file. There are two, a Visa and a Mastercard. I called the 800 number for Mastercard and pressed '1' for account information.

"Your balance owed is ten-thousand-eight-hundred-seventy-two dollars and seventy-seven cents."

Frantic, I pressed zero five or six times until the computerized voice promises me that customer service will be with me momentarily.

I can't stop my leg from jiggling as I wait for a human voice. My heart is pounding.

Jay's blown through more than eight thousand dollars credit on gambling. Or—something.

A live voice interrupts my thoughts.

"This is Monica. How may I help you?"

"Monica," I cough. My throat is dry with fear and anger. "This is Susan Glasser. I need to cancel our account."

Monica asks for the usual security information.

"We can't cancel your account, but we can cancel your card. Is that what you want? You'll still be billed for the balance due."

"Yes. Thanks."

"What is the reason, please?"

"Umm…what are my choices?" I try to laugh, but it comes out half sob.

"Oh, we just document the reason for our records. Did you find a better interest rate elsewhere?"

"No. My husband…spent money without telling me. I need to get things back under control."

"Oh. I'm sorry. I can take care of that for you."

"Can I prevent my husband from getting another card with my name on it?"

"If you get a joint card, you will both have to sign the application."

Jay will forge my name no matter what safeguards I put into place.

"Thanks. Just cancel for now."

"Will do. Here's your confirmation number. Is there anything else I can do for you today?"

Can you turn back the clock for me?

I write down the confirmation number and hang up. I call the second credit card company and discover the card has a balance due of over twenty thousand dollars. The balance was less than a thousand dollars at the time we moved.

What in the hell is Jay doing?

Next, I call Star.

"Star? Hi! It's Susan."

"Hi there! What's up?"

I blurt out the events of the weekend. Star listens without interruption.

"Get out while you can. Jay is completely out of control."

"And I'm in debt up to my eyeballs. I think I might be hanging out at your house for awhile if that's all right with you."

"Of course, it is."

"I'll call Dale and have him take the dogs."

I call Tom and Karen, tell them the whole, ugly story

and ask if I could be late for work on Monday.

Tom says, "I think you need to talk with your attorney as well."

"I'm calling her next."

"Keep your keys and cell phone on you. Sleep with them. I'm serious!" says Tom.

Chapter Fifteen

૭>કર્ણ

I sleep in fits and starts. My throbbing shoulder drives me out of bed to the medicine cabinet in search of the hydrocodone prescribed for my back. I find the bottle at the back of my makeup drawer. It's empty. Jay again.

Really?

Frustrated, I toss the bottle into the trash and take four Ibuprofen instead. Back in bed, I fall into a light sleep. The worries about the future reflect in my nightmares. Around four in the morning I get up, shower, and start the coffee maker—nothing like adding a little speed to my current levels of adrenaline.

How Jay manages to work, gamble and have an affair, I have no idea. I wish I didn't care, but I do. I care because I let him into my heart. The pressure I feel in my chest every moment of every day tells he still has hold of me. But it's time to save myself. I try to keep busy, not think, not grieve. But the ache won't go away.

Tom and Karen drop by a little later to check on me, give hugs and more advice. As I wait for the bank to open, I pack a file box of important documents, including my investment information, to take to the office for safekeeping. I call the toll-free number to check the balance on my personal accounts and hold my breath waiting for the electronic voice to tell me the funds are intact. Jay's reach hasn't extended that far.

I drive into town and park at the bank at nine o'clock sharp. I enter the bank and go to the first customer service desk, where a hefty middle-aged woman greets me.

"I'm Ann. May I help you?"

"Yes. You sent notice about a bounced check and I need to review the history of my account and figure out what's going on. When I wrote the check, I was under the impression we had well over ten thousand dollars in that account."

The woman collects names and account numbers and punches buttons on her computer and keypad. She prints out the account history since we opened the account and pushes it across the desk to my sweating hands.

I review the details. The overdraw total at the bottom of the page is no surprise at this point, but the amount of money withdrawn from the account in the last few days takes my breath away.

Two and three thousand dollars at a time? His spending spree started less than a week ago.

"I need to stop payment on all the checks that are pending and close the account," I say.

"If you can cover the pending checks, it will save you a significant amount of money," says Ann. She proceeds to review the various fees and overdraft costs.

"I have some investments managed out of an account in Chicago. Can I transfer money to insure the current outstanding balance is covered, and then close the account?"

"No problem." Ann smiles like she knows what I'm

going through. "Can you tell me about what's going on?"

"My husband…ah…well, he's on some sort of spending spree…I don't know." To my embarrassment, I start to cry. "He's doing a run on all the credit cards and accounts. I just need to stop it."

"I've seen that happen before," says Ann. "You're doing the right thing."

Ann proceeds to type, print receipts and close the account, and open a new account in my name. The whole process takes twenty minutes, giving me time to control my tears and disappear into a dull gray place in my head.

With all transactions complete, she says, "So at this point, the checks are covered. The account is closed."

"Thanks so much," I say. "I appreciate your help."

The woman pats my hand. "Let me know if there's anything else you need."

I hate it when people feel sorry for me.

I head to work. All of a sudden I feel dizzy and pull over to the side of the road. I gasp for breath as the panic attack washes over me. My heart pounds. I suck for air but can't get a breath. Frantic, I searched the car for a paper bag and find one behind the front seat. As I put it to my mouth, I smell stale French fries. My skin buzzes like electricity is flowing through me and my fingers tingle.

A few breaths into the paper bag help, but the dizziness and tingling remain. I use every tactic I can think of to reduce my symptoms. I breath in through my nose and out through my mouth, try to relax my arms and shoulders. I try to go to my 'happy place,' floating on a canoe in the middle of the lake in Wisconsin. I turn on the radio to the NPR station. Samuel Barber's *Adagio for Strings* is playing, a piece that brings up deep grief even on a good day. Breaking down, I sob for everything I've lost—deep groaning sobs like I experienced when my father died.

After some time, I'm empty. I dig around in my purse to find a tissue. As the blood flow returns, my hands warm, my breathing calms and my thoughts quiet. I feel drugged, heavy and sad. My marriage is over. I once counseled women who had endured abuse from their crazy husbands for years and kept hoping their lives would change, but nothing had changed. Instead, the abuse increased. Sociopaths have to win at whatever game they choose to play, leaving hurt and confused victims in their wake. They might keep promises for awhile, but then they revert. Jay played the supportive husband and then drained all our accounts behind my back.

"Okay," I say out loud. "Things are going to be different. I can't do it alone. I need to ask for help."

I pick up my cell phone and call the office.

"Hi, it's me," I say to Karen.

"Hi. You okay?"

"Not really, but I will be. It's bad. He's blown through over thirty thousand dollars in credit cards and our bank account. I closed the account and covered the outstanding checks with some personal funds. That's all I can do for now."

"Oh, Susan, I'm so sorry," says Karen.

"I can't tell you how much I appreciate your support. I'll make it up to you."

"Don't worry about that. What's the next step?"

"My immediate next step is to ask for today off. I'm pretty useless right now."

"Okay. It's a slow day and I can handle the desk. Are you going home? Is it safe?"

"I assume Jay is at work, so I think I'm all right at home for awhile."

"Call me later today and let me know you're doing okay."

I end the call, start the car and head for the house.

When will I feel at home again?

I sit at the counter to think about my plans for the next few days.

Should I make arrangements to buy the house? It could be the easiest thing to do at this point. I could change it, remodel, make it mine. Am I crazy for wanting to stay here? I know I have friends who care. That's reason enough.

I'll keep my checkbook and bank cards on me at all times. Jay stole checks before, he'll do it again. Jay and Silvia are alike in that way. Why does Silvia need the money? Is she a gambler, too?

How the hell did this happen? I never understood why women couldn't see the red flags that were clear to everyone else. Falling in love really does blind you. Now it's obvious I had plenty of warning signs. It's a good thing I have my own money, otherwise leaving would be impossible.

I call Rosie and then Star to give them updates. Star tells me to come to the store until closing so we can go to her house together. A quick call to Dale and I have a temporary home for the dogs. He asks few questions. I'm grateful for that.

The Water Master

Once on the road, I check my rear view mirror often, afraid either Jay or Charlie is following me. I see no one until a squad car pulls in behind me. Dale is keeping an eye on me. The policeman doesn't leave until I am safely inside the herb store.

❧

Sweetums greets us at the door and follows us down a short hall to the guest room.

"This is yours for as long as you need it."

I look around the small, comfortable bedroom. The double bed takes up most of the space. It is covered with a handmade quilt in green and gold. Four photos taken of the same tree at the height of the four seasons hang on one wall, and a wall sculpture of the tree of life hangs above the bed.

"I've got one bathroom, so we'll be sharing, but you can hang towels on your door and there's room in the closet and dresser for clothes. Make yourself at home and I'll start dinner."

I unpack the few items I brought with me and stuff my cell phone in my pocket. I look around for the charger and realize I left it at home. That was dumb. My phone has a little less than a full charge. I turn it off for now.

The smell of garlic draws me to the kitchen.

"What can I do to help?" I ask.

"I'm just making spaghetti. I'm doctoring the Ragu, so if you could cut some onion to add to the garlic, and pull some oregano off the plant in the living room, I'd appreciate it."

I find a cutting board and a knife and begin chopping onion. Onion tears flow. After adding the onion to the simmering garlic, I find the oregano and lop off a small branch and a few leaves of basil for good measure.

Back in the kitchen, I say, "Your herbs look so healthy! When did you plant them?"

"I start them in the winter and by Solstice I can usually put them outdoors. I harvest numerous cuttings over the summer. And as you can see, they last long into the winter, as long as I bring them indoors. This is a great place for growing herbs. Hot and dry!"

"They smell wonderful. Can I add some basil to the sauce?"

"Absolutely!"

We cook in companionable silence for a few minutes, finish up the pasta and sauce, serve plates, pour wine and sit in the breakfast nook. The sun has long since set. Star pulls the shade over the darkened window by the table.

As we eat, I ask, "How did you get started in Wicca?"

"I felt disconnected from Christianity and eventually found my way to Wicca. My interest in herbs helped, and after I opened the herb store, people were naturally drawn to me for book recommendations and ritual suggestions. I decided to study with a High Priest in Seattle, and it took some time to get my Third Degree High Priestess designation. I really never intended to start a coven, but I saw a need for it in our area. Ronny was a regular customer and asked to study under me. By the time he earned his second degree initiation, he and I decided we should lead a coven. I enjoyed his company and his energy, but there was no romantic relationship there. He's gay and has a partner who is a born-again Christian."

"How can that relationship work?" I ask.

"It seems to work for them, but I couldn't do it."

After cleaning up the kitchen, I excuse myself to go to bed. Star walks to the guest room with me, turns down the bed and wishes me a good night's sleep. Grateful for her warm acceptance, I tear up again after she leaves the room.

The sheets smell of lavender. I smile through my tears. Star provided the perfect calming touch to an otherwise disturbing day.

༁

Late the next afternoon, Dale shows up at the office. He smiles at me over the counter. He has a really nice smile.

"Are you okay?" he asks. "You look a little pale."

I haven't been thinking much about how I look lately. I run my fingers through my hair, realizing I'd done nothing to make myself presentable. And Dale is more perceptive than most people.

"It's been a rough few days," I say. "How are the dogs doing?"

"Great. No problem at all. Do you want to go out for a beer or something? It'll give us a chance to catch up."

"Yuck. Not beer. But maybe a glass of wine?" I reply.

"Sounds good. I want to give all of you an update. Then we can go."

"Okay."

The Water Master

A few minutes later, with the last patient out the door, Karen, Tom, and I sit down with Dale in the break room. Marisa is still with a client.

"I need all the info you have at this point," says Dale. "What I've given to the DA so far is enough for an arrest warrant on Silvia, but I want to make sure she has the most accurate data. Have you made any changes to the information you sent me previously?"

"We fine-tuned some entries," says Karen.

"Do you need that today?" asks Tom.

"Yes. Can you print it out for me? I'll also need an electronic copy sent to my email."

"I'll do that for you. It will just take a few minutes," I say as I stand up.

Ten minutes later, I return to the break room with Dale's copies. Conversation stops.

"Were you talking about me?" I ask, with a faint smile.

"Yeah, actually, we were," says Tom. "Sorry, but we thought Dale should know what you've been dealing with."

"Well, Dale," I say. "Looks like you won't need to buy me that glass of wine after all."

"Sounds like you need one, though," says Dale.

"I'm definitely up for it," I say.

"Then we're still on," says Dale. "But first let me share some information with you about our progress."

Dale explains that when Silvia is eventually arrested and served with search warrants he will attempt to have her thrown in jail on a Friday to ensure she will be locked up through the weekend. This will give the police time to thoroughly search her property and provide a chance to see how Charlie might respond.

Dale has also been in touch with the investigators at Medicare, Blue Cross and Group Health. The separate investigations have turned up the same patterns of fraud and embezzlement. Each will file their charges, which are Federal, on the following Monday, causing another warrant to be issued. Hopefully, the timing will be such that Silvia will remain in jail, and Federal bail will be high enough that she will stay there.

"So, it will be months before we have to have our case together for court."

"It'll be a relief to have that bitch in jail!" says Karen, under her breath.

"I'm worried," says Tom. "Do you think Silvia and Charlie are dangerous?"

"Possibly." Dale pauses and then lets out a deep sigh. "Probably."

"I don't feel safe!" I say.

"I'll have squad cars doing drive-bys and checking in with all of you on a regular basis for awhile," says Dale.

"If you watch enough TV, you know that surveillance rarely prevents retaliation."

"I know," says Dale, "but it's better than nothing."

"Anyone can hide from a squad car," I say. "You can see them coming from a mile away around here."

Dale reaches over and pats my arm. "I promise we'll do our best to make this as painless as possible."

With that, Dale stands up, and I am once again struck by his height. His presence makes me feel safe, but I know better. My thoughts are jumbled as I gather my belongings and follow Dale out of the office to his car.

At the door of his car, I hesitate. Even though I know my marriage is over, Jay doesn't. This is a friendly drink with Dale, but Jay will be furious if he discovers it.

"Do you mind if I take my own car?" I ask.

"No problem," says Dale. "I'll meet you at Francisco's over at the strip mall."

"Is that the little restaurant by the herb store?"

"That's the place!"

I get into my car and check to make sure my 'to go' bag is still in the back seat. Even though I am staying at Star's, there is still the possibility of needing to make a quick exit. I touch it like it is my safety talisman—the only thing really mine at the moment—and drive off to meet Dale.

We find a quiet booth in the back of the Italian restaurant. The smell of garlic makes me hungry. I order white wine. Dale chooses a local beer.

"I'd like some garlic bread!" I say.

"Sounds good. I'll order some calamari too."

Dale waves the waitress to the table, and she takes our order.

"So, I want to hear your story about Jay from the beginning," says Dale.

I sigh as look away. Tears burn as I blink them back. Dale's patient demeanor and kind eyes say he has all the time in the world to listen.

"Can I tell you something first?"

"Sure. What?"

The Water Master

"On top of all the issues I had with the irrigation, I think Jay stole my mother's wedding rings, and dug around in my underwear drawers for what, I don't know. It creeped me out. And my journals went missing in October."

"You're kidding!"

"There's been so much going on. Is there a way you can find my rings? Do you think Jay pawned them?"

"Give me a description later and I'll have someone check out the pawn shops."

"Does Charlie have other friends?" I ask.

"Not likely. Everyone pretty much just puts up with Charlie."

"Except Jay. He seems to like him," I say.

"Right. So give me some history," says Dale.

"A few nights ago—"

"No, I want to hear it from the first day you met him till now."

I blink a few times.

"Okay, but why do you want to know?"

"It helps me know you better, and therefore understand him better. I have a feeling I'm not done with him."

I feel a chill. "What do you mean by that?"

"There's a few things not adding up. Just tell me the story."

I scooch back into the corner of the booth and put my legs on the bench. Leaning my head against the wall so I won't have to look at Dale, I tell him how Jay and I met, how he made me feel, how in love we were, that it wasn't until later I noticed he never mentioned family and he seemed to have no close friends. I share some of my family history, my dad's patent, my inheritance, and Star's theory that Jay pursued me for my money. Then I review the most recent events, including the move out West and the details about his change in personality once we arrived. Now and again, I sneak looks at Dale. His expression never changes. He gives no hint of how he feels about my story. But, he is so focused, I have a feeling he will later write notes of what I say, word for word.

By the time I finish talking, I had plowed through the garlic bread and the calamari, along with two glasses of wine. I turn in my seat and face him.

"I'm so sorry! I've eaten everything!"

"I sneaked in a few bites here and there. Nervous eating?"

"No. I'm starving. I've been so stressed lately that I haven't eaten much, or well, for that matter."

"After hearing your story, I can understand why."

I look down at the crumbs surrounding my appetizer plate. "I've made a mess of it too—in more ways than one," I say.

"I'm not surprised by it. People like Jay can fool the best detectives and prosecutors in the country—and they have. The fact that he fooled you shouldn't be taken to heart."

"So, what's next?" I ask.

"I'm going to follow up on some things. My biggest concern right now is your safety. Have you contacted the domestic violence services?"

"No. I should, but I don't want to. I'm staying with

Star, and I removed my important papers and my personal valuables and I've told the Elwins, Star, and my neighbors what's going on."

Dale's eyebrows shoot up in surprise. "How'd you know to do all that? Most of the time I'm begging women to do exactly that, but they won't."

"I've led a secret life as a counselor. I know the drill. Do I want to do the drill? No. I feel like an idiot. But I know it's the right thing to do."

"Good job so far, then. You're pretty amazing!"

I smile. "Oh, yeah, I'm amazing all right. I dump my whole life, such as it was, to come to the desert and support my loving husband who turns out to be a psychopath!"

We are both quiet for a minute while Dale eats the last of the garlic bread. I look into space.

"What's going on up there?" asks Dale, pointing to my forehead.

"I was just thinking how nice everyone is. The Elwins, Marisa, you, Star. I've never had friends like this before."

"Maybe you never let people be friends like this before," says Dale.

I chew my lip as the tears threaten to overflow once more. Dale reaches across the table and squeezes my hand.

"You're gonna be okay. I'll make sure of it," he says.

I take a deep breath. By telling this caring man my story, I feel like a weight is gone. But, I don't want to be his pity case. I sit up and square my shoulders.

"I'm ready to do whatever's necessary," I say. "It's clear I have no marriage, so tell me what you need."

"First things first," says Dale as he wipes his mouth with a napkin. He takes a sip of beer. "Have you made a decision about letting us into the house for a look around?"

"Oh, yeah. That request was lost in the shuffle. Whenever you want, it's yours. I'll need to be there to let you in. Just let me know."

"We'll be there before you leave for work tomorrow. How's that?"

"Good."

Dale pulls out his cell phone and taps a few buttons.

"Louie? Dale. We're on at the Glasser place tomorrow at seven."

He ends the call and stuffs his phone back into his shirt pocket.

"Wow. You're really chomping at the bit, aren't you?"

"I have been for a year. Let's get this thing rollin' and see what we find."

The waitress clears off the table and we chat a little more about the area, the summer heat and favorite vacation spots. As he walks me to my car, I realize how easy it is to talk to him. But he is just doing his job.

Dale follows me to Star's house and walks me to the door.

"I think you're as secure as you can be for now. All I ask is that you call me every morning before you leave and every night when you get home. I'll keep a close eye on you."

Puzzled, I ask, "Isn't that more than you usually do for women in my situation?"

"Yes. See you tomorrow." Dale turns and walks down

the steps to his car. I wave goodbye, and close and lock the door.

☞☜

I am at the house by six-thirty the next morning. As I let myself in the front door, I hear a vehicle approaching and recognize the chugging of Charlie's truck. I rush inside, shut the door, and peek through the blind. Charlie slows the car to a crawl and glares at the house. A few minutes later, a van and two squad cars pull up to the front of the house. Dale unfolds himself out of one squad car, along with a pretty, petite woman in plainclothes. I meet them at the door, and as I let them in I see Rosie running toward the house.

"Are you all right?" asks Rosie, panic making her voice squeak.

"Sorry to scare you, Rosie," I say. I explain about the police search. Rosie pales.

"I hope they don't find anything. That would be awful if the Clements were murdered in your house."

"I'm not thinking about that yet," I say. "I'm just taking this a day at a time."

"Okay. Let me know if you need anything. What do you want me to tell all the other neighbors? You know they'll be asking!"

"Just tell them the truth. That's the best idea, don't you think?" I reply.

"Okay. I just don't want to share anything confidential."

Rosie wanders back to her house and I go inside

mine. Five technicians are milling around, radios squawking, gloves snapping, cameras flashing, preparing to do a thorough search of the house. My house. Without warning I feel weak in the knees and sit on the floor in front of the door.

Dale rushes to my side. "What's wrong?" he asks, looking worried.

"It all just hit me," I say, head in my hands. "This is awful."

Dale pulls me up and puts his arm around my waist. "Let's go to the kitchen. Have you eaten?"

"No."

"Then let me make you some coffee."

Dale sits me at the counter and rummages through the cabinets for a coffee cup.

"I take my cream and sugar with a little coffee," I say in an attempt at levity.

"Gotcha."

Dale starts a pot of coffee to brew and leaves to talk with his team for a few minutes. I stare at the cabinets I have yet to refinish. Once the coffee pot beeps, he returns and pours me a cup. He slides half-and-half across the counter, along with the sugar. I doctor my coffee and take a few sips.

"Thanks, Dale," I say. I take a few more sips and begin to feel human again.

"Cereal or toast?" asks Dale.

"Cereal. Cupboard next to the fridge."

The sweetness of his care washes over me.

Dale fixes me a bowl of Wheaties and I eat without

noticing. I can hear the crew moving furniture around in the living room and in the bedroom.

"What are they going to do exactly?" I ask.

"They'll be pulling up carpet, using black lights to look for body fluids, looking for anything that's unusual," he says.

I shiver. "I'll be at Star's, so take all the time you need."

"Uh-huh," says Dale as his attention is drawn to the activity in the living room.

"I'm better now. I'll get out of your hair."

"Okay," says Dale distracted by the on-going activity.

I smile. *Men. Singular focus, no ability to multi-task.*

I find my purse and car keys, preparing to leave, but then I remember Charlie's drive by the house.

"Dale, one more thing. Charlie drove by the house about six-thirty this morning and gave it a good hard look."

"Thanks for telling me."

"I think he's Jay's spy."

"Could be," says Dale.

"Hey," I say. "Tell these guys to take a look under the garden. Isn't that where the bodies are always buried?"

"Why did you say that?" he says.

Jarred by the harshness of his voice, I say, "Um—I was trying to joke around? Bad joke, huh?"

"No. Seriously. I don't take anything for granted. Why did you say that?"

"Other than that's where the flood was, no reason. Really, I was joking."

Dale searches my face. "I might take you up on that."

"Crap. I wish I'd never said anything," I say. "Explaining this to Charlie is going to be hard enough as it is. A torn-up back yard is going to send him right over the edge!"

"Don't worry. We'll take care of it," says Dale, distracted again.

"Easy for you to say," I mutter.

෨෴ඐ

I am out of sorts when I arrive at work. I give Tom and Karen an update on the events at my house, and call Star to confirm there is no chance I will return home again anytime soon.

"Do you mind having a long-term roomie for a while?"

"Sure," says Star. "Meet me at the store after work and you can follow me home."

The day moves along in an easy rhythm for a change. The patients are pleasant, and everyone has the right insurance information. I appreciate a non-stress day and we close the office at five without incident. I call Dale, as promised.

"Hi, Dale. It's Susan."

"Hi! How was your day?"

"Uneventful. And yours?"

"Ah. Well. Somewhat eventful."

I feel the familiar clenching of my stomach. "What did you find?"

"I'm not ready to talk about it just yet. But your house is, ah, unlivable at the moment."

"Can I come back and pick up some clothes?"

"You'll need one of us with you."

"That bad?" I ask.

"Remember when I said our crew always tries to put things back the way they should be?"

"Yeeeaaahhh."

"Not sure that's gonna happen."

"Well, shit! Do we have a John Wayne Gacy situation?"

"I don't think we'll be tearing down the house or anything, and I don't think there are thirty bodies in the basement, but we have found some clues that are leading in a couple of different directions and we need more time. We had to take some—ah, items with us."

"Well, I was planning to remodel anyhow," I say.

Dale laughs. "Great attitude. Are you going to Star's?"

"I'm meeting her at the herb store and following her home."

"Have a good night and call me in the morning. I'll have someone meet you here about seven."

"Okay. G'nite."

I end the call. It is hard to remember a time when my life wasn't upside down. Since coming to the desert, nothing has been in my control. I counted on a happy marriage and a daily dose of gardening to make me content. None of that materialized. At least Star is willing to let me stay at her house. I don't want to be alone.

I scan the parking lot as I pull into a space in front of the herb store. I had done this all the time in the city, where I was more vigilant about possible dangers. Any unfamiliar cars? Anything out of place? So, I make sure to park right by the front door of the herb store, and leave room between me and neighboring cars.

∞•∞

Charlie watches Susan get out of her car at the herb store. He is furious.

How dare she let that asshole search my house. MY HOUSE! She will pay for this.

∞•∞

Star is waiting on after-work customers and the store is busy. I curl up with a magazine in the oversized chair. Star nods toward the teapot on the table in front of me and I make a cup of chamomile tea with lemon. I love the sweet, grassy taste of the chamomile. I close my eyes and breathe in the scent of the store. It is tea tree oil with a hint of mint and cinnamon, and an overlay of the ever-present Nag Champa incense.

Star finishes up with her customers and puts the CLOSED sign in the window.

"I'll be a few minutes while I close out the register," says Star.

"No problem. I'm reading an article about the healing wonders of Cat's Claw."

I'm not really reading. I'm staring at the page and thinking confused thoughts about the search at the house.

What happened there?

"I'm ready!" says Star.

I snap out of my thoughts and set down my tea cup and magazine.

The Water Master

"Do you want me to wash this?"

"No. I'll take care of it in the morning. Let's get out of here."

Chapter Sixteen

❧

Now that I'm staying at Star's, I feel better than I have in weeks. I'm finally able to sleep and now have the mental space to relax a little.

I hear Star in the shower, so I go to the kitchen for coffee. A mug, a pitcher of milk and a sugar bowl sit on a placemat in front of the coffee pot. Star's thoughtfulness is touching. I sip my coffee as I look out onto the gray morning of mid-winter.

I hear Star shuffling back to her bedroom and yell out, "Can I use the shower?"

"Yeah, it's all yours."

Taking my coffee with me, I walk to the guestroom and grab my clothes for the day before going into the bathroom. The shower beats on my back and head, and I use Star's lavender shampoo and cream rinse. Of course, I forgot to bring my own. After drying off and lathering my body with rose-scented body lotion, putting on my makeup and blow-drying my hair, I'm ready to take on the day.

Star sits in the breakfast nook eating oatmeal and reading the morning paper.

"There's oatmeal if you want it."

"Thanks. Do you have raisins?"

"In the pantry, middle shelf."

I find the raisins and cinnamon, add them to my oatmeal and sit across from Star.

"You're in the paper today," says Star.

"What?"

"Here." She hands the paper across the table. "Front page, regional section."

Heart sinking, I read the article.

An unnamed source informed this reporter that police were searching a home at 100206 E. Wayne Rd. in Pasco. The current residents, Jay and Susan Glasser could not be reached for comment. Police declined to comment. The house is rented by the Glassers and is owned by Charlie Gottschalk, 500102 S. Eaton.

"Jay's going to see this and go ballistic, to say nothing of what Charlie will do," I say with disgust. "I'm going to call Dale."

Dale answers on the fourth ring.

"Sorry. Just got out of the shower. What's up?"

"Have you read the paper?"

"No, but I bet there's a blurb about our search?"

"Yeah. What's going on?"

"Between you and me, I'm the unnamed source. I wanted to leak some information to let Charlie know we're still looking into the Clements' disappearance."

"How thoughtful of you!" I snap. "Now what do I do?"

"We'll work it out! Don't worry."

"You realize on top of all this, you guys are throwing Silvia in jail soon, right?"

"Yep. Trust me. There are methods to my madness."

"I hope you know what you're doing. I'm pretty scared here."

"Let me talk to Star and you run over to your house to get the rest of the stuff you'll need. I have a guy there waiting for you. And, Susan, can you do me a big favor this morning?"

"What."

"Once you collect your things from the house, go back to Star's and stay put. Don't go to work. I just want you to stay at Star's house for awhile."

"I've got a job to do!" I say, my voice rising. "The Elwins need me!"

"Calm down. Steady there, girl. I want you where we can keep an eye on you today. The article in the paper is going to up Charlie's game, and I want you to be prepared for whatever he might do."

"So, how is not working going to help?"

Dale hesitates.

My heart pounds. Now I'm pissed. "Are you using me as bait?"

"In a sense, yes." Dale sounds very businesslike in a situation that is bad business for me.

"You've got to be kidding me! Is this even legal?"

"I think you can be really helpful right now. Someone will be keeping an eye on you today. I guarantee you'll be okay. I just want you in one place in case Charlie decides to do something stupid. You'll be fine."

"Dale. Really. You don't know that. You don't know what Charlie, or for that matter Jay, is going to do and neither do I."

I slap the phone into Star's hand and stare at my breakfast, arms crossed and foot wiggling, while Star says,

"Uh-huh...Okay...Yeah," throughout her conversation with Dale.

"That was a very one-sided conversation," I say like a spurned lover.

"He told me to tell you that he already contacted Karen and told her you won't be at work. The police will watch the office as well."

"Star, I hate to drag you into this. It doesn't sound like we're safe."

Star smiles. "I'm okay, so don't worry about me."

I'm completely baffled. "What the hell is going on?"

"Susan, you have to trust Dale. He's onto something."

"Fine!" I feel like a petulant child. I want to be home, somewhere I could call home, feel at home, feel safe. Nothing is right and I feel used.

"So, I have nothing to read, nothing to accomplish this morning. Is there anything I can do for you here?" I ask.

"I think a day with no worries is just what you need. I have books, magazines, TV and stereo. Relax, take a nap. Sound good?"

"Do I have a choice?"

I finish my oatmeal while Star prepares for work. We leave the house together and I see an unmarked police car parked along the curb. If I notice it, then Charlie or Jay will, too. That is fine with me.

When I arrive at the house, a squad car is parked in the driveway and a uniformed officer who looks like a teenager, pimples, greasy forehead and all, gets out of his car to meet me.

"I hate to ask you this, but can I see ID before we go in?"

I sigh. "Sure."

I dig around in my purse for my wallet and pull out my driver's license. "That's me."

"Thanks, Mrs. Glasser."

I shudder at the name and rush to say, "Call me Susan."

"I'm Officer Merrifield."

I nod. Merrifield leads the way to the front door, unlocks it and holds open the screen door for me while I walk in.

I freeze mid-stride.

Furniture is pushed to the walls, the carpet is gone, floorboards are missing. Pieces of the wall under the front window are gone, as well as the window sill.

I turn to the officer.

"What the hell!"

"Ma'am?"

"Jesus! Dale said your people were 'neat?' This is a disaster!"

I burst into tears. Officer Merrifield takes a step back, surprised at my outburst.

I wipe my nose with my sleeve. I have no tissues and hope I can find some in this mess. I step over the holes in the floor like they are land mines and find more chaos in the bedroom. Pieces of the carpet are cut out, the wall above the bed as gone, the insulation visible. I continue to cry as I find a suitcase in the back of the closet and pack as many things as I can. The bathroom is intact, but I can tell where items have been moved and returned to the general area where they were found. I stand by the toilet and blow my nose on scratchy toilet paper trying to calm down.

The Water Master

This is it. All of the hopes I had for a happy life in the country have been snatched away by a crazy, sick husband and a psycho landlord. None of it makes sense, and I am appalled at how easily I've become a victim. I take a deep, shuddering breath, stand up straighter, run my fingers through my hair, and determine that this is never going to happen to me again.

I find my meditation pillows and the athame that Jay presented to me when I became his student. While it is a ritual instrument, it is still a knife. I slide it into my hand-tooled, leather sheath and put it into my purse.

Officer Merrifield carries my suitcase and toiletries out to my car for me while I look in the kitchen. The tiles are marked with little circles of magic marker. I don't want to see what is within them. Looking out the back door, trenches run in a grid throughout the back yard and the garden is pile of dirt.

Did they find bodies back there?

I grab my cell phone charger and leave the house as if demons are chasing me.

"Thanks, Officer. Sorry for the meltdown."

"No problem, Ma'am. Let us know if there is anything else you need."

My drive back to Star's house is uneventful, though I find myself looking in the rearview mirror more than usual and am grateful to see the unmarked car a few car lengths behind me.

Letting myself into the house with the spare key Star gave me, Sweetums greets me with leg rubbing and swishes into the kitchen to lie on the cushion under the window.

The Water Master

I pour myself another cup of coffee and slide into the breakfast nook. I stare out the window, feeling bleak. *When I met Jay, we went to dinners, shows, took short trips, cooked together. When did I choose this path of pleasing him and ignoring my own needs? Why didn't I notice that he was not focused on enjoying me, but on molding me?*

If I had refused his offer to be my teacher and guide in Wicca, would that have made a difference? I don't think so, but it gave him one more thing to be smarter and better at. Jay is so charismatic. He made me feel like I was at the center of his universe, and I'd never had that experience before. But he changed from being a loving and attentive boyfriend to a controlling and manipulative husband.

Removed from his influence, I can see my role a little better, but it will take a long time to figure out. Right now I have to focus on the danger I face.

Late in the afternoon Dale calls me.

"I'm at the front door, can you let me in?"

I hang up, walk to the front door and peek through the spy hole. Dale peeks back. I open the door.

"Hi," I say with no enthusiasm.

"You look….not so good," says Dale.

"Yeah. Well, I was at the house."

"Pretty bad, huh?"

"I'm sure you've seen it. It's a demolition zone."

"Susan, I really didn't think we would find that much evidence. I'm surprised at the huge amount of evidence we found. The lab needs time to process everything."

"So what do I do in the meantime, and why are we playing cat and mouse?" I slump against the closed door and put my face in my hands.

Dale reaches over and taps me on the top of the head. "Hey. Believe it or not, I have a plan."

I look at him with dejection. "I don't."

"You will. I know this feels like shit right now, but we're going to get through this."

I look in his eyes. He looks sincere. He actually looks—*oh, dear*—handsome. *No. No. He's a cop, a detective. He's going to use me to play this little game, and then he'll be done.*

"Can you get us something to drink?" asks Dale as he steps down into the living room.

"What do you want?"

Dale look at his watch and sighs. "Water, I guess."

I smile. *I'm having a glass of wine. Too bad for him!*

After pouring my wine and preparing a glass of ice water with lemon for Dale, I settle myself on one end of the couch. Sweetums jumps up on my lap for a tummy rub. Dale loosens his tie and runs his hand through his hair.

"What did you find at the house?" I ask.

"Enough to know that it's a crime scene. We found evidence of blood underneath the living room carpet and beneath the paint job on the window sill in the living room. The bedroom showed a lot of blood spatter above the bed and on the walls—"

I shudder. "Jesus. And I was walking around that house without knowing any of that!"

"Charlie did a good job of covering it up. Except he didn't notice the blood on the kitchen floor."

"Neither did I. The tiles are speckled with all those colors—who would notice?"

"I did, the day I was at your house."

"I remember you looking at the floor. How did you see that?"

"Practice," says Dale, with sadness. "I noticed a few spots around the edges, where the floor wasn't cleaned as well."

"I guess it's obvious the Clements were murdered there."

"We think so. We just don't have any bodies. We need the lab work. It would be normal for Charlie's fingerprints to be found in the house, since it's his house. It's going to be very difficult to prove he did it."

"So, now what?" I ask.

"It's complicated," says Dale. "I wanted you here today so I didn't have to worry about you, but I know I can't keep you here. Go to work as normal. One of my guys will follow you around and keep an eye on the house, but we can't have someone here all the time. So, I'm going to give you a present."

He reaches into the pocket of his sport coat and pulls out two small items about the size of my car key device.

"What are they?" I ask, as he hands them to me.

"GPS tracking."

"What?"

"Keep one on you at all times, I'm going to put the other one on your car. That way we'll know where you are."

"What do you think Charlie will do?" I say, as the reality of the situation dawns on me.

Dale looks serious. "We don't know. That's the problem. If he murdered the Clements and thinks he got away with it, he might target you. I think in his mind, all the bad stuff that's happened is your fault. You moved here, took Silvia's job and suddenly she's in trouble. He can't or won't see that Silvia made her own mess. And now you let us search his house, where he likely committed a murder."

My throat goes dry and I wipe my sweating palms on my thighs.

"I just thought...he was j-just a...an...ignorant man," I stuttered. "Not a murderer."

Dale takes my hand and holds it. I stare out the window and sigh.

"Do Charlie and Silvia actually know about the embezzlement investigation?"

"I'm sure they do. You shared enough with Jay for him to tell Charlie. And I'm sure Charlie told Silvia. They know something's up."

"If they realize Silvia's in trouble and Charlie knows he's under suspicion for murder, why are they still hanging around? Why aren't they acting like normal criminals and getting the heck out of town?"

"They think they're smarter than we are," says Dale. "They think they can win."

"I'll do what I have to do." I look into his eyes. "But promise me you'll move fast on this. I can't live like this. If something doesn't change soon, I'm moving back to Chicago."

Dale doesn't break his gaze. "That's motivation enough, because I'd rather you didn't leave town."

The Water Master

I pull my hand away. "Then get on it," I say.

Dale spends a few minutes showing me how the GPS works. I put one device in my purse, then walk outside with Dale and watch as he attaches the other device to the wheel well on my car. As I wave goodbye to him, I see the unmarked car follow Dale out of the subdivision. All of a sudden, I feel exposed. I hurry back into the house and lock the door.

࿐

Charlie and Jay meet for a few beers at the tavern in downtown Pasco.

"We have to figure out our next steps. Where does that bitch get off letting the cops in my house?"

"Calm down, Charlie. I'm sure it's nothing," says Jay.

What are they looking for at Charlie's house and why isn't Charlie telling me anything about it? He is such a dumbass!"

"Everything will be just fine," Jay says.

He takes a swig of beer and tries to swallow his frustration.

I wish Charlie had a few more brains and a little less odor. Whatever Susan's up to, she's getting a little too chummy with that cop. She's still my wife. She's mine and she will pay. I just have to wait for the right time.

Chapter Seventeen

ঌৄৢ

Gathering the coven during the holiday season is no easy task. Various parties and family gatherings of the coven members prevent the group from holding a Yule ritual on the Winter Solstice. Star decides to have a small Yule celebration at the house a week before Winter Solstice, and on a Friday night instead of the usual Saturday. The coven members draw names for gift-giving, which will be part of the simple ritual. The wind blows hard, and dark, heavy clouds spit rain as I drive home from work.

Star's car is already in the garage.

"You're home early," I say as I walk into the warm kitchen.

"I decided to close. Business was horrible today. The weather kept everyone inside."

"A good book and a hot fire would've felt great today," I say.

"If you'll settle for a gas-burning fireplace, go ahead and turn it on," replies Star.

I go into the living room and flip the switch to the fireplace. With a whoosh, the gas flame comes on. Sweetums plops herself down on the rug in front of the fireplace screen and grooms herself.

The Water Master

With reluctance, I leave the heat of the fire and walk back into the kitchen to help Star unload some groceries. A crock pot of chili has simmered all day. Star is mixing up cornbread and I start the salad.

"Is anyone else bringing food?" I ask.

"Appetizers and dessert. That's about it." Star blows hair out of her face.

We work together in the kitchen for a few more minutes when the doorbell rings, announcing the first guest. Ronny carries a plate of bacon-wrapped water chestnuts, which I almost rip out his hands.

"I love these things!" I chirp. "It's been years since I've had one of these."

Ignoring Ronny's struggle to remove his winter coverings, I rush to the kitchen to unwrap his treats.

"Yum," I say as I bite into the first of many I will eat tonight. "Nothing like it."

Realizing I've left Ronny to his own devices, I yell back to the living room. "Sorry, that was rude!"

Ronny laughs. "No problem. At least you were happy to see me!"

I set the platter down and go back to the living room.

"Let me take your coat," I say.

He hands me his things and I carry them back to my room. By the time I return to the living room, the whole group has come through the front door at once and I busy myself arranging appetizers and ensuring everyone has something to drink.

The group settles in the living room. Star and Ronny haven't told us what the ritual will be tonight.

The Water Master

Ronny stands up. "Yule is the celebration of the return of the light as represented by the rebirth of the Sun King. In early Christian times, in order to get the locals to comply with Christian beliefs, the church determined that three days after the Solstice, a celebration of the birth of Christ would occur. For pagans, this day was already celebrated because this was the day when the daylight was noticeably longer. Hope was rekindled on this day. Winter was halfway over, and the promise of warmth returning to the land to bring food, crops, new lambs and calves and a release from the cold of winter could finally be imagined.

"While it is more likely than not that Jesus was actually born in the spring, the symbolism of Jesus' birth is much the same as that of the sun returning to warm the earth. Both promise salvation. Both give us hope for the future. Both are a celebration of new life."

Ronny sits down and Star stands up. In her hand she holds a goblet and a bottle of wine. She pours the wine into the goblet and says, "As the cup is female and the wine contains the spirit of the Sun God, conjoined, they become the truth and the life and the future."

She holds the goblet in front of her and says, "Tonight we share our hopes for the future. The Sun God is coming back to life, in all of his strength and virility. The Goddess is weakening as she prepares to give birth in the Spring from the sowing of his seed. Take a moment to meditate on how the light is returning to your life, and prepare to share."

Star turns the lights off and the flicker of the fireplace reflects on the walls. The room grows quiet as the coven members settle into meditation. I sit on the floor, legs crossed beneath me and close my eyes. I slow my breath and focus on the light playing inside my eyelids.

What light is in my life at all right now? The man I once loved is a poor representation of the Sun God. If it weren't for my friends…oh yeah. They are my light. They're the one thing I can count on. I completely misread Jay, so how can I trust these other people who supposedly care for me?

As I think this through, I lose myself in the meditation and when Star rings the bell to end it, I still don't have an answer.

I open my eyes. Star leaves the lights off, allowing the dark to maintain the mood and offering a little privacy to each person as we share.

"As I pass the goblet, please share how the light is returning to your life, sip from the goblet and pass it on with a 'Blessed Be.'"

Ronny takes the goblet first. "I will share more of my spiritual life with my partner, without fear, to allow light back into my life."

He sips from the goblet and passes it to a round woman with a sweet smile named Renata.

"To let more light into my life, I will listen better and give advice less quickly."

The group laughs. We all know exactly what she is talking about!

As the cup passes from person to person, I find myself relaxed and mellow. I'm not thinking about my response.

The goblet pushes into my hand, warm to the touch, waking me from my reverie. As I look into the red liquid I say, "With the help of my friends, I will live in peace and will not accept fear."

I hear gentle sigh of approval coming from the circle. I sip the wine, pass it to Star and say, "Blessed Be."

Star says, "I will let the light return to my life by letting things be."

She sips from the goblet and says, "Blessed Be!" She holds the cup up above her head and says, "As the warmth returns to the earth, the ground will be fertile for new seed growth. Tonight you have begun preparation for planting. Nurture the seeds of your intuition. In your mind's eye, maintain the vision of the promise you've made to yourself this night and celebrate the coming of the Sun each day."

I wonder if and when the sun will ever brighten my life again.

༺◦༻

IMBOLG- INITIATION

*"...to these I will teach things
that are yet unknown..."*

༺◦༻

Chapter Eighteen

❧

Since the discovery of murder in my house, my sleep has been disturbed almost every night now. Last night was worse than normal, each nightmare more terrifying than the one before. First I am standing at the top of a tall building in Chicago, gazing at a beautiful sunrise over Lake Michigan, when I hear someone running up behind me. Knowing I will be shoved over the side to my death, I woke up with heart pounding. In another I am trapped in a locked car. Water pours in through the sides of the doors and I will drown if I don't act quickly. Just before sucking in water, I woke gulping air. The nightmare that made me turn on the light involved my mom and dad reaching to me through choking smoke.

Although Star assures me that her house is my home for now, I feel uncomfortable rooting around the kitchen for a bowl of cereal—a comfort I would have found in my own house on a sleepless night. Instead, I go to the bathroom, gulp some water, empty my bladder and return to bed. Sweetums pokes her head through the partially opened bedroom door, jumps on the bed, sticks her nose against mine and curls up on my lap for a snooze.

I check the GPS on the nightstand for the hundredth time and decide it is best to keep it on me. I sleep in socks, so slide it into my sock. Not the nicest feeling. The cat looks at me in disgust while I maneuver, and then we both settle down once more.

Petting Sweetums calms me, and eventually I fall asleep with the light on. Waking to the alarm at five, I feel like I haven't slept at all. The nightmares nag at me.

Star and I share a quiet breakfast. The thump of the newspaper on the front door gives us both a start. Star retrieves it and we both read for awhile before I leave for work.

As I walk to my car, I search for my cop companion and am relieved to see his car far down the street. I let out my breath when I see him pull in behind me as I leave the subdivision.

I am the first one in the office. I open the front door and a woosh of cold air greets me. I stand inside the front door as the hair on the back of my neck prickles. I hold my breath, listening for any noise, ready to run out the front. I run anyhow, and my cop follower jumps out of his car as I rush toward him.

"Something's wrong in there! I think someone broke in!"

"Is there anyone inside?"

"I don't know!"

The officer radios for backup and we wait. He draws his gun and holds it at his side. I withdraw to the other side of his car. I am terrified. Where are Tom and Karen?

Within minutes, three squad cars arrive with sirens screaming and right behind them, Karen and Tom drive up. Karen's face is white with fear and Tom is grim as they jump out of their car.

"Are you all right?" Karen screams as she runs toward me.

"I'm fine!"

Karen reaches me and hugs me hard. Tom, following and frantic, says, "What's wrong? What happened?"

"I think someone broke into the office," I say.

We huddle together while the police carefully approach the door and go inside. Dale races into the parking lot in his unmarked car and runs over to us.

"Are you okay?" he asks.

"We're fine," I say. "Just find out what's going on, will you?"

We stand next to the squad car, shivering in the cold and in fear. Eventually, all the policemen come out, holstering their firearms, and Dale reaches into his car for his radio mic. I can hear him asking for detectives. He then walks back to us.

"You ready to go in?" he asks with a grim look on his face.

"What'd they do?" asks Tom.

"It looks like they took all of the computers, and dumped files all over the floor. The security cameras are toast..."

"Dale! Our investigation files! They're gone?"

"Relax, Susan!" says Tom. "Dale has what he needs, and we have a backup."

"We do?" I ask.

"You do?" asks Dale.

"Yeah. All the files are uploaded every night to an offsite service. It's going to take awhile, but we can retrieve all of it."

"Whoever took the computers will still be able to see

the evidence you collected. That could be a problem," says Dale. "Phone numbers, addresses, Social Security numbers...what a mess."

Karen wipes away her tears and we walk into the office, picking our way through the items scattered on the floor.

It *is* a mess. All the files that we had carefully reviewed and organized are scattered across the floor in the conference room and hallway. The desks are bare of computers and monitors. Entry was gained by breaking the back window. Somehow the alarm had been tampered with, so whoever broke in had plenty of time to take what they wanted.

I look at the scattered piles on my desk, and notice the drawer where I stashed my jewelry and other personal items for safekeeping is open and empty.

"Dale!" I cry. "My stuff! It's gone!"

"What stuff?" he asks as he walks across broken glass to my desk.

"I hid my valuables here after my rings went missing. They're gone." Tears run down my cheeks and I make no effort to stop them.

Dale sighs and puts his arm around me. "Crap."

This time I lean into him and let him hold me while I sob.

"Dale, it's not just my jewelry. The account info about my money back in Illinois is gone too."

Dale gives me a worried look. He squeezes me and let me go. "We'll find it, Susan. We'll get it back."

Tom calls the insurance company requesting an investigator to come out and assess damages. I wipe my nose, tell myself to buck up, and help Karen determine what else is missing. Nothing can be moved or touched until the police finish taking pictures and investigating the building.

I can't stop shivering. The office is freezing and my nerves are raw. I can only imagine what Tom and Karen are feeling. They've worked in this office for years, and this is the first time trouble like this has ever happened to them.

The inventory of missing items includes all the computers and the personal items from my desk. That is it. The sample drug closet wasn't touched. All the security cameras were busted up by a heavy object, probably a hammer. The files, while scattered over the floors and tables, look intact. The reality of the theft dawns on all of us at about the same time.

"Dale, this is about the investigation against Silvia, isn't it?" asks Tom.

"This certainly isn't your typical doctor office break-in," says Dale as he chews his cheek. "Let's get out of here and go down to the station. We need to do formal interviews with each of you."

"What about the patients?" I ask. "We have appointments today."

"The best we can do now is put a sign on the door. All of our records will have to be accessed from off-site," says Karen. "We'll have to take care of it later."

I scrounge around for a pen and paper and make a sign, providing my cell phone number for calls to reschedule. I'll need to use paper for a few days until we are up and running again. I tape it to the front door, duck under the yellow police tape and join Tom and Karen by Dale's car.

Karen's chin quivers and Tom's jaw works as he holds his anger in check.

This has to be about Silvia. Did Charlie do this?

"Susan, come with me. Tom, you and Karen take your car and follow us, okay?" says Dale.

Without comment, the couple walks to their car. I plop into the passenger seat of Dale's car and blow out a heavy sigh as I rub my earlobe. Dale slides into the driver's seat and looks at me with worry in his eyes.

"You okay?"

"No! Geez! This has all the earmarks of a Charlie event, don't you think?"

"Yeah. It's pretty clear that this is about our investigation. No drugs are missing. It's the only doctor office theft I've seen where the drugs were untouched."

We drive in silence to the police station. Dale takes Tom into an interrogation room and another detective takes Karen. I wait for awhile and Karen comes out. I am waved in by a young woman with a notebook in her hand. She asks the usual questions.

"Do you know anyone who has an issue with the doctor?"

Duh.

"Any patients that have been unhappy with their care?"

"No."

The Water Master

I repeat my concerns that I am the target and the investigation against Silvia is the reason. The detective is intent as she takes notes and asks detailed questions. I am embarrassed answering some intimate questions about my relationship with Jay. Nothing is sacred or secret at this point, so I tell her everything I know. At last, she allows me to leave after a long and exhausting interview.

Tom and Karen are waiting for me. I check my phone for messages, finding quite a few. The three of us locate an empty room and start calling patients back, rescheduling them out a week, hoping we will be back to normal by then. Tom has already called the security company, the offsite computer backup company and the insurance company. Everything is in the works to get us up and running as soon as possible. Karen talks to Marisa, who will call her own clients and reschedule later as well.

By the time we are done, Dale gives us the thumbs-up to return to the office and start the cleanup. I leave with Tom and Karen. Starving, we stop at Francisco's—our usual haunt—to eat, to debrief, and to plan. I pop into the herb store to update Star, and she offers to help clean up.

I feel unsafe everywhere now. Even with my cop-minder following me whereever I go, I know that I have gone too far interfering with the Gottschalk family plan.

༅ঌ৽ঌ

It took four days to clean up, repair the window and reschedule all the patients. It took many hours of work to reorganize the files. A spot check of files indicates no paperwork was stolen. I double-check the Clement file. It remains undisturbed. Tom moved all the files back to the storage facility, and he and Karen contacted a scanning service to back up the paper files.

"It's amazing what you think about when you've been robbed," says Tom. "I worry about what those assholes will do with the confidential medical information they have. I will feel terrible if it harms any of my patients."

"Some things you just can't plan for, Honey," says Karen as we open up the office for the first time since the robbery. "Susan and I will send letters to our patients warning them to keep an eye on their personal information."

Still furious that my personal space was violated, I organize the reception area with my new computer and monitors. After the computer techies leave, everything looks the same. Nothing feels the same.

Dale stops in.

"Despite our assumptions about who committed the crime, we have absolutely no evidence. No fingerprints. No footprints. No video. Nothing. We all know it was probably Charlie and Silvia or someone they hired," Dale says. "Jay must be involved, because someone took your personal items, but no one else's belongings are missing. Susan, I promise I want to keep looking. In the meantime, a police officer will still follow you to work and to Star's house. Do you know anything about where Jay is?"

"I haven't heard a word from him. The divorce is in process, but I feel like he's not done with me. It's only a matter of time."

The Water Master

It's going to be a struggle to find a new normal.

"I'll keep in touch as we find out more information," Dale says. He squeezes my arm before he walks out the door.

I call Nancy O'Rourke, my financial advisor, in Evanston, Illinois. After telling her about my problems with Jay, we decide the safest route is to change my account numbers and devise new passwords.

"Susan," says Nancy, "Let's make your old password a safe word, just in case."

"What do you mean?"

"You've been in denial about your wealth long enough. I wish you had listened to me in the past. It's time you accept the fact that you are rich and being rich is dangerous. If you contact us under duress and we ask for your password, give me the old one, okay?"

I sigh in frustration. *I never asked to have money, and look where it got me.* "Then what?"

"Then we contact the police."

"It sounds like you've traveled this route before." I say.

"I have. Many times. And usually with less stubborn people." she replies.

"I've never considered this level of security."

"You weren't ready to hear about it until now," says Nancy. "It's time you take your wealth seriously, don't you think?"

"I know. I think I finally get it—although a bit too late."

"Hopefully, it's not too late."

The Water Master

❧

The weeks after Yule fly by with no new information about the office break-in. Jay doesn't contact me and I am settled in at Star's house. I continue to visit the dogs when I can, though Dale is busy and often unavailable. He offers to give me a key to his house, but I'm not comfortable intruding and it feels too intimate. I try to avoid thinking about my plight by staying as busy as possible, and now Imbolg is already here.

Imbolg is the halfway point between the Winter Solstice and the Spring Equinox and represents the return of the sun, fertility and initiation. Star plans to initiate two coven members to First Degree. They have completed the traditional year and a day of study. If I had remained Jay's student, I would have been initiated as well. He's already initiated me into his evil darkness. I want nothing but a peaceful life.

The Saturday of our celebration dawns dark and cold, no different than the past week. An inversion traps the Columbia Basin in freezing fog. Still air is heavy with the pulpy acid smell of the paper mill downriver. Ice covers everything outdoors in a crystalline white sheet. It feels as if the sun has disappeared forever.

I'm in charge of preparing cakes and ale for the initiation. Never having had success with anything related to yeast-containing breads, I make two loaves of zucchini bread—one for the coven and one for Dale. I mull wine in the crock pot and taste-test throughout the afternoon to ensure it has the perfect sweet taste to symbolize the warming earth, waking to spring.

356

The Water Master

Late in the afternoon, I pack up my ritual gear and drive over to Dale's house in the fog. Whenever possible, I show appreciation for his care of my dogs by offering homemade goodies and bags of dog food. As I pull into Dale's driveway, the dogs stand side by side at his front window, barking like crazy. Before I can get out of the car, Dale opens his door. Brighid and Zeus push past him to greet me, jumping around my feet, whining and barking until I hand Dale the still-warm bread and bend down to love on them. Chaos reigns as I make my way inside, until Dale calls all the dogs to the back door and lets them into the yard.

"That's the most energy they've had all day," laughs Dale. "They've been in a funk with this horrible gray muck."

"I don't blame them. I feel as foggy as the weather," I say.

"Got time for some coffee or a glass of wine?" asks Dale.

"No. I need to get going. I promised Star I'd help with setup tonight. She's got a lot on her plate."

"Something special going on tonight?" asks Dale.

"Initiation."

Dale looks puzzled. "And what is that?"

"Don't worry. No one sacrifices any animals or anything." I laugh. "It sounds so weird, doesn't it?"

"Yeah."

"I don't know much about it. I've never been to one. When Wiccans have studied the basics of the craft for a year and a day, they are initiated to First Degree. I guess you're a real witch then," I say, making air quotes.

"As opposed to not being a real witch?" he asks, smirking.

I sigh. "Every religion has their rituals. I don't think you'd think twice if I told you I was taking communion at church. Body of Christ and all that?"

Dale shrugs. "Yeah. I guess so. I've read a few books on Wicca, but have never been to a ritual. I think I'd be uncomfortable."

"It's not for everybody. I'm not even sure it's for me," I say.

"You sound sad about that."

"I am, a little. I like Star's coven. Everyone is accepting, and I like the subjects we study. But Jay's the one that introduced me to Wicca. It's hard to separate my feelings about Jay from my feelings about Wicca. It's confusing."

"I can understand that. Star's a great gal. I can't imagine she'd be bothered if you decided not to pursue it."

"I know. I'm holding on by my fingernails to some sense of normalcy, and my job and the coven keep me grounded—and seeing my doggies, of course!"

Dale smiles. "I'm always glad to oblige!"

"I wish I could stay, but I need to go."

I open the back door, dogs come flying in, and I hug and pat and whisper doggie-talk to them for a few minutes.

"Thanks, Dale," I say as I walk out the door.

By the time I arrive at the ranch, most of the coven is there. The two initiates are dressed in black robes. Everyone mills around, waiting for the ritual to start.

The Water Master

I find Star in her usual spot in the kitchen.

"Am I late?" I ask. "I didn't expect everyone to be here."

"No, you're not late. We do the initiation first and we're about ready to go."

"I need to get my robes on," I say as I turn to leave the kitchen.

"Oh. I should have told you. Only initiates can be at the ritual. I wanted you to come early so you can arrange dinner. A few of the others will help you."

Disappointment evident in my voice, I replied, "Oh— okay."

Star walks up to me, looks me in the eye and says, "Really, I'm sorry I didn't tell you. I thought you would know that. It's my fault, and please don't take it personally."

I mentally shake myself and say, "Of course. I should have known. I just wanted to see what it was like."

"I know. Someday you may get your chance!" Star replies in a teasing voice.

"We'll see," I say.

"We'll come and get you when it's time for ritual."

"Okay."

I help a few others with dinner preparations, placing flower seed packets at each table setting and arranging a centerpiece of dried and fresh flowers. Star has made chili pepper jam for each coven member, and I set a jar next to each plate.

Just as we put the finishing touches in place, Ronny beckons us to the ritual circle.

The Water Master

Despite the bone-chilling fog, the mood within the circle is light. The initiates look relieved and proud to wear their new white stoles. The ritual includes planting seeds in a pot of fresh soil to symbolize the beginning of life as Spring approaches. But I feel wooden from the never-ending pain of betrayal and exhausted by the daily grind of watching my back.

During dinner, I slam down my food, finishing before the others and start the cleanup on my own, anxious to go home and go to bed. I don't even want to talk to Star, who doesn't seem to notice. As I prepare to leave, I pull my phone out of my purse to check for calls and see a '911' text from Dale. *The dogs! What happened?*

I dial Dale's number.

"What's wrong!"

"Hi. Thanks for calling me back." Dale sounds calm.

"What's the 911?"

"One of Star's neighbors called the police. They noticed someone snooping around the outside of her house. Is she there?" he asks.

"Yeah. Let me find her," I say. Panic and anger well up inside of me.

Jay again! Or Charlie. Did someone break into the house?

I rush to find Star. We close ourselves in a small room off the kitchen and put Dale on speaker.

"What happened?" asks Star.

"Someone's been seen snooping around your house. Be careful when you go home."

"Will one of your officers be there?"

"Yeah. We don't think anyone broke in, but take a

careful look around and make sure nothing's missing."

"Will do." Star seems so calm. My knees are shaking.

I end the call and we just look at each other.

"Let's go," says Star.

We delegate the rest of the cleanup to the coven members, giving the keys to Ronny to lock up. I follow Star down the dark road into town. When we arrive at the house, a squad car is outside. A female uniformed officer exits her car, introduces herself as Officer Meyer, and follows us into the house.

Sweetums jumps off her usual spot on the couch and rubs against our ankles. She doesn't appear bothered by the excitement. We take a quick inventory of the house, checking windows and doors. In the meantime, Officer Meyer walks the perimeter of the house. She yells for us from the back yard.

We hurry toward her voice and find her shining her light on a window screen lying in the grass under my bedroom window.

"Oh crap!" I say.

"I assume the screen was on the window when you left?" asks Officer Meyer.

"I think so," I say.

We check the window. The theft prevention bar had prevented a break-in.

"We probably interrupted the guy when your neighbors called us," says the officer.

"Did you get a description?" asks Star.

"It was dark and foggy. She said she saw a tall man walk up to the side of the house. He was dressed in dark clothing. They couldn't see hair color or anything."

We look at each other. "Jay," we say in unison.

"Jay?" asks Officer Meyer.

"My soon-to-be ex-husband," I say.

"Okay, then. Let's talk," she says.

া৵

Jay grins. He can see it now. Susan all freaked out and afraid to sleep.

I knew I couldn't get into the house this time. But knowing how scared she'll be when she sees that screen laying on the ground, makes me so horny, I'll fuck the first thing I can find.

He hears the sirens long before the cops reach the house. He is out the back fence and down the irrigation service road on his way to Flower with the biggest hard-on he's had since Thanksgiving.

I'm having way too much fun. Too bad it will have to end soon.

া৵

An hour later, Star and I debrief as we drink our evening tea on the couch.

"What do you think he's after?" asks Star.

"I don't know what's left. I think he's trying to freak me out, which he has!"

I hear scratching noises at my window most of the night, but I'm too scared to open the blinds to see what — or who — might be there. In the first light of dawn, I move to the couch in the living room and drift into a troubled sleep.

Chapter Nineteen

༺♦༻

The atmosphere at work is tense after the break-in. Tom and Karen finally decide to take some time off. They've had enough. Silvia's arrest is imminent, and they want to rest and prepare for the publicity that is sure to follow. We decide that Marisa will work her normal schedule, and I will work in the afternoons. Marisa and I will leave together at the end of the day.

Dale calls me at work a few days after the Elwins leave for their Oregon Coast retreat.

"Hi! What's up?" I ask.

"Today's the day," says Dale.

I gulp, my mouth puckers with sudden dryness.

"You're going after Silvia?" I ask.

"Yep. Late this afternoon. Did the Elwins leave?"

"Yeah. It's just me and Marisa."

"When is her last appointment?"

"We won't get out of here until after six," I reply.

"I'll send a car over to keep an eye on you two until you leave."

"Thanks, Dale. I appreciate it."

"Have dinner with me?"

"What?"

"Have dinner with me. I need to talk to you. And I want to make sure you're safe."

"Um. Okay," I say, confused. "Where?"

"Meet me at McGivers."

"All right. I'll get there about six-thirty."

I have a radio by my desk, which I keep tuned to local news, waiting to hear about Silvia's arrest. All afternoon I hear the same news over and over again—gang member arrested, rain in the forecast, boat accident on the river, school bond on the ballot. As five o'clock approaches with no news, I worry that Silvia has somehow outsmarted the cops. Karen and Tom call a couple of times during the day. Each call is the same.

"No, I haven't heard anything." — "Yes, I'm all right." — "No, Dale hasn't called me."

Throughout the day I feel for the new security alarm under the desk to reassure myself that if I need it, help will be on the way. The GPS in my sock is irritating but I'm not about to remove it.

At last, the five o'clock news reports: *"Silvia Gottschalk, age 69, was arrested today for alleged embezzlement of an undisclosed sum of money from the medical office of Dr. Thomas Elwin. Gottschalk will face arraignment on Monday."*

I feel vulnerable. My desk is directly in front of the door. If someone wants to take a shot from across the street, they can. Dale made sure one of the good guys would be in position so nothing like that would happen, but for my own peace of mind, I move to the break room to complete my work.

Marisa sends off her last client and we leave together. As I walk to my car, I scan the parking lot and beyond.

Is that Jay's car? No.

The Water Master

I jump when a car backfires in the distance. My hands are icy and sweat runs down my back. I make sure Marisa is safely out of the parking lot before I leave, with the unmarked police car following me. My heart hammers in my chest. Despite the police presence, I don't feel safe.

❦

Charlie screams at Jay. "What the fuck did she do to deserve this?"

Jay shrugs. "I thought that asshole doctor was making that stuff up. Why would Silvia steal money?"

And between Charlie and me, we don't have enough money to bail her out. After I pretended to break-in at Star's house, my gambling and whoring binge reduced our funds in a big way. But it was worth it. I have to up the ante a little. I'm not done with Susan yet.

Jay squirms and adjusts himself. Charlie leers at him.

"Jesus boy! We got problems. Get your head offa yore dick and help me figger this out!"

❦

McGivers Pub perches on the north bank of the Columbia River. It is a two-story structure with parking below and the restaurant on the second floor with windows overlooking the levee and the river. The décor is sports bar/eclectic, but the food is known to be fresh, and the chef has an excellent reputation for creating tasty combinations. A bike path runs along the top of the levee, and in the warmer months, while eating a lunch of salmon salad, patrons can enjoy the sun sparkling off the river and watch the bikers, runners, walkers, boats, and skiers. A

365

park borders the river on the Kennewick side, and houses cling to the top of the ridge above it. But it is dark, and I'm not thinking about the view. By the time I see Dale waving at me from a booth by the windows, I have worked myself into an anxious mess.

"Hi, Susan. I ordered you a glass of Riesling. Hope that's okay."

"I need it. I'm a nervous wreck. I feel like someone is watching me, and it's not one of the good guys."

I take a sip of wine, grab a breadstick and begin munching.

"So, here we are. Life is about to get very sticky and now you want to talk to me about what?" I say.

Dale looks out the window into the darkness. Weak moonlight reflects on the choppy water.

"Well—I think I told you I was working on a hunch about something and—well, I need to tell you something. And it's not good news for you."

I stop chewing and set the breadstick down. The waitress approaches the table for our order. Conversation stops while I order a bowl of clam chowder and Dale a club sandwich.

After she leaves, I say, "So tell me." I rub my sweating hands on my thighs.

Dale leans forward and folds his hands on the table. I notice that his sport coat stretches across his broad shoulders, and I look at his hands. He has nice hands.

"I think Charlie and Jay lured you here."

I blink. "That's ridiculous. They didn't even meet until Jay came out here to look for a place for us to live."

"Well, I don't think that's true," says Dale. "And the reason I don't think it's true is because Jay is Charlie's son."

My body turns to ice as the blood drains to my feet.

"Can you excuse me for a minute?"

"What's wrong?" asks Dale.

"I don't want to throw up at the table."

I scoot out of the booth and rush to the bathroom. I lock the door behind me and throw up in the sink. Dry heaves follow, and I gulp and sweat through them until there is nothing left. I do not want to be here. Not at this restaurant, not in this situation and not in my body. I wash my face, cup water to my mouth to rinse it of the taste of bile, and lean against the sink to stare in the mirror. Hollow eyes, a red nose, and a flushed face stare back. I look as sick as I feel.

Oh, how I love to fall apart in public.

I rinse down the sink, wipe off the counter and stagger back to the table. The waitress delivered our food while I was gone. My soup is untouched and congealing, making me feel sick again. I lay my napkin over the top of it so I don't have to look at it. Dale says nothing as he watches me.

"You okay?"

"What do you think?" I spit in a harsh whisper.

The waitress reappears. "Is your food all right?" she asks.

"I'm sorry," I say. "I'm not feeling very well. I don't think I can eat."

"I'll take the soup and take it off your check," says the waitress.

I notice her name tag reads 'Tammy.'

"Is there anything else I can get you?" she says.

"Hot tea?"

"Sure. I'll be right back."

"Dale, can we go somewhere else? I can't do this in public!" I beg.

"Charlie is parked up the street. I don't want you to leave until we have a plan."

"Charlie is waiting for me? I think my plan is to catch the next plane to Chicago!"

"And I think that if you can help, you'll be happier in the end."

If daggers could fly out of my eyes, Dale would be impaled.

"The only person I'm responsible for right now is me! I've been screwed financially, emotionally, and geographically. I came to this godforsaken place to be a good wife, and all I've been is an unknowing and, frankly, stupid victim. I won't agree to let you use me either. I need to go home. I want to go home."

I try to hide my tears from the other diners by staring out the window and blinking. I know there is no home in Chicago. I'll have to start over alone, with acquaintances but few real friends. I made real friends here—at least I thought so. I don't trust my judgment right now.

"This sucks for you, Susan. I know. And I'm sorry. Sometimes I get so wrapped up in the excitement of an investigation coming together that I forget there is a human being whose life has been turned upside down. I'm really sorry. I'm sorry."

The Water Master

Dale can't look at me. I know he cares, but that matters little to me right now. We both stare out the window until I can get my breathing back to normal one more time. My thoughts fly.

What does this mean? Who am I married to? My name isn't even real! How will this end?

Dale reaches across the table and puts his hand on my arm. "Will you be all right if I keep talking?" he asks in a soft voice.

I look out the window as tears flow again.

This is not real. It can't be.

I take a few shaky breaths.

"Tell me," I say.

"I've been working a few theories since the Clements' disappearance. Once I met you, and you told me about Jay's—well, Jay's abusiveness, I suspected he was Charlie's missing son. He and Charlie connected right away, and you described a dramatic change in Jay's behavior after they spent time together. So I looked into it, and—it adds up."

"How? How does it add up?" I am impatient, panicky. This might be a theory to Dale, but it is my life!

"All right. Okay," says Dale, trying to calm me.

"As you know, Jay has a gambling problem. He takes after his father. His Aunt Silvia bailed out both of them whenever they needed money. She had a never-ending supply, and we now know where that came from, don't we?"

I nod, feeling numb.

"Jay's smart. You know that. After he graduated from

high school, he was arrested for stealing money from his employer, a pizza place that has since gone out of business. It was his first offense and he never did any jail time. Charlie and Silvia took care of it. They paid the owner back and conveniently helped Jay get out of town by sending him to college.

"He was a smart kid. There's no argument there. He earned his degree in Electrical Engineering at the U-Dub and found a job at Hanford. His job didn't require a security clearance. He never missed work and was the poster child for the great American work ethic. But when he wasn't working, he was hitting casinos up and down the valley, whooping it up with prostitutes and drugs. He finally went too far and owed a bad guy big money. His life was threatened. He needed to escape. Charlie and Silvia bankrolled his disappearance. It's likely his mother got wind of it and thought it was about time he paid the consequences. My guess is she fought with Silvia and Charlie about it. I don't believe she normally spoke up. She was married to Charlie, and who could survive that without wimping out?

"Jay's mother and Charlie had serious problems after Jay left. I think she was done covering for everyone, but then she and Charlie had that mower accident and she lost her foot, Charlie lost his toes. I think that accident was planned, but Charlie's such a klutz, losing his toes was his own stupidity. And it's more likely than not that she was actually Charlie's captive after that point. In fact, I wonder if she really died of natural causes!"

I interrupt. "I never saw his diploma. I had no idea he

was from Washington. I thought he was from Milwaukee. He even had that funny Wisconsin accent. And what's with his last name? It's not the same as Charlie's."

"He's a chameleon, Susan. He managed to get a fake ID when he left the state."

"That's just crazy! How could his family have allowed him to self-destruct like that?"

"Who knows? I've seen it before."

"I guess I have too," I say. "I've had clients that spoiled their children, but to the extent of resorting to embezzlement?"

"Embezzlement, physical violence, emotional duress and manipulation."

"I assume Jay isn't his real name then?"

"Jason Gottschalk."

I can only stare in disbelief at Dale.

"He told me his position at Hanford requires security clearance. How did he get secret squirrel clearance with a fake name?"

"His job doesn't require a security clearance. He lied. He's good at it. Hell, he's great at it!"

"How come no one recognized him when he came back here?"

"He was a fat and frumpy kid, much like his father. After he left town, he must have cleaned himself up, lost weight, and taken advantage of his mother's genes. I've seen pictures of his mom. He looks like her."

"Does Charlie have any other crazy children hanging around?"

"He has two daughters. One left home as soon as she

turned eighteen. She's in Seattle. It appears she has a good job, is married with a few kids and doing well. To my knowledge, she's had no contact with Charlie since her mother died. I couldn't find any information on his other daughter."

"So why me? Why did he target me?"

"No offense, but you were Jason's perfect target. You don't have much in the way of immediate family, and you're trusting—"

"Not anymore!" I say.

"—and you have a lot of money that you aren't spending. Some of this is still theory," Dale continues. "I'm still gathering evidence, but I think Jay wanted to return to his family. With his mother out of the picture, he and Daddy could gamble and whore around all they wanted, and Aunt Silvia would finance their bad habits with no question. Marrying you meant even more money for him, or so he thought. You had a good credit rating, were responsible, and wouldn't go snooping around his business."

"And I made the mistake of telling him I'd inherited money from my parents," I say.

"He knew that before you told him. Remember, he likely searched out information on the Internet and found a bonanza. By the way, have you checked to make sure your accounts are intact?"

"Yeah. I took care of all that. I've never had to touch that money until recently, when I had to cover all those bounced checks. Damn him anyway!"

I begin to cry again. I sip my tea to give my hands something to do.

"So here's the rest of the story," says Dale. "After some investigating back in Illinois and Wisconsin, we found that Jay applied for jobs back here right after he met you. And his dad had just the place for him to live. Unfortunately, someone lived there already."

"Oh my god! He killed those people just so Jay could move in?"

"Maybe there's some other reason. Maybe he just likes to torment people, and they were easy targets. I don't know. But I do know that something bad happened in the house, and we will get to the bottom of it."

"So what you're telling me is that Jay—Jason, wined, dined, and seduced me to marry me for my money?"

"Yes."

"So, is he trying to get rid of me now?"

"You were the ticket back to Washington and another source of income. And maybe he just liked having you in his life like a cat with a mouse. Sociopaths get off on manipulating people for their own gain, and I think he found you a bit of a challenge, so it kept him interested until he got back home and could go out to play with Daddy again. I'm sure he's angry about you finding your own job, because it removed you from his control and gave you the opportunity to make friends that he couldn't influence. I don't think he expected that. What's odd is that he seems to have disappeared from your life without a look back, and hasn't been bugging you, has he?"

"No. And that's what's so spooky. He wanted me around all the time, and then he just left. No phone calls. Nothing."

The Water Master

Dale pondered that for a moment. "Maybe he and Charlie are playing hard and he's distracted. I don't think it's going to last, though. Now that Silvia's been arrested, he'll want you around again, to punish you for interfering."

Taking a deep breath I say, "Now what do I do?"

"I have an idea," says Dale.

Dale tells me his plan. I'm not sure I can do what he asks, but I am certain that I can't walk away. I am caught in Jay's web, and I will extricate myself and make Jay pay for stealing my heart and my money. After our long discussion, the adrenaline wears off and my appetite returns. I order chicken noodle soup and gobble all it down. Dale has a short conversation with our waitress, Tammy, and motions me to follow him back to the restroom, where Tammy has placed a 'closed for cleaning' sign.

Dale takes me into the bathroom and pulls out a wire device.

"Take off your shirt," he says.

I just look at him.

"It's just business. I need to hook you up."

I pull off my shirt and stand in front of him, glad I am at least wearing one of my better bras.

Dale shows me how to hook up the microphone and where to tape it so it won't show. As soon as I can, I put my shirt back on and shrug my shoulders to make sure the wire holds.

"There you go," says Dale. A sheen of sweat covers his forehead. I don't think it's warm in the bathroom. In fact, it's cold. My mind elsewhere, I am completely oblivious to the picture he has in his head at the moment. "You can take that off if you want. Just wear it when you know you're going to meet with Jay."

"I'll take it off when I get home," I say. I look at myself in the mirror to see a haggard woman. My hair hangs in a listless jumble around my pale face. My eyes look huge. "Oh, Dale! How could this have happened?" I moan.

Dale reaches for me as I sway, and pulls me to him to keep me from falling to the grubby bathroom floor.

"Deep breaths! Deep breaths!" encourages Dale.

My breath is ragged as I inhale trying to hold back sobs. One man and one decision altered my life beyond recognition. I can't believe that Jay's kindness and attention was fake, but, looking back I now see that it felt unreal from the start. My deep need to be wanted trumped my common sense.

I am so mad at myself!

As my head clears, I hear Dale's heart hammering under my ear. I pull away from him and turn on the faucet to splash cold water on my face. Dale stands over me, ready to catch me if I get woozy again. His presence is both comforting and annoying.

Don't kill the messenger.

"Better?" he asks.

"Yeah. Thanks."

We remain silent as I dry my face. I take a deep breath. "Let's go. I want to go home—I mean, back to Star's."

As Dale walks me to my car, I feel exposed. I look around.

"Just keep walking and talking to me, okay? Charlie's

down the street, but I have enough unmarked cars here, I'm sure he knows we're watching him. He won't do anything."

"Does anyone know where Jay is right now?"

"His car is at the hotel parking lot at the Casino, so I think you can guess."

"Thanks for keeping an eye on me."

"The next step is getting Jay to talk to you," says Dale. "Any ideas?"

"I need to think about that for awhile. Can I get back to you?"

"Sure," he says as he opens the door of my car. "Keep your eyes open and don't take any chances."

"Sorry I lost it."

"You're doing fine," he says.

I feel like he's trying to apologize for something he didn't do.

It is after ten when I leave the pub. As I drive to Star's, I mull over Dale's story. I realize that the combination of removing Jay's access to all the bank accounts and credit cards, allowing the police to search the house, and Silvia's arrest will provoke Charlie and Jay into doing something drastic and mean to make me see the error of my ways.

My experience counseling addicts has always been frustrating. It's hard to break through their skewed view of the impact of their actions on others. I would, however, much rather deal with an alcoholic client or family than the victims of a chronic gambler. I'd seen families ruined, bankrupt and homeless because they trusted their gambler one more time. Jay had shown no sign of his gambling problem when we were dating. And it wasn't just the gambling. It was the cruelty that completely caught me off guard. He had never shown that side of himself until—when? It was when the truck stalled on the highway, outside of Kennewick, that I first saw his rage. I chalked it up to the stress of the move. I'd made excuses for him and tried to mollify him after each incident, and ignored the pattern that was forming. Now I have to find a way to meet with him and record—what? His admission that he is Charlie's son? Information that Charlie killed the Clements? I don't think he will admit anything, but I will try. I have to try.

I run my tongue across the fuzz on my front teeth. I want nothing more than to get back to Star's house and brush my teeth. My mouth still has the post-barf taste with added chicken broth. A good dose of Listerine is just what I need. In the meantime, Charlie is out there in the dark somewhere, and I am scared.

Sweetums greets me as I walk into the kitchen. She sniffs my feet, and flounces off to her pillow. Star is in her pajamas, reading a book in the living room.

"Well? How was dinner?" Star asks.

"Informative. I need to brush my teeth and I'll tell you everything."

A few minutes later, I curl up on the couch. Sweetums pops up on my lap and sniffs my face as I let out a sigh.

"It's bad," I say. "Really bad."

As I tell her what Dale has discovered, Star listens, eyes wide.

"Oh, my God, Susan. Do you think it's all true?"

"It fits, don't you think?"

Star bites her lip as she thinks about it.

"Yeah. It fits. How are you dealing with this?"

"I'm in shock. I don't know what to do except try to keep safe. And keep you safe. I'm so sorry you're involved with this."

"I'll be fine. It's you they want. I hope Dale knows what he's doing."

"So do I."

Tonight, I'll take a sleeping pill and disappear into the darkness of a dreamless night of sleep.

∂∞≪

OSTARA - NEW BEGINNINGS

"I am a tide: that drags to death..."
"...that if that which thou seekest thou findest not within thee, thou wilt never find it without thee."

∂∞≪

Chapter Twenty

❧

My ringing cell phone wakes me up. Groggy, I pick it up. "Hello?"

It's Tom.

"Susan! Dale called and told us about Jay. How are you doing?"

I look at the clock. It's after nine.

"Crappy. How are you?"

"We're fine. Maybe we should come back."

"No. You guys enjoy yourselves. I'll be fine. Dale's keeping a watch on me."

We spend a few more minutes talking, and I hang up. I sit up, rub the sleep off of my face and consider my options.

The facts I have to deal with are not ideal—not by a long shot. I have no home, no marriage and no safety. I have to fight off my sense of defeat.

What do I have? A job, a place to sleep, and friends. And money. Yes, I have money. I will protect it and use it however necessary to make a new life when this is over.

As I throw off the covers, Sweetums lets out an angry meow and jumps off the bed in a flurry of fur.

Early April is warm. The longer days provide relief from traveling between work and home in the dark. Flowering trees bloom in neighborhood yards, and the singing birds in Star's backyard wake me every morning. If it weren't for the never-ending waiting game—waiting to see if Jay will eventually talk to me, waiting for Charlie to do something stupid, or worse, harmful to me—life wouldn't be too bad right now. My anxiety grows by the day. Dale's prediction that Charlie and Jay would come unglued right after Silvia's arrest has not come true. It is too quiet—way too quiet.

My calls to Jay have gone unanswered. The divorce papers are ready to be served, but I don't have an address for him. He's gone underground. I'm not sure if he is even working. I tried to call his employer, but the receptionist denied any information based on their confidentiality rules. The only thing anyone knows is that periodically his car shows up at the Casino. I instructed my lawyer to serve him there, but every time the server appears, Jay is gone. The minions of his coven must be serving as lookouts, warning him of approaching trouble and allowing him to continue his narcissistic lifestyle of gambling and sleeping with whomever—maybe Flower, maybe someone else.

Dale had to call off most of the police watchdogs. Most nights, an unmarked car follows me home, but sometimes Tom and Karen are all I have. We all make sure our phones are charged, and I still carry my GPS device, along with my knife in a special ankle strap I bought at the gun store. The wire that Dale gave me remains unused on my dresser.

Silvia's arrest is big news for about a week. Dale's

plan worked in this case. Federal and local charges are pending, and her bail is set at just over a million dollars. No one has bailed her out, which indicates that Charlie and Jay are not flush. Or, maybe, they would rather spend what money they have on gambling. I have no idea. Silvia's local trial is scheduled for mid-summer, and we've been busy preparing our depositions with the Elwins' attorney.

We wait. Dale advises me to remain at Star's house until the murder investigation is over, and Charlie is arrested or my divorce is complete, or both. He checks on me at the office or Star's when he can, and I visit him and the dogs on the weekends.

Dale's theory is that Jay has to be stealing or embezzling money himself in order to keep gambling. I don't think he's been stealing money at all. He is charming the most current woman out of whatever she has and moving on to the next one.

Star and I work in her yard, preparing flower pots and Star's herb gardens for planting. The irrigation is to be turned on in mid-April and the irrigation canal behind Star's house is slowly filling with water. The pleasure I take working in Star's yard helps me get over the disappointment of my own failed attempts at making something out of nothing at that horrible little house of Charlie's. I am relieved I no longer live there, and I couldn't care less about the rent or anything else. I walked away from my furniture and doodads and took only what I cared about—my dishes, a few boxes of holiday decorations, my books, and what was left of my jewelry. Someone can burn the rest as far as I'm concerned. I still have plans to buy the land, if at all possible. But the house is coming down, and I will have to start fresh.

Now that we are done with the intensity of the investigation at work, I take comfort in the routine of our daily work. I'm home every night by six, and I prepare dinner so it is ready for Star's arrival. I help Star at the store on Saturdays. After a few weeks, Star let me run it by myself a few times, while she relaxed or shopped or prepared for coven activities.

If I didn't have the threat of Charlie and Jay hanging over my head, I would have a pretty good life. As best I can, I relax into the daily routine to try to release my anxiety.

Finishing up with the last of the patients, I close out the schedule for the day and prepare charts for tomorrow's patients. It's almost six when we are ready to leave, but Marisa isn't finished with her client. Every night, we leave together — safety in numbers.

Waiting in the break room, Tom pulls out three bottles of water. We sit at the table, each in our own thoughts. Tom stands up and begins to pace.

"What's the matter?" asks Karen.

"Well, I'm really pissed, Karen! The situation sucks. I don't like feeling out of control like this."

"I feel like I've brought trouble to you and I'm so sorry," I say.

Tom looks surprised. "So, is it your fault Silvia was stealing money from us? Is it your fault Charlie is such a dick?"

I'm shocked to hear Tom speaking this way. He slams the water bottle on the table, shooting water out the top. Karen finds a paper towel and wipes up after him. This big man, pacing in the small space, makes me more uncomfortable than I already am.

Marisa floats in with her end-of-the-day calm massage energy. Feeling the stress in the room, she says, "What's going on?"

Tom runs his hand through his hair. "I'm just pissed off. I'm tired of waiting, tired of watching our backs all the time—"

"I know. We all feel that way," says Karen.

Dejected, I gather my purse and follow everyone out the door.

Once in the car, I call Star to let her know I'm on my way home.

"I'm just finishing up. I had a last-minute customer who had to tell me about counting parasites in her poop."

"Yuck! Really?"

"You have no idea what people will tell me. I'll be home in about an hour. I defrosted some hamburger. Why don't you get those started on the grill, and we'll eat when I get there."

"Sounds good. See you in a bit."

Getting out of the car at Star's house, I look behind me and give a thumbs-up sign to the officer who followed me home. He waits for me to go into the house, then drives off.

Once in the house, I lock the door and perform my usual security check of all the windows and doors. I go to my room to drop my purse, kick off my shoes and change into my sweats. GPS and knife still on my ankle strap, I pull a pair of clean socks on and go to the kitchen to start the hamburgers. I cluck for Sweetums and hear no returning meow.

"Here kitty. Here kitty!" No Sweetums. I think I hear a distant *meow*, and I search the bedrooms and laundry room.

Meeoow!

The cat is outside. How did she get out there? I unlock the back door and hear the cat again. She sounds distressed.

"Kitty, kitty!"

Meoowww!

I step into the back yard to search for her, and too late, realize my mistake. I am tackled from behind, and land hard with the heavy weight of Jay on top of me. My breath knocked out of me, I struggle to breathe and swallow my panic all at once.

"Jay, get off me!" I gasp.

He whips me over to my back and sits across my hips.

Can I outsmart him and make him think I am glad to see him?

"Oh my god, Jay! Where have you been?"

"Busy. And you?"

"I didn't know what to do! I couldn't reach you. The police kicked me out of the house. You never called me back. Can you get off me so I can breathe?"

Jay adjusts himself further down on my body. He is obviously aroused and it makes me sick.

I try to remain calm. "Why didn't you call me? I would've talked to you about all this!"

"And why would I call a traitor like you?"

"What did I do?"

"Uh. Let's see. You're trying to serve divorce papers, Silvia's in jail. You let the cops into our house. Duh?"

Jay's demonic eyes are trained on my face.

"Everything got out of control. I didn't think it would get so bad!" I struggle to get out from under him, but he grabs my wrists with one hand and holds them tight.

"Whatever. It's all your fault!"

"How is it my fault?"

"Everything was fine until you stuck your nose in this. Charlie's furious!"

"What does he have to do with it?"

"That's none of your goddamned business! I told you not to get involved, but you did anyhow!"

"I did my job, Jay. Silvia did this to herself!" I struggle again and he holds me tighter.

"If you hadn't stuck your nose in it, no body would have been the wiser!"

"You're wrong about that, Jay. Tom and Karen knew what she was up to before I showed up. They just didn't know how bad it was."

Jay shakes with anger. "You bitch! You made this happen!"

I'm terrified.

I have to get away from him!

I soften my approach.

"Jay, if you let me go, we can go in the house and talk

about this. I'll try to fix it! I love you! I really didn't understand how much you care for Charlie. I'm so sorry!"

Jay looks crazy.

"I think you should tell Charlie your story," he says as he shifts his weight toward my crotch. He grins as he put his hand between my legs and then tweaks my nipple.

Can I play this game? I have to!

"Ooh. I don't think you're in the mood for talking," I say.

"Let's save that for later and go see Charlie," he says.

"Okay. Let me get my purse and keys and I'll follow you."

"Oh no, Little Missy. You're coming with me."

Jay keeps hold of my wrists in a viselike grip, stands up, and pulls me toward the back of the yard. I see the cat tied to a bush, struggling to release her bonds. I can't help her, and I need Star to get home now!

No such luck. Jay grabs me by my hair while he opens the back gate, and as he moves to take my wrist again, I break for it. I'm not fast enough. He lunges for my knees, taking me down hard. I struggle against him and stand one more time. He grabs my ankle and I feel the ankle strap bite into me.

Please, please don't let him notice!

But he does. Straddling me again, this time with my face grinding into the grass, he reaches behind him and pulls up my pant leg.

"What's this?"

I don't bother to answer. I'm toast. No one is going to help me now.

388

The Water Master

Jay unbuckles the ankle strap, throws the GPS back toward the house, and pulls my knife out of its sheath and holds it between his teeth while he yanks a piece of rope and a gag out of his pants pocket. He trusses my arms behind my back and pulls the gag tight between my teeth while catching my hair in the knot.

I have to think. I have to think!

As Jay pulls me up, I step on the toe of my sock and pull my foot out, leaving it lying in the damp grass. I will have to find another spot to drop my second sock, like breadcrumbs in the woods, but I only have two breadcrumbs. My next hope is that the neighbors will see me.

Jay opens the gate onto the irrigation canal. On the opposite bank of the canal is a huge, empty alfalfa field. An unfamiliar car is parked outside the gate on the right-of-way reserved for irrigation vehicles. I struggle against him as Jay opens the trunk and shoves me in, whacking my shins on the edge of the trunk. For good measure, he punches me on the head, and the lights go out.

I wake up in the dark trunk with my head throbbing. The hum of the tires on the pavement fills my ears. It takes some time before I can order my thoughts and pay attention to my surroundings. The trunk smells of oily rags and rubber. I shift, trying to determine what is underneath me. It must be the jack digging into my side.

My hands are asleep, still tied behind me. The rope Jay used is the horrible prickly stuff that pokes into me like a thousand tiny bee stings.

The Water Master

Shit!

This has gone all wrong. I begin to panic, but if I lose it, I have no chance at all. Trying to calm my breathing and think at the same time seems impossible. I have no idea how long I've been unconscious or where I am. The gag bruises the edges of my mouth. I'm thirsty. I begin squeezing my hands open and closed, trying to regain feeling. I bite down on the gag in pain,as the blood flows back into my hands and the pins and needles subside.

I lift my head and move it up and down and side to side to see what I bump up against. The top of the trunk is a few inches above my head. I lie on my side and try to roll over on my stomach, but there isn't enough room. Rolling the other way, I can lie on my back, but it hurts my arms. The sharp edge of the jack is underneath me, with a thin carpet between me and the jack.

If I could just get the rope over that edge...

The car slows. I hear the crunch of gravel under the tires and rushing water to the left of the car. A loud mechanical noise increases in intensity until its throbbing fills the air. We must be next to an irrigation canal. The car stops, and I hear Jay open the driver door and slam it shut. The car rocks a little.

The trunk opens. I am blinded by a flashlight.

"Hi there, Little Missy," says Charlie. "How was yer trip?" He laughs.

Hands grab my shoulders and ankles. They lift me out of the trunk, drop me on the gravel, and walk off beyond earshot. Sharp edges of basalt rocks poke and bruise me from head to toe. The nearby water chills the air. It sounds like a raging torrent compared to what I've noticed in the sluggish irrigation canals near my house.

Is it the river?

I squint and look around. No, it is definitely a canal. In the moonlight I can see a little. Looking past Jay's feet, I see the gravel road we had just driven on and the cement sides of a huge canal falling off to the right. I take in my surroundings.

The waxing moon is just above the horizon. It wasn't out yet when I arrived at Star's house. In fact, it was just dusk. Jay must have driven for at least a couple of hours, maybe more. He could have driven for miles or gone around in circles.

Jay and Charlie are talking, but I can't make out what they are saying over the noise of the irrigation pump and the rushing water. Turning my head to the right, I see the car, and beyond it is a small corrugated metal shed shining in the pale moonlight —no bigger than a garden shed— with a dim light glowing through a grubby window.

Shit, shit shit!

Panic rises in me again and I whimper. Jay and Charlie walk toward me and grab me under my arms to lift me up. They half drag, half push me toward the shack. I quit fighting them to prevent them from hurting my arms.

Charlie opens the door, and in the pale light of the lantern on the shelf that runs across the back of the shed, I see a dirty mattress on the floor with a sleeping bag thrown over it and a plastic yellow bucket. Two pieces of plywood lean against the wall under the window.

Jay throws me on the mattress.

"How's this for your new home, Honey?" he says.

I breathe hard, again fighting off panic.

"I figured since you ruined my house, the least I could do was offer you a place to sleep."

Charlie grins down at me. The lantern lights up one side of his face, leaving the other in shadow. His eyes gleam, and he looks as though he is having the time of his life.

"Awright, Little Missy. You can scream all ya want. I promise ya, yer in the middle of bumfuck nowhere and with the sound of the water an'all, no one's gonna hear ya. So I'm takin' the gag offa yer mouth and we're gonna have a little conversation."

Charlie reaches behind me and pulls up on the gag, ripping out some hair and scraping the sides of my mouth. I yelp. I lick my dry lips and taste blood. My head pounds.

"I hear ya got some money you ain't sharin' with yer husband here. This here's a friendly reminder that it's time to give it up. If yer real nice and just sign it over, you kin go home and we're done with ya," says Charlie.

Not likely!

"And if I don't?"

Jay reaches over and grabs my hair, pulling my face toward his. I cry out as he jerks my head back and forth.

"Oh, I'll get it from you one way or another," he says.

"Why? What do you need it for?" I cry.

"Bail money, for starters," says Jay.

"I covered your bills and overdraws. Isn't that enough?" I spit.

Jay slaps me across my face. Stunned, I shrink back from him.

"Why are you holding on to all that money anyway?" Jay shoves his face into mine and screams, "You're such a tightwad! You live like you make minimum wage! Thrift stores, cheap furniture. We could've had everything we wanted, but no, not my little frugal wife. She wouldn't share if her life depended on it. Oh wait, your life does depend on it! Funny how that worked out. It's time to give it up!"

"Why don't you use all the money Silvia stole?" I say.

Jay laughs a wicked laugh. "Yeah. Right."

Charlie looks at Jay, pride in his eyes. "Yep, she did! She been doin' that fer years, Jason! Where ya think all that money's been comin' from that I been givin' ya all this time?"

A look of surprise comes over Jay, which he tries to mask.

"I thought you were giving me the money Mom left me."

He doesn't know!

"She left you nothin', son. Nothin'. She never had no money!" Charlie snorts and spits. I turn my head away from the glop that lands next to me.

"So, Dale was right," I say. "You are Jason Gottschalk!"

Jay slaps me hard. "So your boyfriend's been nosing around, too? Charlie, I think the secret's out." Jay winks at me and leans in. I try to pull back, but he grabs the back of my head and whispers right next to my bruised lips. "Yep. He's my dad."

"What do you guys want from me?" I start to cry. I can't help it.

"Aww, po' baby," says Charlie. "What do you want from me?" he mimicks.

"I told you. I want your money," says Jay.

"What?"

"I want your money. You have a bunch of it that you aren't spending anyhow. We'll pay for Silvia's lawyer and then maybe buy me a new house, since you ruined the one we had. Oh, and I'll pay for my next wedding!" Jay laughs. "Let's call it my life insurance policy."

"That money is mine. Besides, there's no way I can get to it all at once," I say.

"You're going to cash it out and put it in my own little account."

"Jay, it's not that easy."

Jay reaches for my breast. This time as I back away, he follows me and shoves me back on the mattress, lying on top of me. I can feel his hardness and want to vomit. Charlie leers down at us. I lose focus and feel faint.

This can't be happening!

"So here's what you're going to do, my sweet wife," says Jay as he grinds up against me and whispers in my ear. "You're going to call your bank tomorrow and get whatever you need to cash out your accounts. You're going to have to sign some forms, so you're going to tell them to overnight it to an address that I'm going to give you. Once I have the money, you and I can talk about your future plans."

Jay laughs as he rolls off me. Charlie grabs his hand and pulls him off the floor. Jay bends over me and shoves me onto my stomach. He unties my hands and puts the rope in his pocket.

The Water Master

As Charlie picks up a battery-operated drill from the floor and pulls a handful of long screws out of his filthy coveralls, I roll over and sit up. "You know, the cops will be looking for you as soon as they know I'm gone." I rub my wrists.

"No biggie. I've disappeared before."

Charlie grabs the lantern and the pieces of plywood. The men leave the shack, pulling the door shut behind them. I am left in darkness as they board up the window. Then I hear screws screaming into metal as they board up the door. I scream and bang on the door, begging them to let me out. The car starts and gravel crunches as they drive away. The roar of the water and pumps shut out any other sound. I sit, rubbing my wrists, straining to hear anything other than the hellish pounding outside the shack. My head hurts. I feel the large knot on my forehead where Jay punched me. I was knocked out for a long time and suspect that I was drugged. The drug must be wearing off because the pain of my injuries intensifies as the minutes tick by.

By this time, they be looking for me. Star will have come home by now and found the cat tied up in the back yard. I'm sure she called Dale and he'll be all over this. I was so stupid to think I could fool Jay. Why'd I do that?

Then I got mad at Dale.

Couldn't he have arrested Charlie by now? But why am I blaming Dale when Jay and Charlie are the bad guys.

I cry, try to stop myself, and then quit caring. After I cry myself out, I wipe my nose on my t-shirt and feel around for the bucket. After relieving myself, I push it to the far corner of the shack.

Charlie and Jay will be back tomorrow morning. Jay isn't thinking this through. How can I disappear first and then call my bank? He must be following Charlie's lead. Charlie isn't too smart. He has some kind of sick hold over Jay. Jay will be a prime suspect in my disappearance. He'll probably be arrested before he will ever see the money. What is he thinking?

My head pounds. I lie down on the smelly mattress, put my nose into the crook of my arm to avoid the stink, and try to calm my thumping heart. I remember a client, a woman who had been held captive and raped by her husband over and over again. My goal was to help her return to a normal life, but now I realize how impossible that would be.

Nothing will be 'normal' if I live through this. Charlie has murdered before. Jay is following in his footsteps. Charlie has to know he is a suspect in the Clements' disappearance. Is he going to disappear with Jay, or does he believe he can outsmart the law?

I am exhausted and thirsty and in pain. I fall into a fitful sleep, waking now and then to put my face into a new pocket of fresh air near the floor, and at last to pull the greasy sleeping bag over me during the chill of the night.

I wake up in the dirt, my face at the bottom of the door. Even in my sleep I tried to worm away from that horrible mattress. I imagine Charlie sleeping on it—or worse—and right away I lose what little food I have in my stomach. After the heaving is over, I notice daylight coming in through the tiny cracks between the metal panels in the shack. I try to see outside, but to no avail. There is nothing but the irrigation canal on one side, a high bank on the other and the gravel access road. The roar of the water and pumps continues. I try screaming a few times, but quit to save my strength.

As the sun rises, so does the heat in the shack. I am so thirsty and am tormented by the sound of the rushing water just outside my dark and dingy prison. I feel around in my pockets and find a mint, which gives me temporary relief. I try to imagine what Dale is doing right now. Is he looking for me? I scan the shack in the dim light, but see nothing I can use as a weapon. The plastic bucket is no good, although the thought of throwing its contents on Jay is appealing. I stand up and check the strength of the shelf. It holds my weight as I hang on it.

Maybe by hanging onto this, I can swing my feet out and kick the first person to open the door. That might give me the benefit of surprise and give me a chance to run. If one of them is down, I might have a chance to fight off the other one, especially if it's Charlie.

The noise outside prevents me from hearing their car until it is right at the door.

Two doors slam shut. Screws shriek as one of them removes the plywood. I am blinded by the bright sunlight as they wrench open door. I grab the shelf, I kicking out with both feet and hit flesh. I hear a body fall and a grunt. My feet hit the ground, and in two strides I jump over Jay and make a run for it, glancing at Charlie's shocked face as I run past him.

Ha! He underestimated me!

The basalt gravel cuts and tears at my feet. I gather

speed despite the pain, losing my other sock as I run. I hear footsteps behind me, and Jay tackles me to the ground.

Shit! My back gives out with paralyzing pain and I am helpless once again.

I scream. Jay slaps his hand over my mouth and pulls me to my feet. My knees and feet are cut and bleeding, and Jay clamps his hand so tight around my mouth and nose that I begin to lose consciousness. Just in time, he moves his hand and I gasp for air.

Jay shoves me toward the shack. Charlie has a big grin on his face.

"Y'never cease to saprize me, Little Missy. Ya got 'im good, dincha!"

Jay throws me to the mattress. The pain in my back takes my breath away.

"Hello, my wife. How are you today?" At least Jay is breathing hard. I take whatever satisfaction I can get.

"I've been better," I whisper. "Did you bring any water?"

"Why, yes, I did," says Jay.

"Give me some," I gasp.

"Sure." He opens up a water bottle and holds it out to me. I reach for it and he pulls it away, toying with me.

"But first you have a phone call to make," he says. Charlie walks up behind Jay, blocking the light.

"Do you have the number?" I ask.

"Of course, I do, my sweet. I think of everything."

I try to smile at him. "Yes, you do."

Trying a different tack, I say, "Jay, I've been thinking. Since you need the money, I can give you some. You don't have to do this."

Jay grunts. "You were pretty clear that your money was off limits."

"But I'm beginning to think you're right. I should have been more generous and I'm sorry."

"Then maybe you can tell me why you closed our account!" Jay slaps me across the face.

I stammer. "I had to. We were bouncing checks!"

"That was my money, you bitch!" Jay slaps me again.

I let the tears flood my eyes and I am sure Jay wants to see them flow. I say, "I'll make it right."

I'll go along with this until I can get away..

Jay grins. "Too late now!"

My breath is ragged with panic as Jay coaches me on what to say to the bank. I can't think. Nothing makes sense. He writes down an address in Pendleton, Oregon. Grabbing my hair, he drags me to the car where I sit with the windows up so the noise outside can't be heard over the phone.

"If you don't do everything exactly as I told you to, things will only get worse. You get it? Put her on speaker phone. Just do what I say. Got it?"

I can't look at him. I nod. I'm terrified.

He punches in a number and hands me the phone. I ask for Nancy and wait a few moments, listening to elevator music—an incongruous situation.

"This is Nancy. Can I help you?" The familiar voice of my financial advisor brings fresh tears to my eyes.

"Hi Nancy. It's S-s-susan Glasser."

"Susan! How are you?"

"Oh, fine."

"You sound out of breath. Are you okay?"

"My back is giving me some problems. That's all."

"What can I do for you?"

"I'd like to make arrangements to move my investments out here."

"Really? You found a new advisor?"

"Um. Yeah. I just thought it would be easier to have someone close by."

"Oh." She sounds disappointed. "Well...all right. You know the drill."

"Yeah."

"What's your password?"

I take a deep breath, knowing this answer could save my life. I freeze. My mind won't work. What s it?

"Ummm. Oh, it's Daddy101945—pound, exclamation point."

Silence. No response from Nancy. She got it.

"What would you like me to do?" she asks.

"Just send me whatever forms I need to sign to get this started. It's kind of an emergency."

"It would have to be, wouldn't it? Can you give me any idea what's going on?"

"No. It's personal, but it needs to happen as quickly as possible."

"What's that noise?" asks Nancy.

"What noise?"

"It's a shushing sound."

"Really? It must be some kind of interference. I live in the middle of nowhere," I laugh.

Jay grabs my hair to get me to hurry up.

"Let me give you the address." I read the address from Jay's note.

"That's an Oregon address?" questions Nancy.

Jay didn't think this through either.

"Um, yeah. Jay drives through there regularly and it's easy for him to pick up the mail."

Jay tightens his grip on my hair.

"If you could send that Fed Ex overnight, it would be the fastest, okay?"

"I'll take care of this immediately. It won't be long." She's trying to comfort me.

"I really appreciate your help."

"How's everything else going?"

Can I give her another clue?

"Ah, it's kind of hard to get used to the desert. If it weren't for the irrigation, nothing would grow here."

Jay grabs the phone and ends the call.

I have to buy time. Someone will find me, I am sure of it.

"You talk too much."

"She would have known something was up if I didn't visit with her. She's been my advisor for years!"

"Well, now all we have to do is wait for the mail."

I'll be okay. Nancy will contact Dale. She'll mail papers to the address, and Dale will have someone watching for it, waiting for Jay to pick it up. I just have to live through the next few days.

Jay pulls me out of the car and drags me back to the shack. My back screams in pain, and I want to.

Charlie leans against the door and spits tobacco in my direction. "I wonder how we should entertain ourselves now?" he says.

Jay leans over and kisses me hard on my bruised mouth.

"Oh, I think I know what I want to do!" he says.

Charlie chuckles. "Well, boy, I'll leave ya to 'er. I'll be in the car."

Jay pulls the door shut and pushes me down on the mattress. He stands over me as he unzips his pants. I try to play along, feeling sicker by the moment.

"Oh, Jay. I'm so glad we can be alone. I love you so much. You don't need to do this. I'll give you the money. I know we can make it. I love you. I love being with you."

The words fly out of my mouth as fast as I can think them. I reach up to pull Jay to me and he grabs my wrist, bending it, enjoying my pain and the power he has over me.

"You don't love me, Suze. If you did, you would have done what I told you to do." He drops to his knees in front of me, pulls my wrists up over my head and nuzzles my breasts with his mouth. He is too strong for me to fight, so I don't.

"I'll do whatever you want. Please don't hurt me!" I sob.

"Oh, yeah? Then take off your clothes."

He lets go of my wrist and I pull off my top. Jay is very aroused. He pulls a knife out of his back pocket. With a start, I realize it is my athame.

He holds the knife in front of my face. "Take off your pants." I do, though I move carefully, wincing in pain as my back spasms. Jay places the end of the knife between my breasts. In one quick motion he cuts through my bra and it falls to the floor. He pulls me to him and kisses me, forcing his tongue so far down my throat that I gag.

What happens after that, I will forever try to forget and never be able to.

He becomes an animal, taking me from behind, raping me, making me do things and say things that leave me feeling filthy. I try to make him believe that I want his attention, but it makes no difference. I give up, turn off my mind and become a rag doll, unable to resist his violent attack. When he is done with me, he picks up the knife and with an evil grin carves his initials deep into my upper arm. The pain is torture. I can't help myself. I scream.

"You're mine, you know. You always will be," says Jay as he zips up his pants. "See you soon, baby."

I search for my clothes.

"Can you leave me some food, some water?"

Jay opens the door. "Charlie! She says she wants food and water."

Charlie's shadow falls across me. I fumble with my t-shirt as I try to cover my breasts. Charlie gawks. "Boy! You got good taste!" He leers at me. "Wish I had it in me. I'd do 'er meself!"

Jay says nothing. Charlie throws three bottles of water into the shack along with a few packages of beef jerky.

"There you go, Little Missy. Don't say I never gave ya nothin'."

The door shuts, they screw the wood back on, and I curl up into a painful ball of shattered spirit with bruised and bleeding skin. I weep.

Chapter Twenty-One

❧

Star's phone call brings tears to Dale's eyes. He knows as soon as he hears her voice that it is bad. His stomach lurches when they search the backyard and find the GPS. He can picture exactly what happened. Susan's heart was ahead of her brain and she was so concerned about the cat, she didn't think about why the damned thing was not in the house.

Damn it! I've tried so hard to stay ahead of Jay and Charlie and I just haven't been able to. Since the captain had to withdraw funds, I had to personally hire that investigator to keep an eye on Susan. But that guy had just come on duty to watch the house when Susan was taken out the back. Jason is no dummy. He timed everything perfectly, including setting up the 911 call that took all the squads to a different part of town. The tire tracks and two sets of footprints in the gravel tell me what I already suspected. Jason and Charlie have her and I have no idea where she is. Silvia must know something about where Charlie hides his secrets.

Dale's anger fuels his lights-and-sirens drive to the jail to talk to Silvia. She stares at him as he asks her where Charlie took Susan. She stares and grins.

"What are you going to do for me if I tell you?" she says.

That starts a whole new laundry list of things he has to do.

Will the DA agree to a deal? When can we meet with the judge? Would Cap allow it? All of this takes time and the clock is ticking. The tire tracks may hold some clues about the make and model of the car. Gathering the information will take time. I feel so helpless. I don't know where to look.

༄•⚬

Star is frantic. Her cat is fine, other than some rope burn on her neck and a new fear of doors. But she feels responsible. Jay entered her house through a little known weak spot in a crawl space window. She should have known about it. In all the years of protecting victims, no one has ever tried to get into her house. She looks for clues everywhere. She finds nothing other than Jay's hand and knee prints in the dirt of her crawl space.

༄•⚬

I have no idea how long I can last with three bottles of water and the salty beef jerky. I have to pace myself.

After Jay's attack, I sleep very little, unable to stop my mind from replaying it over and over in my head. I've lost some blood. My pants and shirt are soaked with it. I can't move my arm without searing, shooting pain in my arm and neck. I hear muttering voices within the pumping thrashing sounds outside. The only escape is sleep.

I doze off and on until early morning. When it is light enough to see, I explore along the floor, looking for possible escape routes. I dig into the ground with my fingers where the most light is shining in, only to find a steel grid

405

underneath the dirt. I can't dig out.

The only possible weapon I can use is the shelf. I pull and wiggle it, but it is tightly screwed to the wall. I sigh in frustration. There is no way out.

I lift my shirt sleeve off the wound where Jay carved his initials, starting a fresh trickle of blood. Seeing that crooked "JG" makes me woozy. *Jason Gottschalk...Jay Glasser. If I survive this, what will my married name really be? What does it matter anyhow? He plans to be a widower. He has every intention of taking my money and killing me. It seems like all I can do is wait and hope Dale finds me in time.*

I sit on the mattress with my back against the metal wall, now growing hot with the rising sun. I move to the other side of the shack.

I try to imagine where I am in relation to our house. Irrigation canals run roughly parallel to each other in a general east-to-west direction. By the position of the rising sun, the canal is on the east side of the shed, so it must be curving in a north/south direction. This is a huge canal compared to the ones running near the house. It must be a main channel.

I think back to the bike ride along the irrigation canal with Rosie, wishing I had asked more questions. All I know is the water comes from the mountains.

Maybe I am up north near Yakima? If the address is in Oregon, maybe I am somewhere south near Pendleton. How will Dale ever find me? If this shed is Charlie's secret getaway, I can't be too far from home.

That calms me a little.

Yes. I am close to home. Dale will find me any time now.

406

The Water Master

I have too much time to think. All the crap I've kept at bay through the distractions of school, work and now my ugly marriage, rush up to slap me in the face.

I failed to see Jay for what he is. I should have known better, but I'm the perfect victim. All that time I spent counseling other people should have been spent working on my own shit. If I had, I might not be in this mess!

I was twenty-two when my mother died of a stroke. One minute she was standing in the kitchen, drinking a glass of wine, and the next she was dead. I had barely started my own life when my mother's was over. Dad was never the same after that. He drank more, and kept to himself, locked in grief and loneliness. Within two years, he died of a heart attack. Ruthie married her high school sweetheart and started dropping kids. She and I never talked about the pain of losing our parents, and never really supported each other. I isolated myself from close relationships and focused on my career.

Ruthie and I are not that different after all.

"That bastard just sucked me right in," I say out loud. "And I was too fucking blind to see it!"

All those clients I "helped." Did I really? Or was I just playing with their heads? Did I do more harm than good? I remember some clients yelled at me and stomped out of my office, telling me I was full of shit. Were they right? Could they see what I couldn't?

Then a memory pops into my head of the elderly woman who was married to an alcoholic for years. Her family forced her into counseling, hoping she would leave her husband. She 'yes, deared' me for weeks and did nothing to change, eventually disappearing into the land of no-shows. But a couple of years after I last saw her, she called out of the blue to tell me that her husband had died. Drank himself to death. She wanted to thank me because she knew, without a doubt, that his death was not her fault because of what she had heard from me.

Thinking of that poor old lady calms me down. My thoughts stop racing, and I fall into a light sleep.

I wake up in the late afternoon, hot, stiff, sore, and stinky. I eat some beef jerky and drink a little more water. I fall back to sleep before sunset, and when I wake up the next morning, I am pissed off.

Everything hurts. I stand up on bruised and scabby feet, groaning.

I have to move.

I limp back and forth the few steps space allows. One, two, three. One, two. One, two, three. One, two. The fog begins to lift.

Giving up is too easy. Today will be different.

I stretch my back. It hurts, but I will deal with it. My knees are scabbed over, bruised and stiff.

I can't physically fight my way out of this.

My attempts to convince Jay I still love him were futile.

He doesn't care. He has one goal in mind, and that is stealing my money and then getting rid of me.

I relieve myself in the yellow bucket once again, holding my nose against the rising stink.

My sock is still out there on the gravel road. Someone will find it. When they come back to get me, maybe I can drop some pieces of beef jerky or a water bottle along the way. What else is there?

The pain makes me awkward as I stand up. I lose my balance and kick against the bucket, knocking it over.

Great. Now I can't even throw my piss on them. If I live through this, I'll be a helluva lot more careful with men! Jay wants everything his way. I thought if I made him happy, he would make me happy, but it didn't work that way. The more I tried to do what he wanted, the less he cared about what I wanted. I gave myself over to it, and never imagined ending up his prisoner. I want out and I am getting out! That asshole isn't going to kill me! I'll have to take a chance on whatever opportunity comes to me.

I am anxious, scared and hungry. I sip a little water and doze off.

Chapter Twenty-Two

❧

When the call comes in from Susan's financial advisor, Dale is all over it. He sends up two helicopters and notifies the Irrigation District that it is likely Susan is being held captive along one of their canals. He rushes to their office to meet with their management team and review the system maps. One of the guys knows Charlie used to disappear for hours when he worked for them. It was usually when he was sent to the Palouse to repair a pump or check for a canal breach.

The Palouse is huge. Hundreds of square miles of rolling hills, wheat and potato farms. Where is she?

The information Nancy provided indicates the crime will move across state lines into Pendleton, Oregon, so now the damned FBI is involved and they are mucking up my plans. I don't have time to tell them all the details. I've been trying to take down Charlie for the last year. He is mine! Susan has to be somewhere in the Palouse. Maybe she's close to the Oregon border. Oh, shit! That grassfire! They sent out extra crews to fight that one. I hope it's nowhere close to her.

❧

I wake to what I think is full daylight. I have no idea what time it is. I smell smoke and started to panic.

If there is a fire nearby I'll roast alive.

The Water Master

I pee in the bucket, groaning in pain. My nether regions are in bad shape. I can't withstand another rape.

The only time Jay avoided me was when I had my period. If only...

Since my pants are already bloody, I'll tell Jay I'm having my period. But the blood is dry. So, I pick the scab off the carving in my arm, take off my sweats and soak the crotch with fresh blood.

"That should do it," I say.

Soon after, I hear their car approaching. I gulp some water and resolve to get as much information out of them as I can. If I manage to escape this prison with my life and my mind intact, I am going to take these bastards down.

Charlie and Jay remove the board and open the door. Smoke filters the sunlight, but the sudden brightness still blinds me.

"We're baaack," says Charlie.

"I can see that," I say.

"Hello, wife," says Jay.

"I'm so glad you're back." I don't even try to sound sincere.

"Good. Charlie, go wait in the car."

Jay sits down next to me and pulls my hair, exposing my neck to him. He bites it.

"Ow! Jay! That hurt!"

"Get used to it, baby. I want you bad."

"I, um...I'm having my period."

"Yeah, right. I don't believe you."

"Really, Jay." I open my legs a little, and he sees the fresh blood on my pants.

Jay snickers at me. "Well, that shouldn't keep you from taking care of me!"

"Whatever," I whisper.

I know what Jay wants, and I do it for him, hoping he will finish.

When he is done, Jay buckles up and goes out to get Charlie.

"Any word on Silvia?" I ask.

"Why do ya care?" snarls Charlie.

"I feel bad. I wish I hadn't gotten involved."

"Too late for that!"

"Maybe it's not, Charlie. Maybe I can do something for you."

"Like what?"

"If I knew a little more about what's going on, maybe I can help you guys. I really want to make this up to you."

Charlie looks at me with distrust.

"Why th' change in yer attitude?" he asks.

"A few nights alone and a lot of time to think. I didn't realize how much the two of you care for each other. Charlie, you're my father-in-law. I never gave you a chance."

"I don't believe you!" says Charlie.

"I can see why. You and I got off on the wrong foot. But I've thought about it. I'll do whatever it takes to make sure Jay is happy, and he won't be happy unless you are."

This is so lame. Jay won't believe me, but maybe Charlie will.

"What are ya gonna to do fer me?" asks Charlie.

"I think I can get the police off your back about what they found at the house."

"How ya gonna do that?"

"Charlie, she's full of shit," interrupts Jay.

"I'll tell them that you told me the blood at the house was because of a murder/suicide and you were afraid someone would think it was your fault so you buried the bodies…" I answer.

"That's crap. It weren't no murder/suicide!"

"I know that and you know that, but the cops don't."

"Charlie, shut UP!" yells Jay.

I begin talking louder, with more insistence.

"Dale likes me. I think he'll listen to me."

Jay's face darkens. "Have you been messin' around with him?" he yells, grabbing my hair again.

I'm cutting my hair short after this is over.

"No! No, Jay. I don't like him. He's trying to manipulate me. I can tell. He thinks if he's nice to me I'll turn against you guys. I don't want to do that. I really want to help you! Look, I know you need money. I'm fine with that. I also know you need an alibi. I think I can get you off the hook. I just need to know what to tell them. Maybe I could tell them that you're getting senile, or that you got nervous when I was digging around the garden and told me the bodies were there."

"The bodies ain't there and yer not telling no one I'm senile!" yells Charlie.

"So why were you messing with our irrigation?" I ask, my curiosity getting the best of me.

"Because I knew how much Jason hated havin' ye work in your yard. He wanted you inside with 'im!"

I let that sink in. Charlie is one weird dude.

Who would do that?

"Anyhow, Charlie, if I do this, they're going to want to know what you did with the bodies. The worse that's going to happen is you'll be charged with something like interference with a dead body or whatever you call it, and if we go the senile route, you'll probably get off completely."

"No one's gonna say I'm senile," he screams. "I'm smarter 'n all a 'em! They're so stupid! The bodies are right under our noses—"

"Charlie!" yells Jay. "Shut up!"

"Well, it weren't no murder/suicide!" he huffs. "That Andy Clement was a good friend until his wife changed his mind about me. I didn't want them living in my house no more, so I put an end to it."

"Charlie! Shut up! She's playing you!" yells Jay. He turns to me and slaps me hard. Blood spouts from my lip.

Stunned, I lick the blood off my mouth. I know I'm not fooling Jay, but Charlie is mine. I press on. "Where are the bodies, Charlie?"

Charlie laughs and spits out the side of his mouth. "Where no one will ever find 'em. And, Little Missy, I know you'll be seein' 'em soon."

Charlie just admitted to murder. Is that enough?

"Charlie, for the last time, shut the fuck up!" yells Jay. "She's up to something."

I'll shut up now. My efforts sound stupid even to me. Jay knows it, but at least I got a rise out of Charlie.

"Come on, you guys. Let me go. I promise to give you the money when I get it. If this all stops now, no one is in trouble and I'll vouch for Charlie. Jay, you can, too. You can say we moved here because you were worried about your dad and you had no knowledge of the Clements or Silvia's activities. I'm the perfect alibi."

"I'll have none of it!" says Charlie.

"Me neither," says Jay. "I don't trust her. She's a goody-goody save-the-world type. She's lying to us."

I say nothing. Jay stands up and Charlie walks out to the car.

"Susan, when this is done and I have my money..." He kneels in front of me and stares straight into my eyes. "...I'm going to kill you. You know that, right?"

I swallow the lump in my throat.

Jay stands up. "I'm going to fuckin' kill you! But before I do, you'll wish you were dead!"

He grabs me and half drags me to the car and shoves me into the back seat. Jay ties my hands behind me once again. I don't bother to struggle.

> ❧

Dale focuses on the rolling geography below him, oblivious of the radio chatter and the thump of the helicopter blades.

Where is she? Where is she?

Flames and smoke make it impossible to see anything but what is immediately below them. The pilot follows the path of the canal. Dale's eyes follow it to the horizon and sees nothing but the water and gravel road giving way to a fog of smoke. His eyes water and he coughs. Blinking a few times to clear his eyes, he realizes the spot below him is a small shack.

The Water Master

"That was it! The shack!"

He directs the pilot to go in low and slow and he sees a lonely sock lying on gravel in front of the shack.

Is she there?

The helicopter lands in a field on the hill above the canal. Dale flies out of the cockpit before the aircraft touches the ground, slipping and sliding down the hill to the access road. He stops cold.

The door of the shack is open and it is empty. Her sock lays limp about twenty feet from the door. Blood stains cover the sock. Dale's mouth goes dry. He pulls a flashlight out of his pocket and shines it into the shack. Blood everywhere. Her bra, cut and bloody on the mattress. Empty water bottles. A bucket with blood and urine. Dale covers his mouth as he tries not to gag. She is hurt and she is gone. Those fucks are always one step ahead of him.

This has to stop now!

The last chance is Pendleton.

ন্ত০৩

As soon as we drive onto the road, I try to get my bearings. Smoke fills the air, making my eyes burn and drip with tears. A brief opening of clear air gives me a distant view of Rattlesnake Mountain out the right window, but to the left, flames lick through the tall grass along the side of the road. I realize I was held captive far away from home, northwest of Pasco in an area of rolling farmland.

The freakin' middle of nowhere, in an area empty of all but fields of potatoes and desert. No one would have ever found me here.

The Water Master

Charlie yells at Jay, "Watch out, dammit! We should have left earlier like I tol' ya. This fire's a hot one!"

Jay seems too calm given the wall of fire heating up the car. I don't want to die this way. I mewl in panic.

"Shut the fuck up! Both of you!"

Jay's knuckles grip the steering wheel as he peers through the smoke. For a moment I consider finding a way to escape from the car while they are focused on getting out of the fire, but then I'd be left at the side of the road and would burn to death. I freeze in terror and hold my breath as flames jump the road in front of us.

Where are the fire fighters?

The inside of the car bakes. Sweat pours off Jay and I can smell Charlie's funk over the smell of the smoke. I have an urgent need to pee.

"Jay, get us out of here!" I scream.

Jay mutters, "This got a lot worse all of a sudden."

Jay swerves past a burning tumble weed and all at once the flames are behind us. I lose it.

"You asshole! What is wrong with you!" I sit back, pull back my leg and kick him in the head.

It pays to be flexible.

"Shit! Charlie! Take care of her!"

Charlie reaches back, grabs my hair and throws me against the door.

"Shuddap you cunt!" he screams. He shows me a knife. "I'll cut ya and lick the blood offa ya if ya don't shuddap!"

I stare at him, spent, my breath catching in my throat. I try to stop myself from wetting my pants. I am only somewhat successful. This isn't going well at all.

Jay drives south on back roads: some gravel, some paved, through barren and deserted little farm towns with a few buildings or a gas station at an intersection. Vehicles traveling these roads are few and far between, so signaling a driver for help is not an option. My only hope is that Nancy contacted the police after I called her, and somehow I will be saved wherever that package is going to be delivered.

I stare out the window, my mind racing, preparing for the opportunity to escape. I wiggle around to try to open the door as we roll to a four-way stop, but Jay has activated the child-proof lock.

Jay catches me wriggling as he glances in the rearview mirror and yells, "Lie down and don't move!"

Charlie leans over the back seat with a dirty rag in his hand.

"Come'ere, girl. We don't want ya seein' nothing."

He grabs me by the neck and pulls me toward him to cover my eyes with the blindfold. He shoves me back and growls, "Stay outa sight." He pushes me to the floor.

Time passes in silence until I begin to hear increased traffic noise. I assume we are in Pendleton, and Jay is stopping the car at traffic lights. I try to keep track of the number of turns in my head, but soon lose count. Jay is trying to keep me confused, and it works.

I rub my head on the floor a few times and am successful at creating a crack in the darkness. I crick my neck to look through the bottom of the blindfold.

Charlie says, "Pull ova there in that parkin' lot and I'll wait fer ya."

As the car turns, I note a tall, beat-up sign that says: GROCERIES.

Jay parks, shuts off the car, and says, "I'll be back in a few minutes."

"Stay put, Susan. If you move, Charlie has a gun and knows what to do with it. Pretty soon you'll be signing your name to my fortune." He giggles. "After that. Well… you'll see."

"Charlie, if she moves, don't kill her. Just take her legs out so she can still hold a pen."

Charlie says, "Hurry up, I gotta pee."

Jay steps out of the car and closes the door.

Now might be my chance. I rub my head on the floor until the blindfold creeps up above my eyes.

"Charlie, do you have any water? I'm really thirsty," I say.

"Quit yer whinin'. Pretty soon it won't matta."

"Charlie, please!"

I sit up and peek out the window. We are parked next to a pair of green dumpsters in an isolated corner of an abandoned old grocery store. No one is in sight.

Charlie grunts in disgust. I lie back down and tuck my face under the driver seat so he can't see the blindfold is above my eyes. I feel Charlie bump my arm with the water bottle.

"I can't drink it unless you help me," I say.

"Jesus H. Christ," he says, as he turns around in the seat. "I'll be glad when yer dead and gone."

The Water Master

I peek out. Charlie's arm hangs over the back seat and his hand wiggles the bottle. I work my way into a crouched position and see he's paying no attention to me. He is looking out the window, distracted.

I get my feet under me and lean forward as if I am rooting around for the bottle. He is muttering to himself about his need to pee, and I take my chance. In spite of the pain, I push myself up and over the seat and head butt Charlie as hard as I can. Through the fog of my own pain, I see Charlie slump against the window. I dive over the front seat, landing my head in his filthy lap as I maneuver my legs into the driver well and sit up in the driver's seat. The keys are still in the ignition. I use my knee to pull the locking device toward me and manage to slip it into my mouth long enough to bite down on the panic button.

The siren is deafening. It wakes Charlie. He moans.

I have to get out of the car!

I back up to the door and grab the handle and pull. Nothing happens.

Damn! It's locked!

I feel along the door handle with my numb fingers, pressing every button I can. One window goes down, and then another, and at last I hear a click. I fumble for the door handle once again, and it opens. I spill onto the pavement.

I struggle to my knees and stand up just as Charlie gets his wits about him.

"Get back here!" he screams as he opens his door.

Charlie isn't capable of chasing me down, but he does have a gun. I run as fast as I can with my arms still tied behind me.

The Water Master

Get out of range!

I run back and forth like a crazy chicken as I head for the street.

I am out of the parking lot and onto a quiet side street in a matter of seconds. I hide behind a tree and stop to catch my breath. I am in an old, deserted business district. No one is in sight. Evidence of safety is just a few blocks down the street, where cars drive on a busier thoroughfare. I run toward them, fighting for breath.

As I near the intersection to step into traffic in hopes someone will stop and help me, a man steps out from the doorway of a building just ahead of me. Too late, I realize it is Jay, a package in his hand. I sideswipe him before he has time to react, knocking the package to the ground. He reaches for me and misses. I hear his feet pounding behind me. My side cramps. I am almost to the main street when sirens scream and squad cars approach from all directions. Breathless, I slow and look behind me. Jay stands in the middle of the street with police surrounding him, guns drawn, yelling at him to lie on the ground. I sink to my knees.

❧❧

Dale crouches down next to me.

"You all right? Let me see you. You look like shit," he says in a gentle tone.

I give a weak laugh and then begin to sob. Dale plops down next to me and lets out a deep sigh as he hugs me and rubs my arm.

"Ow! Stop rubbing!"

The Water Master

Dale doesn't let go, but lightens his grip on me.

"I was ho-ho-ping you'd find me," I hiccup. "What took you so long?"

After dealing with captivity, I endured the humiliation of the ER exam. The doctor took smears from my vagina and rectum, photographed my bruises, and treated the cuts around my mouth and arm. Jay's carved initials were re-opened and stitched. He'd carved to the bone in places, but appeared to have missed the tendons. I'd received IV antibiotics and a prescription for more. Future appointments were set up to test for various sexually transmitted diseases, something I couldn't even consider in my current state.

The hot shower pounds my neck and shoulders. It doesn't dull my anxiety. I stand in the shower until the water cools. I turn off the tap and step out of the tub. I wrap my sore head in one of Star's best fluffy towels, and dry off with another. I take a quick look in the mirror and then turn away. There is too much damage. I'll have to visit a plastic surgeon, or cover Jay's jagged artwork with a tattoo.

During my ordeal, escape plans must have kept my pain at bay. Now, pain is front and center. I take a high-powered pain pill prescribed by the ER doc. I wrap up in my robe and limp out to the living room, where Dale and Star wait.

With difficulty I sink into the couch and Sweetums jumps on me and touches her nose to mine in greeting. She curls up in my lap, her motor running and closes her eyes. I sigh as I run my hands through the cat's soft fur.

"I'm so glad Sweetums didn't get hurt," I say.

Star smiles. "I think her pride was hurt. She huffed around here for awhile."

"You look much better," Dale says.

"Better than what? A beat-up old hag?"

Star laughs. "I'm just glad it's over with and you're back with us."

"*You're* glad?" I say. I pull the towel off my head and rub to dry my hair. I stop. My scalp hurts too much.

"When I got home and you were gone, and the cat was screaming from the back yard, I totally panicked. I called Dale right away. We found your sock and the GPS. I thought you were dead."

"So did I!" I say.

I tell them what happened to me, from start to finish. I leave out a most of the details surrounding Jay's vicious attack. Despite Dale's tough demeanor, he cringes as I share my story. I was raped before he could find me. He saw the bite marks on my neck. Only the ER doc had seen them on the rest of my body. Dale will see the pictures at some point. I stop thinking about it.

Dale rubs his head in frustration. "We were just steps behind you. After Nancy called and told us about your clues, we sent up helicopters to look for you. Finally, I convinced Silvia to help."

"Silvia? Why would she help?"

"She didn't really want to, but when we agreed to discuss a plea deal on the embezzlement charges, she agreed.

She had no problem throwing her own family under the proverbial bus. She told us where Charlie's hangout was. I had no idea you'd be that far out of town. By the time we got there, you were gone. We already had our people watching at the address that you gave Nancy, but had no idea what kind of vehicle you were in. Setting off the car alarm led us to Charlie, and of course you know the rest."

"So now what?" I ask.

"Jay and Charlie are in jail. I'm asking for no bail. If either one of them is released, your life is at risk. The DA has your statement, and that will help as well."

Star says, "I'm still trying to piece it all together. Why would Charlie kill those people, and how is this thing with Silvia related to Jay?"

"I don't have the whole story worked out, but here's what I think happened," says Dale. "Jay—or Jason—had serious problems with gambling from the time he was a teenager. His mother wanted nothing to do with sending money into the bottomless pit, but Jay was the perfect boy in the eyes of Silvia and Charlie. Silvia bailed him out of trouble for years. Charlie gambled as well, which caused a rift between him and his wife. He blew through all of their money. Like father, like son."

"You got that right," I say under my breath.

"At one point, Jason borrowed money from some bad guys in Oregon and couldn't pay it back. Even Silvia couldn't come up with that much money. Jason was scared and knew he was in trouble, so he decided to take off. He moved away, set up a new identity, but Silvia continued to send him money when he needed it. His mother begged

Silvia to quit giving Jason and Charlie money. She must have known that Silvia was stealing it. She'd probably realized that Silvia was embezzling money from the Elwins. Soon after Jason left, his mom lost her foot in that accident. I don't think it was really an accident, but Charlie's sick way of showing his wife who was boss. If she couldn't get around, she'd be dependent on him and he could abuse her however he liked. Too bad he was such a klutz and cut off his own toes!"

"But why would he murder the Clements?" asks Star.

"That's the info that Susan squeezed out of Charlie. He murdered them because Andy wouldn't be his friend anymore. Charlie blamed Amanda Clement for that. From what I can gather from neighbors, the Clements were friendly and outgoing until Andy started hanging around with Charlie. Charlie somehow influenced or maybe even blackmailed Andy to gamble with him. Amanda eventually put a stop to it. The couple must have made an agreement to cut off the friendship with Charlie. My guess is Charlie couldn't take the rejection, and decided he didn't want their presence as a constant reminder of it."

"I don't think Charlie likes women very much," I say. "Nothing he's done makes any sense. It makes you wonder how he became so damaged."

"He's crazy," says Dale. "He clearly knows right from wrong, so, I doubt he could use an insanity defense."

"Why did Jay want to come back here?" I ask.

"His dad offered him a free place to stay. Charlie probably cashed the rent checks you sent him and gave the money back to Jay. He wanted his boy back. His wife was gone, so no one would interfere with their good times. I don't think Jason could resist. He'd met you already, Susan. He knew he was going back to people who would look after him and let him do whatever he wanted. He just took you along because you were an extra insurance policy—more money—and he could look more normal."

"There's nothing normal about him," I say.

Star reaches over and gives my shoulder a squeeze. I wince.

"Ooooh. I'm sorry!" says Star as she yanks her hand back.

"Everything hurts!"

Dale sighs. "We still have charges and trials. This ordeal could last a long time."

"As long as they're all in jail, I'm good," I say.

The phone rings and Star answers it. "It's for you," she says and hands me the phone.

"Hello?"

"Suze, it's Ruthie! Are you all right?"

"I am now, Ruthie."

We talk a few minutes. I share the highlights of the last few days.

"When are you coming home?" asks Ruthie.

This stops me short.

Home?

"I don't know, sis. I think I'll stay here for awhile. But I do want to come back and visit with you. We have a lot to talk about."

As soon as I hang up, the phone rings again. Karen and Tom heard the news and are calling to check on me, and tell me to take as long as I need to rest before coming back to work.

"Do you still want me?" I ask.

"Of course we do!" says Tom.

"Thanks," I say. "I'll be back to work in a few days."

Dale, Star and I talk a little more, but I am falling asleep. The cat is warm on my lap, and I am drowsy from the hot shower and the pain pills are kicking in.

"I need to go to bed," I say.

Dale stands up with me and gives me a gentle hug. "You're a real trooper, Suze."

"Yeah, yeah. When are you going to dig up those bodies?"

"As soon as we figure out where they are."

"They're under the shed," I say through my yawn. "Right under our noses."

❧◦❦

I sleep almost eighteen hours. I feel stiff and sore, and my internal clock is confused. I want breakfast, but it is dinnertime. Star makes me French toast and bacon for dinner as I sit at the table and stare out the window.

"Star, you said something about being a safe house before. What did you mean by that?"

"I volunteer with the domestic violence program. Sometimes, women need a place to stay that isn't at the shelter."

"You do that?"

"Yeah."

"That's amazing! I'd be nervous letting a stranger stay

with me, particularly if it put me in danger."

"I don't worry about it too much. Dale and his guys know me and keep an eye on the place when I have company."

"Dale really seems to understand the DV victim, doesn't he?"

"He has a big heart. He gets it."

"I never, ever thought I'd be a victim. But here I am."

"I doubt you'll be one again," says Star as she sets down a plate of French toast in front of me.

"No. I doubt I'll ever be in a relationship again."

"Never say never. Use what you learn and move on."

"Easy for you to say," I say.

"Not really. I had to learn the hard way too."

"Not you!" I reach for Star's hand.

"It can happen to anyone, Susan."

"Who was yours?"

"Dagan Moore," she says.

"That's why you got so freaked when I mentioned his name!"

"Yeah. I didn't want to say a whole lot, but I knew right then that you were in trouble. I watched Jay and you and saw me all over again."

"How long did it take you to get out?"

"I was really young, eighteen. I met him at a bookstore in Seattle. He was giving a talk on his first book and I was mesmerized. I found out later, I was one of many female groupies. He reeled me in with his dark eyes and intelligence, and then held me on his hook by making me think if I just did a little more, a little more, a little more, he would be happy with me. I degraded myself for three years, trying to get him to stay with me and love me. Finally, my parents stepped in. They insisted I go on a family trip with them. Dagan couldn't join us. He threatened me that if I went, he wouldn't be there when I got back. Something clicked. I decided to test him. I went with my family, and when I got back he was there, begging me to stay. I left."

"Did he hurt you?"

"He threatened me, pushed me around a few times. Enough to keep me in line."

"It's scary how easy it is to fall for a guy who seduces you into believing he's knows what's best," I say. "Especially when your spiritual life is tied up in the relationship like mine was with Jay."

"It's hard to see what's happening until you can get some distance," says Star.

"Not only am I not going to get into a relationship again, but I'm staying away from any kind of organized religion or group. I don't trust myself. I might get sucked in again!"

Star gives me a sarcastic hurt look. "I was hoping you'd join my coven!"

"Ask me again in a year," I laugh.

☙❧

After a few more days of rest, I return to work. Karen and Tom are thrilled to see me, and Marisa offers free massages for the rest of my life. I don't want her to see my bruises, so I put her off. It might take awhile for me to let

429

anyone touch me, but I know Marisa's hands will help me heal.

The newspaper, TV and radio are full of the news of Charlie's arrest, Jay's deception, and my kidnapping. I am grateful I don't know many people yet. It is hard enough with my friends hovering over me. Star lets me stay at her house indefinitely. I call my beloved financial advisor, Nancy, and thank her over and over again for a detective job well done. My money is safe.

Dale stays busy with long days of work making it difficult for me to go visit my dogs. And, I miss him. I miss my dogs. I wish he would at least check up on me, but he doesn't. And he doesn't return the few calls I make to him, either.

At last, a few weeks after I return to work, Dale stops by the office at the end of the day to give us an update on the charges against Silvia. I can't stop smiling.

"Silvia has three federal counts of fraud against her, plus the embezzlement charges. I think she'll be in jail a long time," says Dale.

"What are the chances of getting some of our money back?" asks Tom.

"Once all of her assets are assessed, the lawyers' fees are paid and the insurance losses are added up, you'll get a portion of the assets. I'm not sure how much that will be."

"Something's better than nothing," says Karen.

"And what about Jay and Charlie?" I ask.

"The bodies under the shed have been identified as the Clements. I think we have enough to put Charlie away for a long time. He'll likely die in prison. As for Jay, the kidnapping, rape and extortion charges will be a shorter sentence than Charlie, but it will be years before he's out. They're both still held without bail."

"That's a relief. I don't mind telling you that I have nightmares about being kidnapped again," I say.

"I can understand why," says Karen. "I can't imagine your terror!"

"I wouldn't want you to," I say.

Dale stands up to leave.

"I have to go back to Illinois for a few days to track down some information to complete my investigation. I hate leaving all the dogs at a kennel."

I just look at him.

Dale laughs. "Susan, I was wondering if you would mind dog sitting for me?"

I smile. "I'd love to."

"Oh, I almost forgot something!" Dale says. "I've got a present for you. Hold out your hand."

Puzzled, I hold my hand out, palm up.

Dale puts his hand in his pocket, pulls it out and places my mother's rings in my hand. I let out a little "oh" and stare at Dale with wide eyes.

"How did you…"

"Don't ask," interrupts Dale. "And these are for you, too."

He rummages in his briefcase and hands me a package wrapped in a grocery bag and tied up with a sloppy Christmas bow.

"My journals?"

"Yep." Dale smiles.

"You're not going to tell me how you found either of these, are you?"

"Nope."

I let out a sigh as I bite my lip in an effort to hold back tears.

"I—I can't thank you enough. You have no idea what this means to me."

"Right now you've got some dogs who are anxious to see you. Come by my house tonight for a visit. I'll make you dinner. Sound good?"

"Sounds good," I say, as a tiny piece of my frozen heart begins to beat again.

ABOUT THE AUTHOR

Betsy Dickinson was born and raised north of Chicago, in Waukegan, Illinois. She moved to the desert Northwest in 1992.

She has a Bachelors degree in Earth Science and a Masters degree in Marriage and Family Therapy. She worked in the drug and alcohol counseling field for many years and consulted with business and industry on human resources issues. For over ten years she has been a Human Resources manager for a large school district.

Betsy has traveled to Canada, England and all but one of the fifty United States. She is married with a step-son and owns three rescue dogs. She is a pianist, has owned an herb store, been a Wiccan High Priestess, and generally led a non-linear life. She draws on all of these experiences to develop intriguing scenes in her debut novel, *THE WATER MASTER*.

Visit Betsy's website at:
www.betsydickinsonbooks.com

DOMESTIC VIOLENCE
Are you a victim?

Abuse is a repetitive pattern of behaviors to maintain power and control over an intimate partner. These are behaviors that physically harm, arouse fear, prevent a partner from doing what they wish or force them to behave in ways they do not want. Abuse includes the use of physical and sexual violence, threats and intimidation, emotional abuse and economic deprivation.

If you feel as if your partner or a loved one's partner is becoming abusive, there are a few behaviors that you can look out for.

Telling you that you can never do anything right.

Showing jealousy of your friends and time spent away.

Keeping you or discouraging you from seeing friends or family members.

Embarrassing or shaming you with put-downs.

Controlling every penny spent in the household.

Taking your money or refusing to give you money for expenses.

Looking at you or acting in ways that scare you.

Controlling who you see, where you go, or what you do.

Preventing you from making your own decisions.

Telling you that you are a bad parent or threatening to harm or take away your children.

Preventing you from working or attending school.

Destroying your property to threatening to hurt or kill your pets.

Intimidating you with guns, knives or other weapons.

Pressuring you to have sex when you don't want to or do things sexually that you are uncomfortable with.

Pressuring you to use drugs or alcohol.

For help or more information,
contact the National Domestic Violence Hotline
at
www.thehotline.org
or
1.800.799.SAFE(3224)

Be safe.

CPSIA information can be obtained at www.ICGtesting.com
Printed in the USA
LVOW10s1159090316

478425LV00004B/5/P

FICTION
$19.95 US

THE WATER MASTER

BETSY DICKINSON

A TALE OF MURDER, DECEPTION, SURVIVAL AND REDEMPTION.

Susan Bradley, searching for spiritual renewal, falls in love with the spellbinding Jay Glasser—her Wiccan High Priest and mentor. After a whirlwind courtship and marriage in Illinois, she and Jay move to the desert Northwest community of Pasco, Washington. Their creepy and obnoxious landlord, Charlie Gottschalk, brags about being the local watermaster and neighborhood watch guy, but Susan suspects he is more than that as he interferes with her marriage. Jay's unusual friendship with Charlie changes him for the worse—much worse.

When Susan begins her new job in Dr. Elwin's office, discrepancies in the files thrust her into an embezzlement investigation that leads to none other than Charlie's grouchy sister, Silvia, as the thief. Detective Dale Freeman directs the investigation but has his own suspicions about Charlie as he reopens a cold case involving the disappearance of the previous tenants of Susan and Jay's shabby rent-to-own house. As Dale and Susan venture further into uncovering the deceit and destruction the Gottschalk's have left behind, Susan's closely held secret, once revealed, puts Susan in life-threatening danger. Can Susan survive the flood of evil unleashed by the watermaster?

ISBN 978-1-935993-79-7
51995

Nightengale Press
A NIGHTENGALE MEDIA LLC Company
www.nightengalemedia.com
©2016 All Rights Reserved
Visit www.betsydickinsonbooks.com

9 781935 993797